Madhumati

Anshuman Rai

Invincible Publishers

First published in India in 2017 by Invincible Publishers

ISBN: 978-93-86148-92-6

Digitally Printed at Replika Press Pvt. Ltd.

Invincible Publishers
G-120, Sushant Lok III, Sector 57, Gurgaon-122002

To my daughter,
Rhea

Acknowledgment

From the moment, I was taught how to elicit the first syllable by my mother, to the time my teacher held my hand and helped me draw the alphabet and onward to the times when friends lent me books to read, and the English professor taught me an advanced course in modern novels, there are way too many people I must acknowledge for my first novel. I thought about it a while, and to make it short, sweet and safe, I can just say that I would like to thank my family, teachers, friends and colleagues.

I would like to think that a large part of the novel comes from the fascinating imagination of my daughter Rhea. She is that one special person in my life who is always inventing games and cooking up stories, and I would like to thank her from the bottom of my heart for helping me come up with much of the creative section of the novel. And if it were not for her caring mother, my adorable wife Rajani, she would not have grown up to be this amazingly wonderful child.

I would like to thank my Dad and my Mom for always being there when I needed them. My brother, Dr. Raghwendra Rai, is the best elder brother that one can possibly have, one who I look up to, and one who I can always approach with the issues I face. It always helps that his better half Dr. Meenakshi Rai is an avid book reader.

I would like to thank all my colleagues at Shree Shankaracharya Technical Campus, where I teach computer science. A big thank you to all the guys and girls for taking their time to read through the manuscript and give their feedback.

It was heartwarming to get to know that so many of my friends wanted to know about the book, especially those from IIT Kanpur days, who took out time to get in touch on Facebook and inquire about the novel. A special thanks to my dear friend Mr. Randeep Singh Bagga, whose timely financial remuneration for work done on a project helped me to finance the publication of this work.

I would like to thank the staff at Invincible Publishers, you guys are really the best. I believe Aditi Saxena is a creative genius when it comes to editing unlike any other that I have ever known or will come to know. Sneha Agrawal's work on the book cover left me speechless and Ajay Setia's coordination and managerial skills in managing the entire project were superlative.

Last but not the least, I would like to thank you, the reader, for making the decision to purchase this book and taking the time to read through the pages of what I promise will be a story you will cherish in more ways than one. I can never thank you enough!

Prologue

Duality is at the heart of things, every coin has two sides. If one were to look closely, one can find examples of two perfectly antagonistic concepts or things like bad and good, heavy and light, dark and bright, man and woman, foolish and wise, hate and love, silence and music, hard and soft, cold and warm, cruel and kind, devils and angels, anxiety and calm, long and short, all paired and in co-existence with each other with the only exception of God who exists as one supreme being, and can only be experience in oneness with the divine.

In post-independence India, two brothers, Darshan and Darpan, lived happily together. They were *darshniks*(philosophers), much like fire and water, different and yet inseparable. Darshan means presence, while Darpan means a mirror. Much like their names, their natures also reflected this duality. Darpan was the younger of the two and liked to argue and debate, while Darshan was the quiet, reflective thinker who liked to answer questions that were posed to him.

They were both very fond of games and since they had a lot of time at their leisure, they spent it playing nim, go, reversi, backgammon, chess, checkers and the occasional charades or pictionary. Darpan was fascinated by the existence of duality in all its myriad forms. He would constantly breach the subject with Darshan, who would patiently try to answer his questions. Sometime, even the wise Darshan was flummoxed by some of Darpan's perplexing questions. Over a period of time, a game began to take shape in the minds of the two, the game of finding and contemplating duals, and then examining the nature, course, fate and other philosophical outcomes from the game.

As soon as they had formalized the game of Dual, a storm started brewing and a voice thundered from the heavens.

It was Narayana, God himself, who spoke, "Darshan and Darpan, I am pleased with the two of you, as you have proved yourself worthy of being called philosophers. I would have given you a boon, but knowing very well that you do not wish for material possessions, I shall grant you the company of my two lovely daughters, Vani and Deeksha. As and when you play the game of Dual, Vani and Deeksha shall guide you in your quest of exploring the true nature of things.'

Vani, the younger daughter of Narayana, was sound personified, made up of the most beautiful intonations that one can imagine. Vani was also called Kavya, for she stood for poetry, the nine muses and perhaps poesy herself. Deeksha, the elder daughter, was grace in motion. She was also called Pushpa as she was like a flower; the fragrance emanating from her carried the very essence of knowledge to those who seeked it hungrily.

Vani chose to be the benefactor of Darpan, to be the voice for his mirror, while Deeksha chose Darshan as her partner to grace his presence with the element of ceremony.

The brothers felt like little boys who had been offered candy. As soon as Kavya took her place next to Darpan and Pushpa sat next to Darshan, the brothers rolled the special dice that they had prepared for the game of Dual. The dice tumbled to a halt; one showed opulence, while the other showed economy. Darpan and Darshan looked at each other, expecting the other to speak something that would help decide the next step.

It was Kavya who spoke, 'Darpan, you have always been curious to understand the duality inherent in things. This is just one of those pairs. Let us travel to ancient India where a young girl is about to begin a journey. I will speak for you and you shall be my eyes.'

Part 1
Madhumati and Sisters

The Empire of Simhas

Vani waxed eloquent on Opulence,

For her face was wisdom, her eyes, a dalliance of art.
Her lips, the guardians of song,
Such was the beauty of Madhumati.
And he sculpted desire in the beat of heaven.
In the land of the *Nataraj*, Sibu ruled with love.

He was a moth to her flame,
She was the wind and he was the vane.
Theirs was a tale of love, pride,
Ambition, art and some things vain,
Dance and music trickled down
From the heavens like rain.

The Gods eulogised the might of the empire of Simhas,
With the ruler of the jungle on their coat-of-arms.
The king, Narsimha, a mighty warrior
And Shiva's devotee,
Ruled fairly with love, candour, grace, wit and repartee.

Lord *Nataraj* graced the empire over the coastal Indies;
From the Malabar across to the Bay of Bengal,
Drained by the mighty *Cauvery*,
And flanked by the majestic Nilgiris, standing tall.

Madhumati sang paeans, hymns and odes a plenty,
Of valour, happiness, bravado and gaiety.
Sibu danced to the sound so beauteous,
And Madhumati, a consort,
A *nrityanagana*, a poetess, like a ditty.

The land was vast, a never ending paradise,
Mountains, rivers, flatlands,

With mangroves and coastal beaches.
Crop ripened, milk flowed
And honeysuckle bloomed in every flowerbed.
A land so bountiful,
That it could breathe life into the dead.

Soil fertile, sedimentary, rocky, alluvial and drained,
The Cauvery, virulent,
Enraptured, a symphony she played.
Amidst the gorges and the ravines of the ghats,
Draining the water through the rocks
And land and way past.

Mung, Urad and Horse-gram grew in the savannah,
Not a foe to fight, no one a pariah.
Cattle were reared, and the bulls worshipped,
Copper and other precious metals were smelted.

Sheep, goats and crops brought an abundant harvest,
While trade brought about a new zest.
The Iron Age introduced new age Pottery,
Trade in ceramics, sandalwood,
Mango, citruses and the charcuterie.

Temple construction in the empire
Received royal patronage,
They served as representatives of the might,
And glory of the kings of the age.
Of the types of the temple, there were three score,
The first *Nagara*, the second *Dravida*
And the last *Visara* to fulfil the lore.

Characteristic of the *Nagara* style
Was the lofty tower or spire called the *Shikhara.*
Nagara adopted regional characteristics too
Like the temple at Lingaraja.
Dravida was identified by *garbhagriha, vimana,*

Gopuram and *mandapa.*
G*arbhagraha* being the sanctum,
V*imana,* the stories atop,
And G*opuram*, the lofty gates,
And the hall with carved pillars – the *mandapa*.

The temples of the empire spoke its grandeur,
The *ShivaVihara* being the Toast du Jour.
The deity, the lord of the universe
Ensconced in the *garbhagraha*,
Complemented the humble abode of *Natarja*,
Mount Kalisha.

Three entrances to the shrine
Were guarded fiercely by the Dwarpalakas.
To one who enters the Gopuram,
What a wondrous sight he beholds!
Scenes from the *ShivaPurana*,
And women holding various *Kalasas*
Were depicted on the walls.

The main shrine was divided into five numbered areas,
Garbhagraha, *KalaMandapa*,
KalyanaMandapa, and *Vadya Mandapa*.
And the Shivalinga housing
The power of *Brahma*,
Vishnu and *Shiva*.
The sanctum was guarded outside
By the mighty deity, *Ganesha*.

The chamber for housing
The lord himself was the *Garbhagraha*,
The courtyard for cultural activities was the *KalaMandapa*,
The corridor for marriage ceremonies
Was the *KalyanMandapa*,
While the one for the musical performances
Was the *VadyaMandapa*.

The temple walls consisted of intricate carvings
Telling stories from the *ShivPurana*,
While one wall *speaks of Vidya Samhita;*
A dedication to the *bhakti* of Shiva
Through devotion to the linga,
And the description of India's rivers, mountains,
Flatlands and other geographical areas.

While on other walls, one could see the *KhelSamhita*
And the *YudhSamhita*,
Which discussed Gods & Goddesses,
Particularly, *Vishnu*, *Brahma* and *Krishna*.
On another wall were depictions
From *Nritya Samhita*,
Uma Samhita, *Maitri Samhita*,
Grihastha Samhita and *Sangeeta Samhita*.

On the inside walls of the courtyards were frescoes,
From the legend of *Rama* to Krishna's dalliances.
The frescoes recited the tales of
Rama's victory over Ravana,
And Krishna's victory over Kansa,
Putana, Bakasura and Aghasura.

The temple on the shore or The Samudra Shiva Mandir
Encapsulated Shiva's beauty,
Beautifully sculptured, was the mandir,
Like a chariot of the almighty.
A combination of the three shrines,
Brahma, *Vishnu* and *Mahesh*,
Spoke of the Lord of Creation, Lord of Preservation
And the Lord of Aakrosh.

A lion statue sat guarding
The front entrance to the *garbhagraha*,

The lion is shown carried
By an ancient technological wonder, the *vimana*.
Pillars with intricate carvings
Were found in the courtyard,
And statues of voluptuous dancers
Were strewn all over the corners, a plethora.

Relief work on the walls
Depicted the creation of the universe,
From the fire in the sun, the cool in the moon,
To the churning of the oceans.
While precious gems were embedded
In the eyes of the idols on the wall,
They shone and beckoned mesmerisingly,
On whomsoever their light were to fall

The temple seemed like a fantasy chariot
Made to fly in the skies,
With Vishnu as the Charioteer, Brahma as the Creator
And *Shiva* as the Apocalypse, behind.
To where it may go, it remains to be seen,
For in one direction there was a sundial,
And in the other, a wind vane.

The King was an avid practician
Of religion and dharma,
And was the only one allowed
With the priest in the *garbhagraha*.
The full moon nights, called Poornima, were special,
When the temple celebrated with pomp
And splendour, a fiesta.

The state was governed by the King
Who was its almighty head,
And he ruled along with his other feudatories,
The Samantas, whom he led.
The Samantas, once upon a time,

Were Kings in their own rights,
But alas! had been defeated,
With their kingdoms surrendered,
And cash and other tributes to the King, indebted.

The king meticulously followed the practice,
Of granting land to the Brahmins,
Religious persons and institutions
Were not the only ones to benefit,
For not far behind were state officials,
Ready and forthcoming to take credit.
Decline in trade prompted the decrease
In the minting of coined money,
Land was typically granted to the donee
And was exploited by him tax-free.

On the land granted thus, the King had no authority,
And the donee could manage as he chose
And issue, any decree.
At village level, the local people enjoyed
A high degree of autonomy,
They looked after the administration
With the help of a self elected local body.

A typical village had two types of assemblies,
The Ur and the Sabha,
The Sabha was made up of inhabitants
Of the area dominated by the Brahmins.
Wheres the Ur consisted of people
From non-Brahminical settlements.
These assemblies looked after the temples,
Public works and tax collections.

There was a gradual increase
In the number of people from various castes:
Sudras, Kayasthas, Chahmanas, Rajputs,
Paramaras, Pratiharas, and *Chandellas*.

Some believed they were the descendants,
Of *Sakas, Kushanas* and *Hunas,*
The Rajputs gradually settled in Rajasthan,
And emerged as the supreme warrior class.

Art, literature and the sciences
Found here a burgeoning haven,
Beginning with the Tamil translation
Of the glorious epic, the *Ramayan.*
The language of pre-eminent scholars was Sanskrit,
And in this language bloomed the texts -
Vinoda Rangini and *Mridu Bharat.*

Narsimha made military ascents on India
And navy campaigns on Sri Lanka,
And annexed much of the Malabar, Ceylon and Kerala.
The Simhas waged war against modern day Indonesia,
And making victory, assimilated the people
Of other tribes and intelligentsia.

The Simha military consisted
Of a standing army, or the *agrasena,*
While those recruited for a special occasion,
Were called the *visheshasena.*
Band of soldiers from guilds
And mercenaries too, the *nipunasena,*
And troops of allies and friends, the *bheetsena.*

The enemy troops were called the *shatrusena,*
The forest tribals and warriors
Were named the *vanasena.*
Of the classes of the Simha army, there were six score,
Vanawasis being the last and *Charawahas*
Placed at the fore.

The forest-dwellers, and the tribesmen were the *Vanawasis,*
And the once-cattle-lifting-marauders

Were the *Charawahas.*
Such was the division of classes,
And the ranks of the infantry men,
That the hierarchy of one dissolved into the other
Like ink flowing out of a fine fountain pen.

The Simha army had a regimental system,
And evolved war machines,
They used elephants on battlefields,
Swordsmen with swords,
Archers with their bow and the cavalry.
The *DwarRakshak* were the guardsmen
Of the palaces of *Narsimha,*
And when times required,
Doubled up as fierce and mighty *Goliaths.*

The Simhas were also great architects,
Construction workers and builders,
For they had built intelligent canals
To guide the waters of Cauvery.
To secure irrigation, they had obstructed
The mighty Cauvery with dams,
Brilliant was their understanding of architecture,
And in it they had achieved mastery.

The artisans flourished under the grace of his majesty,
Narsimha the great,
Fine figures of *Siva* and his consort *Parvati,*
In bronze they made.
No less fascinating were the figurines of *Vishnu,*
And his consort *Lakshmi,*
The Nayanmars, the *Saiva* saints,
And other notables from the *Hindu* coterie.

Tatva

Deeksha extolled the virtues of economy

The nine wise sages, Kala (Time),
Dravya (Substance),
Kama(Love), Karuna(Compassion),
Dosha (Deficiency),
Kalpana(Imagination), Vidya (Education),
Kreeda(Games) and Mithya (Falsehood)
Came Together and Performed a Yagna.

They began chanting in perfect synchronicity,
Govinda Jaya Jaya, Gopala Jaya Jaya
Radha Ramanna Hari, Govinda Jaya Jaya
Achyutam Keshavam Krishna Damodaram
Ram Narayanam Janaki Vallabham
Hare Ram Hare Ram, Ram Ram Hare Hare
Hare Krishna Hare Krishna, Krishna Krishna Hare Hare

The Lord was pleased and appeared,
A flute in his hand
He played a mellifluous mystical melody
And out of the nothingness
That had pervaded time & space
Was born ether, which permeated
All space-time.

The sages then began beating their drums
And the emptiness reverberated with a boom;
A primordial sound that made ether resonate
And a shockwave went travelling
Through space-time.

Ether began to heat up and liquify
Within moments, coagulation began
Followed by a Brownian motion.
As a form began to emerge,
Tatva, the essence of all creation,
The father of Prakriti, was born
And the sages started chanting,
Om Tat Sat
Om Tat Sat
Om Tat Sat
Or Aum, Tatva is the truth.
As Tatva began to stabilise
The nine sages began to give it a conscience.

First came Kala, who set the wheel of time
In motion in Tatva, forever binding
Cause and effect together as causality.

Second, Dravya gave Tatva mass,
Thereby it began to acquire inertia
And started gravitating towards itself.

Third was Vidya, who enunciated theories
Of Language, Logic, Algebra,
Trigonometry, Calculus and Computation.

Fourth was Kalpana, who created dreams
And let loose in the infused Tatva,
A myriad of imaginative forms.

Fifth came Dosha, and he introduced wanting,
Needs, desires and gaping holes
To be fulfilled in Tatva.

Sixth was Karuna, who introduced feelings,
And the concept of Emotions.

Seventh was Kama and he inspired Love;
That vital ingredient
Which is the source of all life.

Eighth was Kreeda, who created games
That could be played; abstract, yet real.

Finally, Mithya infused fallacies,
Enigmas, dogmas and sowed
The seeds of Maya.

And now Tatva, the father of all creation,
Shimmered in a silvery hue,
As if he held all the secrets of existence.

Discourse on Materialism

After Deeksha had finished recounting the creation of Tatva out of economy, Vani began speaking, 'So what have you learnt from this story so far, Darpan?'

Darpan reflected, 'I have only managed to get a glimpse of an ancient empire, vis-a-vis the very act of creation. I do not know what to make of it.'

Vani offered her wisdom, 'It seems like you have not been looking for the pearls of truth hidden as messages in the story. The empire that I have described, speaks of the empire's magnificence and beautiful creations, in it like temples, the art and the management of people, land and the armies. It mostly speaks of a material world created as a playground for a King. On the other hand, the portrait painted by Deeksha speaks of an age eons ago, when time itself did not exist and economy in words, deeds and art was a thing of virtue. This world pertains more to the soul and the conscience, tending towards the more gentler philosophical tendencies in man.'

Darpan countered, 'Are you implying that materialism is a waste, when so much can be achieved by simple acts of a gentle artistic hand.'

It was Deeksha who replied, 'You still fail to see the complete picture. The two worlds are different, yet bound to each other through a common theme, which is that of 'the material' and its creation and purpose in life. One cannot exist without the other. If there was no act of creation, surely empires would not exist and without the possibility of empires in future, creation would lose its need for existence.'

Darshan summarised the discourse, 'Thus, we must choose wisely when pursuing materialistic pleasures, balancing the need for satiation via physical objects with the cravings of the soul.'

Vani began singing a rhyme and the others joined her.

Before there was time,
And the Gods were not nigh.
There was you, my love,
In my life all this while.

As we take our first step now,
And watch the time fly by,
Matter melts, rivers flow,
Space warps around and entwines.

Tonight, you'll be mine,
As I hold you in my arms,
And sing a sweet love rhyme,
As form begins to swell to a tide..

Will you stay by my side?
Will you be my one true guide?
And tell me the secrets
Of the material life.

It's only you in my eyes,
The rest is a surprise.
As we witness creation,
And the birds take to flight.

Are you the child, heavenly and divine,
That plays, sings and cries?
I will hush you to sleep,
Gently and tenderly, with a lullaby.

The next roll of the dice displayed artifice and nature.

The Neighbours

Vani began her rhyme describing artifice,

Of the folks next door to the Simhas,
There were four,
The *Suryas*, The *Chandras*, The *Ashwas*,
The *Meenas* and their folks of yore.
The Suryas ruled over much of Tamil Nadu and Kerala,
While the Chandras, ruled over
The rich Cauvery drained Karnataka.

The Ashwas controlled
Much of modern Andhra Pradesh,
And the Meenas governed
The black soils of Maharashtra.
The Simhas had a central government
While the neighbours enjoyed local rule,
Narsimha held royal court
At the city of *SimhaGadh*, the capital.

The Suryas' land was rich with coffee,
Spices, sandalwood and tea,
The Chandras had sugarcane, grapes,
With ragi, millets and rice in the granary.
The Ashwas took to greenhouse farming
For vegetables and toiled in the arid land,
While the Meenas grew cotton, sugarcane and grapes
In the black soil, so goes the legend.

There were temples, palaces, court-houses
And concert houses all over the raj,
Nrityabalas danced, royal visitors were entertained,
And the environs filled with song,
Aditya was the King of Suryas,
While ChandraPani lead the Chandras,

Chakravarthi presided over the Ashwas,
And the Meenas were lorded over by Paramhans.

Suryas, Chandras, Ashwas
And Meenas reported to the Simhas,
In the matters of administration, revenue collection,
Military, society and traditions.
The emblem and the flag of the Suryas
Marked the Sun in its full fiery form,
While the Chandra flag bore
The face of the Goddess Luna
Riding the winter storm.

The Ashwas' insignia was the Chariot
Of the Lord driven by horses,
And that of the Meenas was a mermaid of the sea
Spraying water through her fins.
Together the five kingdoms were called the PanchTatvas
And they rejoiced in their friendship,
Harmony and peace.

Rock-cut pillared halls resonated with music
That sounded divine,
Rock-cut structured temples
With carvings of figures, entwined.
Temples there were polygonal, star shaped,
With multi faceted columns,
Garbhagrahas, Kalasha, Mandapa, Shikara, Gopuram,
Circumambulatory and steps.

Stupas of the Buddhist craft
And temples in Dravidian style,
Stupas with *Chaitya* halls
And the monastery – the vihara.
The gateways to the Stupas were called the *toranas.*
The majestic *toranas*
Displayed the influence of the helens.

Temples of the five states had a sanctuary or a *Vimana*,
Which tapered upwards in a pyramid
To a portion called 'the *Shikhara*'.
The Vimana contained a dark enclosure
Housing the diety – the *garbhagraha*,
An entrance gaped from the eastern side,
While walls surround the others.

The anthem of the Suryas
Sang of their light and its magical realms;
'Oh fiery Sun, shine your glorious light
On us mortal beings,
Bring life forth to all
And let water, seed, wind,
Fire and earth sing beauteous songs.
Let there be no place hidden
From the rays of the sun
And the reign of the Simhas,
Bring fame to the king Aditya
And eternal joy and happiness to his faithful subjects.'

The song of the Chandras
Celebrated the divine union
Of the masculine and feminine;
'Moonlight shine on us ecstatic lovers
And bring your shine to the dew drops on flowers,
Let the nectar drip, the fireflies dance
And lead us in your white light amidst the gardens.
For tonight is the night
When Rati and Ravi become one
And celebrate their togetherness.
Let Luna the divine deity
Bring eternal love's light
In the life of the star-crossed lovers.'

The music of the Ashwas

Spoke of a warrior's undying spirit
And ferociousness;
'Oh mighty warrior,
Bring forth the strength of Hercules
And the spirit of Achilles,
For you are stronger than ten elephants
And braver than a hundred lions.
Guide us to victory,
Lead us to a righteous path,
And do it with grace,
For yours' is the battlefield to storm,
Arrows fly, swords flash and the warriors dance.'

Lyrical poems of the Meenas
Delved into fantasy, deception, and illusions;
'Oh queen of the ocean Meenaskhi, do not delude us
And deceive us with your games,
Show us your paradise and reveal the secrets
That have been held by the seas.
Let the mythical creatures,
The fantastic palaces and creations of
Maya be revealed.
For we wait with baited breath to
Bask in your grandeur
And rule in water, air, and land.'

All the five kingdoms came together
To celebrate the divine feminine;
They revered goddesses *Kali, Saraswati,*
Parvati, Lakshmi, Durga and Devi the divine.
The kingdom of Suryas worshipped the creator
Of the alphabet, Saraswati.
Saraswati, the consort of *Brahma,*
Was the goddess of learning, mathematics,
And also that of the arts, music,
Magic and eloquence.

Many consider her the divine mother,
And the mother of all life,
Since her divine energy united
With Brahma's awareness and beings came alive.
Saraswati was also the river goddess
And her name translates to *the flowing one*,
She is usually shown seated on a lotus blossom throne
Accompanied by a white swan.

She has four arms,
Signifying her power that extends in all directions
Proving that she holds knowledge, deeply spiritual.
Two of her hands hold books and beads
With the other two hands, she plays the *Veena*,
(The Indian lute)
Such is the grace bestowed on the kingdom
Of the Suryas by Saraswati, the astute.

Lakshmi, the wife of *Vishnu* - the preserver,
Is the Chandras' chief deity,
She was born from an ocean of milk
Standing on a lotus flower.
She is the goddess of fortune, prosperity,
Wealth and beauty.
She represents all that is masculine
While *Vishnu* exudes all the power.

Lakshmi and *Vishnu* are seen riding the giant eagle
Garuda across the land,
They have a son *Kama* who is the God
Of romantic love, *Cupid's hand.*
Lakshmi is attended to by white elephants,
And *Sita* is one of her reincarnations.

In the form of *Sita, Lakshmi*
Plays the perfect wife to Lord *Rama*,

Once a year, on a full-moon night in November,
Women clean and light up their homes, praying
That *Lakshmi* will grace their abodes.
She lives in the sky, with the most beautiful of jewels,
The stars like the *Nakshatra*.

The Ashwas are warriors, hence worship *Durga*,
One of the Devi's avatars.
She is invincible in battle, and to destroy the
Buffalo monster,
Was created by the Gods.
She killed the beast
By taking a weapon in each of her ten hands.
She is *Shakti*, responsible for fire, water, earth
And air; the supreme Mother Goddess.

Parvati, Shiva's wife, is often seen with him
In statues and paintings,
She is also Durga, or the ten armed goddess of warfare,
Kali is one of her incarnations.
Parvati means a mountain girl and she is the daughter
Of the Himalayas,
This is *Uma*, the tiger riding goddess
Worshipped by the Meenas.

Artisans worshipped the divine
By exhibiting stitch, pattern, motif and color.
Craft was relegated to the artisan
And design reserved for the professional designer.
In ancient India, the designers were called the *shilpi*,
And belonged to various guilds
And schools throughout the country.

Their works of art included carpets,
Papier mache, brocade,
Stone inlay and design motifs.
Innovation exhibited in form, proportion,

Color and in the artists' display of skills.
All artists worked together in a factory
Called the *karkhana,*
And named their handicrafts as *dastkari,*
Karigiri, hastakala and hastashilpa.

Hindu ornamentation and ancient craftsmanship
Worked together hand-in-hand,
Cotton and silk and muslin was weaved
In the textile mills, with a hum.
Some silks were called after
The evening dew, or *shabnam,*
While another variety was called the *abrawan,*
The evening water.

Pottery, metal work, leather work,
Bamboo work and cane flourished.
Some were used for carrying water, others for weaponry,
Some for clothing,
Some for ornaments and guilds,
And some others to construct houses and sheds.
While the workers were kept well,
A class grew wealthy and burgeoning.

Then came the various handicraft goods
And knick-knacks,
Fishing traps, baskets, cradles,
Biers, bridges and umbrellas,
Mats, musical instruments, chairs, cots and waterpipes.
Such was the craftsmanship
That it always left the people amused in surprise.

The weaponry of the army were the *Muktha,*
The *Amuktha* and the *Mantra Muktha,*
Mukhtas were thrown, Amukthas were not thrown,
Mantra Mukhta were discharged by the Mantra.
Bows and arrows were

The chief weapons of the Mukhta,
The fire weapons were called the *agneya astra*,
The paramount of them being the *agni bana*.

Agni bana had three recipes: *agni dharana,*
Visvasaghati and *ksepyo agni yoga*,
Visvasaghati had the powder of zinc, khumbi, lead,
With Turpentine oil, wax and charcoal.
Astra means a missile while *agneya astra*
Denotes a firearm,
A small gun is referred to as a *tupak*,
And the engines of war, as *yantram*.

Agnicurna, or gunpowder, was composed
Of four to six parts saltpetre,
One part charcoal of *arkha, sruhi and* one part sulphur.
Other trees burnt in a pit and reduced to powder,
Were used in ancient rockets
Taking the place of actual guns in warfare.

The *Bindipala* was a heavy club
Which had a broad and bent tail end,
It was meant to be used by the warrior
Having placed his left foot in the front.
The various uses of this weapon included cutting,
Hitting, striking and breaking.
It was like a *kunta*, but with a big blade
Like a scythe meant for hunting.

A hand gun or a musket which rightly
Pierced the mark, is called the *Nalika.*
Straight in form and hollow from the inside,
It discharged vicious darts when one had it ignited,
The small one with a little hole at the end,
Measured sixty *Angula*.

Through the touch-hole,
A breach which contained wood,
Fire was conveyed to the charge.
It was carried by foot soldiers,
But the big gun was conveyed by carts.
The balls were made of iron, lead or other metals,
The word Nalika, in the sense of the firing gun,
Was used as a signal for the unwary King.

The *Cakra* is a circular disc
With a small opening in the middle.
It was of three kinds: of three,
Six and eight spokes each.
Five or six ways there were to use it at war,
Be it felling, rending, breaking,
Severing, cutting or whirling.

Another weapon of war frequently mentioned
In all kinds of accounted warfare, is the *Tomara.*
It was of two kinds, a javelin
And an iron club or a *sarvayasa.*
It was used in combination
With arrow or straight feathers,
And helped delivering blows to
The eyes and hands of the enemies.

Another weapon of war in the shape
Of a tooth, is the *DantaKantha*,
It is made of metal, has a strong handle,
A straight blade and is used in two movements.
A noose for killing the enemy
In one stroke is called the *Pasa,*
Attributed to the god Varuna.
It consists of two or three ropes.

The *Masundi* was an eight shaped cudgel,
Furnished with a broad and strong handle.

Its name comes from the root which means,
To breaking into pieces and cleave.
It was perhaps akin to the Musala.

The *Parasu* is a battle axe
Attributed to the Lord Parasu Rama.
Its blade is made of steel and has a wooden handle.
A heavy rod of iron with one hundred spikes
On top is called the Gada;
In twenty different ways it can be handled.

A staff in the shape of a hammer
Is called the *Mudgara*,
It was used to break heavy stones and rocks.
A bucket like instrument curved on both sides,
With an opening made of iron is the *Sira*.
It is as long as a man's height.

The *Sataghni* meant that which had the power
Of killing a hundred at a time.
It looked like a *gada* and was in length four cubits.
It is generally identified with a modern canon,
And hence, in war was used as a projectile weapon.

Prakriti

Deeksha began expounding a theory on nature,

Tatva began to lose its inertia
And acquired momentum.
Thus was born entropy
And heat, leading to enthalpy.

Soon Tatva began to metamorphose
Into a myriad of clusters and shapes
The *tribhuja*(triangle), the *aayat*(square),
And the *vritta* (circle).

The shapes then began a dance
Describing geometry
Forming lines from points
Formulating the concept of infinity
Starting from nothingness and
Extending in all directions.

Within moments, these shapes
Transformed and gave birth to abstracts.

Out of Time, in Tatva, emerged fate,
And from Fate and Geometry
Emerged Synthesis.

Out of Algebra in Tatva, emerged Recursion,
And from Recursion and Geometry
Emerged fractal forms.

Out of Language in Tatva, emerged Music,
And from Music and Geometry

Emerged the concept of Beauty.

Out of Emotion in Tatva, emerged Expression,
And from Expression and Geometry
Emerged the notion of Art.

Out of love in Tatva, emerged *Rasa,*
And from R*asa* and Geometry
Emerged the first musings of Philosophy.

Out of dreams in Tatva,
Emerged the poetic construct,
And from poetic construct and Geometry
Emerged the first glimpses of divine poetry.

Out of Games in Tatva, emerged Laws
And from Laws and geometry
Emerged the first Books of Knowledge.

Out of Fallacies in Tatva, emerged Conscience
And from Conscience and geometry
Emerged the Soul.

Soon, all these entities,
Synthesis, Fractcal forms, Beauty,
Art, Philosophy, Poetry,
Knowledge and the soul
Intermingled and merged together as one.

Thus, was born the consort of Tatva,
Prakriti, the mother of all creation.
She is the universal consciousness
That pervades all through time
And defines the very nature of existence

Over the course of eternity

She is creative, beautiful, artisitc,
A philosopher, a poet, a savant,
And one who is blessed with a beautiful soul.

She guides matter, ether and other forms
In their course through time,
As they chart out their trajectories
Through the constantly churning flux
Of space and time stretching far out infinitely.

Discourse on Realism

Vani teased Darpan, 'You had your eyes glued on me, yet you were all ears for Diskha, Darpan. You should be able to tell me the key takeaways from this part of the story.'

Darpan pleaded ignorance, 'I still do not see much beyond the plain words. I learned about the four powerful neighbours holding sway in their respective fields of influence. Diskha, on the other hand, gave me a brilliant description of the birth of nature herself.'

Vani coddled Darpan as if he were an infant, 'You are such a child Darpan, relishing the outer chocolate coating of candy, forgetting to enjoy the mushy, gooey center. The story has now moved on from materialism to realism. While materialistic pursuits create an artificial world, seeking bliss in simpler things leads to a life closer to nature.'

Darpan brightened up in an instant, 'So, we should all quit the pursuit of the artifices of matter, time, space and most of all money to lead a more fulfilling life by being closer to the elemental nature of things.'

Deeksha held Darpan's gaze and spoke wisely, 'Well, you can't avoid the artificial world completely, Darpan. Surely, the ego is the biggest artifice and is essential for the existence of a civilized world, without which we will be reduced to beastly animals. Also necessary are the artifices of success and the joy one derives from gifting material possessions. The ultimate artifice is the artifice of life itself, as the flesh and bones that we are made of are built to perform physical tasks and derive tangible pleasures.'

Darshan summarised, 'Again, it looks like one must walk a tight rope, balancing the reality built on artifices on one end with the surreal or spiritual aspect of nature on the other.'

Vani started reciting a poem and the others caught her dream for themselves.

I dream, of a dreamcatcher in my sleep,
That can catch my reveries
And hold my thoughts, like a tree.

I feel, the need to be free,
As the morning lark sings to me
Of love's beauty and gaiety.

I hold, you in my arms and weep,
For its you that I need,
Just like I crave sugar and the sweet.

I see, a kingdom of glee,
Where hearts rule lovingly
Where we live in peace.

I hear, the sound of the waves,
Crashing on a distant shore,
Bringing joy and happiness
For eternity.

I love, the feel of your lips,
As they brush past my buds,
And suckle tenderly.

I wake up, next to you in bed,
Dreamy thoughts in my head
And a love, heavenly.

The next roll of the dice showed hands and feet.

The Sisters

Vani began a poetic description of the hand
That shapes destiny, work and success.

Renuka had quintuplets
And fondly called them *panchgani*,
They were like the five fingers of her hand.
The pinkie, the ring, the middle,
The index and the thumb,
Nubile, rotund, tall, lithe and voluptuous.

Urvashi, Ritambhara, Madhumati,
Menaka, and *Kamakshi*;
Blessed in the arts, romance,
Warcraft, delusion and wizardry,
Fond of music, emotion, drama, dreams and theory,
They were a band of sisters, a sorority.

Together they went to school and studied hard,
Each a master of their own craft.
Urvashi in war, Ritambhara in Maya,
Menaka in witchcraft,
Madhumati, a jack of all trades,
And Kamakshi in matters of the heart.

Their playtime was full of fun and frolic,
But at times some were left sad and melancholic.
For they were all lovelorn and smitten,
By the handsome Sibu. Alas! into the forbidden fruit
They had bitten.

In their dreams each wished for their Prince Charming,
Who would pluck their heart strings,
Fill their life with things charming.
None was aware of the loves of another,

Went on with their lives and left all to wonder.

What was it, on might ask, that kept the sisters
So in love with each other?
So different they were, qualities apart,
Yet stayed together.
The days were filled with harmony,
With song, dance, music, charade, drama and wizardry.

Yet the great guru of Madhumati,
Acharya *Durvasa* had predicted,
That this harmony will not last,
Some harm would be inflicted.
And the sisters would sooner or later take to fight
Over some thing or the other, when the time was right.

Kamakshi was like Love cast into life,
For she had the eyes of a doe,
A waist taut like a well strung bow,
And hips that swayed lusciously, to and fro.

She could entice men and make them swoon,
A fragrant garland on her person, she would festoon.
She would beckon them with a coy demeanour,
To her side, her playgrounds,
And if lucky, to her chamber.

She could put the Lord of Desire, *Kama*, to shame,
Such was her coquetry, such were her games.
She could steal hearts and injure with a look,
What she had learned, could not be found in a book.

For her teacher was the great guru *Vatsyayana*,
Who taught her *Kama, Dosha, Shastra* and *Rasayana*.
She fancied men and toyed with their hearts,
With her anklet adorned feet
And her eyes as sharp as darts.

Her bosom was round and voluptuous, a heaving sight,
She carried her narrow waist with a dainty plight.
Luscious lips, bounteous hair,
Rosy cheeks, nature's delight.
A rose apple, a cherry tart,
A strawberry mousse call her, you might.

She could dance like a goddess
And invoke Cupid with her moves,
Make men go into a frenzy and get into the groove.
At times she would summon the finest wine,
And intoxicate the Gods, men and women
Until they lay supine.

Wherever she went,
The women looked at her with envy,
Her entourage consisted of beautiful women,
And handsome men, a bevy;
None could take their eyes off of her for an instant,
They all longed to be rather close to her, than distant.

Menaka held the key to magic and grandeur,
She could turn frogs to princes,
And princesses to manure.
She could cast a spell to last for years,
And cause all kin to break down in tears.

She knew all about potions, spells and witchcraft,
For she was clever, adept, cunning and deft.
She could make rain fall, sun shine or moon rise,
And could drive many a strong men
To near death fright.

She was tall, elegant and carried on her person a wand,
And transform many a thing with a sleight of hand.
People from near and far sought her advice,

And pleaded to turn fields of dust into gold
And bad men into mice.

Her teacher was the magician *Chakram*,
Who taught her *Jadu, Tona,* and *Mantra Vidya.*
She learnt it all and used it well,
For arousing fear, awe, pleasure and *mrigya.*

Wherever she went, throngs of people followed,
To see her person in a light haloed.
By the craft of wizardry, and all things spooky,
She would utter what sounded
Gibberish and gobbledy-gooky.

She had once materialised gold out of thin air,
And there was this one time,
When she left a man dangling by his hair.
She was charming, curious, adventurous and haughty,
At times though, she turned difficult and naughty.

Like this one time she transformed
Prince *Singham* to a croaking frog,
And his charming bride,
Princess Deepika, to a mangy dog.
The King Nataraja and his subjects
Looked at her with much suspicion,
For some say, she could even survive
Swallowing a poisonous scorpion.

Ritambhara was a savant, an avid pupil of *Mayavi,*
Who taught her *Maya, Chalava*
Or deception and the art of delusion.
She could fool many with just a story,
Or pull a rabbit out of a hat, in all its glory.

She could build dreamy castles out of thin air,
Or make the ones with sand that disappear.

She made meddlesome mazes, labyrinths and layers
Nobody in the vast kingdom could escape, from where.

She was fond of puzzles, quizzes and rhetoric,
And all things quaint, curious and esoteric.
She could answer the most complex queries,
And make wizened witches look like fancy fairies.

She had wisdom and an ocean of knowledge,
A shrewd persona, a petite figure
And a profusion of kismet.
For she had escaped many a delusions set by Mayavi
Through her wit, presence of mind and skulduggery.

At times, she was hard to figure out
As she puzzled you, coaxed you and threw you about
In a whirlpool of thought, grandeur and delusion,
Which ended up creating a complex illusion.

While sometimes, she was almost childlike,
Eager for a picnic, an outing,
A walk in the clouds or a hike on the mountains.
She would stroll in the fields, her head lost in thought,
Sometimes it came to a naught,
At others, it came to a lot.

Once she created a replica of the royal palace so real,
That the King himself could not tell
The fake from the ideal.
For many she remained an enigma, a puzzle,
Oh, what thoughts occupied her mind, none could tell.

Urvashi was fierce, strong, adamant and wise,
Feared by all who came in her line of sight.
For she was equally skilled
With the bow and the sword,
Some say she could defeat Hercules with a single blow.

She lived like an ascetic yet, what a beauty!
Her hair in a bun, eyes - a limpid pool,
Could send men into a tizzy.
She could arch her nubile body like a well strung bow,
And kill fighters like a hunter would hunt a sow.

She was fond of the game, taking well to the *shikar*,
Hunting deer, prized wilder-beasts, cattle and wild boar.
She was fair in sharing what she brought home,
But always chose to carry on in her hunt alone.

Her guru was the fierce and raging *Durvasa*,
Who had taught her the martial arts.
She had performed and excelled at many a *yagna*,
And earned boons from the pleased Gods.

She would win every competition
She chose to partake in,
For she was the first to wrestle,
Fight and drive home the stake.
She would wear a proud smile back home for her guru,
Who sometimes chose to call her Puru.

She was more like a man, an alpha fighter,
Star of the King's infantry, a brave solider.
Ferocious like an animal, a crouching tiger,
She was for many, a knight in shining armour.

Madhumati was just a child, a free spirit, a vagabond,
The one who sang, played and with nature
Was to be found.
None could instruct her or hold her in their midst,
For she was like a gushing river,
A waterfall, a spray of mist.

She pranced around the kingdom and listened to them
Vatsyayana, Durvasa, Mayavi and Chakram.
She could remember what they preached
And recite it all,
The secret depths of her memory, none could tell.

She knew the spells of love, the war hymns
The maya rites and the magic crafts.
She grew up with the combined knowledge of the four,
Of what use it would be, none knew anymore.

Her guru was the wise and saintly *Drona*,
Who taught her peace and forgiveness, above all.
He taught her love for nature and things simple,
And to look for joy in things, that God made beautiful.

In her childishness, he saw the divine,
In her playfulness, the equine.
Her innocence reminded him of creatures bovine,
And she matured into a woman, like a bottle of wine.

He never sought to restrain her or calm her down,
Her temerity and gusto never caused him a frown.
For he loved her like his own daughter,
And was glad that in her, a pupil he had found.

Above all, her love was for music and dance,
And she would take to the temple, given a chance
To indulge her senses in *Raga, Rasa* and *Nritya*,
Little did she know that she would rewrite *Sahitya*.

Panch Tatvas

Deeksha started describing the details of the feet,
As if she harboured fetishes as secrets.

Prakriti started playing games with Tatva
She played a truant most of the times
And got the better of the father
Winning with her notorious ways.

Out of her haughtiness and naughtiness
And the pranks of her childish games,
Emerged Maya, a creature of illusion.
Tatva was smitten and fell for her.

Tatva and Maya took to each other
Like a bird takes to flight
And spreads its wings,
Like a mind takes to thoughts and dreams,
Like a horse gallops and stretches its legs.

Soon they were giggling and snickering
Like children in a secret garden.
They took to running wild and smothering
Each other with affection.

Out of their love were born
The *Panch Tatvas*, the five daughters,
Ritu, Pavan, Jal, Dhara and *Jyoti*,
Who seemed to have been
Plucked from eternity.

Ritu was the queen of seasons,
Pavan, the princess of wind,

Jal, the carrier of water,
Dhara, the earth
And Jyoti, the light and warmth of fire.

Together they stood for the dance
Of joy and change,
Love, life, magic, and the warrior's way.
Pavan flowed like a love song
Through ether and spacetime
And brought with her a cool breeze of fluxions
That made Prakriti feel like a love child
Let loose in a bower of enchantment.
She took the sage Kama as her guru.
Pavan was blessed as a lover and a romantic.

Jal, typically, was seen carrying a pitcher
On her person, as she brought relief
To the parched earth,
That lay waiting for her calming embrace
In the omnipresent Prakriti.
She took the sage Vidya as her guru.
Jal was blessed as a magician and a life giver.

Dhara was steady as a rock
A pillar of strength for others to lean on.
She took all burden on her mighty shoulders With ease
And released Prakriti of her sorrows.
She took the sage Mithya as her guru.
Dhara was blessed as an illusionist
And a creator.

Jyoti was all fire and soul.
She was a brave-heart who led the sisters
To victory in the face of calamities,

As she brought her unquenchable energy
To rescue Prakriti from a cold demise.
She took the sage Kreeda as her guru.
Jyoti was blessed as a fiery sentimentalist
And a warrior.

Ritu was like a child, a poetess,
Fickle, dreamy and artistic.
She took the sages Kala and Vidya
As her gurus,
And was found dancing and singing
The hymns of ancient rites and rituals,
As she brought about
A metamorphosis in Prakriti.
Ritu was blessed as a poetess and
A game changer.

Discourse on the Limbs

Vani coaxed Darpan into a discussion, "I am sure you enjoyed the visual description of the ladies, Darpan. What do you make of Madhumati and her sisters as well as Ritu and her sisters?"

Darpan rubbed his hands in glee, "While you described the beauty of these girls, I closed my eyes and imagined myself surrounded by them. But when Deeksha took over, I was mesmerised by the sheer artistic abilities of Ritu and her siblings. However, I fail to see how they relate to hands and feet."

Vani explained, "Well, if only you had not lost yourself imagining these beautiful girls around you, the message would have been as clear as water to you. Madhumati and her sisters are like the five fingers of the hand; the thumb - voluptuous and bossy, the index helping the magician in the sleight of hand, the middle having attributes of all the other fingers in parts, the ring finger associate with illusions as it is the one on which we put a ring, while the little finger comes into play in artistic pursuits. Ritu and her siblings are like the feet - grounded in the basic element of nature, while still possessing the dexterity of arts, hence giving the feet the requisite adeptness for dancing."

Darpan began to get the picture, "So, I guess the hands are what perform all the work like love, magic, dance, illusions and art, while the feet put things in motion with dance.'

Deeksha added, 'Not only are the hands and the feet fundamental to expressing motion, they are also inseparable. The first thing a child learns is to examine things with his hands, but he cannot do so unless he learns to use his feet and reach those objects. Also, one cannot imagine any kind of locomotion, without the combined use of hands and feet.'

Darpan put an end to the discussion by saying, 'Hands and feet bring us in touch with the real and the artificial'.

Vani broke into a lyrical rhapsody and the others could not help but hold on to their beating hearts.

'Cos, I feel you in my arms,
As when a mother holds a child,
When I count till five,
I feel like dancing the jive.

It's your fingers that I hold,
By my hand and I feel guilty
Of not being there to help you
When you walked and fell.

It's your feet I rub,
I feel the warmth in my hands now.
I put an anklet around them
And hear the twinkling bell sounds grow.

As you hold my hand
And lead me to the dance floor,
I feel the ground shake and jar,
The rhythm's like a downpour.

We can dance, we can dance,
We can dance,
Till the sun draws down,
Till the moon blooms up.

'Cos, the stars house in our eyes
As we speak,
And the moonshine narrates
The joy that you bring me.

The next roll of the dice showed ears and eyes.

Ritu

Deeksha started elucidating to the eager ears,

.

Prakriti woke up from her slumber
And manifested Prakasha (Light) to being.
She called upon Ritu to play with Prakasha.

Ritu, playful and naughty
Started dancing and singing with Prakash

Ritu began a dance which was eclectic
For it involved all the elements of Prakriti.
She threw Prakash all around,
But it disturbed ether.
She manifested in Prakash
Synthesis, fractcal forms, beauty,
Art, philosophy, poetry,
Knowledge and the soul.

Prakash became artificial, recursive, vain,
Abstruse, deep, poetic, pedantic and soulful.
This destroyed the very essence of Prakash,
Which was contained in his simplicity,
His purpose;
That of living as a pure life-giving energy.

Prakriti was miffed and called upon
Vidya and Kala.
Kala and Vidya decided to educate Ritu again.
Kala tested Ritu with a simple question,
"Tell me Ritu, what is that

Which can be seen, heard, felt,
And yet can never be experienced in full?"

Ritu was flummoxed and felt stupid.
She replied, "I do not have a clue, master."
Kala answered, "Ritu, as the Kalachakra (wheel of time)
Passes, one grows memories,
Especially of dear ones.
These memories can never be
Experienced in full
Because no matter how hard you try
You will forget parts of your experiences."
Vidya then asked her, "Tell me Ritu,
What is lighter than air
And thinner than water?"
Ritu was perplexed and feigned ignorance.
Vidya answered, "Well, it's Vidya (Knowledge), my dear."

"We hope we have left you wiser
And more prepared for your tasks."
Prakriti then asked Ritu to create the seasons.
Ritu engendered Sheeta (Winter),
Basanta (Spring),
Grishma(Summer) and Varsha(Rains).

Prakriti was delighted
But as soon as she saw the seasons,
Her joy turned to anger.
Sheeta was full of raging fire,
Basanta had extreme showers,
Grishma contained the onset of life,
While Varsha brought with it extreme cold.

Prakriti could not bear

The sight of Ritu anymore.
Ritu pleaded with her for another chance.
Prakriti first set Prakash right
And then corrected the seasons.

She then assigned a seed to Ritu
And asked her to play with it
Along with Dhara.
Ritu and Dhara started playing with the seed
But soon a battle of egos, did proceed.

Ritu said, "The seed is mine and
I alone shall develop it."
While Dhara interjected, "I have all it takes
To pop it."
While they argued and wasted their time,
The seed slowly began to rot with slime.

It disintegrated and the task was lost.
Prakriti was furious,
Making Ritu and Dhara run
As fast as their legs
Would take them to their homes.

Madhumati

Vani began her lyric on the eyes,

Madhumati was playing in a mango orchard
When Drona arrived,
He said, 'O sweet child,
Get ready for a test as an exercise.
Since you are a jack of all trades
And the master of none,
You must answer questions about war,
Magic, love and illusion.'

He began with love and asked,
'Tell me what is the difference between love and lust?'
Madhumati replied, 'Someone has said,
Some love is fire, some love is rust,
But the cleanest purest form of love is lust.
However, I beg to differ with their opinion
And put lust itself to test.

Lust is carnal, a kind of beastly desire whole,
While love is angelic, a need felt by the soul.
Lust is fleeting, it lasts for a moment,
And is instantly satiated,
While love lasts for a lifetime
And lives forever, once initiated.

Love and lust are like companions,
Fire from the hearth and embers from the cinder,
Long after the fire of lust has died,
The embers of love still smoulder.
Lust is never chased after and is easily acquired,
While love is not easily granted
And is not for the weak hearted.'

'Attagirl, Madhumati. Now explain to me
The art of lovemaking.'
'Lovemaking, my Guru, is a sacred ritual
Where you are granted passage by following rites.
The first and foremost is holding,
Cuddling and embracing.
When the lover is comfortable
In your presence you must hold them tight.

One can then proceed to wrap their thighs
Around the lover's thighs,
You can play with their hair and start with a kiss.
The first kiss can be a simple peck on the cheeks,
This can be followed then
By a passionate smooch on the lips.

A little tongue can be used to the enhance the foreplay,
And some objects like sweetmeats can be inserted,
If you like it that way.
After the kiss comes the *Aalingam*,
The entwining of the lovers' limbs.
When the lover is ready, the paramour
Can part her thighs to be stroked and caressed.

As she gets comfortable,
He can proceed to enter her gently with finesse.
She will make a sweet moan
And utter the name of the lover from her parted lips.
The lover can then kiss her over the bosom
And knead it gently.
As the man enters her over and over again,
The lady will reach ecstasy.'

'Well said Madhumati. Now tell me
About the various types of magicians.'
'Guruji, I will answer this question in two sections,
In the first I shall answer the question

By the words that I have memorised,
And in the other I shall answer
With what my heart says.

The first type of Magician is the *Handman,*
The one who makes use of the sleight of hand.
He usually has cards up his sleeve for card tricks,
And does not wear a cloak or carry a magic wand,
He also uses fake fingers and thumbs and wears bands.

The second type of magician is the stage magician.
He uses props,
Elaborately prepared sets and instrumentations.
He takes aid of assistants to perform his acts,
Mostly composed of vanishing acts and illusions.

The third type of magician is the street performer.
He is into juggling balls, throwing swords
And catching them in mid air.
He balances himself on stilts
By walking on bamboo poles,
Or walks a tight rope high across two pillars
Over a bed of burning coals.

But let me now answer the question
As my heart truly feels,
For I believe the best sort of magician
Is the one who steals,
Hearts with a smile, kindness with a glance,
And has magic in his eyes and glamour in his stance.'

'Supreme endeavour, Madhumati!
Now tell me about the various charms.'
'O Wise One, I shall begin with the charm
For the wild beasts.
Thou shalt make fun of destruction and famine
And the beast of the earth

Shall run away from you into a ravine

The stones of the field shall be
In the same league of play as thee
And thou shalt be at peace
With the field-playing beasts.
And now, I will describe the charm
Against trouble, in general.

Thou shalt be delivered in troubles six,
Yea, in seven and evil touch shall escape thee.
He shall redeem thee from death in famine,
And the power of the sword
Shall win over wars with ways feminine.

That thy tabernacle should be left in peace,
Thou shalt know,
And there shall be regular visitations
To thy habitations and thy love shall grow.
Finally, I'll tell you the charm against enemies.

Aloha, salvation flows from God,
I will trust and not be afraid,
For my strength and song flows
From the lord *Jehovah*, a dear friend.
My salvation is delivered by him,
Just like the constellations, the heavens
And the stars do not grow dim,
And shall not surrender their light.

Darkened will be the sun and will not shine bright,
And from the moon, will be taken away
Her lovely glow, white.
There shall be trouble at the evening tide,
And he is not, before the morning ride.
For some of them, shall spoil us,
And the lot of them shall rob us.'

'Superb Madumati. Now explain in detail *Maya*,
Chalava and delusion.'
'Gurudeva, the artifice of Maya is all around us,
First and foremost in the form of nature.
For surely the trees, the skies, the earth, the sun,
The moon and the animals are all delusions,
But there is a subtle and very important difference
Between Maya and delusion.

While delusion can come out of our own selves,
Maya always finds a way to manifest externally.
As an example, we can delude ourselves
Into believing that we are God-like,
But Maya would make us play, laugh
And love and be child-like.

At the far end of the spectrum is Chalava,
The art of deception,
It is for the corrupt, the deceitful
And those who enjoy commotion.
For Chalava intends to fool a person
Into believing that something exists,
When truly it is fake or surreal
Or unreal like ghosts and spirits.'

'What mastery, Madumati. Now can you explain
The planetary spirits to me?
'Spirits exist for all the seven planets.
The spirits for *Saturn,* slender and tall,
With a lean body and a fierce countenance,
Are black in color and shine
Out of varying forms.
Swift is their motion, like the wind,
Attended at times with an earthquake as a norm.

Their particular forms include a King,

Bearded and carrying a tarragon,
Leaning on a crutch, an old woman.
A boar, an eagle, a black garment, a dragon
A book and a pair of scissors,
A mango tree and a bearded old man.

The spirits of Saturn follow the south-west wind.
They arrive at first with a terrific brilliance,
Silver'd earth, fairer than snow
Is the sign of their appearance.
Their office is to sow hatred, cause agitations,
Evil thoughts and discord.

To plunder, kill and commit heinous crimes,
Which shall be permitted by Providence divine.
They rule over Saturday,
And are invoked on the 1st, 8th, 15th, and 22nd
Hours of that day.

The spirits of the *Sun* appear in a rotund full body,
Sanguine and gross, in gold color
With a tincture bloody.
They are glorious and regal in their appearance,
Their motion is like a bolt of lightening,
Accompanied by powerful thunders.

Their particular forms are a King with a sceptre
Made of dandelions,
A Jester with a sceptre, a Prince with a crown,
A dinosaur, a rooster, a lion,
A sceptre, a beige garment and a dandelion.

The spirits of the sun are under the northern winds,
Their sign causes massive perspiration
In the invocators.
Their nature is to acquire quartz, sapphire,
Diamonds, carbuncles and rubies,

And lead one to obtain grants and benevolence.

To dissipate enmity, to further honours,
And to relieve infirmities,
These spirits are said to rule over Sundays.
The hours are the same as that of Saturn's.
The spirits of the Moon appear
Generally in a huge and full stature,

Mellow and phlegmatic, with the hue of a dark cloud,
A puffed up countenance,
With eyes red and soaked with water,
Bald heads and teeth like those of a wild boar,
Even a great tempest at the sea,
Their motion can bring forth.

There will appear an exceedingly great rain
For their sign, about the circle.
Their particular forms are a King
Like an archer riding upon a foe,
A midget boy, a fierce hunter with arrows
And a bow.
A bull, a foe, a barrow, a goose,
An emerald or golden coloured garment,
And a many foot'd creature.

The spirits of the Moon rule over Monday.
They are accompanied by marvellous
And jolting blasts of the west wind during the day,
With drizzle, wisps of clouds and hail,
When powerfully invocated.
Many a tempest have been raised
At their invocation, by God.

Its in the Lunar spirits' nature to give copper,
And to carry artefacts from place to place,
They make horses swift and fill them with grace,

And bring in the open, the secrets of a person,
That one may discover.

The spirits of Mars appear mostly
In a body, lithe and slender.
A mangy countenance, of the color of mud,
Swarthy or flaming red, with horns,
Like a hare's and condor's claws.
They come bellowing like wild bulls near,
And fire burns wherever they move;
The sign of their appearance is thunder.

Their particular forms are:
A King armed, standing on a stool,
An armed knight, a female with a sword and buckler,
A lamb, a mare, an orange garment, a muffler.
A horn, a ram and a load of wool.

These spirits rule over Tuesday,
And travel with the east wind.
They are best called upon the day,
When the time is for Mars,
For they cause the living to turn dead.

They are invoked to cause battle, morbidity, turbulence
And to perform strange exploits.
The Mercury spirits make an appearance
In a body of middle stature,
Barren, fluent, of an amiable speech, prudish, yet fair.
Taking the form and shape human, having bright
And clear color like an armed knight,
They move like amber colored clouds.
The invocator draws forth unforeseen tragedies
And fear is a sign of their appearance.

Their particular forms are a King carrying a spiral wire,
A fair damsel, a mallet holding woman,

A hog, a robin, a half goat - half woman,
A pipe or a sceptre and a cloth of changeable color.

These spirits generally come with the south-west wind,
It is believed that they rule over Wednesday.
Their nature is to give all sorts of metals,
To calm judges,
To expose all things of daily life - past, present
Or future, and to bring victory to the day.

They teach adventure and all the archaic sciences;
To modify bodies composed of elements,
Typically from one form into another,
To give life or infirmities,
To heal the poor and condemn the rich,
They bind as well as release spirits,
Open obstructions and enrich.
They can be brought to visual appearance easily.

The spirits of Jupiter appear with bodies
Divine and Greek,
Or at times with a potbellied gait
With a motion terrifying, awkward, or meek.
Albeit, with a timid countenance
And a mild mannered speech,
They have the color of iron.

When they move,
They bring about treacherous thunders,
And brilliant, spectacularly vivid lightnings.
Their appearance can generally be
Surmised by numbers,
Of faulty and horrid forms, like dragons
And beasts of the jungle.

Their particular forms are a king with a drawn sword
Riding on a horse,

A boy wearing a tunic, clothed in long garments,
An angel crowned with a laurel,
And adorned with flowers,
A lion fiercely roaring, a seagull, an azure garment,
A box tree, a sword and a horse.

They rule and govern over Thursday.
They usually come with the southern wind,
Very strong and mighty, akin a hurricane.
Their nature is to purchase the love of women,
To cause men happiness and joy,
To calm arguments and discussions,
To win over enemies,
To heal diseases and cure sicknesses,
And to rebuilt what is gone and destroyed.

The spirts of Venus have a voluptuous stature
And fair bodies,
Graceful and pleasant countenance,
Of colors silver or green.
They move like a nebulae, their upper parts
Are golden and melancholic,
You can tell of their arrival by the appearance
Of handsome maidens.

Their particular forms are a King with a distaff
Riding on a camel,
A lamb, a camel, a glove, a naked female,
A silk or cotton ornament, foliage, the herb savine.
They govern the day of Friday
Which is the day of Venus, divine.

They come with the furious west wind,
Mixed with gentle zephyrs and divine music,
Delightful to hear.
They provide gold and lead men to a life gilded,
Cause engagements, procure happiness,

Take away disease and calm natures.

They are readily invocated,
As per the ancient *Theurgists.*
Confined to visible appearance,
In time and space limited, compared to the other spirits
To which they are likened.'

'Marvelously said, Madhumati.
Now explain to me the different types of *Vyuha.*'
'Well, there are many different kinds,
But my favourite is *Matsya Vyuha.*
The warriors arrange themselves
In the shape of the reefs of an ocean,
And any oncoming assault is greeted
By them shaped like shoals of fish.

The warriors arrange themselves
In the shape of small fish for guerrilla warfare,
Like *matti, bangada, hilish, bhetaki,*
Salmon, cod, *rohu* and the pomfret.
For those manoeuvres requiring large numbers
Of warriors and fanfare,
They take the form of a shark, a whale, a tuna,
Or a hammerhead.

The warriors move through enemy lines like fish
Gliding with their fins,
And neutralize their enemy like a hammerhead
Driving home its pins,
Also at times, the smaller fish can take the shape
Of a large animal,
And fool the enemy with deception
And take them down in the ocean, abysmal.

The other Vyuha that I am very of is the *Hasti Vyuha,*
In it, the warriors arrange themselves in the shape

Of a group of elephants.
And make any enemy cower with their sheer
Size and might,
To cover up their large tracks, they confuse
The enemy with chants of Hallelujah.'

'Masterfully done, Madumati. Now humor
Prince Singham with your wit.'
Madhumati found the Prince
Taking a walk in the palisades.
She invited him to the auditorium
And asked him to take a seat,
'Prince Singham,' said she,
'Let me entertain you with my repartee.'

'Of Angels and Demons, I will speak in a hushed voice,
Angels hold the staff of goodness bread,
While the Evil hold their sepulchres.
Angels have a halo,
While Demons feast like vultures,
All good in this world has to fight the evils of vice.

Let me tell you the story of an Angel,
Arjun, who fell in love with the devilish Dana.
Arjun flew on the wings of God,
And carried goodness in a satchel,
While Dana was the worshipper of the Mill,
Factories, the *Karkhaana*.

While Arjun laboured to relieve pain and suffering,
Dana rejoiced in merriment and mischief making.
She was always found hatching devious schemes,
With which she could rob the hearts of men
And their sleep.

Arjun first met her at the gardens of Babylon,
And looking at her luscious body, fell into a lurch.

He fell for her, hook, line and sinker,
While for Dana, it was just another heart to tinker.

Arjun met her in parks, gardens,
Museums and lakesides,
And took her to ball games, expo's,
Theatres and boat rides.
She seemed sweet, kind, generous and divine,
Little did he know that for her love,
He would soon pine.

He gave his heart to her and did not think twice,
While Dana flirted and danced,
And was jubilant in her vice.
She would fly with evil spirits
And coax them to plunder
The city's peace, until the citizens would surrender.

One fine day, he saw her making love to a fiend,
And his heart broke in two,
How could she do this to a friend?
She never met him again and hence began his sorrow,
It felt like his life was finished,
That there was no tomorrow.

He drowned his pain in cheap liquor, tea and cigarettes,
And took to playing, in seedy bars,
Jazz tunes on a trumpet.
She would walk in often, hand-in-hand with her lover,
Arjun sealed his broken heart and put it in a clover.

Ever since then, the sealed clover
Has been thought of as a bad omen,
If you like this tale, please pass it amongst men,
Sing it merrily, or sadly, for six pence a song,
But remember, if you have love, make it last long.

Discourse on the Sensory Organs

Vani encouraged Darpan to speak, 'Darpan, now you have come to know about the lives and qualities of the two lovely ladies, Ritu and Madhumati. Considering your temperament, I hope you did not fall in love with either of them.'

Darpan confessed, 'To be very frank, I would love to have the love of both these women in my life. It looks like Ritu is naive as she failed in the tasks assigned to her by Prakriti, whereas Madhumati came out victorious. While I would love to have Ritu as my daughter, care-free, restless and innocent, Madhumati can play a doting mother to me, kind, generous and wise beyond her years. I do not, however, see how Ritu is related to the ears and Madhumati to the eyes.'

Vani explained, 'Its very simple, if you can visualise the allegory which you have very well imagined. Ritu is the intuitive mother, the fairy godmother to the seasons of nature, who uses her ears more than anything else to listen to the crying child and rush towards him to correct things. Madhumati, on the other hand, is more of a controlling mother, the one who looks anxiously all over the house for her child, making sure he does not get into accidents, fights or other such troubles.'

Darpan sighed, 'So we are not supposed to be all ears when working, or merely a set of eyes looking out for signs of trouble?'.

Deeksha concurred, 'Exactly. The ears are windows to the mind, while the eyes are the front doors. One must be careful to let in both light and sound and then act accordingly.'

Darshan added, 'From now on, I will always listen to my heart and look into the recesses of my mind'.

Vani started dancing and singing out of sheer elation and the others could not help but join in the merriment.

So long, I've been looking for these eyes,
And wondering if you see what I do,
The loveliness of you, the magic of you,
When I am near you, holding you, caressing you.

Oh, when I look into your moist eyes,
And when I hear your honeyed voice,
I loose all the sense of place and time,
And my heart beats as if in a rhyme.

If only I could be near you all the time,
I would give all that I have,
To see you like my sweet child,
Rocking and rolling, as I sing lullabies.

Would you mind if I closed your eyes,
With kisses, like butterflies.
Would you flinch, if I teased your earlobes
As I suckle on them as if sipping wine.

Lets dance out of here into the glade,
Into the woods and the creek by the cove.
Lets make sweet and taboo'd love,
As you become my eyes,
And I hear your stifled cries.

The roll of the dice showed mouth and navel.

Pavan

Deeksha began an exposition of the mouth.

Prakriti, still simmering
From her jinxed episode
With Ritu, began fixing the seed.
But soon, she got tired
And felt the need to ask for a helping hand.

What the seed needed was love,
And she decided to beckon Pavan for the job.
She found Pavan, carefree and dancing
In a flux infused mass amidst the firmament.

She began telling Pavan a treatise on life
Starting from the *Kalpa Vriksha*,
And the *Vata Vriksha*,
Ending her story at the Tree of Life.

She described the role of Basanta,
As the harbinger of goodness in which
The seed sprouts,
Grishma as the kiln in which
The seed stratifies,
Varsha as the torrent in which
The seed germinates,
And Sheeta, the placid calm in which
The seed hibernates.

She waxed poetically about the virtues of love,
What it can do to a young sapling.
How tender nourishing care
Can transform a mere dot in

Dhara into a *florida conspicua.*

What she wanted from Pavan
Was a gentle coaxing lullaby
For the sleeping child
That would allay all its fears
As it lay dormant in its infancy
Waiting to come out in
A spurt of floral abundance.

Pavan took to the task
And began swaying her steps.
She stuck to her rhythm for a while,
But soon got bored and broke the hymn
And developed a haphazard,
Shaky, scary rhythm.

This made the seed scared
And it cocooned in on itself.
The seed felt life seeping away from itself
As it started crumbling to a powdery mass.
Within moments, the seed had disappeared
And life was lost.

Prakriti raged and ranted and cursed Pavana
And called forth Kama.
Kama came to know about the incident,
To enlighten Pavan, was his major intent.

He asked Pavan, 'Tell me child,
Why does Pavan flow?
Why does Prakash glow?
And why does Dravya show?'

Pavan was clueless and maintained
A poker face.
Kama replied, 'It is love my child,
The supreme force which makes
Things come to life while being
Gentle and mild.

By this time Prakriti had sown another seed,
And had the issue of love resolved.
She charted a task for Pavan:
It was to bring Jal gently down.

Pavan summoned Jal and asked her
To use a pitcher
To make it shower over the seed
And do it quicker,
But Pavan's tone was bossy,
Haughty and rude.
Jal dropped her pitcher and left,
Unsettling dust in a plume.

Pavan knew that she had
To make a quick exit,
She had aroused Prakriti's rage
And did vex it.

Kamakshi

Vani's poem turned towards the navel.

Kamakshi was frolicking in the garden of the ShivaVihara
When Vatsyayana arrived.
He took her to a private corner
And into her ears whispered,
'Oh, child of mine, you have achieved much
In the tutelage Of Kama, but have you excelled,
For I must test you now and see if you have truly
Come out of your shell.'

Kamakshi, overcome with emotion,
Echoed his sentiments and said,
'Guruji, that you find me worthy of your *shiksha*,
I am led to believe that you must
Have entrusted me with a task worthy of greats,
For I know you hold all the knowledge of the art
Of love, seduction, pleasure and hate.

Vatsyayana mentioned two tests:
One, a questionnaire and another, a practical.
The questionnaire contained a set of assorted questions
On the art of love and arousal.
And to steal the heart of Prince Singham
And leave him wanting, was the practical.
With this he said, 'Let's now begin the questions
Which are five in total.

'Tell me, oh Kamakshi, the various categories
Of men and women.
Kamakshi replied, 'The various categories
Of men are as follows:
The men are of three kinds – bull men,
Hare men and horse men;

While the women are either mare, a female deer,
Or a female elephant.

'Very good, dear. Now explain the embraces
Mentioned in the Kama compendium.'
'Oh guru, the embraces are four in kind,
Rubbing, piercing, touching and kissing.
When, under some pretext or other,
A man walks alongside or in front of a woman,
And with his body touches her body,
It is called a touching embrace.

There is no fixed schedule or timing
Or order between the embrace and the kiss,
Or the pressing and scratching with the nails
Or fingers.
But this thing should be done beforehand,
Before the beginning of the sexual union rites.
At the time of the sexual congress,
One may make striking and other sounds.

As the intensity increases, scratching with nails,
Or pressing with them is practiced,
Especially when going for a journey,
Or when a spiteful lover is reconciled.
But it is not usual to press with nails,
Except in cases that the lovers are very passionate.
Together with biting, it can be employed
By those, to whom this practice is agreeable.

The following are the various kinds of bites:
The swollen bite, the hidden bite, the point,
The jewel and the coral, the line of point,
The broken cloud, the line of jewels and the hare's bite.'

'Excellent, my disciple. Now please elaborate
On the various ways of lying down.'

Kamakshi spoke, 'The deer woman
Has the following three ways of lying down.
The wide opened position, the yawning position,
And the Indra's wife's position.

In low congress, the elephant woman should
Lie in a way to contract her bottom.
While in high congress, the deer woman
Should lie in a way to widen her bottom.
In an equal congress,
They should lie in a natural position.
In a low congress, to satisfy their desires, the women
Should make use of medicine.'

'Well done again dear. Now please speak
About the various types and modes of striking.'
Kamakshi replied, 'Sir, the the following
Are the various places for striking:
The head, various points between the breasts,
The shoulders,
The *jaghana*, the back, the middle part of the body,
And the sides.

The four kinds of strikings can be distinguished as:
Striking with the back of the hand,
Striking with the fingers contracted,
Striking with the fist
And with an open palm of the hand.'

'Bravo Kamakshi, you impress me. Now tell me,
How do you create confidence in a girl?'
Kamakshi spoke, 'The first three days, lovers sleep
On the floor and avoid things sexual.
Also, food is consumed without seasoning
It with alkalis or salts.
For the next week, they should bath ensconced
In sounds of musical instruments.

They should dine together, decorate themselves
And visit their relations,
They should pay attention to those
That have come to witness their conjugation.
On the eleventh or twelfth day,
The man should start in a lonely place.
This will result in building in the girl, some confidence.

The man should make attempts to win her over
And create confidence in her,
But must restrain from arousing
In her, any physical pleasure.
Women want gentle foreplay
As they are of a tender nature.
He should embrace her in a way
That lasts a long time and feels tender.

When the girl welcomes his embrace,
He should put a tambula or a betel nut in her mouth.
If she refuses, he should coax her
To take it, with mollifying words and mirth.
However shy or furious a women may seem,
He should use appeals and kneel at her feet.
When giving her the tambula, he should softly kiss
Her mouth, not making any movement.

When he is able to win her over in respect,
He should then make her talk,
And let her tell him things
About which he knows nothing.
If she does not converse with him,
He should not frighten her, or balk.
If a man slowly gets her to open up,
He should win her confidence and everything else.'

'Good job Kamakshi. You have bettered yourself

With every response.
Truly you have mastered the art of Kama, Rasa,
And their eternal dance.
Now let's head to the gardens of Prince Singham
Where he plays games,
And you must ensnare his heart and leave him
Wanting or your talents will be put to shame.'

Kamakshi wandered into the gardens
Of the royal palace and found Prince Singham.
She had a plan in mind with which she intended
To play him like a game.
She transformed herself into a beautiful doe
And started frolicking in his sight.
It was not long before Prince Singham
Took to chasing the doe with all his might.

The doe sprang and leapt and playfully jumped
Through the garden over walls;
She ran around the trees, trod over the springs
Of water and jumped over the corn.
Prince Singham and his entourage chased her
On a chariot armed with his weapons,
The doe ran far out of sight for it was a steady sprinter
And left Prince Singham forlorn.

The Prince saw the doe's foot prints
Etched about in the muddy fields,
He turned his chariot and searched through the thicket,
The bush and the mango trees.
He spotted the doe hiding behind a bush,
Looking oh-so-lovely, with limpid eyes.
Prince Singham uttered a *mantra*
And on his bow appeared the *Pasa*, with ropes.

Out of the corner of the eyes, the doe saw Singham,

And leapt for joy again into the woods.
Prince Singham let go of the Pasa,
The noose flew straight towards the animal's legs.
It missed her by inches,
The doe now knew Prince Singham's intent.
She scampered even faster around the trees,
As if the path itself was bent.

But soon the doe got tired,
And it started huffing, panting and came to a rest.
Prince Singham chanted the mantra
And again the Pasa on the bow appeared.
He let go of the Pasa, with a twang
And it flew straight towards the resting doe.
This time, the noose got him in bull's eye
And had him in a bind.

To Singham's surprise, as the Pasa tightened,
The doe transformed into a Canary,
And it flew away to a tree and chirped,
Tweeting a song that sounded merry.
Singham could not believe his sight
But wanted to capture the bird, 'It's Maya',
He said and turned his chariot, chanting a mantra,
And got on his bow, a *Pinjara*.

A Pinjara is a cage which was meant to catch
The canary and keep it inside;
Little did he know that the little bird
Could put up a big fight.
She moved swiftly, hopped and skipped
And flew straight through the branches.
Whenever she could manage,
She also threw at the chaser, some tiny twigs.

The bird sang in merriment and flew high
In the clouds and was not to be seen,

Singham gave up the chase and rested,
And at last, tried to glean.
The trail that the bird had left once,
She left it for the clouds,
But could not be found no matter where he looked,
Up, down, round and about.

Suddenly it started raining and the winds blew
With a mighty roar,
And the bird flew low to escape the winds
With her wings it attempted a deep soar.
Singham jolted his chariot into a frenzy
And chased the bird to a pond.
He managed to corner her down,
Right at the banks where the water met the sand.

Now the bird was tired of flying
And battling the winds, she needed rest.
So she lay itself down on the bank,
As if she had just made itself a nest.
Singham shot the Pinjara and captured the bird
In the cage and finally put her to rest.
Satisfied with the catch of the day,
He put the singing bird close to his breast.

Yet again, the cage collapsed as the bird
Transformed itself into a dolphin and swam away.
Singham was left fuming and perplexed,
But took off his clothes and jumped into the fray.
He swam after the dolphin but she
Kept giving him the slip,
She sang and snorted and sprayed water
Out of her snout; she even did a flip!

Singham finally managed to catch up
With the beast and caught her by the tail,
But the dolphin gave him a tail-slap

And slipped away, like a water filled pail.
Singham then caught hold of her fins,
But the dolphin head-butted him in his shins.

Finally, he got the better of her,
When he caught hold of her neck.
He managed to strangle her
With all his might and said, 'W*hat the heck.*'
He dragged the dolphin out of the pond
All the way across the water,
And tied it with a rope so it could no longer
Go anywhere or disappear.

He was fooled yet again, as the rope turned to dust
And the dolphin to a mermaid.
She was so beautiful to look at
That out of joy, Singham went mad.
He caught her in a wild embrace
And said, '*I will never let you go.*'
She gave him a quick slip
And then started rocking to and fro.

She said, 'O Prince, you have freed me from a curse,
But now I must leave.
I have taken form in earlier lives, of a grazing animal,
A bird, a fish and even a tree.
I thank you from the bottom of my heart,
But I must go back home now and we must part.'

Singham begged, 'Please don't go, my dear.
I am in love with you.'
With this, he ran towards her in a blind hullabaloo.
As he touched her, she decomposed
Into a million butterflies,
Each of a brilliant color, that took to the skies.

Discourse on the Feeding Organs

Vani egged Darpan on, 'So Darpan, what do you think of Kamakshi? I am sure, she has now become your fantasy and the object of your affection. '

Darpan complained, 'All I remember is Kamakshi's curves and Pavan's light heartedness. I also remember the fact that Pavan messed up simple tasks like giving tender care, affection and love, when she is supposed to be good at it. Also, Kamakshi seems like a master of the art of love, which she proved by enticing Prince Singham over and over again with her love games. Somehow I fail to see the connection each time and it beats me as to how Pavan is related to the mouth and Kamakshi to the navel.'

Vani spoke, clearing his doubts, 'Its fairly simple, but you don't get it since you are a visual thinker and do not read between the lines. Pavan is the first breath of life for a child, who breathes her in through the mouth, just like all children are supposed to come out of Narayan's mouth. Kamakshi, on the other hand, is the mother to whom the child is connected via the umbilical cord, which acts as his physical conduit for nourishment and forming taking. It signifies a physical as well as an emotional connect with the navel.'

Darpan let out a whistle, 'Now that I think of it, it was staring me in the face the whole time. So I understand that children derive nourishment from the mother via the navel in the womb, but are supposed to let go of her once they are born and their first breath of life is via the mouth.'

Deeksha affirmed, 'Yes, but that is not it. In oriental philosophy, the mouth and the navel are considered the cleanest of all parts. We can meditate on the navel and derive a connection with the soul, whereas the mouth is foremost, a medium for air, thereon of water and food, and finally of the most beautiful invention by mankind, language.'

Darshan added with a wink in his eyes, 'I guess there is a reason why children suckle on their thumbs and toes'.

Vani had tears in her eyes as she thought of the first lines of the poem she was about to narrate.

Be gentle my love,
And speak as if I am a child.
Treat me like a flower,
'Cos over me, you have all the power.

Hold close your mouth,
And let me feel your breath on mine,
As we kiss, our lips meet,
And the night is on our side.

Let bees suckle on dripping nectar,
And birds peck in sweet ecstasy.
As fish glide, jump and wave their goodbyes
To the sweet waters of Santorini.

Bring me sweet surprises on long nights,
As I dream of you
As the Sheikh of Arabia,
The Prince of Persia.

Let me feel your body next to mine,
As purple skies surround us,
Deep velvet ensconces us,
Mahogany is all around us,
And the Gods bless us.

Kiss me again, my darling,
For I long to feel your tender touch,
And wish that this dream never ends,
As you, my love, plunder my heart.

The roll of the dice showed tongue and teeth.

Jal

Deeksha began a discourse on the tongue.

Prakriti was now a raging ball of fire
And she needed the help of Jal
To calm the *doshas* in her many layered attire.

A calm fountain,
A spray of water,
A mist, a cloud, rain,
Or even better, a gushing river,
Replete with waterfalls,
Canyons, ravines, crevasses,
Lakes, sea shores,
Oceans, reefs, glaciers, corals
And sandy beaches
Was what she had for a plan.

She summoned Jal
And asked her to create first, the oceans;
And from the oceans
And the melting ice-lands,
Thundering rivers, that meander their way
Through the terrain
And crash in majestic waterfalls,
Creating misty sprays,
Rainbows, reefs, little puddles of joy,
Morphing into magical chasms,
Ponds, fjords, and lakes,
Finally forming mangroves
At the deltas surrendering into the seas.

She summoned Jal and put her to the task.

Jal began sculpting the icebergs,
From which she extricated the oceans.
She then took to the task of
Engineering mighty rivers
By causing massive rifts in the terrain
That she hoped would fill up
With surging water,
As the icebergs melted
And the oceans swelled.

But to her dismay, she had miscalculated.
The icebergs were too many in number
And began melting sporadically
And way too fast.
Pretty soon the oceans
Began welling up with water.

The oceans overflowed
Into the water laden rivers
Causing havoc, as the rivers swelled up
To monstrous proportions
Of meandering swells.
Prakriti, who needed a panoramic display
Of aquatic splendors,
Was left gasping for breath.

She shrieked in horror.
First, she diverted the course of rivers.
Then, she summoned Vidya
To set things right.
Vidya decided to enthuse
Her student in her art.
She questioned Jal,
'Tell me child,

What is that which can be seen and admired,
But should not be shown too much?
Also, it is more often than not,
A fool's paradise?
It remains a quirky science
And some call it fake.'
As Jal feigned ignorance,
Vidya answered with grace,
'It's magic, that which
I have imparted the best of.
Now go ahead and do your best.'

Prakriti, though enraged,
Decided to test Jal again.
She wanted Jal to calm the unstable stars,
As they were now full of raging fire.
Jal came up with a plan;
She decided to release steam
Into the core of stars.
She watched in horror,
As her plan fell apart.
The steam caused the stars,
To diminish their gravitational pull
And they exploded and fell apart.
Wisely, she left before she could meet with Prakriti's fire.

Menaka

Vani, on the wings of poesy, spoke of teeth

Menaka was playing at the annexe of the royal Auditorium
When Chakram found her.
She was turning a pillar into a column,
And a lamp to a chandelier.
'O Menaka, come out and leave your childish tricks
Because you must take a test,
Which examines your knowledge of magic, potions,
Tricks, spells and the rest.

Together they left for Chakram's cottage
Where he practiced his art,
And when they had found solitude,
Chakram thought he would start.
The first task, he spelled out, pun intended,
Was to display the knowledge of magic,
And the other was to surprise Prince Singham
And leave him with something tragic.

Chakram asked Menaka, 'Tell me, O Magician,
What is down magic and up magic?'
Menaka replied, 'Magic as practiced
In the middle ages is called Down magic.
It combines the art of whiz-craft, spell-logic,
Voodoo and hex crafts.
It utilizes lotions, amphoras, simple visualizations,
Chants and bracelets.

Up magic is performed to bring about a union
With gods and is called Devotional magic.
The powers of nature are conceived
Either as angelic or satanic.
The powers are controlled in conjunction with spirits,

Using words and names of sacred Gods.'

'Bellisima Menaka, you have done well.
Now tell me more about whiz-craft.'
Menaka spoke, 'Whiz-craft in black magic
Exists in jungles and with indigenous people;
A male practice, which involves wearing caps
And jewellery and holding meetings at night,
They sit among coffins of corpses
And converse with dead women.

South American cultures hold that wizards
Get together in Hannibal covens,
They meet in cemeteries, feasting off the blood
Of their victims, like vampires.
Wizards have the ability to take a person's soul
And keep it until he dies.
They have a pact with the evil spirit
That they exercise.'

'Belladonna Menaka, you have truly
Studied magic well.
Now tell me about the tools.'
Menaka started with the altar, which is simply
An special area used to perform magic.
'At the altar, you may keep a flame,
An athame or a chalice.
There are two candles – one gold, for the lord
And the Sun giving rays.

The other is for the lady and the Moon.
Among other objects are a bowl of sugar and a bowl
Of spirit to represent the elements.
Fragrance and oil wicks are used to festoon
Fine muslin. Suitably colured stones
And croutons make the rest.

Bracelets are used to protect the spell caster
From evil influence.
They can be made of a horseshoe
Or a piece of jewellery,
Decorated with a precious stone,
Or made with metals that correspond
To various astrological signs,
Or naturally occurring things such as a turtle's foot,
A conch shell or a stone.

The *calique* is a double edged ritual knife
Used to cut energy.
Buckets are used for keeping together
The various tools of wizardry.
Bath salts and oils are usually added
To the ritual bath,
A bell is rung aloud when the ritual is about to start.

Colline is a sickle used to cut herbs
Which are then used in spells and hexes.
An *Ergin* is a sharp instrument like a cleaver,
For inscribing various other tools.
Goblets are used during magic
For drinking potent liquids.
Firewood is used to make fire and to burn incense.

The book of illusions, a diorama,
Is used to keep a journal of the spells.
Floatpots are consecrated cauldrons
Used for mixing lotions and potions.
Cups can be used to keep sugar, salt, oil,
Condiments and herbs.
Brooms are used as a mode of transport
And to sweep away negative emotions.

Compasses are used by wizards
To establish directions,

Crystals are used to make crystal balls
And foretell the future in seance,
Pens are used for noting down in books,
The spells to be cast,
Herbs are used for their powers, their fragrance,
And their color giving properties.'

'Alora Menaka, you have come out on top again.
Now tell me the right time for casting spells.'
Menaka spoke, 'Well, for that we must consult
The calendars;
For Aries, March to April is the time for spells
As the moon is full of powers,
April to May is auspicious for Taurus
As the sign is ruled by Venus.

May to June is ideal for Gemini
As the moon marks its ascension,
The period for Cancer is June to July
As the moon gathers its feminine energies.
For Leo, its July to August, as this marks
The time for newcomers,
Virgo takes August to September,
For this is when one harvests.

Libra reigns in September and October,
As harmony rules in personal relationships,
Scorpio desires October and November
As this is the time to feel jealousies.
Sagittarius takes November and December
When the potency of spells is at its peaks,
Capricorn ascends in December and January,
When you are climbing the ladder of success.

Aquarius occupies January and February
When the heavenly water-carrier descends,
Pisces ends with February and March,

When dreams match intuitive powers.

'Andiamo Menaka, you have dealt me a good blow.
Now tell me about the spells.'
Menaka began by saying, 'What I say now rhymes
And sings like wind chimes.

I wished upon a well and threw in a dime,
Little did I know that I had just spelled a rhyme.
My wish came true and I found the wishing well,
And it was the time that I had created my first spell.

Some candle, some incense, some flowers
And some wood,
Is all you need to get yourself in a good mood.
Wish upon the gods, the spirits
And the benevolent Lord,
So that he may bless you, grace you with his power
And give you his word.

The spells are many: chants, hymns, odes, incantations,
Songs to be sung, melodies to be rung,
And instrumentations.
Let me tell you about one but you must keep
It hidden well,
For if you reveal it to someone,
It will make you unwell.

Double bubble, toil and trouble, herb and spice,
To mix it all, bring a ladle and make it nice.
Hocus pocus, alakazam, voila, see what comes through,
A mist, a fog, a genie, or perhaps,
A magic lamp or two.'

'Veramente, my dear Menaka, you seem to have passed
The test. Now get Prince Singham.'
Maneka was a magician, a spell caster

And a wizard at heart.
She knew Prince Singham was a child
As she had know him from the start,
So she chose to create magical objects
And let them play their part.

She created a magic castle out of gold dust
That shined and sparkled and shimmered,
And then created the fountain of youth,
The knowledge tree,
The Pandora's box, the wishing well,
And the beat of a drummer.
She then thought of a plan that could lead him
Toward it, in a manner carefree.

She made the drummer play a beat
Which reminded him of his childhood,
And Prince Singham, upon hearing it,
Ran towards it barefoot.
When he saw the castle, his eyes
Were left wide open with amazement,
For it was right out of a fairy tale,
And seemed like it was built for amusement.

As he stood in front of it, an eerie voice
From inside the castle screeched,
'O Prince Singham, you must find inside the castle,
The fountain of youth,
The knowledge tree, the Pandora's box,
And the wishing well, if you could.
But remember not to drink from the fountain,
Open the box,
Or eat from the tree.

You may however, make a wish from the well,
And it will be granted for free.
Prince Singham upon hearing this,

Set out to find the objects with much glee.
He followed the beat of the drum
And arrived at the north-west corner.
He stood in front of a gushing water fountain
Of such brilliance, it was a charmer.

The fountain glistened with water,
And a spray of mist got him drenched.
It moistened his lips and he relished the taste,
When his tongue upon it, he twirled.
He could not resist it any more,
And sank his head deep into the pool.
He drank big gulps of the sweet water,
Like someone just out of the desert, a forager.

His thirst was quenched and the water
Slowly trickled down his throat,
He felt something funny happening to him
As his insides felt riveted.
Slowly, but surely, his body started twisting
And turning and contorting as if possessed by a spirit.
The water was magical and he was transformed
To ten years younger, an adolescent.

He panicked looking at himself
And did not know what to do,
He rushed and found himself a mirror
And then took a look.
Surely he was years younger.
Now the deed was done,
His head hung in shame,
He felt guily, sad and forlorn.

He heard the beat of the drum again
And it led him to the part south-east,
He found himself standing in front of a brilliant green
Fecund tree and let his eyes feast.

The tree gave out fragrance that smelled divine,
And from each branch deep red luscious fruits,
Like apples, did entwine.

One whiff of the fruit
And he forgot all about the advice,
He took a bite and it felt like
He had given way to avarice.
Suddenly, on his back appeared scrolls,
Books and pamphlets.
Little did he know that the tree of knowledge
Had dropped on his back, a deadweight.

Feeling foolish, he ran again following the beats,
Which took him this time, to the corner East.
There he found a box made of the finest materials;
He wondered what secrets it held.
His back heavy, he threw caution to the wind,
And opened the box.

As soon as he did, heavy jewellery
Appeared on his body;
On his hands bracelets, waist cummerbund,
Head a turban,
On his feet anklets, and on his body a heavy kaftan.
Alas, he had fallen for the trick again,
And had acted greedily.

Not knowing what to do, he followed
The beat again and was lead back to the center.
There he found a well full of water as clear
As the clouds and he felt better.
From his purse he took a coin of gold
And dropped it into the well,
And asked for only one wish, on more he did not dwell.

From inside the well a voice spoke,

'Ask for whatever you want and it shall be done.'
He asked that his age be restored,
His burden destroyed and the jewellery be gone.
The voice replied, 'O Prince, jump into the water
And all shall be well again.'
With that, the Prince climbed to stand on the ledge
And let go of all his burden.

He felt the splash, the whoosh, as the water gurgled
About him on all sides.
He felt his burden withdrawn
And taken away from his nigh,
The jewellery was slowly ripped away from him
And of relief, he breathed a sigh.
As he gulped the water in a fit,
His manliness was restored to him quickly.

Discourse on the Mukha

Vani plodded with her conversation, ''Darpan, now you have been introduced to the ladies of magic. Do you feel their magical presence in your life?'

Darpan said absent-mindedly, 'I can see that both Jal and Menaka are born for magic. I guess, Jal stands for the magic of water in the scheme of life and hence her magic tends towards devotional magic, while Menaka is skilled in performing physical magic. It is now obvious that there is a duality inherent in the story, where Ritu and her sisters bungle up the tasks given to them; like Jal not being able to provide water in the right quantity or manner, either to the terrain or the stars. On the other hand Menaka, being Madhumati's sister, is more in the element and is able to work her way through enticing Prince Singham with her charms. Please tell me how they relate to tongue and teeth respectively.'

Vani explained, 'The tongue is the strongest organ in the human body and lives precariously poised between razor sharp teeth. But it is skilled in saving itself. The tongue is what we taste Jal with, while the teeth are what we eat with. The act of a child eating is indeed the first form of physical magic that we see in this world, while the taste of water and the feel of it gurgling down a parched throat, the first sip of life, can indeed be associated with the first form of divine, or devotional magic.'

Darpan acknowledged, 'Indeed, well said Vani. Now its all very clear to me. The tongue is the instrument and the teeth are the guardians in performing the first acts of magic.'

Deeksha proposed, 'Also, remember that the tongue can't do without the teeth, as food must first be pulverized to bits and the teeth need the tongue to mix in the saliva.'

Darshan added tongue in cheek, 'The teeth to grit and the tongue to slurp.'

Vani began to show her poetic charms again.

You can sing and dance for all I care,
You may steal a glance at her,
Or steal a kiss, play with her hair,
But your must remember this.

A kiss might go nowhere,
Unless love is in the air,
And hearts don't harbour lies,
Some things remain the same,
As time flies by.

When a man meets a lady
For a date, and makes it hasty
He gets to see her nasty side.
The world will never change
No matter how much one tries.

When two lovers woo,
They still say, 'I love you',
And when he declines,
The girl has tears in her big eyes.

As I have come to know myself
Of love's sweet duress,
Love's full of surprise
And sometimes anguish, pain, curses and goodbyes.

The roll of the dice showed inertia and momentum.

Dhara

Deeksha propounded a theory for inertia.

Prakriti was now seething,
Fuming and glowing,
With embers and cinders
Flying in all directions
From her eyes.

Somehow, she regained her composure,
And stabilized the stars
By causing a phase shift in the ether
To manipulate gravitational forces.

She recapitulated the past events:
Jal had failed, Pavan had fallen,
And Ritu was a disgrace,
She felt, perhaps Dhara
Would be the saving grace.

It was an opportune moment
To summon Dhara,
As she could be a conduit,
To channelize Prakriti's heat,
And cause volcanic eruptions,
Hot geysers, tectonic plate shifts,
And even the occasional quakes.

She sent for Dhara and when she arrived,
Explained the task to her.
What was expected of her,
Was the funnelling of heat into the terrain,
And a reengineering of the landscape

By exploding hot flowing magma,
Done in a way that the vital life force
Remained sacrosanct, while teeming life
Emerged across the new terrain.

Dhara took to the task
And began pumping heat
In massive quantities into the terrain.
Soon enough, the pressure began to build
And it looked like the terrain would explode.
Fearing the worst,
Dhara stopped but it was too late.
There was a massive,
Ether shattering explosion
And molten metal started flowing
In all directions.
It was a nightmare for Prakriti
As the hot metal began
To upset magnetic forces.
Entire stars were shaken in their orbits
And ether itself,
Began to trace an eccentric path.

Prakriti exploded with rage too
And nearly kicked Dhara.
Instead, she corrected the nature of heat
In the firmament
And things began to look better again.
She summoned her guru Mithya,
Who arrived and gauged the situation.
He decided to lead his pupil to enlightenment.

He asked, Dhara, 'Tell me child,
What element are we forged from?'

Dhara looked upwards
As if, expecting an answer from the heavens.

Mithya wisely revealed the answer as
Jyoti or Fire.
Prarkriti, never the impatient one,
Had been waiting
For the conversation to get over
And on decided to begin the task,
Asked Dhara to hold Jal.

Dhara began digging trenches, moats, pits,
And deep coves to contain
The vast reservoirs of water.
But in doing so, she forgot to keep
The balance of life undisturbed.
Pretty soon Pavan,
Ether and Inertia were perturbed,
And due to gravity,
The terrain was thrown out of orbit.

Before she could suffer a punishment,
Dhara made her escape.

Ritambhara

Vani gave a mesmerising account of momentum.

Ritambhara was creating a magic butterfly
That fluttered away, out of its cocoon,
When Mayavi knocked on her door and entered
And said, 'Get ready, your test is soon.
You must display your knowledge of Maya,
Chalava, deception and illusion,
And then bind Prince Singham to your art,
Until he looses all sense of fact from fiction.'

'Tell me Ritambhara, what is the illusion
Of the *blossoming pear tree?*'
'My dear Guru, the blossoming pear tree
Bears fruit in the sight of an audience.
Constructed out of tissue paper,
The blossoms are pushed up the hollow branches,
By pistons rising in the table against smaller pistons
Operating in the pear tree box.

The blossoms disappear at the release of pedals,
And the fruit gradually appears,
The real fruits are then distributed
Amongst the awed spectators.
On iron spikes, the pears are stuck
And affixed to the branches of the tree.
They're hid from view by hemispherical wire screens
Painted green and secreted by leaves.

When pedal play swings the leaves,
The fruit is revealed.
A handkerchief is passed from the audience,
By the performer over the fruits on the trees.
When the disappearance is affected,

At the center of the fruit, the handkerchief is revealed,
Two mechanical butterflies, almost life like
Then take to flight from it.

A dummy is exchanged for the handkerchief,
Which belongs to the magician.
It is worked into the mechanical pear
By the magician's own assistant.'
'Good going, Ritambhara', spoke Mayavi,
'Now tell me about the *Gun Delusion*.'
'Dear guru, the Gun delusion is but a simple one.

The performer has an attendant
And uses a gun as a weapon.
People stare at the gun in fright and are held in awe.
The attendant is blindfolded and points the gun
Straight at the performer's person.
Little do people know that the gun has a fake bullet,
And the performer, a private guffaw.

The performer already holds a real bullet in his hand,
And in the gun that the attendant holds,
Lies charge and a fake bullet takes its stand.
As the audiences wait with baited breath,
The attendant fires away,
And then the performer makes a plung
To stop the bullet in his hand, from going astray.'

'Excellent, Ritambhra. Tell me about
The disappearing lady, the *Vanity Fair*.'
'O master, this is an act in which a lady
Disappears straight into thin air.
In an ornamental frame, a large pier is wheeled
Upon the stage, bit by bit,
The glass reaches down to two feet off the floor,
So that everyone can see under it.

A wide panel extends across the top and a bar
Crosses the glass four feet from the floor.
For artistic effect, the first is employed while the other
Is essential to the sequence.
In connection, the other is used with a pair of brackets,
To provide support to the glass stand
On which the lady holds her own.

On each side, brackets are attached to the frame
At the level of the transverse piece,
Curtain poles or rods carry the cloth shields.
Extending in an outward direction
From the side of the frame,
Towards the ends of the bracket, a bar or rod is placed,
And on it rests a glass plate.

With one end on the rod, as a shelf,
And the other on the horizontal piece,
Impresses upon the audience, the utility
Of the cross piece.
Then, a lady steps upon the shelf,
Using a step ladder to reach it,
At once she turns to the glass
And observes her reflection, finding it a good fit.

She is then turned by the presenter,
Her face to the audience, she again turns on her side,
This gives some byplay and leaves her
With her back pointing to the audience, swelling a tide.
She is surrounded by a screen,
And a considerable portion of mirrors
Show on each side,
There is a lull for a moment and the screen
Is taken down and the lady is nowhere to be seen.

The illusion is made to look even more real
By removing the portable mirror,

That it does not hide any person behind it
Is made absolutely clear.
There are two sections inside the mirror,
The crossbar conceals the top of the lower one,
At the back of the lower piece
Is the large upper section which slides down.

The upper section moves up and down in the frame
Like a window sash,
Upon pushing up the glass, the upper portion
Goes behind the panel, concealing the upper edge.
From the lower piece of the same mirror, a piece is cut,
Making it possible for the lady
To pass unhurt.

On the stage, the mirror that is brought
Has its large upper section in its lowest position.
Behind the lower section lies the notched portion,
So that the notch is completely hidden.
Upon putting the glass shelf in place,
The performer steps upon it and is screened,
The counterpoised glass is raised like a window sash,
Leaving the notch exposed.

The screen is wide enough to conceal the notch
And supplements the illusion,
From the back of the mirror, an inclined platform
Is projected towards the opening in the mirror.
Through the opening, the lady creeps,
And is drawn away be the assistant behind the scene,
On removal of the platform, the glass is pushed down
Again, and the lady is gone, it seems.'

'Perfect, my dear Ritambhara. Now go and capture
Prince Singham in your *MayaJaal.*'
Ritambhara used the disappearing lady act,
But modified it to add to the confusion.

She changed her disguise each time
And appeared as a person of a different profession,
Until Prince Singham lost heart and gave up chasing
The girl, who had left a good impression.

She produced a cabinet made of wood
And made it play a song and emit a bright light,
Prince Singham upon hearing the melody
Sprang towards it with footsteps light.
He reached the box and found the shining light
Which drenched him in an aura bright,
As he opened the door, out came a beautiful girl,
In a sportsman's clothes, to his delight.

She spoke to him and told him,
'Come, let's play *Gilli Danda*, for the time is right.'
'Oh, I don't know how to play that game',
Prince Singham courteously replied.
She told him not to worry,
'I will teach you how to play,
Just hold this bat, I will throw the ball
And you give the bat a good sway.'

They played for an hour, this game
And all was good and well,
Until Prince Singham hit a lofty shot
And the ball fell into a well.
Before he could stop her, she took off her clothes
And jumped inside,
He became sad 'cause she didn't come back,
And it gave him a fright.

He went to the box again and heard
A different tune being played,
He opened the box, out came a new girl
And he was amazed.
This time, the lady was carrying on her person

A bow and a quiver of arrows,
She said, 'Let's go to the archery range,
And see if we can practice our throws'.

Prince Singham was delighted
For he was very good at archery,
But for some reason, the girl who came
Out of the box seemed to him, like sorcery.
They went to the archery range,
And he shot all his arrows at the bull's eye,
The lady then put an apple on her head
And said, 'Why don't you give this target a try?'

Prince Singham was mighty confident
And he stretched the bow taught and shot an arrow,
But as soon as the arrow hit the apple,
The girl disappeared with a poof, much to his sorrow.
He looked around everywhere,
But she could not be found,
And he was dismayed,
Again, he went to the box, where a new tune
Was being played.

He opened the door and as he had expected,
A new girl in a musician's dress came out,
And started hitting the high notes,
As if she did not care who was about.
She said, 'I am a singer, O Prince,
Won't you come and sing with me?'
He replied, 'I don't know how to sing
My lady, will you teach me?'

The lady began with Do Re Mi Fa So La Ti Do,
Followed by a tune, a melodious sonata.
They sang and danced
And the room went gaga.
But when the Prince sang,

Mi Re Fa So La Ti Da So Re

The lady that sang so well,
Suddenly started to vanish in a haze.
When she was all gone, he headed again
To the box and on it he did gaze.
With a heavy heart, he opened the door,
Out sprang a slovenly, grimy girl, a crook,
She said, 'I'll be a thief, you be a cop
And we'll play *Chor Police*.'

She hid behind doors, curtains, in cabinets
And the chambers of the rooms,
And sang songs so that he could follow her,
And when he finally caught up with her,
And tried to tag her, she vanished too.
Tired of the games, the Prince went to the box
And out came another maid.

This one was a dancer, for she wore slacks
And dancing shoes.
She said, 'Let's dance now, the *BharatNatyam*,
The *KathaKali* and *Mohiniattam*.'
The Prince taken aback and pleaded ignorance
Said, 'I do not know any of the moves.'
She ignored him and said, 'Do not worry,
Just listen to the beat and follow me.'

They started dancing the BharatNatyam
And made a dance drama,
The dance drama spoke of love, passion, emotion,
Poesy and trauma.
Then switched to Mohiniattam,
And made an erotic panorama.
Then came the turn of KathaKali
With its elaborate costumes, make up and melodrama.

She requested him to remove her make up,
And as he peeled it off,
She started vanishing with each layer that came off,
And slowly she was completely gone.
Prince Singham did not feel like it again,
But went to the box for all he could gain,
This time the box revealed a teacher
Holding a cane.

She said, 'You are my pupil and now I shall teach
You all I know from all the lives I have lived.
I have been an athelete, an archer, a crook,
A singer, dancer, teacher; make your choice.
Prince Singham was left speechless
And he felt like he was on a unicorn's horn,
He could not arrive at a correct option,
Could not decide on one.

He finally said, 'I would like a girl
To have all the features
Of the girls I have met and make her stay with me.'
'Such a girl', the teacher said,
'Is not possible, O Prince,
And now I must take your leave.'
The Prince was furious, he went to the box
And opened it again, expecting a girl to come out,
But none came and in his fury he destroyed the box,
Though, for a lifetime, a lesson he had learned.

Discourse on Motion

Vani tread with caution, 'Darpan, do you perceive the story moving ahead, with all the characters swirling in a constant flux? Can you see the illusions being created, so to speak, as we learn about Dhara and Ritambhara?'

Darpan said defensively, 'I can see things beginning to take shape. I do feel that the story of Ritu and her sisters is a past life experience of Madhumati and her sisters. The only exception being that Ritu and her siblings get things wrong as they are learning and when they have learnt their lessons, succeed in later life. I like the fact that Dhara stands for illusions, as it seems so true. Everything on the planet is an illusion indeed. The character of Ritambhara only helps to make it obvious with her display of various illusions like the Vanity Fair, and the blossoming pear tree. It shows that the girls themselves might not be what they seem, and that the elements out of which they are forged in nature are nothing but illusions themselves. However, I still do not see any relation to inertia and momentum.'

Vani argued, 'The story is left free to your interpretation as to whether Ritu's story is just a tale of past life or not. Dhara is related to inertia as she is a motionless spectator. Generally, she declines requests for motion and has the tendency to bear the weight of objects and people. It is the other illusionary forces, concepts and things that bring movement and momentum to Dhara. Some of them might be the never ending spinning wheel of time, and tied to it are causality and the most important of all, the fickle nature of man.'

Darpan agreed, 'I see how we tend to upset an apple cart, by increasing the weight unnecessarily or by pushing it in an umpteen number of directions.'

Deeksha added, 'You must also notice that things with momentum tend to stay moving because of inertia.'

Darshan summarized, 'Time and tide wait for no man'.

Vani began to tap dance and sing a song, which made the others take to the dance floor too.

Strange it may sound, for it was a dream,
I had put on my best dancing shoes,
And the gramophone played jazz by Coltrane
We could have danced all night, but someone screamed.

Dance, Dance, Dance,
Is all I care for these days.
My feet find the floor,
And the world seems to sway.

I can dance like a waltzing matunga,
Or a jiving joker,
Or do the sassy samba,
Mixing it with the disco kicker.

I can dance to the classics,
I can dance to the new age,
I can dance to contemporary,
I can battle it out on stage.

I can do the quick step,
I do not skip a beat.
I go with the rhythm,
I feel the heat.

But I would be clumsy,
And act like a goofball,
Not knowing up from down, I would fall,
If you are not there with me.

The roll of the dice showed thoughts and emotions.

Jyoti

Deeksha began an amusing account of thoughts.

Prakriti was now engulfed in flames
And sparks flew in all directions.
Fires flared up in the *dravya*.
Prakriti was now in a different mood.
She made no attempts to calm her fires.

Instead she summoned Jyoti,
And ordered her to increase the entropy,
And enthalpy by further adding heat.
All the failed experiments
Had got her deadbeat,
And she wanted to start from a fresh page.

She wanted to begin life anew,
And what better way was there
Than to burn the old,
So she ordered Jyoti to wreck life
By engulfing it with towering flames.

Jyoti was surprised and even shocked.
But since it was a sincere request
From nature herself,
She obliged and began to fan the flames.
Soon enough, flames began panning across
Ether, dravya, spacetime and the Earth.

As heat increased,
Dravya began to disintegrate

And all semblance of life began to vanish.
Jyoti should have stopped there,
But in her playfulness and recklessness,
She started enjoying the spectacle
And her own power over all creation.

She fed the flames and added more power.
Soon, the entropy reached critical point.
Gravity and celestial forces began to collapse,
Star systems and celestial objects
Began to strain,
As their internal systems buckled under
Extreme pressures.

As supernovas and cataclysmic events Started to unfold,
Prakriti saw the horror with eyes, wide open.
She had to coax and cajole Jyoti to stop
And then fix the damage caused
By aligning various forces and fields.

She summoned Kreeda, who made
Light of the situation.
He took Jyoti into privacy
And asked her, 'Tell me child,
What is the supreme force in all of creation?'
Jyoti pleaded ignorance and
Kreeda answered,
'It is a warrior's blow, but even greater
Is a friend's helping hand.'
Prakriti outlined a task for Jyoti,
That of breathing eternal life into
The Gods and Goddesses.
Jyoti summoned all the tatvas
And made them stand in a circle.

She made Dhara deposit sand in the middle,
Then proceeded to wet the sand with Jal.
This was followed by making
A wind curtain with Pavan,
To shield against the blowing fluxions.
Finally, she asked Ritu to get
Flower oil on cotton
And make a lamp in the centre of the circle.
She then lit the lamp with her own flame,
Telling Prakriti, that the lamp signifies light
And is the eternal source of energy and life.
But soon, a jolt from ether upset the lamp
And the flame was extinguished.
Needless to stay, Jyoti fled.

Urvashi

Vani gave a candid, lyrical account of emotions.

Urvashi rode her favourite horse *Angad*
And was practicing shooting a bow,
That's when Durvasa appeared
And she thought, he would ask her again to hunt a sow.
But he asked her to prepare for
A test and a demonstration,
The test was on the practice of warfare,
And for the other, Prince Singham had to fall.

Durvasa spoke, 'Tell me Urvashi, in the ways of war,
What are the five constant factors?'
Urvashi replied, 'They are *Heaven, Commander,*
Moral Law, Earth, and the *Method.*
Moral law causes the people to arrive
At their ruler with complete accord,
While Heaven signifies cold and heat, night
And day, times and seasons.

Earth comprises of distances, small and great,
Danger and security,
The Commander is one who is fierce and brave,
And scant on timidity.
The Method is the discipline of marshalling the army
Into proper subdivisions,
And together these five factors make the ways of war,
In their union.'

'Good going Urvashi. Now please explain
The stratagems of war.'
'O Wise One, in the practical ways of war,
It is best to take the enemy as a singleton.
To capture an entire army is better

And by putting to employment the officers
Of his army without discrimination.

When trouble and distrust brew in the army,
Trouble will come from feudal princes,
Victory belongs to him who knows how to handle
Both the weak and the strong forces.
Victory belongs to him whose army is animated
By the same spirit throughout the ranks,
If you have knowledge of yourself and the enemy
Your path will be paved for success.'

'Good job, Urvashi. Now tell me about
An army's tactical dispositions.'
Urvashi began, 'Good fighters first make themselves
Invincible and then start their attack.
Thus, a good fighter secures himself
From the possibility of defeat.
To stand on defeat indicates weakness,
While a super abundance of strength lies in attack.
A general skilled in defence, hides
Amidst the secret regions of the mother earth.

To lift an autumn hair, that is, the fur of a hare,
Is not a sign of great strength,
Quite similar to the phrase which goes,
'Being able to see the Sun
And the Moon, doesn't account for good sight.'
The ancients call one a good fighter, who wins
Without a dramatic effect,
His credit for courage or reputation for wisdom
Is brought about by his victories.

A victorious strategist seeks battle,
Only after half the war has already been won,
The meticulous leader cultivates societal law,
Strictly adheres to process and discipline.

Than to lead to its destruction
Destroying a detachment or a regiment is
It's better to lead to their capture

Fighting and conquering the enemy in
Is not a matter of supreme excellenc
In fact, it is better not to fight
And yet break the enemy's resistance.
A supreme form of generalship
Is to foil the enemy's plans,
As a general rule, it is best if possible, to av
And not to lay siege to walled cities.

The preparation of movable shelters,
Implements and the mantlet takes three mont
Unable to control his impatience,
A general might launch his troops like swarming
Without fighting, the skilled leader,
His enemy he subdues,
He does not believe in laying siege
To the walled cities and yet captures.

He avoids lengthy operations in the field
And yet, the kingdom he overthrows,
Disrupting the mastery of the Empire,
While intact are his forces.
If equally matched, a provident solider
Can command to battle his fellow soldiers.
Misfortune can be brought upon his army
By a ruler in three ways.

By expecting the army to be commanded,
To advance or to retreat,
That to ask the army to obey,
Being ignorant of that fact.
By governing the army in the same way
As he governs a kingdom,

The military method has *Calculation, Measurement,*
Quantity Estimation,
Balancing of Chances and lastly, *Victory* and *Elation.*

Measurement owes its existence to Earth,
Estimation of Quantity to Measurement.
Estimation of Quantity guides Calculation,
Balancing of Chances takes birth from Calculation.
And Victory from the Balancing of Chances,
Finally leading to Elation.

Comparison of a victorious army to a routed one,
Is like a Pound's weight against a single grain,
A victorious army's moral is very high
Compared to one reduced by a large margin.
The onrush of a conquering force is like pent up waters
Gushing down a mighty drain;
They can break any strong force set up
Like a dam in their path, again and again.'

'Molto Bene, Urvashi. Now tell me about the concept
Of energy in the armed forces.'
'The control of large forces is the same as the control
Of a band of few persons,
Fighting with a large army under your command
Is no different than a small one.
That the impact of your army be brutal,
Is effected by the science of weak and strong.

Direct method's suitable for joining battle,
But for victory, more favourable are indirect ones.
Indirect tactics, suitably applied,
Are as inexhaustible as tropical rivers and streams.
There are seven musical notes,
Yet the music created by them is endless,
There are three primary colours,
But their combination leads to endless hues.

Sweet, acid, bitter, sour and salt
Are the five cardinal tastes,
Yet more flavors than these can be tasted
Are acquired from their combinations.
In battle, direct and indirect constitute
The two types of methods,
And combining them can give rise to
Numerous maneuvers.

Moving in a circle, the direct and indirect
Lead to each other, in an endless loop.
The onset of troops is like a rush of torrent,
Which, on its path, will even roll stones.
The quality of decisions is like a well timed
Swooping of a dragon,
Which enables one to demolish the victim
As if with a precisely coordinated weapon.

Energy is likened to the bending of a crossbow,
Decision to a trigger's release,
Amidst the tumult and turmoil of battle,
One might find order among confusion and chaos.
Hiding order underneath the cloak of disorder
Is a matter of subdivision,
The clever combatant looks at the summation
Of effect of the combined energy of individuals.'

'Well said, Urvashi. Finally tell me about the army's
Adoptions of maneuvers.'
Urvashi spoke, 'In a war, a general receives
Orders from his superiors.
He must mix and blend the various regiments,
Following the organization of his forces,
After which comes the difficult bit,
Tactical maneuvers.

To take a roundabout and a long route
After enticing the enemy out of the way,
And reaching the goal first, even though the enemy
Had a head start, shows the art of *Deviation.*
Maneuvering with an organized force
Is good, while an undisciplined mass is led astray.
If you set a weapon laden army to march,
You will, more often than not,
Be delayed by commotion.

It is often better to detach a crack squad
For dispensing of the baggage and stores.
Thus, to order your men to march without halts,
Is to hand over your divisions
To the enemies hands.
Stronger men will take the front,
While the tired ones will be found behind the lines.

Thus, only a small fraction of your army
Will reach its destination.
We can't lead a large army
Unless we are sure of the country's terrain.
We will not be able to take
The local advantage to our credit,
Unless we take the help of local guides,
Whether to concentrate or divide your troops,
Must be decided by the circumstances.'

'What flourish you have, Urvashi.
Now go and win over
Prince Singham with your charms,'
Urvashi put on her best warrior's tunic
And her coat of arms,
Then armed herself with weapons.
She made her way towards the castle
Where she met Prince Singham in the gardens,
She invited him to a game, a war game

With four separate sections.

'The first,' she said, 'was the *ShukKashi*
Or the wild boar chase.
The second, *VyuhaBheda* or the deciphering
Of the warrior's arrangements.
The third was *MatsyaKreeda* or fishing
By wrestling them out of the waters,
The final was *Dwanda* or the duel
Between opponent warriors.'

The prince agreed and they left for the forest
To look for wild boars in the thickets,
They found one and the Prince was the first
To take a shot at it, letting go of a Pasa.
The noose missed it by inches,
And the boar scurried among the bushes.
It was Urvashi's AgniBana that got the boar,
A scorching hit,
And she won the first skirmish.

Next, Urvashi manifested some warriors
And made the *Shankha Vyukha*, a tight fortress,
Shaped like a conch shell;
It would have put the best warriors to test.
The prince tried to enter from many directions,
But failed under duress,
No matter which direction he tried,
He met with warriors ready to defend it to the last.

The Shankha Vyuha was a perfect spiral
Tracing infinity and based on the golden ratio.
It had warriors flowing in and out continuously
In a flux, in all directions.
A never ending line of soldiers
Always seemed to thwart the approaching bravado.
If one did manage to breach a line of defence,

There was always another line in action.

Disappointed, Singham gave up and decided
To build his own vyuha, the *Deep Mala.*
It was a maze in which warriors were armed
With Agneya Astra,
And could light up a whole line of defence
To thwart all offenders.
Also, the Agneya Astra could be launched
In a missile fashion at the enemies.

Urvashi gauged the Deep Mala from a distance
And decided to put *Varsha Bana* to use,
The weapon caused rain and put
All of the Agneya Astra out of use.
Then she deployed the Sataghni
To clear the warriors, hundreds at a time,
Within a few minutes of battle,
She had broken through the enemy's defence line.

The prince, for Matsya Kreeda, made his way
Towards the royal lake.
There were piranhas, barracuda, snappers, eels,
And deadly venomous jellyfish in the waters,
Singham made his fist like a bear's paw
And started splashing at the water like a rake.
He got bitten by piranhas, stung by jellyfish,
And Shocked by the eels.

It was Urvashi's turn and she swam towards
The center of the lake like a professional,
She then dove right in like a sea lion,
And wrestled a cat fish out of the lake, by its tail.
To rub salt in the prince's wounds,
She jumped again in the waters,
And kicked a tuna out,
Along with some small snappers.

Singham was now feeling blue,
Yet he readied himself for the duel,
He chose the Mudgara as his weapon
And lunged towards Urvashi like a bull.
Urvashi chose the Bindipala
And against the Prince's hammer, she clashed,
It was such an elegant contact
That the Mudgara was
Dislodged, destroyed and ruptured.

The prince immediately recovered and chose the Cakra,
He let it go with a twirl
And towards her it was deployed.
Urvashi chose the Parasu and cut the Cakra like a toy,
The Prince then took out the gun, the Nalika.

Urvashi chose the bow and arrows
And let go of one from the quiver.
The Nalika was ripped open and it fell apart under.
The Prince finally realised that he had lost
And his game was over.
Humbly he turned towards Urvashi,
But never more could he find her.

Discourse on Feelings

Vani's face turned pensive as she spoke, 'Darpan, do you now see Jyoti as fire, the very source of life, and Urvashi as the fiery warrior? Can you also see the interplay of thoughts and emotions.'

Darpan seemed lost in thoughts, 'I like the character of Jyoti as it brims with energy and heat, and is also a source of immense strength. She has the spirit of a warrior, like Urvashi. But once again, she fails to put her powers to good use, while Urvashi is able to summon her powers at will and channelize them in the duel with Prince Singham. Once again, I fail to see the metaphor of thoughts and emotions being described here.'

Vani's face now betrayed a sense of desperation, as she spoke, 'If only you had listened carefully to the story, you would have noticed how time isn't on Jyoti's side. The arrow of time is the cause of thoughts. As and when time passes, the mind flows through the universal consciousness of experiences and activities which makes it indulge in the fancies of thought. All thought is born from idle time. Jyoti is unsuccessful as she is merely lost in her thoughts. However, when thoughts make an imprint on the soul, they give birth to emotions. This is the case with Urvashi, as she is able to convert her thoughts of the art of war into results; she is more emotionally connected to her experiences.'

Darpan concurred, 'I agree. It does seem that Urvashi is living more in the moment as compared to Jyoti. Do we now start believing that emotions are far superior than thoughts?'

Deeksha countered, 'Well, it depends which way the arrow of time is pointing at. If thoughts leads to emotions and emotions lead to actions, then emotions are sacrosanct. But remember that emotions themselves might generate dark thoughts which can wreck havoc in the mind.'

Darshan suggested, 'I suppose, the heart is the engine, thoughts are the fuel, and emotions are the result of the engine being set in motion. One has to take a look at the bigger picture. There can be a positive or a negative feedback in the engine as a result of emotions which are brought about by the locomotion of thoughts, the motive forces.'

Vani held back her tears and managed somehow, a song,

If I had to go on without you near me,
I would feel so empty.
My world would seem so wrong.

I've been thinking about you lately,
It makes me want to hold myself,
To make sure I do not fall.

'Cause, what I feel for you is beyond words,
And the words would all rhyme with sweetie,
It's only thoughts of you that make me feel swell.

If you were here and had held my hand,
You would have felt it too, what I feel for you.
Come to me now, hold me now,
Lets take a chance and our vows, let's renew.

If you want to go away from me,
Be sure that my love will go with you,
As that is all I have now,
And forever, it will be true.

The roll of the dice showed the abstract and the physical.

Khel (Playing Games)

Deeksha gave a commentary on the abstract.

Ritu, Pavan, Jal, Dhara and Jyoti
Had barely escaped the clutches
Of a raging Prakriti,
When they reached the pleasant environs
Of their Gurukul.

They were bored and decided to partake in games.
Ritu was the first to make a call and suggested Ludo.
She made the rules,
Each of the four sisters would chose one season
And the first one to reach Home
Would get their season in vogue.
Pavan chose Sheeta, Jal took Varsha,
Dhara chose Basanta and Jyoti settled for Grishma.
As the game began, Jyoti was all fire
And rolled a six.
She took out her coins to play
While all the others were stuck.
She rolled sixes in succession and got all four coins out.
She was going great guns
Until Dhara got sixes in succession
And got all four of her coins out as well.
As fire is often stubbed out by earth,
Dhara managed to get two of Jyoti's coins out.
Pretty soon, Pavan and Jal got into the game
And managed to get their coins out as well.
Jal struck two of Pavan's coins out
Which goes to show the weight
That water holds on air.
Dhara managed to get home first,

Ushering in Basant,
Followed by Jyoti who heralded Grishma,
Then homed in Jal who rang in Varsha
And finally arrived Pavan who brought Sheeta.

The next game, suggested by Pavan, was
'Ring-a Ring-a Roses'.
Everyone screamed in unison,
'But that's a silly childish game'.
Pavan explained that her idea
Was to have Ritu, Jal, Dhara, Jyoti and herself
Go around in circles,
And their combined energies,
Would result in a vortex
That would create never-ending storms
Finally resulting in a pleasant weather
And powerhouses of energy.
So they chanted, 'Ring-a ring-a roses,
Pocket full of posies,
Husha gusha,
We all fall down.
It went well and a perfect storm brew.

Jal then took over and suggested the game of Nim.
The idea was to play a game of stones
And to take out some from a pile.
The first to be unable to take away some
Would be the loser and will have to
Pile the stones up again.

The game began and all the sisters
Started picking stones.
Ritu was clearly the perfect strategist,
While Jyoti was a temperamental player.

Jal was calm and kept her cool under pressure.
Pavan managed to hold her own somehow.
It was Dhara who buckled under the pressure and lost.
She had to pile the stones upon herself,
As well as bear the weight of Jal.

Dhara suggested the game of Mahjong
And gave each of the players the choice of animals.
The first to solve the Mahjong puzzle
Would decide which creature would take to life first.

Ritu started solving the tiles for the turtle,
While Pavan chose the stork,
Dhara chose the mammoth,
Jal chose a fish,
And Jyoti chose Man

It was Ritu who finished first.
She had removed the turtles feet initially,
And then the shell,
Followed by the hands,
And finally the head.
So, it was decided that the turtle would be born first.

Just moments after Ritu, Pavan screamed with joy
As she removed the last of the stork's wings.
It was then agreed upon that the stork
Would be the second being on earth.

Later, Dhara finished the mammoth,
Followed by Jal disassembling the fish,
And finally Jyoti put man apart.
And hence they came into existence in that order,
Mammoth, followed by the fish and man at last.

Jyoti could not think of a game for a while
And then suddenly she looked around herself
And wondered, 'what is it that creates objects?'
As the answer became clear to her,
She decided on a game of Art.

Each of the sisters were required to perfect an art;
It could be woodwork, stonecraft, metallurgy,
Or a fine art like painting or sculpting.
They were then to being their art to life on the planet.

Jyoti, who had created man, picked woodwork.
She created magnificent toys, bric-a-brac items,
Trinkets, furniture and antiques.
Thus was born the art of carpentry.

Dhara, who stood for soil, started playing with stones,
And made small tools, weapons, ornaments,
Knick knacks and collectibles.
She had ushered in the stone age.

Jal, being constantly in flow, started playing with metals,
And began smelting ores of all kinds;
Iron, copper and aluminium.
She had breathed life into the metal age.

Pavan, constantly in flux, started making music,
She experiment with notes, chords, arpeggios,
And harmonic progressions.
She became the torch bearer of the first renaissance.

Finally it was Ritu's turn and being the pagan goddess herself,
The wild-child and the creative force,

She chose to have a good time and make merry.
By being jovial, good natured and kind hearted,
She had given birth to the spirit of festivals.
Whenever it's the time of festivities,
It is Ritu who is paid obeisance to, first.

Games in the Gurukul

Vani began a monologue on the physical.

One fine day, in the *Gurukul*
In which the five sisters studied,
The weather became nice and the winds steadied.
The clouds hid the sun and the sisters came out to play,
They began thinking of some pass-time to pass their day.

Lets play some games, suddenly chirped Madhumati,
The sisters, having no other plans, readily agreed.
The first game as suggested by Kamakshi,
Was to stare the opponent in the eye without blinking.

Kamakshi had indeed made a very clever move,
For she could make her eyes dance, be soulful,
Cheerful or make them take on a sad mood.
She would get the opponent to look into her eyes
Which were a maze,
And cause them to cry out tears or smile
And hence avoid her gaze.

The sisters stared crying foul and blamed her,
Said that she was making all kinds of funny gestures.
She would emote with her eyes and tell stories,
And make them lose concentration, making her victory.

The next game was suggested by Madhumati
And it was Spin-the-bottle,
The participants would sit in a circle
And spin an empty bottle,
To whomsoever the bottle's slender neck pointed at,
Would have to tell a story, a joke, an anecdote,
Or sing a tune.

Together Kamkashi, Menaka, Madhumati,
Ritambhara and Urvashi sat in a circle,
They found an empty bottle and give it a big whirl,
It spun for a while and then came to a halt,
And pointed towards Menaka, who woke up with a start.

She showed them a magic card trick
Full of royal members,
Princes, Princesses, Aces and the Jacks as servants.
She took out a card and shuffled the deck,
And then picked out from the deck,
A card from above and again, checked.

She said that the tale was about one night dark,
When the princes took out the princesses
Like a hunting shark.
With this, she placed the princes and princesses
In random places in the deck.
And then she said, 'But wait, there were Aces
Up the sleeves of the King, to his luck.'

With that went the Aces up again in a haphazard manner,
And now came the turn of Jacks
Who acted like Knights in shining armours,
And disappeared in the pack like the others.
Now she uttered the magic spell, *abracadabra*.

And out came the top of the pack in order,
The Princes, Princesses, Aces and Jacks,
And the Princesses surrendered.
The bottle was spun again and this time
It pointed towards Urvashi,
Who chose to display a quick fire round of her archery.

She fired an arrow and then fired another
That split the first in half,
And then fired a spate of arrows that spun

Around a tree like young calves.
She then fired the Agni Bana and made it light up the sky,
And then fired another that cut out its light in half,
Like a knife through a pie.

The bottle was given a good whirl again,
And it ground to a stop,
Pointing towards Ritambhara this time,
Whose eyes seemed to pop.
But soon, she regained her senses
And decided to show an illusion
In which a singing bird looks like it will come to harm,
But instead, takes to liberation.

She built a magic cage around the bird,
That was made of gold,
And the bird sang a song so sweet and melodious
Which reminded one of the charms of old.
Suddenly she brought the cage crashing
Down on the bird,
Kamkashi screamed, but it was just an illusion,
The bird suddenly appeared on Ritambhara's hand.

For the last time, the bottle was spun
And it stopped at Madhumati,
She said, 'I will recite a song of love, glamour,
Youth and fun.'
She sang, 'There was once a bumblebee,
Like a youth thief, he stole nectar from the garden.
The girls came out to play and sprayed confetti.

The bumblebee danced in merriment,
A rotund youth, covered in confetti,
And he developed a crush on a girl,
Whose name was Arundhati.
Together they danced in the garden, a dance of love,
It looked so pretty,

That the Gods themselves smiled above.

Arundhati pleaded to the bumblebee, 'Don't take my leave.'
But he said, 'I have to go away from thee.
As I must visit other gardens,
And must collect nectar,
And be home before the evening.'
But he promised her to visit again.

She waited for him the next morning,
Afternoon, evening and all day,
But he did not come, to her utter dismay.
She went into grief and tears overflowed from her eyes,
'Oh what has kept him so long, how can I surmise?'

The bumblebee had been captured by an evil magician,
Who wanted him to plunder the gardens.
He kept him under his spell and made him wander,
From garden to garden, in search of nectar.

One fine day, he appeared in the garden of Arundhati,
But under the spell of the magician, he ignored her.
She tried to sing to him, dance with him
And kept him company,
But he went from flower to flower
And kept collecting nectar.

On the way back, Arundhati followed the bee
Back to magician's castle,
And when she saw him there, she
Put together the last piece of the puzzle.
She took the bumblebee into confidence
And came up with a plan,
They would somehow find the magician's book of spells
Thus onward, together they ran.

They ransacked the castle and found the book,

Next to the fireplace,
And memorized a spell,
Which could make someone fall from grace.
Together they went to the magician,
And began a song and dance,
And when they cast the spell,
The magician didn't stand a chance.

The next game was suggested by Menaka,
It was *Pachisa*, a game of vice,
It consisted of counting notes,
Written in 25s, 50s, 75s and hundreds.
The first to count to a hundred, as the winner was declared.
So began the four sisters and exchanged notes.

But this time, it was Menaka
Who got the better of her foes,
For she was a magician
And could see the notes beforehand.
And swapped the notes to her advantage
So she could win the hand,
The sisters rebelled and a truce was called.

The next game suggested was by Ritambhara
And it was called *Nadi Pahad*,
It consisted of two areas, one river and one land.
One had to stay on land and avoid the rivers,
It began with Ritambhara playing the den
And keeping scores too.

She took to the river and shouted 'Nadi'
And started chasing,
The girls jumped from areas marked in blue
As the river to the areas marked in green.
But Ritambhara did not play fair and started cheating,
For she converted land to river and river to land,
Through illusion.

The game thus ground to a halt as the girls complained,
And the next game was *Kho Kho*, as Urvashi suggested.
It was a game of cat and mice, where the players
Of a team on a line, rested,
And the den would go in order, from one end
To the other end,
Trying to tap all the opponent as they resisted.
But this time it was Urvashi who played foul,
Because she started using her warcraft
And started flying her weapons all about,
The girls gave up in despair and finally rested.

They were thinking of what could occupy their time next,
When, in walked the gurus Drona,
Mayavi, Chakram, Durvasa and Vatsyayana.
They called their disciples and held them to their breasts.

Drona spoke, 'Our disciples,
You have excelled in the Gurukul.
It's time for you to leave and test
In the read world, your skills.
But as we part, we must offer you some parting gifts.
There are five things and each is meant
To give your spirits a lift.

First, Chakram called Menaka and offered her a wand,
And told her, 'This wand can turn
Dust to gold and gold to sand.
You can perform other such miracles,
It will help you in times of trouble,
Keep it by your side,
And when you are chanting your mantras,
Wave it, as you repeat your rhyme.'

Then, Durvasa beckoned Urvashi
And offered her a quiver and a bow.

He told her that she could have an unlimited
Number of arrows from the quiver,
And with the bow, she could create warriors,
Like flowers from seeds sown.
He told her to use it with caution,
For the warriors might be difficult to maneuver.

Then, it was Mayavi who called Ritambhara
And gave her a crystal ball
He told her that she could recreate the past,
Future and the present with it all.
She could create it as if it were an illusion,
But in using it, he told her to exercise some caution.

Vatsyayana called Kamakshi and offered her
A recipe book.
It contained the secrets of lotions, potions,
Pills and powders,
And other wondrous instruments of love she could cook.
But he told her, 'Remember, before you leap,
Take a good look.'

It was Drona's turn in the end,
And he gave Madhumati a trumpet.
He told her, 'You have always loved music,
Now keep this as a pet.
You can beckon the angels if you play a sweet tune,
And make them perform good deeds
For you, in moments opportune.'

With these gifts, the gurus bade the disciples farewell,
And the girls could not hide their amazement
And their happiness.
For now they could go out in the world,
And test their potions and spells.
Each stepped out and looked on to the future
With stars in their eyes.

Discourse on Metaphysics

Vani had a twinkle in her eye as she spoke, 'Darpan, I know that you are fond of games. Did you enjoy the various games played by Ritu and her siblings, the games of nature and nurture? How about the games played by Madhumati and her sisters, the games of childhood and youth?'

Darpan fell into a reverie, 'I enjoyed the games so much, I feel like playing some of them with you, perhaps we can do that later. I especially enjoyed the idea that the order of creation was determined by a game of Mahjong. It was fun to watch Madhumati's sisters cheat at games, as it is so common and natural to happen when we play games as children. However, can you explain how these relate to the abstract and the physical?'

Vani broke into peals of laughter, 'You are such a baby for wanting to play these childish games. It's interesting to note that the games that Ritu's sisters are abstract games defining the order of things, the heralding of seasons, etc, while the games mentioned later are physical games like *Kho Kho* and *nadi pahad* which require some strenuous physical exercise. On the contrary, in life, we play physical games as children and as we mature, we tend to turn towards abstract games.'

Darpan began to wonder aloud, 'So the abstract can precede the physical and it can be the other way 'round as well?'

Deeksha explained, 'Yes. Not only that, but also the fact that the abstract and the physical are interlinked. Notice how *nadi pahad* can be correlated with the game of seasons. '

Darshan finished the discourse, 'All work and no play makes Jack a dull boy, especially if all he does is abstract reasoning all day long.'

Vani, in the mood for song and dance again started,

Oceans apart, the mist and the spray
Let it all come down on me, what may.
If you will be gone all the time,
I will surely go insane.

If the world does stop spinning,
And you go on winning,
I will remember the games
That we played on the gate
Of your house, that stood on the hill.

I took out the marbles,
You rolled out the dice,
As we waited for a big surprise.

You were the jock of the pack,
I was a tomboy in school,
Together we defined the cool.

We were always found playing till late,
Whether it was football or cricket,
Down the alley and in the back lanes.

Of all the games that I can remember now,
Are the games you played with my heart.
I hear the laughter, I spill the tears
But the games are over now.

If you leave me forever,
I will sulk and quiver.
So carry your cool
And the schoolbag too
And give me kisses, one or two.

The roll of dice showed beastly and angelic.

Part 2
Love

Pashupati

Deeksha began describing the bestial forms.

The daughters of Maya had transformed Prakriti.
Her rage had converted her into a monster.
She had now become luminescent like a trillion stars,
Nothing in the known universe could calm her.
To channelize her immense energy,
She decided to create a being that would be mortal
And yet, have mythical qualities akin to Maya.
She wanted this creature to rein in the erring sisters.

In her rage and pride, she forged out of Tatva, Pashupati.
He was a mighty beast,
A hulk of a giant,
A leviathan on the vast terrain.

He stomped, trod and trampled the earth,
He swam, raged and fought agains the oceans,
He flew, seared and soared through the skies,
He was the majestic king of beasts.

He was destined to rule over the jungles,
Skies, oceans, deserts, swamps,
Marshes, savannahs and the distant oases.

He had skin like the hide of an alligator,
For it was hard, toughened to withstand extreme weather.
He had on his body, an armour made of the toughest metals,
Which made him seem invincible to his rivals.

He had the cunning of a lizard,
The grace of a flying bird,

The ferociousness of a lion,
The might of a mammoth,
The force of a thousand ship's armada,
The stratagem of hoards of army ants,
The beauty of a shoal of fish,
The temerity of a pack of wild dogs,
The naughtiness of a group of monkeys,
The patience of a snail,
The rigidity of a giant redwood tree,
The handsomeness of a Greek God,
And most of all, an undying warrior spirit,
Of battle hardened soldiers of the past.

Pashupati was an elegant dancer,
A skilled musician,
An artist,
A magician,
A gifted poet,
A true friend,
A wise philosopher,
A tough teacher,
A handsome sportsman,
A leader of youth,
A creator,
An illusionist,
A Godlike figure,
An adept sailor,
But most of all,
He was a warrior,
The kind that had never,
Graced the ageing planet,
Or rather, the kind that would exist
Only once in the history of the universe.

Sibu – the Dancer

Vani took to singing about dancing angels.

Sibu was in seventh heaven
As he had a dance performance in the Kingdom.
It was a play on eternal love
And he had seldom felt such bliss,
For he sang with joy from the mountain tops,
And swam in the rivers and climbed trees and danced
Under the moon and stars.

The awaited night came and the Samudra Shiva Mandir
Was decked like a bride,
The Garbhagraha was lit, seemingly with a million lamps,
And the pillars were adorned with flowers of vivid hues,
The whole compound was bathed in incense
And it felt like Yuletide.

The path to the temple from the shore was spread
With gold dust,
And the gates were decked with foliage
And flowers and the rest.
The Shikhara flew a flag at half mast,
Which bore the emblem of the Simhas and looked
As if it was star cast.

Various stalls had been set up around the Mandir,
That sold eatables, or knick-knacks
Or antique things of yore.
Music streamed in from a stall,
Where a shehnai was being played
By one the performers.

The shehnai player played *Raga Viraha*,
And it sounded like it spoke of Juliet and Romeo,

Layla and Majnun, Shirin and Farhad,
And of all the lovers who were cast together at first
Before their love grew wayward.

There was a *Ferris Wheel* which was tall
And shaped like a *Sphinx*,
For whenever the wheel spun about its top,
A mouth opened to reveal a secret opening,
From which a joker would come out and fall
To the ground, with a flop.

The performance was to be held in the Vadya Mandapa
In the dance section,
And for it, a stage had been set up
Resembling a colossus.
However, it could be titled and lifted
And made to swing from side to side,
And pretty soon a crowd started streaming
In from all directions.

The sisters arrived looking like princesses
And wearing beautiful sarees.
Madhumati wore a Patola silk with an ornate border,
One with zari embroidery.
Ritambhara was in Kosa silk with a floral pattern,
While Kamakshi flashed a Kancheepuram
With a backless blouse to entice the men.
Urvashi was dressed in a Tussar silk saree
With geometric designs,
And Menaka looked ravishing in Kota silk, art nouveau,
Colored in a flashing neon hue.

The ladies took their seats in the front of the crowd,
But all waited for Narsimha and Singham
To make their entrance.
Narsimha arrived in a chariot led by eight horses
And looked regal amidst the gentry.

Singham came next in a tunic, riding a horse
And leading the cavalry.

The show was titled *The Fakir's Chrysanthemum,*
A sufi mystic devotional dance drama.
It was supposed to capture the length and breadth
Of India, a panorama.
Sibu had practiced and practiced
Until he could dance
No more,
For he knew *Bharat Natyam, Manipuri,*
Kathak, Kuchipudi,
Oddissi, Mohiniattam and *Sufi*, to name a few.

To begin, Sibu had mastered the Mohiniattam,
The erotic dance with
A heavenly glow, divine music, tinkling silver bells,
And a beauty unmatched, Mohini.
Her tulip eyes, cast a spell with her celestial dance,
The enchantress, the Ragini.
Close your eyes a while to imagine
This enchanting sight by yourselves.

Mohini is the glamour icon and this is a dance,
Not of destruction, but of enchantment
Ruling in the very air you breathe, in the music
And in the tinkling toes of merriment.
Sibu's androgynous features helped him act
Out the part of the enchantress;
Imagine, that in order to steal the *amrita*,
She commands you to shut her eyes.

The churning of the mighty oceans went on and on
In a never ending storm.
They were no ordinary disturbances,
Arising in the abyss of the oceans,
A hundred thousand leagues beneath the surface,

Those were not the elements that whipped up
The ocean's calm.

This was not a climatic upheaval
To determine the seasons,
To determine the destiny of the Universe.
The whirling of the mountain *Mandargiri* continued,
With the serpent,
Vasuki entwined around it, all bent.

The churning was done by the *Devas* and *Danavaas*,
Performing the churning of the ocean
To get to the essence of life and existence.
The reward was *Amrita*, an elusive potion,
That, for which every living being is thirsty
To achieve immortality and elation.

The churning of the ocean went on and on,
Whipping up mountainous waves,
A great liberating power capable of crushing the earth,
Such a great force.
Out of the ocean came all the precious treasures
That it had stored in its depth;
Out came the *Kamadhenu*, and the *Kalpavriksha*,
And ultimately *Lakshmi* from within the earth.
All were relinquished by the Devas.

For what they all wanted dearly was *Amrita*.
At last, the great storms were allowed to subside,
Mandargiri stopped whirling
And *Vaasuki* came to rest by its side,
The Daanavas, true to their nature, grabbed the *amrita*.

Ah, Lord. Mighty Saviour, come and save
The Universe from this awful calamity,
Darkness enveloped the land, while amrita
Fell in the hands of the Daanavas,

And Maha Vishnu, the saviour of the Universe,
Came to the rescue of the deities.
He arrived in the form of Mohini, the enchantress.

With Mohini within their reach,
The Daanavas forgot all about *amrita.*
Enchanted by her sight, they started dreaming in daylight.
Oh, what use is *amrita*, immortality,
When this divine form fills your vision and senses,
With the celestial dance, the enchanting dance,
Mohiniattam, the dance of the seductress.

The Hindu pantheon came to be used to represent
The fundamental struggle,
The battle between Good and Evil.
From the depths of the nether world,
Came the Daanvas to fight the Devas.
Hence came Mohiniattam, to save the *amrita*,
The dance of the enchantress.

Sibu was also trained in the Bharat Natyam,
Dance of the southern end,
A dance form which is said to have derived its name
From *Bharatha* Muni,
Secondly, the dance itself is signified by
Bharata, in all its finery.

It has been maintained by another school of thought that
Bharat had composed;
Bha, which stands for *Bhava* or facial expression,
Ra which stands for *Raga* or a musical note,
And Ta which stands for *Tala*, rhythm.
These three form the important aspects
That are most important in the art.

Bharat Natyam has been divided
Into three distinct categories,

Nritta, *Nritya* and *Natya*.
Nritta is pure dancing where the focus
Is on *tala* or the time measures;
In *Nritya*, there is a fusion of *Nritta,*
Or pure dance and *bhava*.

To the *Natya* category belong the dance dramas,
Wherein, each character is represented
By a different dancer.

An important aspect here is the *Angasudda;*
Perfection of the movement of limbs.
To this effect, the sinuous and lyrical lines of
South Indian temple sculptures
Are adapted to suit the dance form's regalia.
The sculptured carvings are also relevant
To the temples of Southern India.

The various schools of Bharatnatyam may have differed in time,
But this difference is superficial.
Basically, they pertain towards
The one spirit – the Divine,
Because of its universal and spiritual quality,
It appeals to one and all.

The sculptor finds form with beauty.
The religious in the painter finds
A spiritual appeal in the colors;
And the philosopher, esoteric implications.

Odissi is what Sibu learnt when he travelled
To the amazing East,
He learnt where the form had its origins,
In the temples of Orissa.
As cultural life has temples as their seat,
There has been an association of Odissi
With the day to day activities of the Mandir.

The rhythms, *Bhangis* and *mudras* used in Odissi
Dance have a unique blend,
It primarily depicts the theme of infinite love
Between *Radha* and *Krishna.*
The earliest mention of this dance is found in
Natya Shastra by Bharata Muni.

There are four styles: the *Avanti*, *Dakshinatya*,
The *Panchali* and *Odra Magadhi.*
There are also mentions of seven styles: *Souraseni*,
Magadhi, Karnata, Kerala, Odra, Gouda and *Panchananda.*
Siva and Parvati images are found with the Siva in *Tandava.*

We find the mudra of *dhyana*, *abhaya* and *bhumispara*
In the dancing form of *Heruka* in Tandava pose
At Ratnagiri, Orissa.
Every inch of the Konarka temple
Is sculpted with carvings,
Of dancing girls and musicians.

There are dancers holding cymbals, drums, mirrors
And flutes, showing vivid expressions from the dance form.
The most fascinating of all is the *Alasa Kanya,*
The gesture of relaxation,
And *Nayika bhavas* in the Konarka temple,
Which are considered the highest forms of expression.

From the past, we know of the practice
Of dedicating dance girls,
To the temples, in honour of the Gods.
Devadasis or dancing girls dedicated to Gods,
Belonged to the temples in Orissa.

The main *bhangi* of this form is the *Tribhangi,*
Supposed to have been taken
From Sri Krishna's Tribhangi,

And the *Chauka* pose (half seated) of Lord Jagannath.
There are a few other *bhangis* that are important,
Such as the a*dabhanga, abhanga* and *atibhanga,*
Which are very special to the form of Odissi.
There are other *Abhinaya* and *Chandirka*
Such as a*bhimana,*
Sukachanchu, mardala, akunchana, sarakhepa, etc.

Odissi has a rich variety of mudras.
According to the *Shastras*, they are,
Asamjukta hasta (Single hand),
Samjukta hasta (Double hand) and
Nrutta hasta (Dance hand).
Others include g*abhakya,* b*ana, baloya, tambhula* etc.
In Odissi, there is the *Natabatala* system in place, which is,
Jhampa – 7 beats, *dhruba* – 14 beats, *matha* – 10 beats,
Rupika – 6 beats, *tripata* – 7 beats, *Kuduka* – 12 beats, E*katali* – 4 beats,
Ada tali – 7 beats and *adi tala* – 8 beats.

Apart from these talas, there are *Fati tala* – 7 beats,
And the N*isaruka tala.*
Different *chhandas,* like the *jhoola* of *Tisra chhanda.*
Pahapata of chatusra chhanda,
May vary according to their *jatis,* such as *tisra,*
Chatusra, Khanda, Misra, Sankirha,
Different types of *bhavas, rasa, Nayaka,*
Caris, Mandalas, Bhramari, Karana and Utbhavana.
The inevitable include the *bhramari, ekapada, and biparita.*

In a Kuchipudi village, they refer to their art
As *Bahagavata natakam,*
And Sibu had learnt well this dance form.
Other names for it are *Yakshaganam, Veedhinatakam,*
Or Bharatam.
Kuchipudi may be the *Kelika* of classical texts.

It is believed that the erstwhile saint, Siddhendra Yogi,
Was the originator of the dance,
Or perhaps he was instrumental
In getting the folk dance-form rid
Of its obtuseness and gave it a classical base.
The origin, probably lies in the dance oriented
Around Siva Leela,
Which thrived in Andhra Pradesh.

The tradition of singing and interpreting *Geeta Govinda,*
Had been introduced in the areas bordering *Kalinga Desa.*
Narayana Teetha, the celebrated composer
Of *Krishna Leela-Tarangini,*
One believed to be the Guru of *Siddhendra Yogi,*
Who came to Puri on his way back from Varanasi,
Might have brought the Geeta Govinda
Tradition of music and dance with him.

Perhaps it's best to say that Siddhendra Yogi,
Composed *Parijata-apaharana* as a dance drama
And made the male members,
Of Brahmin families perform it as a devotional exercise.
The drama also set the tradition
For the development of *Kalapams.*
Siddhendra's work is better known as *Bhama Kalpam.*
Authors on dramaturgy in Sanksrit,
Know Kalapam as a poem written in one metre.

Kalapam is an innovation on the classical
Uparupaka Srigaditam,
With stress on presentation of a single bhava
By means of *nritta* and *nritya.*
Bhama Kalapam is essentially a dialogue between,
Satyabhama (Sri Krishna' consort)
And *Madhavi*, her maid.

It is said that originally, Krishna and Gopika also figured in it,

And at the beginning of a performance,
Madhavi (*Vidhushika*),
And Gopika entertained the audience
With music and dance.

With the entry of Krishna,
A romantic dialogue ensues between Gopika and him.
It enfolds into a highly philosophical dissertation
On *atma – paramatma*,
The relationship is interrupted occasionally
By the jester, Vidushika.
This sequence was fashioned into an independent item
Known as the *Golla Kalapam*.

The jester takes the place of Krishna in the dialogue.
Again, Kalapam led to the evolution of the Veshakathas,
Which, in due time,
Developed into the *Pagati veshams*,
Performed by the itinerant Kuchipudi artists with ease.

The Kuchipudi fair is based
On *Srimad Bhagavata* and the *Ramayana*,
And is classified under *vachikaabhinaya*.
Each artist is required to sing the lyrics,
Which enables him to get the emotions easily.

The music of *Kuchipudi* is adapted
Straight from the style of *bhajana kootams*,
Of Andhra Pradesh villages.
It is sizzling, lively and offers immense potential,
For variegated rhythm patterning,
While sounding rustic and genial.

In the procedural and technical aspects, Kuchipudi dramas,
Confirm to Bharata's formulation of classical dramas.
The performers here however,
Derive scientific sustenance,

From *Abhinaya Darpana* of the Nandikeshwara's oeuvres.

A performance starts with *Gurustuti* and Naandi,
Followed by Poorvaranga
Consisting of *Punyaha Vachana*,
Indradhwaja praushta, *Dhoopa*, *Deepa*,
Pushpanjali and *Ambastava*.
All through, the prefatory rituals of Daravus
(music, movements and mime)
Are executed, creating an effect that is scintillating.
Prahlada natakam, Rama natakam, Usha parinayam,
Chenchu Lakshmi, Sasirekha parinayam, Nala charitam,
Dhruava charitam and Tripura are among the popular
Dramas in the repertory.

The most celebrated of these works is the *Bhama Kalpam*,
Which deals with the famous
Episode from the Bhagvata,
In which, the proud Satyabhama demands
That Krishna should bring to her
The celestial *Parijata* plant from Indra's garden.

The play which starts with a lively
Pravesa Daruvu, employs
The Samvada and the *Abhinaya daruvus*,
Numbering to about ninety in count.
Bhama Kalpam is performed on three consecutive nights,

And Satyabhama remains behind
The curtain held by stage attendants,
Throughout the opening night's performance.
She throws over the curtain
The ornamented plait of her hair called the *jada*,
Studded with 27 stars, symbolising the constellation,
The five-hooded mythical serpent
And Lord Vishnu's golden image
With ten of his incarnations.

The recitation of devotional shlokas is done by the *Sutradhara,*
He offers *arati* to the *jada,*
This is called *jada bharatam* for long enough.
The curtained look of Bhama
Is a performed challenge,
Provoking and questioning the excellence of one's artistry,
To cut the plait off,
In full view of the audience.

In this play, Satyabhama is *swadhinapatika,*
Kalahantarita and *vasakasajjika.*
The eternal oneness of atma and paramatma
Is the essence of Bhama Kalapam,
People were impressed
By the balanced presentation of *natya dharmi,*
And *Loka dharmi.*

The Kuchipudi performers employ
Seven types of *Tandava,*
With variations in *Gati,*
Karana and *Chari,*
And the Desi five-fold *Lasya.*

Manipuri dancing was learned by Sibu
Where it had developed in the North East,
With two simultaneous traditions,
Hinduism and Animism.
The festival invoking the village gods, *Laiharoba,*
Consists primarily of the dance of the priestess.
It describes the concept of cosmology,
Which is primitive.

The basic theme in Manipuri
Is that of Lord Krishna and Radha,
Uncountable gurus and artists have delved deep into
Vaishanavite Sangeet Shastras,
Literature as well as manuscripts,

Available in Manipur on dance and the sciences of music.

Taking inspiration from them, they increased
The repertoire of dance movements,
Talas, rhythm patterns and musical compositions.
They evolved their own system of music and dance,
And even wrote various manuscripts.

Throughout the year, each and every
Social and religious festival,
Is heralded by celebrating the various forms of dance
And music, for example,
Dances with drums like *Dholak*, *Dhol*, *Khajari*,
Dhafat during the *Holi* festival,
Dances on clap rhythms at the *Ratha Yatra* festival.
Dances with swords and spears at *Durga Puja*,
A dance with *Kartal* and drum during the Natpala,
Dances with cymbals at the *Jhulan Yatra*,
On different social occasions such as births,
Marriages and before *Rasleelas*.
The theme of the childhood pranks of young Krishna,
As well as the divine love of Lord Krishna and Radha,
Pervade in most of these festivals.

Rasleeas and *Sankirtans*
Are highly developed dance forms,
Displaying the highly aesthetic religious feelings
Of the people of Manipur.
Rasleelas go on for 8 to 10 hours in the temple courtyards
From dusk to dawn.
Tears of joy are shed by the religious people of Manipur,
Who experience the real spirit of the lord, as their own.

All the technical elements mentioned
In the Sangeet Shastras,
Are found in *Rasleelas*, such as *Nritta* (Pure Dance),
Nritya (Interpretative Dance) and *Natya*.

The theme is expressed through four kinds of *Abhinaya*.

The songs are sung in the *Padavali* language
Such as *Brajabali*,
Old Bengali, Braja, Sanskrit, and now in Manipuri too.
A variety of talas infuse the songs,
Ranging from four beats,
To sixty-eight beats with their various rhythm patterns,
As well as dances on Nritta and Nritya Prabhandhas.

Manipuri dance is one of the most graceful
And lyrical dance styles of India.
The swaying movements of the neck
And the torso are inspired,
By the bamboo trees lilting in the breeze.

The movements are rounded, continuously mingling,
Into each other like waves in the sea.
Equal emphasis is given to the movements
Of different parts of the body.
The meaning of the song is conveyed
Through hand gestures, facial expressions,
And body movements in a subdued, dignified
And suggestive way.
In the *Rasleela*, thirty to forty girls
Wear gorgeous costumes and sway.
Their costume consists of a mirrored stiff skirt,
The upper half-skirt and a veil which creates
An ethereal effect.

In *Sankirtan*, male dancers
With *Kartal* and *Mridang,* wear white dhotis,
And turbans creating a serene and dignified atmosphere
With their presence.
In the festival dances, women wear an embroidered
Hand-woven *phanek* with stripes,
And thin white scarves.

A traditional classical Manipuri dancer
Faces a great challenge,
To present these dances in the modern theatre.
She should first have a thorough knowledge
Of techniques,
An expertise of the traditional dance
And other related aspects,
And then should present it, keeping intact
The original spirit and form.

Kathak is the art of the right use of movement,
Gesture, posture and pace,
Within and taking the unending flow of *laya.*
The dancer, more or less,
Creates a pedantic beauty
Of form, expression,
And rhythmic utterance in a uniquely recognizable union.

Moreover, the dancer is free to change
The course of dance,
In compliance with the *rasikas'* responses,
And the courteous challenges or the environs,
That the percussionist may offer at times in stance.

The body of the dancer does not participate in the mundane
In this dance,
It is transfigured and honed to the ends of the dance.
A body so adapted, becomes the *ang*,
And the *ang* acquires a pivotal role in the dance.

Two conditions, that are inter-linked,
Have to be met by the artist.
The dancing figure should look winsome
All along, not all wounded,
And the performance should never look mundane,
Like every day life.

For the first, the artist must give up the use
Of representations of the Divine,
In say, *vandana;* to not look into the eye
(As *Durga does,* for example).
And second, care should be taken with respect to posture,
The intermediate moments of no activity, that separate
The completion of one pattern,
From the beginning of another,
Or in anticipation of a re-enactment in dance
Of an intricate pattern,
Thrown as a friendly challenge by the percussionist.
The disruption from daily life shown
In the bodily movements of the dance,
Is made evident by the presence of make believe
In the basic *bols* of *tatkar.*

The syllables *Tehi, Tha Tha, Tha*
And Pra do not sound different from one another,
But, they are considered variant.
Nritya demarcates the daily from the artistic
In three ways that are apparent.

First, there is no hiding of the distinctive gait of the *taala,*
Or the moment of its *sama* in *abhinaya.*
Secondly, everything from daily life
May not find its representation.
In presenting, for instance, a panghai-ki-gat, the strain,
Of pulling a full big bucket of water
From a well or drain.
It can not be portrayed by a dancer by facial distortion.

Finally, everything is shown with such love and detail,
With such delicate markings of line and movement,
With arms and fingers composed to look like the holy grail,
And with such delicate use of glances and bodily turns,
That contemplative attention,

Would remain stuck to the display on stage,
Instead of going astray for the lack of visual drama.
If the dance portrays thematic items as suggested,
By and large,
The representational elements will gather after it
And help in the narrative process of the drama.

Discourse on Human Nature

Vani spoke as if she was in a dream, 'Darpan, did you find the sudden appearance of Pashupati, the manly warrior, a welcome reprieve from the pervading femininity in this story, until now? What do you think of Sibu's dance skills?'

Darpan was pensive as he spoke, 'I am awed by Pashupati, the mighty king of beasts. Actually, I am in a way, scared of his powers. At the same time, I am fascinated by Sibu, for the fact that he has mastered so many dance forms ranging from the erotic Mohiniattam, to the artisitc BharatNatyam. It's also interesting that Pashupati rhymes with Madhumati and Sibu with Ritu. I wonder if there is a connection. Once again, I would like you to explain the bestiality and angelic characteristics portrayed in the two stories.'

Vani explained, 'Well, you might be right about a connection between Madhumati and Pashupati, and between Ritu and Sibu. Once again, it's left to the interpretation of the story's listener. Pashupati's arrival signals the arrivals of the beasts, the fearsome, the awe-inspiring and the nerve-wracking elements in our lives. While we delve into the senses, the human body, materialism, and the esoterics of metaphysics, we digress and explore the possibility of man endorsed by the beast-like form of Pashupati - a warrior and angelic in the form of Sibu, a dancer.'

Darpan continued, 'So, we can say that the warrior is bestial in nature, while the dancer is angelic and both of them can be found in the form of man.'

Deeksha added, 'Yes. The warrior is also a dancer in the game of war; what is bestial must surely possess some angelic qualities. On the other hand, an angel must possess a dark side as well.'

Darpan summarized, 'For he shall be the master of all beasts, birds and mankind, who rules over angels and devils.'

Vani had fire in her eyes as she recited her poem.

Drowning in the seas of desperate sadness, I cry
And feel the beast rise in me,
It seems that my human side is slowly changing,
I can't deny what I feel.

I can feel the goodness dying in me,
As I feel the sickness rising,
Taking over my body,
And my soul for eternity.

The demons are calling out to me,
While the angels pull me back.
I can't seem to hold back
My thoughts and my feelings.

Have I got the fever, mother?
Or do I have the chills?
Will you make me take a pill?
Or will you say, in your cool manner, don't bother?

Has love finally done me in?
Or has hate drowned me in sorrow?
As I carry a burden of sin,
And toil from the day's work, on my barrow.

The roll of the dice showed spring and fall.

Rati and Ravi's Milan

Deeksha spoke in prosody about spring.

Prakriti had now become a sheer mass of pure energy.
Creating Pashupati had made her even more energetic
As she fed on the energy from the surrounding ether.
Her energy content soon reached critical mass.

Suddenly, she exploded into trillions of supernovas;
It was a cataclysmic event,
That reminded one of Tatva's creation.
As energy flew about in all directions,
A brilliant light began to shine across the firmament.

Thus was born Ravi, who came to be associated
With a glorious day,
And with all the goodness in the universe.
Ravi also stands for the onset of all things good,
And is the God of auspicious beginnings.

As light got distributed via ether through the firmament,
Prakriti began to cool down and condensation began.
Entropy decreased and so did the enthalpy,
And *dravya* began to revert to crystalline form.

Within moments, Rati, or Nisha, or Rajani,
The very essence of night itself was born.
She stood for dark powers, mystical beings,
Dreams, nightmares and vivid, despondent thoughts.

Rati and Ravi then began a celestial dance.
The Gods played music that enthralled Prakriti
And she began to blossom with flowers,

The seed itself being brought forth to life.

Wherever Rati and Ravi went,
Their path was strewn with flowers.
The five daughters of Maya were not left untouched either.

Ravi made Ritu shine with his creative energy,
While Rati made Ritu cold, distant, effusive and abysmal.

Ravi led Pavan through ether by adding heat,
As storms brewed and swift currents began forming.
Rati made Pavan morph into a breeze at night,
A soothing lullaby for the tired dreaming souls.

Ravi caused Jal to evaporate and clouds began to form.
Rati then caused the same clouds to condense into dew,
And the night dew transformed into morning dew,
As a foggy haze settled on flowers in the morning.

Ravi caused the seed to burst out of Dhara,
While Rati was the reason the seed lay dormant,
This contrasting dance laid the foundation of life.

Ravi caused Jyoti to acquire a burning incandescence,
While Rati led to the celebration of Jyoti in festive moods.
Jyoti gained as Ravi came to being with the day,
And she let her light shine when Rati took over the night.

The five sisters then conspired together,
And began to plan the union of Rati and Ravi.
Ritu set the mood by making the scene romantic,
Pavan made a zephyr blow over the ether,
Dhara led flowers to spring all over in glorious colors,
Jal brought about a dreamy drizzle,

And Jyoti made the love candles light up.

The mood was so romantic,
That Ravi took Rati in his arms,
And carried her to his dwelling, the fading stars.
When they reached the dwindling lights,
Ravi spoke to Rati,
'Let moonshine be the melody,
Let sunshine be the rhythm,
Let morning dew be the intoxication,
Let the dandelions be the drummers,
Let birds take to flight,
Let angels take to song,
Let the devil play along,
As I make love to you, darling,
All night and day long,
For it seems like I was made for you,
And you for me, for all eternity.'

Rahu and *Ketu* began devouring the light in the universe,
And a hallowed haze fell all over the ether,
As *dravya* itself began to close in on itself, in love,
And the angels came down from the heavens,
To sing merrily about love's glory.
The devil himself started dancing with his trill,
And played a symphony to summon the mischief makers,
Who began to laugh, play pranks and cause trouble.
As night became day, and day merged with night,
Ravi and Rati became one in a divine union.

Later, Rati was blessed with a daughter, Radha.
She was joy personified.
Adorned with anklets, bangles,
The *maangtika* and the *kardhani*,

She brought music with her, wherever she went.
She was so beautiful to look at,
That the onlooker, upon seeing her face,
Would later see her face in flowers, Gods,
Goddesses, children, men, women, trees,
The wind, the firmament, the stars and even in ether.

She was destiny's child,
And when she was born,
Vishnu incarnated as Krishna, a divine lover,
Who later took Radha as his consort.
When Krishna played his flute,
She danced to his tunes;
A celestial dance that described all of life,
The flight of birds,
The merry-making of children,
The sprouting of the seed
Bursting out of *Dhara* in joy,
The swimming fish,
The teeming fauna,
The abundance of flora,
The magic of creation,
The sorrow of destruction,
The anticipation of an invitation,
The flourish of the artist's pen,
The dreams of a poet's thought garden,
The surroundings - romantic, mystic, rustic and sylvan,
The dreariness of a rainy day,
The fancifulness of a dance,
The creaminess of milk,
And of reservoirs of honey,
That lay trapped in the bower,
And of morning dew in the glade,
The cotton-like flakes of first snowfall,

The fearful onslaught of the rushing tide,
The restlessness of a sailor on a moored raft,
Dwindling on the morose seas,
As he waits for Zeus,
And Persephone to dance
Amidst the anemone, periwinkle and starfish.

Radha was the fierceness of desire,
And the onset of youth's fancy,
In a poetic, prance-y, piquant, yet pragmatic way.

The Fakir's Chrysanthemum

Vani, the poetess, began singing a poem on fall.

The Fakir's Chrysanthemum begins
With a journey from the British Isles,
From where, Princess Diana sailed in an armada
Of ships and navy sailors.
The play showed the armada with cloth stitched ships,
And *Sibu* danced together with a bevy of dancers
To represent the stormy seas.

For the part with the journey, he chose *Kathak*
As the dance form,
For with its *Bol*s, he could make the sea
A raging deity, telling a tale,
With his *Ghungroos,* he could make the sounds
Of the ocean's spray and foam,
And finally, with *Abhinaya* set to *laya*,
He could display the tribulations of setting sail.

Sibu set the beat of the ocean with his Ghungroo,
The EkTaal, DuTaal and TeenTaal,
And then twirled round and round
From one side to the other,
To display the whirling of waves.
The music for the ocean was set
In *Raga Bhairava*, the norm,
And thus began *Sundara Tera Roopa*,
Or Beautiful is Thy Form.

Sibu started doing the mudras
Displaying the ocean as a feminine deity;
He begain with the *Mattali,*
Which symbolised the ocean
As the passion of a young woman,

And then moved on to *Katibhranta*,
Which was like the moon,
And then again the *Pristaswastika,*
Which denoted a meditative ocean free of calamity.

He also used hand gestures, like the *Mushti*
To represent a closed first of oceanic abundance,
The *Pataka,* or the flag of the wayfarers
On distant seas,
The *Hamsapaksha* denoting the flying of birds,
And the *Sikhara* signifying
The underlying mountain ranges.

The armada had set sail for the coast of Indies
In search of spices and precious stones,
But on the way it met resistance in the form of pirates.
Sibu displayed warfare with much pomp and show,
He danced with such ferocity,
That his whole body seemed to glow.

He made the hand gesture of the *Bhramara*,
Or the bumblebee to signify the pirates,
And when the sailors resisted,
Pallava or strength as a sign of resistance.
With eye movements which signify fear,
Angst, bravado and hate,
He moved with the ruthlessness of a warrior
Who is compelled to fight by fate.

The pirates having been defeated,
The armada made its way forward again,
But this time it lost its way
As the navigation system gave away.

The sailor took to the navigation system of old,
Following the movement of the stars,
And Sibu, along with his dancers

Displayed the formation of constellations.

He displayed Aries or *Mesha*,
The Big Dipper, or the *Saptarishi*,
The Pleiades, or the *Krittika*,
And Gemini, or the *Mithun*.

Also Cancer, or the *Karka*,
Leo, or the *Simha*,
Libra, or the *Tula*,
Pisces, or the *Meena*.

Vrishaba, or Taurus,
Vrishchuka, or Scorpius,
Kumbha, or Acquarius,
Capricorn, or Makar.

With the help of stars and constellations,
The sailors were on course again,
And in due time they landed
On the western coast of the Indies.
The dropping of the anchor was displayed
With the sounds made by the Ghungroo,
So was the alight of soldiers on land
And all the hullabaloo.

The sailors, with Diana, set camp on the coast
And waited for the morning sun,
For they were to meet the Prince of the western empire;
Their emblem was the sun.
Dawn arrived and Diana set out for the market
With her attendants,
And Sibu changed the dance form to Manipuri
To show the market amusements.

For here she was to set sight on the *Fakir* Arun
And fall deeply in love,

And for this part, the dance of Radha Krishna,
Manipuri was appropriate, by Jove.
She saw Arun by a banyan tree, singing mystic
Sufi tunes to the passers-by,
And when the mellow sound fell on her ears,
It felt like a lullaby.

Sibu made whirling movements and adorned
Manipuri Dance with the *kirtal* and *mridanga*,
To display the whirlpool of emotions
That was going on in the head of Diana.
The *Fakir* glanced upon the beautiful Diana
And decided to call her a chrysanthemum;
Sibu took to showing the petals of the flower,
Set on the beat of a drum.

The music of Arun spoke of whirling dervishes,
Mystics and divine love,
And of nature's delight, the doe, the dolphin,
The grazing gazelle and the dove.
Sibu put on the feminine Manipuri attire
Complete with the masked veil,
And danced to nature's beat, showing animals,
From an ant to a singing whale.

The Fakir unearthed that which lay in the hearts
Of men and women,
And drove Diana's heart sick with love,
For she was now love ridden.
She swooned, her heart ached and her plight
Was laid bare for all to see,
Sibu danced with various *bhavas* and *abhinayas*
To reveal her soft heart beat.

For displaying the plight of Diana's heart,
Sibu changed the style to Bharat Natyam.
Diana longed to hear Arun's voice in the privacy of her

Chambers, so she ordered her men,
To bring him to her and then to make him sing,
In her presence alone.
Sibu displayed this commotion
With the *Nritta* aspect of Bharat Natyam.

Sibu refused to heed to Diana's demand
Saying that his art was meant for all, not to please just one;
Her solitude and his refusal
Was shown by Sibu in the form of *Nritya,*
The various *bhava* that housed the face of Diana,
As she heard the Sibu's refusal, were marvellous.

Sibu shows at first, disbelief and then a feeling of guilt,
All snowballing in a tumult of sadness
Leading to grief and solitude;
Diana lay stricken and refused to eat;
This part of the play was shown with *Natya,*
Of dramatic magnitude.

Diana finally came up with a solution
And ordered for a gramophone,
She said, 'The gramophone will be used
As a recording instrument,
To capture the sound of Arun's voice and its tone.'
Sibu displayed the gramophone again,
With his dancers in much merriment.

Arun looked at the records
And called them t*avas* or platters,
And agreed to record his voice on the instrument.
This part of the recoding was shown with Odissi,
As a matter of fact.
Odissi is known to display performances like a play
In a dramatic manner.

And thus it was well suited for the display

Of a recoding session in proceeding,
Diana and Arun were always found together
In all those sessions of recording.
Their togetherness was shown with the various b*hangis*
And *mudras* of Radha and Krishna,
And then Diana took to teaching the piano-forte.

She started teaching Arun the nuances of classical music;
This is shown by Sibu with the help
Of the Odissi beats of *Jhampa*,
And also, the *Fati tala*.
Together with the *tala*, he recreated
The magic of western classical music.
On one such occasion, Sibu requested Diana
To sing for him.
The style now changed to Mohiniattam as Diana
Now played a songstress.
She sang and her voice was so sweet,
Soothing and melodious,
That Arun ended up falling in love with her.

Sibu danced a sequence, of Diana
As Mohini wearing trinkets and bells,
And Arun took turns as Vishnu, Devas and Daanavas.
Mohini took to singing, dancing
And carousing with her lover,
They ended up falling in love,
The closing scene showed him taking her in his arms.

Arun gave up his mysticism
And started to sing romantic ballads,
This was again depicted with the various *bhavas*,
And mudras of the Mohiniattam dance.

The final *mudra* of the dance form is the hamsa,
Where the lovers are shown as a pair of swans.
But much to the Diana's chagrin,

Her father came to know about her affairs,
And he comes to India to take her
Back to the distant shores.

This part of the play was shown
With the dance of Shiva, the *Tandava*,
For it displayed the rage of Diana's father.
When he had come to know about her affections,
For a mere vagrant, a *Fakir*, he was torn to bits,
And Sibu showed this well
With aggravated *Bhava* and *Vismaya*.

By this time, the sisters were affected much
With the play's movements,
Kamakshi sang a love tune to herself which rhymed,
Menaka attempted to reconcile her lovers
With some tricks,
While Ritambhara thought of placating
The father by teaching Diana some spells,

Urvashi thought of making
The lovers elope and make a run for it,
While the most hurt of the lot was Madhumati,
Who had been moved to tears.
The one thing is common as a whole,
Was that all the sisters were in love with Sibu,
For he had stolen their hearts.

Kamakshi fell in love with Sibu,
When he danced his eyes during Kathak,
Menaka fell in love with Sibu
When he recited the story of the seas.
Ritambhara gave her heart away
When Arun's started learning classical music,
And Urvashi fell for him
When he lost his heart to Diana and took to singing.

But Madhumati had fallen in love with him at first sight,
His body handsome like Adonis',
And his face like a Greek God's,
He exuded charm and looked like an angel,
An ethereal figure, fit to walk the heavens.
When he danced, his movements were fluid
Like flowing wine.

And when he sang, he could have put a canary
And the morning lark to shame,
Oh! what a voice, what command over meter and rhyme.
Her heart now pined for his glance,
For his touch and his voice,
For she no longer could bear being away from him,
She had no choice.

Meanwhile in the play, Diana's father
Would not listen to Diana at all,
Packed her things and asked her attendants
To carry them off,
He put them away in a specially prepared ship
That he had brought from South Hall,
To cross over the Arabian sea and the oceans
And take his daughter away from the eastern mayhem.

The commotion was displayed well
By the *Shiva Bhairava*,
Fear in the eyes, as well as
The scowl on the face.
Diana and her father left the Indies
For England and braved again, the seas.

Arun was lovelorn and became a wandering minstrel,
A Majnu, a Farhad, a Romeo, a wastrel,
A wanderer, best displayed by the Sufi movement;
For the Sufi dances show whirling dervishes
And saints and other things taboo,

Sibu took to dressing in tatters,
And whirls, twirls and twists as if in torment.

Arun, now helpless, took to drinking
And was found mostly in taverns,
He became angry, abusive, rude and indulged in fights.
Sibu displayed this with the Sufi dance forms
That showed things in bad light.
However, with time,
Arun transformed himself into a saintly persona.

He became a Sufi mystic,
And wandered all over the country,
Singing about love and devotion.
This was natural for Sibu to portray as he
Assumed the persona of a wandering Sufi saint in motion.
As the news of the wandering saint
Travelled by the patrons' word-of-mouth,
The story of the Fakir's Chrysanthemum
Was enshrined forever in the hearts of all Indians.

The play was over and Sibu, as a whirling dervish
Fell to the ground,
There was a standing ovation,
Not one amongst the audience was sitting found.
But most important of all, was the impression it left on the sisters,
For there were tears in the eyes of one and all,
And love housed in their hearts.

Discourse on the Seasons

Vani broke her reverie with her dreamy words, 'Tell me whether or not you liked the passionate story of Rati and Ravi, their divine union? You would be a stone to not fall in love with the charming Radha. The Fakir's Chrysanthemum is the best romantic tale I have ever heard. My heart cries out for Arun as he is heart broken, and the play's end leaves a bittersweet taste in the mouth, much like the last dregs of coffee.'

Darpan admitted with sincerity, 'I have to admit, I would surrender the whole world for just one meeting with Radha. I absolutely loved the whole idea of the union of light with darkness, good with the bad, and woman with man. The Fakir's Chrysanthemum left me in tears. As your narration of the play neared the end, I folded my hands in prayer to God, hoping that Diana would return to Arun. I can imagine Arun and Diana like Sibu and Ritu, like Pashupati and Madhumati, like Krishna and Radha, cavorting, dancing, and playing in God's secret garden, like children amidst dandelions, daisies and pansies. Will you please explain the metaphor of spring and fall?'

Vani started enunciating, 'Rati and Ravi's love is like the spring. When the darkness of winter finds its soulmate in the bright rays of the sun, life springs from the earth and the entire firmament bursts forth with a jolt of joy. The Fakir's Chrysanthemum is the antithesis of spring, that is, fall. Its a melody which speaks of falling leaves, of their changing colors, and of trees turning from their raging autumnal hues to a dead black. The love that Arun has for Diana is the only thing that remains in the form of life, preserved for the next spring, while Diana, the petulant blossom in his life, has faded away, unable to face the bleak winter ahead.'

Darpan blew out a whistle, 'Love is a many splendored thing, just like the seasons, eh.'

Deeksha added, 'It also hurts and heals, just like the seasons which wither and bloom, and the moon that wanes and waxes.'

Darpan finished the discussion with the flourish of a philosopher poet, 'My love is like a rose that sprung in June. *Shall I compare thee to a summer's day? Her smile is like the onset of spring's bounteous blooms.* Poets have used metaphors and similes to the best when composing dreamy poems and lyrics on that tender, sweet, hurtful yet magical feeling they called love.'

Vani was in a pensive mood as she sang,

The autumn leaves fall like a ghoul,
And don't help the soul at all.
My heart does cringe and sing
Sad melodies of spring's reverie,
Of the past, when time was joy and it flew by.

But now, there is a bit of snow and cold lashing winds
That take the rouge from my face away,
Leaving a trail of pale ale
And scars of the rake,
Collecting fallen leaves from the sidewalk.

The heart can't wait for spring-time
When music is swing and ragtime,
Flowers spring in every bower
And grass braids through every glade.

But most of all, spring brings you,
In a cloak bursting with colors that sparkle with joy,
And lays the ground for lingering summer kisses
And lovemaking in the hot afternoon sun.

The roll of the dice showed silence and music.

Pashupati and Ritu

Deeksha spoke of the beauty of silence.

Prakriti lay resting in the cradle of the Gods,
When a devious plan began to take shape in her mind.
She would pit Pashupati against the sisters.
Starting with Ritu, she would make them meet,
And induce desire, worldly pleasures and satiation.

She intended to mix Pashupati's ferocity
With Ritu's timidity,
And achieve the thinning of both of her creations.
She wanted to destroy their egos,
Dwindle their powers,
As they lust for each other,
And go wayward together.

She manifested Swapna, the Goddess of dreams,
And made her take control of Pashupati's mind.
As Pashupati slept in a stupefying slumber,
He dreamt of a chance meeting with Ritu.

In his dream, he saw her as the chalice,
Brimming with sweet wine,
Made with nectar collected from the flowers,
And distilled by clouds themselves into dew drops,
Resting on rose petals and lily blossoms.

When he woke up, he began a fervent search for Ritu,
And much to his amazement, found her right next to him,
Playing amidst wild beasts and foliage.
He approached her with love in his heart,
And trepidation in his soul,

For he feared losing her in the vastness of Dhara.

He spoke to Ritu, 'O child of Maya,
The sweet forerunner of the abundance of harvest,
Hear me as I describe my heart's plight,
For I am smitten by your charms,
And lay myself at your disposal.
Feel free to take me as a lover,
Or cast me aside if you please,
As without you my life is worth nothing.'

Ritu was shocked at first,
To hear such an amorous plea.
But she found Pashupati handsome and charming,
And decided to put him to test.

She said, 'O King of beasts,
I am honored to be the object of your affection,
But I must ensure that your love for me is true.
So you must perform some tasks to prove
The legitimacy of your intentions.'

She said, 'I want to bring the seasons to life,
Basanta to sing, dance and celebrate with joy,
Grishma to burn, rage and scald with ferocity,
Varsha to pour, heal and bless all with timidity,
And *Sheeta* to calm, placate
And soothe with her mystical beauty.'

Pashupati was puzzled by Ritu's appeal,
But he decided to try something that he knew.
He was a good dancer,
And asked Ritu to be his partner in a celestial dance.

Ritu agreed and soon they began an enchanting dance.
Pashupati first held Ritu's hand
And took control of heat,
He threw it around,
As he swung Ritu all over the ether and the firmament.

As heat began to dissipate from Ritu,
Basanta began to show its myriad forms,
Enveloping *Dhara* with mystical creations.
Pashupati then held Ritu by her waist,
Which caused her to moan with desire,
And a surge of intense pleasure coursed through her veins.

Their bodies began to entangle,
In slow erotic movements,
And a warm glow began to emerge from Ritu,
Which caused *Grishma* to acquire a sheen,
Leading to sunny days and bright beginnings.

Pashupati then held Ritu's head,
And unclasped the clutch that held her hair together.
As her locks cascaded down her shoulders,
Pashupati twirled them round and round,
And spread them across the firmament,
Causing clouds to form in the sky,
And streams and rivulets to flow down to Dhara.
Soon, it began raining in a massive downpour,
And Varsha arrived in full glory,
Bringing tumescent life to all of Dhara.

Pashupati finally lay at Ritu's feet,
And tied an anklet around her feet,
He then danced with her to a beat,
Which made a sound

Like the clip-clopping of iron horseshoes on the ground.

As the dance broke in a sudden wanton abandon,
Snow began falling to the sound of the anklets,
While the cold descended from Ritu's feet,
On to Dhara, the ether, the sky and the firmament.
Sheeta had now arrived in full force,
And the cold caused Ritu to squirm.

She desperately sought the warmth
Of Pashupati's embrace.
She fell in his arms,
Collapsing, tired and weakened,
Yet glowing with the love
Of a satiated maiden.
She was now in love,
Or so she thought to herself,
As she looked into the intense eyes
Of her lover.

Madhumati and Sibu

Vani waxed poetic on music.

One evening, on seeing a moment opportune,
Madhumati wandered into Sibu's dwellings
And started singing a tune.
He heard the melody and came out
Wondering who was singing,
And upon looking at Madhumati,
Instantly made a reckoning.

He asked, 'Who are you, oh lovely lady,
And what is this song you sing?'
Madhumati replied, 'I am Madhumati,
I came to visit you as I saw you dancing.
I have seen you dance brilliantly
At the Fakir's Chrysanthemum.
Would you dance for me,
If I were to sing for you, at the auditorium?'

Sibu was taken aback, but he found Madhumati
Very beautiful indeed,
So he gave in to her demands and readily agreed.
He said, 'I agree Madhumati, for you are truly talented,
You have the voice of an angel and are truly gifted.

But first, I must ask you some questions,
Tell me about the various *Ragas* and the *Raginis*.'
Madhumati spoke, 'A Raga is something
That colors the mind with feelings,
A wave of passion or emotions.

Sonic compositions of musical notes (*svaras*)
Are called Ragas.
They have a sequence, a form,

A structure of peculiar significance.
The starting note is called the *graha*,
While the terminating note is called the *nyasa*.

The *vadi* is the predominant note,
Also the speaker, the announcer of the Raga.
It's the note which manifests as,
Or expresses the peculiar characteristics of a Raga.
The dissonant node plays a part in the destruction
Of the melody's character.

For the ascent of a Raga,
You have the notes called the *aroha,*
And the one that determines its structure,
The descent, is the *avaroha*.
Ragas may have different number of notes
In their composition,
And hence may be classified as *odava* (pentatonic),
Using five notes,
Or *khadava* (hexatonic), using six notes
Or as *sampurna* (heptatonic), using all the seven notes.

A Ragini, on the other hand, is like a minor melody,
There are six major Ragas and thirty six minor Raginis.

The Raginis can be conceptualized as beautiful,
Miniscule parts of the Ragas themselves.

Raginis are given feminine connotations.
The term Ragini is oftentimes ascribed as the wife
Of a Raga in some parlances.'
Sibu interrupted, 'O but this is all theory,
Can you sing a melody by applying
Some of these raga and raginis?'

Madhumati said, 'I have tried
And composed a song,

It's called 'O Beauteous One'. Shall I sing it for you?'
Sibu agreed and asked her to go ahead and sing,

Sa	Sa	Re	Re	Sa	Re
1/4	1/4	1/4	1/4	1/2	1/2

Where Sa, Re, Ga, Ma, Pa, Dha, Ni are the notes,
and 1/4, 1/2, 1 stand for quarter, half and full notes, respectively.

Ga	Re	Ga	Ma	Pa
1/2	1/2	1/2	1/2	1/2

O beauteous one, you have made
My heart dance and sing,

Sa	Ni	Dha	Ni	Dha	Pa
1/2	1/2	1/2	1/2	1/2	1/2
Ni	Dha	Pa	Ma	Ga	
1/2	1/2	1/2	1/2		

And my love, it seems like you are the one for me.

Re	Sa	Re	Sa	Re	Sa	
1/2	1/2	1/2	1/2	1/2	1/2	
Sa	Re	Ga	Ma	Pa	Ni	Sa
1/4	1/4	1/4	1/4	1/4	1/4	1/4

Will you please come into my life and be with me

Dha	Pa	Ma	Ga	Sa	Re	Ga
1/4	1/4	1/4	1/4	1/4	1/4	1/4
Sa	Re	Ga	Ma	Pa	Dha	
1/2	1/2	1/2	1/2	1/2	1/2	

Or I will forever be lovelorn and be cast away into infinity.

Madhumati finished a stanza
And told Sibu that this was as far as she had got.
Sibu was impressed and agreed

That she knew far better than a lot.
He agreed to dance to her music
And off they went to the auditorium.
When they reached there, they were surprised
To find a rhythm,

That was playing by itself, perhaps from the trees,
The wind and the ground.
Tin, thak, tha, thaiya it went and Madhumati
And Sibu were both spell bound.
They decided to put the rhythm to good use,
And Sibu put on his best dancing shoes.

Madhumati had decided to sing the music
Of the *Bhramara,* or the bumblebee,
And the flowers in the garden.
She began her song by invoking the names of the flowers:
Malati (jasmine),
Kamala (lotus), *Nilotpali*(bluc lotus), *Kumunda* (lily),

Kusuma(flower), *Kaumadaki*(pertaining to a lily) and *Utpali*(lotus).
Sibu began dancing the Bharatnatyam
And started making mudras.
With hands cupped, he made the lotus,
And with fingers spread open, the lilies.

He displayed the color blue with the expression(*Bhava*)
Of his eyes,
And displayed the fragrance of jasmine
By twirling his body serpentine.
Madhumati now invoked the names of animals,
The *Mayuri* (peacock), the *Vada-hamsi* (the big swan), the *Vihan-gada*(the bird),

The *Kokila* (cuckoo), the *Naga-dhwani*(snake's sound),
The *Kuranji-Kurangi*(the antelope) and the *Hamsa-dhwani* (swan's sound).

Sibu took to Mohiniattam to display the animals,
Dancing with trinkets and bracelets
That he had adorned on himself.

Madhumati now started singing the Megha-raga,
That signalled the onset of rains,
And Sibu took to dancing the Manipuri in a panorama,
He brought out his kartal and mridangam,

And let loose a volley of beats,
Which made the sounds of the clap of thunder
And lightening.
He put on his masked attire
To represent the rain gods,
And then sprang to his feet from the ground
In a display of fertile grounds.

Madhumati now started singing *Raga Basanata*,
Which signified the onset of spring.
With various flowers and trees coming to full blossom,
The environment was shown full of animals and birds
Singing with joy for the season.
The *Bhramara* danced with joy
And found a lot of companions,
Together they started building a bee hive
For the winters.
They would collect nectar from the flowers
And emptied their udders,
Before settling for the night, as the cold
Would give them shudders.

As the hive began to take shape with geometry,
Sibu danced out the various ragas in measures of trignometry,
For it involved the *odava* scales, or the pentatonic,
The *khadava*(hexatonic) and the *sampurna* (heptatotinc).

As the dance reached a point of

Utter pandemonium and commotion,
Madhumati could take it no more,
And when the passage came to where
She had to sing of the Queen bee,
She ran towards Sibu and clasping him in her arms said,
Mi amore!

'Hold me, O *bhramara* divine, I am your queen bee.
Together we shall rule,
In *Basanta* over this garden heavenly.
You can be the King and I shall be your bride,
The whole kingdom of bees
Shall look upon us with pride.'

Before Sibu could utter a word,
She kissed him on his lips.
It was a kiss that began as an exploration and soon
Became a consummate fiery bliss,
From which neither Sibu, nor Madhumati
Wanted to wake up,
For it seemed that if their lips were to part,
Heaven itself would break up.

Madhumati had declared her love for Sibu
And he had fallen for her too.
Together they entwined their bodies
In passion like lovers,
As if they had met after years and had longed for each other.
He held her close to his bosom
And stroked her gentle thighs,
He pleaded with her, 'O my love,
Let me drink from your lovely eyes.

For soon, this dance will be over and you shall be gone,
And without your love, I shall be lovelorn.
After *Basanta*, comes *Sheeta Ritu*, the season of winter,
Which shall stoke the fires, the cinders and the ember.

Madhumati spoke, 'My love,
I cannot be separated from thee,
For wherever you go, I shall follow thee.
In case you become lost and lose heart,
Don't worry, you have my love
And we can begin from the start.'

With this, the dance of the bumblebees came to an end,
Madhumati and Sibu walked away
From the auditorium, hand in hand.
Together they went to the lakeside and saw the sunset,
And looked into each other's eyes, with tears they were wet.

Like a rutting deer and doe,
Kissing under the mistletoe,
Drinking wine that is divine,
He drank from her eyes and her lips,
And letting their limbs entwine,
They made passionate love on the rocks next to the water.

He entered her person with gusto,
And did not let his eyes wander,
Which settled on her bosom,
Her slender waist and her thighs,
Her neck, the small of her back and her restless eyes.
She felt him inside her and let go of a sigh.

She pleaded him not to stop,
Until the morning was nigh.
They made sweet love that was taboo, all night long,
And the birds and the bees next to them did throng,
They took their places in the morning
And welcomed them with a song.

In her arms, he rested after bearing the heat,
And in the lap of water, he found a seat.

He then let her head rest in his lap,
Oh, when love is all around, who needs a nap.

Discourse on Music

Vani stepped aside from the other three as if she wanted to sieve her thoughts before she could begin a discourse on the subtle subjects of music, she then spoke, 'So what do you think of Madhumati and Sibu as a couple, Darpan? Do you think they will make it? Are they meant to be together? How about Pashupati and Ritu? Can you see the King of Beasts have a dreamy romance with the Queen of Seasons? Are you beginning to see the poetry in the story?'

Darpan was amazed by the story and he spoke with stars in his eyes, 'I am now rooting for the two couples. I am now convinced that Madhumati, who is a singer, was a man and a warrior in her past life, while Sibu, who is a dancer, used to make seasons dance to his tunes like Ritu. Please explain how the notions of silence and music intertwine with the story.'

Vani began laying out the details, 'You see Darpan, the game of love between Pashupati and Ritu is like silence, for it is the King of Beasts and he must be gentle with Ritu, careful not to upset her delicate nature and destroy the subtle play that she has with Prakriti to bring about the change in seasons. On the other hand, Sibu is the dancer who dances to the music of love that is Madhumati and together they make divine, erotic and gentle music that is love itself.'

Darpan agreed, 'I can hardly wait to see what follows now as the story unfolds and their love for each other grows. I wonder if the sisters will bring folly to their love lives.'

Deeksha countered, 'A love like theirs, manifested in silence and music, blowing hot and cold, part erotic, part hypnotic seems too good to be true, doesn't it?'

Darpan wondered, 'Like children watching their mum and dad loving each other, we can only wait and watch, I guess.'

Vani broke into a vituperative carmoisine melody and it sounded like it would shatter the window panes.

Zeus spoke, 'Hold me close, my nine Muses,
O Calliope, evoke the feelings unfelt with your hymns,
O Clio, read the parchments from Herodotus,
O Eratoto, delve into the erotic and the tabooed in poesy,
O Euterpe, play your divine flute,
O Melpomene, cast a gloom with a tragic tale,
O Polyhymnia, unveil the hymns of antiquity,
O Terpsichore, strike the lyre and dance like the devils,
O Thalia, bring humour, satire and a divine comedy,
O Urania, make the stars shine with stellar music.'

The heavens began to dance and sing.
It began to rain as a misty fog descended,
And birds began to chirp, chirrup and chatter,
Nymphs took to dancing and pixies scattered their magical dust.

Children became angels and blew the horn,
Women frolicked, flirted, fancied and fandangoed with men.
Men displayed bravado and skill on horses,
While the jester stole the King's crown.

Flowers spread their fragrance in jubilation,
The deer kicked, trotted, and treaded about in anticipation
Of the King of Beasts.
Out he came, the lion-hearted Tiger,
And announced the coming of a prodigy,
Of the likes of Mozart, Beethoven,
Bach and Tchaikovsky.

The dice showed consummation and infatuation.

Pashupati and Pavan

Deeksha's words took to a flight of fancy
And spoke of consummation.

Prakriti was not done yet.
She now wanted Pashupati to have fun with Pavan.
She summoned Kama and with his help,
Aroused in Pashupati's heart,
A searing need to be one with Pavan.

She also manifested Leela, the creative player,
And made her take center stage,
In the life of Pashupati.
Pashupati was to be Krishna,
And Tatva was to play Nanda Rai, his father,
While Prakriti decided to play Yashoda.
Pashupati then put up a show of Raasleela
Or, games of love, along with Balaleela,
Or games of the child,
With Pavan playing his consort, Radha.

As Leela began churning the universe
In her games of childhood and youth,
Pavan began to feel maternal love for Pashupati,
In the form of his mother Yashoda,
And romantic love,
In the form of his consort, Radha.

It was she, who approached Pashupati,
Like a mother beckons to a child to play with her.
She scolded Pashupati for not coming to her earlier,
And asked him to come and sit in her lap.

Pashupati was now in two minds,
His heart was in torment,
Was it Yashoda calling him or Radha?
Leela churned the reals of pathos again,
Pashupati began gurgling like an infant,
And soon scurried over to Pavan like a toddler.
He began cooing in her ears,
As if caught in a naughty act,
And started to placate her,
So that she would forget her anger,
Hold him tight to her bosom and soothe him.

Pavan was also in two minds;
One part of her wanted to console the child,
For it was quite ironical that she was air,
The very essence of life that an infant craved,
On the other hand, she wanted to reprimand him,
For not seeking her out earlier.
She decided to play games with him,
Some of them were mother-child games,
While the others were love games.
She told Pashupati to fetch his toys.
As Pashupati brought his crayons,
Play dough, clay, tempera colors and stationery,
She began readying a sand pit,
With buckets, a shovel and a tumbler.

She wanted to teach the child sandboxing
As a mother teaches a child art,
After which, she wanted to indulge in fun games,
Like clay modelling and papier mache, as a lover.

She asked Pashupati to carry some sand from a lakeshore,
And when he had done so,

She made him take out a bucket load with a shovel.
Then from the bucket,
She asked him to remove a tumbler full of sand,
And empty it upside down on the ground.

Pashupati watched with eyes wide open,
As she carved out the first bird,
The Archaeopteryx from the sand.
She uttered a magical hymn then,
And the first bird took to its fanciful flight.

She then let the child play,
As he made various other birds,
The lark, the pigeon, the parrot and the sparrow,
All of whom took to roosting on lush green trees.

Pashupati was delighted and craved for Pavan's arms.
But she intended to deprive him of some loving,
And shooed him away with disdain.
The child was hurt and moaned in pain.
Soon, Pavan's feelings metamorphosed,
From an indifferent mother,
She changed into a caring lover,
And transformed into Radha,
Who took the crying child in her arms.

She cajoled and coaxed the child to get his stationery.
They drew with brushes and pencils and crayons,
And mixed paper with water and mashed it to a pulp,
To prepare it for papier mache.
Also they kneaded the play-dough,
Until it was soft and workable,
Getting it all over themselves,
And they clasped each other,

All slimy, grimy, wet and lusty.

By now, Pashupati had started
Feeling amorous and lusty,
But Pavan as Radha had managed
To keep him on a tight leash,
By keeping his attention on the job at hand.
They began working in a passionate rhythm,
And gave birth to the first works of art,
Birds, animals, nature's regalia, stars, constellations,
And the first divine shapes of Gods and Goddesses.

When they had finished,
Pashupati and Pavan had stars in their eyes,
And the feeling of having enjoyed
Their first Rasleela warmed their hearts.
But as they held hands and embraced each other,
As lovers madly in love would,
They felt, this was just the beginning
Of the many Rasleelas that would play out with time.

Kamakshi and Sibu

Vaani's poem delved on infatuation,

Kamakshi could neither sleep, nor eat,
And could not rest at all.
Her eyes longed for the sight of Sibu
Dressed in his tunic and shawl.
She writhed in pain and her heart sang
The tune which spoke of love,
Her limbs trembled, her words came out in a stutter
And her fancy took to flight like a dove.

In her fancies, she devised a devious plan,
To make Sibu hers with elan.
She would use the knowledge of potions to create Maya,
As outlined in the book given to her by Vatsyayana.

She decided to create potions numbered 1 to 5,
The one that would make him follow her
Was to be the first potion,
While the other that would make him see her in his dreams
Was to be the second potion,
Another, that would induce him to sing songs to her
Was to be the third potion,
Yet another which would make him fall in love with her
Was to be the fourth potion,
Finally, the last would make him want to make love to her,
And it was to be the fifth potion.

She took out the recipe book,
And brought out a brewing pot,
And then gathered the ingredients, the whole lot.
She then started chanting the incantation,
'Hocus pocus, mix some, stir some carnation.

Put a bit of thyme, a bit of coriander
And something sweet like a honeysuckle.
Mix it with one part ginger to give it a twang,
And let it all simmer,
For this will cause him to follow me like a ram.'
The potion was soon ready and Kamakshi
Applied liberal doses of it on herself.

After anointing herself with it,
She passed by Sibu's cottage.
Sibu was going about his daily duties,
When the potion's fragrance invaded his nostrils,
And like an elephant in musth,
He started following its trail.

The sight of Kamakshi's voluptuous body and swaying hips,
Soon greeted his sight and it made him even more
Mad with desire and wanting.
Kamakshi decided to play the tease
And make him chase her,
So she started a circuitous route around Sibu's village.

First, she took him to the village pond,
And on the pretext of drinking water, got herself drenched.
The sight of Kamakshi's nubile body,
Her hardened nipples,
Her slender waist and her inviting eyes,
All served to add to Sibu's delirium.
Oh that fragrance! That madness inducing potion.
It drove him crazy with lust for her,
He could take it no more and started running after her.

Kamakshi saw him chasing her and laughed inwardly.
She doubled her speed
And rested next to the mango orchard.
She plucked a mango fruit and ate it sensually,
Letting the sweet syrup drip down

All over her lips, cheek and neck.

Sibu could now imagine himself as a bee,
Driven only by his primitive instincts,
Towards the fragrance wafting,
From her and the nectar dripping,

All over her luscious body.
He finally managed to catch hold of her,
And grasped her tight in his hold, kissing her,
Smothering her with affection, like a rutting bull.

Kamakshi pleaded ignorance for his plight,
And shooed him away, disappearing from sight.
As Sibu was left tortured in heat,
Kamakshi had won the day and felt neat.

The next day she started chanting
The incantation for the second potion,
'Mix some strawberries, mangoes and the nectar of oranges,
And let rosemary and thyme entwine,
For when your eyes meet mine,
It will become a dream that you wake up from,
And the sun will then rise.

She dabbed the potion on herself
And passed by Sibu's house
When the moon was high in the sky.
Sibu was fast asleep when the fragrance
Hit him strong again.
He started having a wet dream,
One in which he was chasing Kamakshi
Like Krishna chased for cream.

He saw her both as an angel and a devil at the same time.
The angel played a harp to some divine rhyme,
While the devilish girl came to him in a negligee,

And made sweet love,
Which left him in a sweet reverie.

The angel and the devil girl were then drawn to a battle,
Neither wanted to let go of him
And treated him as if he were cattle.
They began fighting and the devil
Seemed to have the upper hand,
Until another angel came down from the heavens
And threw sand,

Over the evil intentions of the devil
And took the angel to her side,
While Sibu watched helpless,
Not knowing by whom he should abide.
Suddenly, the two angels started playing a sweet melody,
That made the devil lose her mind
And sank her in melancholy.

She left screaming in anger, cursing with spiteful words,
While Sibu and the angelic girl made love to the music
Till the end of the world.
The friendly angel then bid adieu,
And together with Kamakshi, the angel,
Sibu let their vows renew.

He woke up with a start and
Was sweating from head to toe,
'Oh, what a dream, with the angel
And devil as each others' foes.
I must have been enamoured by Kamakshi
So much, that I imagined it all,
In my dream I did not even notice
That from the cot I did fall.

He picked himself up and put himself to bed,
And woke up the next morning,

Feeling like he still needed to rest.
In the meantime, Kamakashi prepared
Her third potion at its best,
She chanted the incantation
And let the ingredients melt.

'Double, bubble, toil and trouble,
Mix a lot of water and cane,
Stir in some curd, sweet syrup and nectarines,
And let the mixture rest on a bed of flowers again,
Till the fragrance is infused with music
And makes the lover sing.'

She doused herself with the potion
And visited Sibu's nest,
Where he lay on his cot, dozing and taking rest.
He was woken up by her sweet fragrance
And began to sing,
While at the sight of Kamkashi, his heart did singe.

She was dressed in a loose sari,
Showing off her bosom and revealing her navel.
It felt like she was the hammer and he, the gavel,
And the ruling had been passed in the court of law,
That Sibu was the mice and Kamakshi, the cat's paw.

For she had him in a vice,
And he sang merry songs and made them sound nice.
'O Kamakshi,' he sang, 'you are my heart's desire,
You are the furnace, the hearth and my love is the fire.

Wherever you go, my heart longs to be with you,
I cannot bear to be away, I cannot bid adieu,
For your musk laden body
Has driven me out of my senses,
And aroused such passion
As a hoard of wild un-reined horses.

Come, rein in my passion
And throw the noose of your love around me,
Beguile me with your charms and steal my sanity.
For you, I would gladly do anything that you wish,
A look from your lusty eyes makes my body rush,
To be by your side, it is all that I now think.
You are a bottle of wine and it's all I want to drink.
Let loose a volley of words and pierce my tender heart,
You were meant for me, I have known it from the start.

Kamakshi kept him waiting still,
For she wanted to stoke the fire
A little more in him.
She left him wanting,
And headed back to make the fourth potion for him.

Again, she began chanting an incantation
From the book of potions,
'To steal his heart with these ingredients,
The betel nut, the leaf and rations.
Mix it with some lime, some cashews, almond
And some raisins,
And allow the betel leaf sweetmeat
To let love rise amazing.'

She doused herself with the betel leaf sweetmeat potion,
And passed by Sibu's cottage
To create in his mind love's notion.
He could not resist the fragrance's powers,
And started following Kamakshi on all fours.

He was so in love, he could not feel
The heat of the countryside,
Nor the need to avoid the *looh*,
The hot gusts of tropical wind that do not easily subside,
He began to feel sick and fell down to his knees.

Kamakshi came running to him on her lap,
And sang a lullaby to the poor soul,
'Sleep well, my love, for your heart and body
Have fallen sick.
Of all the women in the country,
Of whom, you could have had your pick,

You chose to follow me
And for that I am flattered.
Now that we have each other, it's all that matters.
Let's go far away from here and you can build me a home,
We will have elves, fairies, pixies as well as gnomes.

We'll bide our time and grow old with each other.'
Sibu was faint, yet managed a weak smile,
And said, 'We shall do as you please,
For all I care about is you and for us to be together.'

Kamakshi decided to put the final straw
On the camel's back,
And told Sibu, 'Just wait darling,
In a moment I will be back.'
She rushed back to her potions,
And brought out her book and the stirring pot.

And decided to make the last potion,
The one that would make him want to love her
And forget all other notions.
She chanted, 'Rose petals, tulip buds, chrysanthemum,
Wings of a butterfly, and cardamom,

Stir it well, let it rest, and make love
Till the end of the millennium.'
But she fell short of one magic ingredient,
A four leaved clover,
But she left in a hurry,
For she had Sibu's love to discover.

She administered the potion on herself and sat by his side,
Alas, the potion had a backward affect
And reversed the tide.
Sibu woke up from the charms of all the potions,
And started questioning, 'Who are you?
And what is this commotion?'

She pleaded with him to make love to her,
But he left her wanting, he would not listen to her.
All her effort was in vain, courtesy a little mistake,
If one does not know well enough, one should not partake.

Kamakshi was in grief and left for her quarters,
And vowed to get Sibu, for she was a fighter.
She took to revising her book of potions,
And started stirring the pot again
And fetched her ingredients.

Discourse on Affinity

Vani was beginning to feel tired but she carried on, 'Don't the names of Pavan and Kamakshi give you goosebumps. To me, the very thought of Pavan makes me feel the wind blow softly over my face and caressing my hands and body, making me crave the need to be held. Kamakshi, on the other hand, makes me want to reach out to my lover and pull him in a tight loving embrace and devour greedily as I make love to him. What do you have to say to that Darpan?'

Darpan felt shy and stammered, 'Kamakshi's episode with Sibu made me reach out for a pillow as I felt like hugging and sleeping next to a lover. The erotic description caught my fancy, while Pavan's innuendos left me confused about maternal and romantic love. Can you explain the metaphors of consummation and infatuation to me?'

Vani's eyes seemed to lust for a lover as she spoke, 'Kamakshi's love for Sibu is nothing but innocent puppy love, an infatuation, which is never reciprocated. She tried way too hard and if not for one mistake, she would have succeeded in her plans. Pavan's love achieves consummation as the desire she has for Pashupati is more ethereal.'

Darpan questioned, 'Does it mean that puppy love or infatuation can never lead to a state of union and bliss with one's beloved?'

Deeksha answered, 'Not necessarily. But an infatuation must be given time to develop into something more soulful.'

Darshan filled in the gaps, 'I must say, love is no child's play.'

Vani changed into a camise that made the others go va-va-voom. She began dancing the Bolero and sang the Flamenco.

Como si amo, el paso
La palabras de miguel.
I love the way he dances the tango,
The salsa, the bachata and the flamenco.

Love me tender,
Love me sweet,
Never let me go.

For you my darling,
I would cross the rivers,
The mountains and the countries.

It's you in my heart,
In my eyes,
In my soul.

We shall meet,
In the chaparrals,
In the oasis,
And by the bay.

As you hold sway,
Over my body,
With your kisses,
And take me, with one stroke,
To the heights I have never seen,
And I explode to pieces.

The dice showed passion and placidity.

Pashupati and Jal

Deeksha's prose turned towards passion.

Prakriti was having the time of her life.
She had Swapna and Leela
At her beck and call,
But she choose to manifest Karma,
That majestic being,
Who governs the lifecycle of
Work and hardships,
As she now wanted Pashupati
To earn his daily wage.
She also wished for Jal to descend
From her mighty throne of a fancy life,
And experience the laborious
Common existence.
She devised a plan where both
Pashupati and Jal
Would have to work together
To earn their daily bread.

As Karma descended from the firmament,
Pashupati began experiencing a strange vibe.
He began to feel restless and anxious.
The life that he had led
Until then, seemed false,
And he felt that he must toil
Under the sweltering heat of the stars.

At the same time, Jal began
To feel the need to nourish
Someone close to her heart.
Simply flowing across Dhara,

And falling from the skies as rain,
Was not enough to keep her soul satiated.
She wandered across the firmament
Looking for a hard working person to nourish.

Pashupati had made up his mind
To till the land.
With brute strength, he felled trees,
And made for himself a plough,
Which he fastened to a pair of oxen.
He then started tilling the land,
Shouting "Yaah, Yaah" at the oxen
To keep them in tow.

As Pashupati's muscular body,
Gleaming with sweat,
Greeted Jal's eyes, she felt strange emotions
Surging through her body,
Something she had never felt before.
This is the man I must serve,
She thought to herself.
She started flowing in a sweet little
Stream of water.

As soon as the stream reached Pashupati,
He felt a cool breeze waft over him,
And all of his tiredness dissolved
Away in a jiffy.
He managed to till the land,
And with the stream of water at hand,
Began setting up an irrigation system,
To prepare the field for the sowing of seeds.
Soon, the field was soaked wet,
A sight to be seen.

As soon as he had finished irrigating the field,
Jal materialized in front of him.
He was amazed at her beautiful form,
And quickly put two and two together,
As she carried a pitcher brimming with water.
'You must be Jal, a magical element of Prakriti,' he said.

Jal laughed and sprinkled some
Water on him playfully,
Soaking him, while at the same time,
Getting some water on herself too.
As the sight of a water
Drenched feminine form,
Began to dance in front of Pashupati's eyes,
He began to lust after Jal.

Her rotund hips, slender waist,
Nubile body, lithe arms,
Long strands of wet hair and her wet sari
That clung to her heavy bosom,
Left little to the imagination,
And sweet water dripping off
Of her erotic face,
Maddened him with desire.

He could resist her no more,
And ran towards her
Like an elephant in musth.
He grabbed her hair with one hand,
And her wet, slender waist with the other,
And held her in a tight embrace,
While kissing her all over.
She tried to resist him by pushing him away,

But her refusal seemed to turn his resolve
Stronger yet and he dug his fingernails
Into her back
And pulled her closer to himself.

Pretty soon they were on the ground,
Their legs in struggle with each other,
Almost tied to a knot,
Their bodies crushed against the other,
Their lips searching and hungrily devouring
The sweetness of love's first kisses.

As Pashupati made sweet, erotic,
Lusty love to Jal
All night long,
The stream in the field began
To get infested with tadpoles.
It witnessed the emergence of
The first primordial fish,
The piranha: cannibalistic, flesh eating,
Creatures, that would later be found
In the Amazon.
As the piranhas mated and multiplied,
Scratched and bit at each other,
Other fish including the cod,
Seahorse, cherub-fish,
Sea-bass, blenny, and the jawfish took to life.
When Pashupati and Jal climaxed together,
Pashupati uttered a haunting scream,
Jal surrendered in his strong arms,
Feeling that she had found her
Place in the scheme of things.

Menaka and Sibu

Vani's words expressed the rhymes of placidity.

Menaka sat in her quarters playing with her hair,
Thinking of ways to get Sibu to her lair.
She hatched a scheme, devious
Which involved intervention divine,
She would change form into apsaras
To flirt with him and entwine.

She decided to begin with his dreams,
And thus, one night when Sibu went to sleep,
He saw Menaka as an apsara, Rambha to be precise,
The thought of her was all that surrounded him,
And all that he could keep.

He dreamt of wisps of cotton candy clouds
Up above his head,
And that he rose slowly towards the firmament.
As he wafted through the clouds,
A distant light did shimmer,
And he could see the promise of heaven,
Silver, gold and glitter.

Divine music then started playing in his ears,
The flute, the shehnai, the sitar,
The sarod and the drums,
All harmonised in a melody aged for years.
He seemed to follow the music
And raised his footsteps.

An imaginary ladder seemed to float
Down from the top,
On which, he seemed to be walking,
And thought, he would never drop.

Slowly, the planet Earth's environs
Gave way to the Moon and the stars,
And at a distance, the light
Still beckoned him from afar.

The light now started
Changing to various colors,
Red, blue, magenta, crimson, green and viridian.
He could see a distant terrain
Drawing closer as if chained to the stars,
And suddenly it gave him what seemed
Like a never ending motion.

He stepped down onto the planet,
It was lush green with foliage,
Animals grazed, streams of crystal clear water
Flowed and music played.
He was still being carried,
By some sort of an imaginary force.

In some distance he saw nymphs playing,
Next to a stream and some gurgling dolphins.
He also saw, popping out of the water, pretty mermaids,
And grazing the grass were healthy cattle by the glades.

Suddenly, Indra's mighty white elephant *Airawat*
Appeared out of nowhere,
With his trunk, he lifted him up
And placed him on his back somewhere.
They now began a journey
And everything looked far below,
There was merry making all around,
And quite a number of clowns.

They reached a stream and Airawat
Started following the river,
The stream meandered and raged with its force,

Towards a mighty range of mountains.
Airawat started to walk through the mountain range
With what felt like practiced ease.

Nymphs, butterflies and dragonflies graced their path,
While birds of song chirped merrily
And in the stream, took a bath.
The mountain range curved
And the path was very narrow,
But Airawat took to it, like to air does a sparrow.

Suddenly came a ridge and the clouds
Appeared below, thick with thunder,
Airawat turned around and a plateau
Revealed itself from under.
The plateau had pretty girls playing on a swing,
And they made circles and sang songs
That had a distant ring.

On a throne was seated Lord Indra
Himself in regal attire,
And strewn about the place were ruby,
Corals, topaz and sapphire.
Rambha made her appearance
But it actually was Menaka in disguise,
She took Sibu by the hand, much to his surprise.

She led him to play by the stream,
And drenched him with water, he did scream.
The water was sweet, as he felt it in his mouth,
But it was also cold as if it had come
From the mountains of the north.

Sibu was now ecstatic and in his element,
Took to teasing Rambha without impediment.
Together they played the game of hide and seek,
They seemed at times like children, at times like freaks.

Rambha, later made Sibu sit down on a couch,
And started playing some music
By blowing on a conch.
The music was tremendous, the sound
Of a blowing horn,
And it brought forth birds, animals,
Plants, flowers, particularly a rose from a thorn.
She blew the horn again and this time,
Sibu woke up from his sleep,
'Oh, why did I wake up?
Why could I not continue the dream?'
Such were the thoughts that entered his mind,
And left him writhing on his bed and in a bind.

The next night Sibu wondered,
If he would get to see the Apsaras again,
And Menaka passed by his house,
As he took to sleep without pain.
This time, the sequence was the same,
But it was Anjana he found, sitting in his lap,
She poured wine for him
From a decanter as if it was a tap.

She twirled her hair, teased Sibu,
And tugged at his clothes,
He caressed her, cajoled her,
Sang tunes and took her in his fold.
Together they ran and sprang
Through what seemed like heaven,
And enjoyed the company of the other angelic brethren.

This dream came to an end as well,
And all looked dour for Sibu,
He went to sleep again
And Menaka infiltrated his dreams that night too,
This time taking the form of Malini, the enchantress.

She played the game of hanky-panky with him,
And did the serpentine dance.
He lay with his arms around her,
And found her form so enchanting
That he fell in love with her, at once.

He regaled her with tales, stories and anecdotes,
And she listened to him, like a mother on a child, dotes.
Together they seemed like such a happy couple,
Like doves in flight, so soft and supple.

She fled from him suddenly,
And he ran after helter-skelter,
She found a tree in heaven and beneath it, took shelter.
Suddenly, the clouds started appearing,

And a dense mist dropped about,
He ran, looked around and did shout.
He could not find Malini again,
For she was lost like a needle in a pile of grain.

For one last moment he let out a cry,
And found himself sitting in his bed,
His mouth felt dry.
'Oh, it was just a dream again and now
I must go to bed.
I wonder where in my next fantasy will I be led.'

The fantasies started getting more and more colorful.
This time it was Madura,
And she played the tambura,
At times and at others, the mandolin.

The sound of music when hit Sibu's ears,
He was so enchanted by it,
That he felt a weight of a billion tonnes

Lifted from his years.
He ran towards the music and fell for it.

Next thing he knew he was lying prostrate,
It was as if the Dhatura he had ate,
For he felt like he was listening
To a thousand oceans sounding waves,
Crashing together on distant shores,

And a melody that fulfilled exactly what he craved.
He began dancing to a steady beat,
And a *mridanga* appeared in his arms
And added to the heat.
Together the sounds felt a bit depraved.

They were now in a divine union,
Music and dance together, in a holy fusion.
Madura sang about the sunset,
The moonshine and nature's glory.

And Sibu danced to the beats,
And put practice to theory.
His feet did not miss a single beat,
And his heart felt ripped and gory.

The music culminated with a fountain,
Springing from the earth below,
And a sound like a hollow chamber did bellow,
And water then, from it did emanate.

For now where there was a tree,
A giant chasm first and then a pond lay.
But as soon as Sibu saw the reflection,
Of Madura in the fountain,

All was lost.
For what seemed like frivolity, had come at a cost.

The reflection showed the true face of Madura,
Rambha, Malini and Anjana.
For it now showed the real face of Menaka.

Sibu's dream was broken,
And he woke up with a start.
He now knew that all the five women,
Had fooled him and played with his heart.

Discourse on Desire

Vani was beginning to feel a little shy in Darpan's presence. She carried on, albeit with hesitation, 'Darpan, have you understood the love of Jal, the tender feelings she had for the hard working Pashupati, which were almost magical? Also, did you see the folly of Menaka as she tried to lead Sibu, a simpleton out into the world of apsaras and offered him heavenly delights?'

Darpan surmised, 'I can only guess that Jal, being water, did what she could by staying true to her magical powers, while Menaka used her magic in all the wrong ways. I cannot, however, come to terms with the metaphors of passion and placidity.'

Vani explained with vigour in her voice, 'Jal is all passion for Pashupati, a hard working man. She gives up her heavenly ways and comes down to the level of lowly creatures as she brings water to a parched terrain. Their passion is evident in their lovemaking as well. Menaka on the other hand, is placid like the calm waters of Kailash 's Mansarovar. She only changes form, and not her ways. She is decadent, a hedonist who is seeking pleasure, not love. Hence, she fails in her attempt to attain the affections of her lover.'

He concluded, 'So I guess, if we are to acquire the favours of our beloved, we must not sit complacently, but be proactive.'

Deeksha affirmed, 'Exactly. If love is not fire, it is rust, and what is rust, soon turns to dust.'

Darshan summarized, 'As a bard once said, since love cannot accept vanity, passion must be sustained by pain. The hearts of lovers must beat as one, like the words that flow out of a poets' pen. If what I say is wrong, then I did not love and the others may as well have failed.'

Vani threw caution to the wind, broke out of her shy demeanour and beckoned Darpan. She then put on her dancing shoes and turned on the music el Tango de Roxanne.

Roxanne, you do not have to go out tonight,
For you must not sell yourself and your plight.
I will lead you on to the dance floor,
And the angels will take to flight.

The stage is set on fire,
And the sepulchre is a dance room tonight,
Where the satyrs and the fauns prance and preen
To the glory of hundreds of violins, my Josephine.

I shall be Miguel de Cervantes
And you shall be Estrella, burning bright,
As you turn me on,
And lead me to your pale hallows,
And your dainty plight.

We shall sing and drink Bacchus' wine,
And dance to the hymns of Persephone,
As the lyre emits notes of harmony
That break the silence of the skies.

I shall be a troubadour,
A bull fighter,
A savage warrior,
A beastly buccaneer,
To rescue you from all scares and frights.

You cling on to me,
Your body's alluring fragrance pervades all,
And brings closer, things divine.
As we dance away to the stars,
And the heavens ring in yuletide.

The dice showed sensual and platonic.

Pashupati and Dhara

Deeksha spoke of the sensual.

Prakriti got more diabolical with time,
She now wished to impart knowledge to trounce egos.
She manifested Shiksha, the goddess of Knowledge,
And sowed the seeds of the desire for truth,
In the heart of Pashupati.

Not only did she stir the cauldron of Pashupati's mind,
With Shiksha, but also prepared
The ground for Dhara's love.
For in Shiksha, lay the magic of illusion,
Of phantasmagorical creatures
Residing in the underbelly of the terrain.

Dhara was playing in the garden of Eden,
When thoughts of creatures,
Descending from the firmament,
Began to take fancy in her mind.
She also dreamt of Pashupati cavorting with her,
Along with the mystical creatures of the earth.

She could not bear her loneliness anymore,
And decided to look for Pashupati.
She found him resting near his fields,
Waiting for his crop to ripen.

She decided to take the form of a meadow,
Covered in velveteen kusha grass
And bounteous blooming begonias.
Pashupati's sight fell on the magical mystical meadow,
And he rushed towards it, like a child

Leaping towards his mother.

He fell flat on the kusha grass, which was part doob,
And it felt like satin, silk and muslin underneath him.
He took in a whiff of the begonias
And instantly fell in love with them.
He plucked them from the meadow,
And made a laurel wreath,
Which he adorned himself with on his head,
Proclaiming himself the emperor of Dhara.

As soon as he had done that, Dhara appeared,
Bowing gracefully before him, she said, 'O Swami,
I have been waiting for a being like you,
Strong, intelligent, wise, adept in the arts,
Fierce, skilful and a lover,
To grace my meadow,
To take me as a lover,
And to bring to life, this land.'

Pashupati was astonished at Dhara's charms,
But soon her alluring presence,
The fragrance emanating from her,
The aura around her person,
Her voice, like a birdsong,
And her eyes which danced in perfect harmony,
Had the overall effect,
Of making him feel a searing desire for her.

He wanted to possess her,
To feel her body,
And to run his fingers through her hair,
Which were like the first harvest of wheat,
A burst of golden tresses.

He wanted to kiss her peach lips,
That spoke of nature's delights,
To feel her nectarine breath,
On his face,
And to drown in her silken embrace.
He wanted to cuddle her,
Hold her close as he slept next to her.

He wasted no time,
And grabbed her by the waist,
And pulling her close,
Implanted a passionate kiss.
Beginning at first with a tender peck,
He then slowly opening her lips wide,
With his own, as their tongues found each other,
And he made her arch her head back,
While he held her golden hair
Strongly with his arms, pulling her even closer,
Dissolving in a kiss
That seemed to last forever.

When they finally emerged from the lip-lock,
Dhara had love in her eyes,
At the same time, a certain shyness,
For now she was Pashupati's lover.

On the meadow, now, emerged creatures of all kinds:
Fauns, satyrs, dwarfs, elves, midgets,
Fairies and nymphs.
The nymphs began to make music,
The fauns and satyrs took to dancing,
The dwarfs and elves created ruckus,
While the fairies made love with the nymphs.

Soon, animals of all kinds began to come to life
In the meadow.
Sabre toothed cats, wooly mammoths,
Giant ground sloths,
Mega fauna,
Behemoths,
Dinosaurs, like the Tyrannosaurus and
Velociraptors.

As Dhara and Pashupati looked over the fauna,
Dhara spoke to Pashupati,
'These are our children dear,
They will be here for a long time to come,'
And she kissed him softly on his lips.

Ritambhara and Sibu

Vani sang about the platonic.

Ritambhara lay sulking in her privacy,
When the thought of Sibu rose from dormancy.
It was an idea to have him in her arms, but in infancy.
She let her mind wander and thoughts took to fancy.

She came up with a plan, which involved deception,
She would fake herself as an artist,
To gain his trust,
And then talk to him about his craft, his devotion.

She gazed into the crystal ball,
And saw the future clear.
She was an artist, he was under her spell,
And the coast of his heart was clear.

She could not contain her joy and happiness,
For now, she knew she could have him all to herself.
She wondered if she will have to learn all the dances,
But then she figured she could take the help
Of illusion, why take chances.

She uttered some chants at the crystal ball,
And suddenly a puff of smoke raised around her as a pall.
Out she came, dressed in an artist's overalls.
She was now ready to make Sibu fall.

She started to her feet and ran towards his cottage,
To appear at his door,
Wearing a hat covered in plumage.
She knocked on the door and waited for him to come,
And heard his voice answering a welcome.

She stepped inside, introduced herself as an artist,
And said that she wished to collaborate
With him in dance and fantasy.
She said, 'I know the various dance forms,
Classical, modern, contemporary and fusion.

Now let's get to work, without anymore confusion',
Sibu was surprised, for this was an unexpected arrival.
He did not expect a visitor,
At that time of the day, to call.
Yet he introduced himself and seeing an artist,
Folded his hands in salutation.

Together they left for his dance studio, Sibu leading,
Began to think of some dance drama,
Their minds on a hunt.
Ritambhara suggested that they do the Rasaleela,
That she would play Radha, and Sibu, Krishna.

It was a clever move on her part,
For it gave her a chance to flirt.
And while Sibu was thinking of the dance,
She could, at his heart, take a chance.

They started practicing the basic mudras,
And to Sibu's surprise, Ritambhara
Could not get the moves right.
She apologized and made some silly excuses,
For she now recalled that she had forgotten to practice.

She made a hasty retreat,
And bade goodbye to leave.
She promised that she would be back for her part,
To start from where they had left off.

Sibu was amused, to say the least,
And wondered how an artist

Could not recall such a visual feast.
He left for his quarters thinking about the day's events,
And wondered what they would do the next time
To make amends.

The next day Ritambhara gazed into the crystal ball
And chanted incantations,
To make her remember the moves for the day,
She made preparations.
She learnt all she could about Radha and Krishna,
And as a contingency, practiced the battle
Between Krishna and Putana.

She arrived again at Sibu's place
And they left for his workplace,
On arriving there, began practicing the same piece.
Ritambhara had brought a flute
And she played a sweet melody,
She asked Sibu to dance to it,
Fearing her plans could be in jeopardy.

She played the Raga Panghat,
In which Radha carries a pitcher from the lake,
And on the pretext of dancing with Sibu,
Sprinkled water all over his face.

She also got some water over his tunic and his coat,
It felt like they had just stepped out of a boat.
She managed to get herself wet,
And started playing with him in a manner naughty.

Changing her mind suddenly,
She started acting haughty.
All her shenanigans got Sibu enthralled,
Enraptured and crazy,
For she looked seductive, when wet and lazy,
Sibu lost all sense of time and his mind felt dizzy.

He started touching her in places unspeakable,
And to provoke him more, she threw caution to the wind.
She did not restrain him, in fact, drew him even closer,
And to think that all of this had just started
With an innocent game of water.

She then played Raga Balakrishna,
And asked Sibu to pelt stones at her pitcher.
Which she had filled with cream,
And it spilled all over her.

She ordered him then to lick the cream off of her lips,
And Sibu, now completely in her control,
Let go of his self and locked her lips with his.
He licked and kissed and smooched and trolled.

Oh, what a scene it made!
If only, in simple words it could be told.
Cream all over their bodies,
Their limbs did entangle,

His arms slipped around hers and removed her bangles.
She slithered and swept and curled in his arms.
And he welcomed every move of her, with all his charms.
They lay together, a couple in eternal bliss.

Sibu tried to grope her and feel her inside her clothes,
But she shied away saying,
'We will meet in a few days.'
And took her leave.

Sibu was all worked up and in heat,
For she had captured his mind and his heart beat.
For the rest of the day, he could only think of her,
Her sight, her voice, her smell and her demeanour.

Ritambhara rushed again to the crystal ball,
For she had to learn the moves,
But what she saw in the crystals,
Took away her mind's peace, once and for all.

She saw the future and it was not a pretty sight,
For it did not show her in good light.
It showed that she had approached him again
With some dance moves,
But this time Sibu was a bit apprehensive.

For he had been thinking and his mind was pensive,
'How could an artist enter his heart
And make him fall in love,
Was there some hidden motive?
If there was, he had to find it, by Jove.'

When Ritambhara suggested that they practice
Sita Harana, he agreed.
They played the part well,
With Ritambhara as Sita and Sibu as Ravana,
It looked swell.

He was cautious not to let his guard down,
But she kept on with her flirtations,
Running her fingers under his gown.
Since he did not reciprocate her intentions,

It was clear to her,
That he had summoned her,
This time around. He was clever,
Even though she had come over.

When the *Sita Harana* episode got over,
He suggested they play Meera's Bhajans,
And expecting her to know the part,
Let her take lead from the start.

Ritambhara was now caught in a trap,
For she did not know much about Mira,
Or her bhajans or her divinations.
How could she have danced without Sibu's probations?

She tried to play the flute,
But Sibu objected, saying that Meera played the Ektara.
She feigned knowledge and said, 'I know that too,
But hey, Que Sera Sera.'

Sibu had now caught her off guard,
And asked her to sing a *bhaktee geet*,
She tried singing some melody, however,
It was only an old tune that she did repeat.

Sibu was now convinced,
That she was an impostor,
And told her to abscond,
Or else, he would thrash her.

Ritambhara saw all of this in the crystal ball,
And considered it best, to not go to Sibu at all,
So end's this story, and Ritambhara's gall,
She could not bear the pain of her heart's call.

Discourse on Attraction

Vani, by now, had started feeling a certain attraction towards Darpan. In order for him to not hear her thoughts, she spoke louder than usual, 'Darpan, did you like the lyrical and poetic description of Dhara, her folds holding flowers in full bloom? Did you like Ritambhara's artistic ploys that rendered an illusionary world around Sibu?'

Darpan, now aware of Vani's attraction towards himself, shyly confessed, 'The description of the meadows made me lie down on the field and reminded me of the time I was in the south of France amidst the fields of lavender in Provence. I can almost smell the sensual fragrance from the blooms invading my nostrils, making me want to hold someone I love and drown in their loving touches and kisses. I feel sorry for Ritambhara as she could not get Sibu's affection, despite making so many artistic displays. I know I am always testing your patience, but can you explain the metaphors of the sensual and the platonic.'

Vani, now very conscious of Darpan's presence, could barely suppress her feelings and somehow managed a response, 'Dhara's presence in Pashupati's life is erotic as she brings to him a meadow in full blossom, like a life of love stirred by the passions of youth. Ritambhara, on the other hand, takes the path of the artist and Sibu considers it a platonic relationship. Hence, he does not reciprocate her advances.'

Darpan sighed, 'Well, to be frank, I have always been a sucker for platonic romances.'

Deeksha warned, 'But remember, platonic yearnings must be forged with the sensual, otherwise one is left with the feeling of not having felt the full force of the feelings of love.'

Darshan summarized, 'I guess, one must sprinkle liberal doses of lust with love then.'

Vaani, now feeling hot under her skin, began an impromptu sensual poem by herself. To her surprise, it was Darpan who joined in first, as if he could sense her feelings for him.

Where do I begin, where do I start,
How did you make your way into my heart?
It was first a sigh, a hello, a wave of your hand,
And then the thoughts of you pervaded my mind.

I could not shake off the ghosts of you,
That seemed to come to me in my loneliness,
As I went about my daily chores,
Unaware of the growing tenderness for you.

You broke your silence,
And I broke my vows of loneliness,
Time played the devil,
And love was the song.

Soon we were writhing on the floor,
Naked, unabashed, unkempt and unashamed,
As you clawed, I screamed with pleasure,
And the night was filled with sighs and moans.

The next morning was paradise,
As you woke up in my arms,
With stars in your eyes,
And love in your heart.

The dice showed erotic and cool.

Pashupati and Jyoti

Deeksha went wayward with the erotic.

Prakriti couldn't be happier.
The powers of the five sisters were fading,
As they were spent in creating life,
While Pashupati wasted his energies on love.
She basked in the afterglow of her victories,
Of having trounced and trampled
Upon the egos,
Of the daughters of Maya and Pashupati.
Now, she planned to draw
The last nail into the coffin.

Out of her delirium and depravity,
She manifested Mahaparinirvana,
The afterlife and the distillate of
Spirits and ghouls.
Soon after, from the constituents of Mahaparinirvana,
She manifested her daughters,
Moksha and Nirvana.
Moksha was the ultimate release
From all delusions,
While Nirvana was the liberation
Of *atma* (the soul).

She then manifested *atma*, the soul,
And prodded Pashupati and
Jyoti's conscience,
Towards the creation of a being
That would have *atma*.

As if on cue, Jyoti woke up from her slumber,

And felt a raging fire in her belly.
She felt the first kick of life,
As if an egg had been
Materialized in her womb.

She was on fire,
And felt as if she had consumed embers.
Her body craved consummation with another.
She drank a consommé made of
Water and the seed,
Which soon put her to sleep.
She dreamt of Pashupati on a mighty stallion,
Carrying a sword and trouncing an army.
He wore a headdress
Which looked like a turban,
A *sherwani*, *churidar paijama*, and *mojris*.
Behind him was a procession,
With some men playing the *shehnai*,
While others who beat
The *dhol* and the *nagara*.
The women whirled,
Danced and jumped with joy,
While the children stole sweats
From the presents that had been loaded
On top of bullock carts.

Suddenly, she woke to a knock at her door.
To her surprise, it was Pashupati.
He was sweating and panting,
As if he had been running hard.
He broke down in tears,
Fell in Jyoti's arms,
And started to explain himself.

He said, 'I don't know
What has come over me.
I have not been able to eat, drink or sleep.
I have lost my peace of mind.
I have nightmares of life ending,
Of creatures running amok,
And of stars and the heavens falling apart.

Dreams of you are the only saving grace.
I dream that we are together,
And that we have a child,
In out midst, playing in the garden of Eden.'

Jyoti took him by his hand and led him inside,
And made him sit on her bed.
She then brought some oil
Made of betel nut leaves,
Nilgiri bark and the Cinchona bark,
And began to massage Pashupati's head.
She started with his eye lids,
Making sure that they were closed.
She kneaded his eyelids gently,
Making a circular motion with her thumbs.
Then she moved out to his temples,
Using her thumbs again,
She went clockwise,
And counter clockwise, in turns.
At the same time,
Using all of her fingers,
She massaged alternatively,
His scalp and his forehead.

Pashupati was now moaning with delight.
Suddenly, he grasped Jyoti by her hair,

And bending her head towards his,
He implanted a deep lingering kiss,
On her wet burning lips.

The kiss began as a
Soul searching experiment,
And their lips and hands fought for each other.
At first, Jyoti only brushed her lips
Against his in return,
But on feeling the strength of his arms
Around her,
She began to melt under his touch.

She parted her lower lip a bit,
And Pashupati was quick
To explore the opportunity.
He began suckling at her lip,
As if he were an eager bumblebee,
Thirsty for the first dew drops of honeysuckle,
From the tangy tumescent tulip lips of a Tilia.

Jyoti's hands began to remove his turban,
While Pashupati's fingers got busy,
Unfastening the hooks of her kurti.
Jyoti was now like a wildcat chasing a prey,
As she began ripping his tunic off,
And soon the *paijama* came off as well.
Pashupati, surprised at first,
At Jyoti's forwardness,
Began to peel the kurti off of her silken body,
Which was burning with an intense desire.
By the time he got to removing her pants,
It felt like the fabric itself would catch fire.

They lay naked, breathing heavily,
Hot under their skins,
With only one thought on their minds,
To possess the other completely.
Pashupati began kissing Jyoti all over,
As if following a heat trail,
Starting from her hot forehead,
Where he gave her butterfly kisses,
Over her eyelashes,
Which shut under his tender touches.

He then kissed the nape of her neck,
And took her earlobes between his lips,
Teasing them, tantalizing
And tasting the sweat,
That had begun to envelop her burning body.
Suddenly, he gave her a big surprise kiss,
Covering her entire mouth with his,
Parting her lips,
Exploring with his tongue,
Which darted in and out,
Finding her tongue and tasting her sweetness.

Their bodies were now on fire,
And Jyoti had begun writhing,
Squirming and moaning
Like a serpent which comes out
In the rainy season.

Suddenly, she took control
And turned him over,
To sit on top of his nakedness.
She began marking his skin with love bites,
And left hickeys all over his aching body.

As he shivered and trembled,
She held him close
And guided him into herself.

He let out a scream as he felt
Her softness and heat.
She began grinding on top of him,
In a movement that was alternatively,
Circular, soft, hard, long, short,
Filled with pauses,

Warm, cold, hot, sweaty, fragrant and musical.
As she began churning over him,
The animals began to rut,
Clouds began to form,
Bolts of lightening fell from the sky,
Birds began to get amorous,
And flowers began to bloom in the gardens.

Pashupati was now in ecstasy
And kept screaming
Jyoti's name in sheer delight.
He let his hands wander
All over her sweaty body,
Resting at her hips, squeezing them, Kneading them
Gently at first and then grasping them firmly.
He then proceeded to trace
A line down her spine,
While the other hand tickled her navel,
Her belly and her love handles.
When his hands touched the areola,
Surrounding her nipples,
She let out a yelp,
Partly in pain, partly in joy,

For she felt a tingle coarse down her spine,
Ending at her sweet spot.

He then proceeded to kneed her breasts
With his fingers,
At the same time, tweaking,
Tweezing, plucking and massaging,
Her tender and swollen, blood red nipples.

He then rose up from the bed,
And took a nipple in his mouth,
Holding the peak tantalisingly,
Deliciously, softly
Yet firmly between his lips,
While his tongue flickered over them.
At times, he would bite the nipples
With his teeth,
And she would try to drown her scream
By holding her hands over her mouth.

He then turned her over,
And took over the lovemaking,
Entering her with powerful thrusts at first,
And then with tender caressing strokes,
Which made her desire him more and more.
She felt like she was riding a lightening storm,
Only it was an outpour of emotions,
Joy, relief and a tumult of sheer elation.
At times he would leave her to make her crave his touch,
And then enter her with surprise,
Which made her curse his name,
'Pashupati, my darling, my love,
Don't make me wait for you like this.'

Their lovemaking had now reached its peak
As their bodies were now tumbling,
Thrown about like tidal waves.
Like a symphony reaching its crescendo,
Like festivities reaching a climax,
Like an army celebrating an orgiastic victory,
They rocked together
Like peas in a pod.
To and fro they went,
Twisting, turning, screaming,
Moaning, sweating, wanting,
Desiring, needing, panting,
Biting, carousing, pecking,
Needling, tickling, growling,
Scratching with nails, grabbing,
Holding, embracing,
And most of all loving,
As if they were never meant to separate
From each other.

And then suddenly, as clouds burst,
Lightening struck,
Plants sprouted in wild abundance,
Animals barked and roared in ferocity,
Waves crashes on ocean shores,
Birds took to sudden flapping and flippingFflights of fancy,
Bees started buzzing about
Like maddened drones,
The winds started brewing a storm,
Ether began to vibrate with a fierce force,
And all of firmament began to shake,
With the magnitude of a trillion quakes,
As they collapsed on top of each other.
Jyoti let out a loud scream,

Calling Pashupati's name in her delirium,
Wanting only one thing,
To rest forever in his strong arms,
And to bask in the afterglow
Of her newfound love.

Urvashi and Sibu

Vani succumbed in her dreams to things cool.

Urvashi was another one of Sibu's victim of desire.
Where there is smoke,
There is fire,
But this was no joke,

For Urvashi pined for him.
For the first time in her life,
She had felt like she was the game,
And he, the hunter; all was strife.

She could think of nothing,
With which she could win her heart's desire.
She did not posses the magical skills of her sisters,
And was only adept in war's affairs.

She thought of a some games,
More like war games, to be precise,
With which she could entice,
Him, if only she could break the ice.

She then hammered her plan into shape,
To grab the bull by its neck and nape.
She planned to go ask Sibu to play some war games,
So that he could learn more of his dance dramas.

And in doing so,
She could flirt,
Win his heart with gusto,
And make gold from dust.

She found Sibu at his workplace,
And knocked at the door twice.

Sibu wondered who it might be,
Oh, how could he surmise?

He welcomed Urvashi inside,
And she told him about her plan.
To Sibu, it sounded like a clash of clans,
But, he promised to give it a try.

Together they started playing war games,
Where each side had to play
He part of infantry soldiers,
Generals, artillery staff, archers,
And the whole naval brigade.

It also involved a fair amount of role play,
For at times it called for a ray,
Of light to shine on a character that had been dark,
By adding dialogues, raw and stark.

Sibu and Urvashi discussed maneuvers,
Stratagems, and battle-plans.
While sometimes, they immersed themselves,
In a list of items that their soldiers might want.

But Urvashi's plan was only now truly unfolding,
Because her games were an excuse for hand holding,
And hugging and cuddling,
And other activities that were naughty,

Crept to her mind,
For often she would discuss an archer's bow,
And entwine her body with his,
As he took out an arrow.

She would then suddenly discuss a martial sequence,
And hold him close to her body,
As she kept changing her stance,

And pretty soon things got bawdy.

Sibu now reeled under the heat,
For instead of a battle on the charts,
There was a battle in his heart;
Whether to think of Urvashi as an artist,
Or as a lover who owned him from the start.

He decided to fall for the latter,
And gave his heart, for it had started to chatter.
There was music in raindrops, pitter patter,
As they were now engrossed in each other.
He decided to make things more hot,
And said, 'why don't we try the fox trot?
It's a dance which follows the beat of the army drums.
If you hold the drum in your arms, we can be chums.'

He let go of all inhibitions,
And wrapped his arms around Urvashi,
For there was no prohibition,
And things between them got mushy.

They then marched hand in hand,
To the beat of the drums, in a vast land,
Onward, with much delight and ease,
As if the Gods, they intended to please.

The Foxtrot soon gave way to the Salsa,
The syncopated music came out
Of drums made of balsa.
He showed her the shines and the shimmies,
And together they undid a few naughty thingies.

Pretty soon, they were fighting
To get out of their clothes,
And their hands were all over each other,
As it they had had a liquor overdose.

They fell out of line and such was the clammer,

That the beat kept rising, nor did they stammer.
They did not let go of each other,
For they were now writhing on the floor,
What a sight it made, oh brother!

She said, 'Let's turn this into a cat fight',
He said, 'I will do as you wish, if you feel right.'
He let her claw and smash
And drive her arms into his face,
They were making love curry like nutmeg and mace.

Now the music was reaching a crescendo,
And Urvashi used all kinds of innuendos,
She let her hands slip inside his pants,
Sibu felt like a flying cormorant.

He felt a tingling rush,
All over his naked body,
The dance sequence,
Had now changed into a prosody.

They were at each other,
Each trying to get the better of the other.
Legs fought and entwined,
Arms wrestled and entangled.

Urvashi's hair looked dishevelled,
And her demeanour had him beguiled.
For while fighting,
She looked but like a child.

She ranted and raved and cursed and spat,
And together they looked like wrestlers on a mat.
They laughed at each other,
Struggling to get on top of the other.

She smothered him with kisses,
And he responded with fervent sighs.
Oh, there is nothing like a couple that fights,
And then gets on with their way,

Like a small boat floating out of wild seas in a fray.
Urvashi's hair now had a tousled, thrown back look,
She looked like a femme fatale out of a noir book.
She then proceeded to sit on him,
As when a hen does lay,

And made him apologise to her,
For she felt that he had belittled her.
She scolded him,
And told him to set things right.

For now, she was on top,
And suddenly, made a pop.
It sounded like a cork
Had been pulled out of a bottle of champagne,
And Sibu let go of a yelp, as he cried in pain.

She had landed with a flop on top of him,
And he felt like a glass of rum, full to the brim.
He said, 'Let go of me, you vile, vicious vixen,
Had you come to play games, or to play a wild kitten?

You have me in a bind,
And now it seems like you had this planned.
For no matter how I try,
I cannot seem to attain victory.

You have danced your way into my heart,
As if you had thought this out from the start.
You must leave now and leave me alone,
As for this practice, we must postpone.

Until I have thought this through, over and over.
It looks like there is more to you,
Than I have discovered.
You are not someone that can be trusted,
And my turned-on mind needs to be dusted.'

Urvashi grabbed her clothes and was miffed,
She felt like she had just been stiffed.
She left Sibu's place with a heart full of sorrow,
But she thought, there will always
Be another tomorrow.

Discourse on Eros

Vani, was close to revealing to Darpan what lay in her heart, but was able to hold on to her feelings. Instead she managed a few loosely held words out of her confused mind, 'I feel shy discussing the lovemaking with you, Darpan. But I guess it had to happen, given the fact that Pashupati was the king of beasts and Jyoti was fire herself. It had to be with someone, and Jyoti was the fire that consumed Pashupati. Urvashi, on the other hand, tried to play the cool cat and pin Sibu to the ground, a strategy which backfired.'

Darpan hesitated, 'It was a bit too much to take in one passage and I feel like I am on fire myself. I had always expected it to be Ritu. It came to me as a bit of a surprise that it happened with Jyoti. But, you are right, it had to be with someone and given Jyoti's fiery warrior's temperament, there was no holding back. Urvashi tried to do much with her war games but her plans just fell apart.'

Deeksha added, 'Not only did her plans fall apart, it also shows how a warrior must not always play it cool; instead, a fiery approach to life, a certain hot headedness might often be the order of the day.'

Darshan summarized, 'It reminds me of Keats as he had told the knight at arms, pale and loitering, that the sedge had withered from the lake and no birds sang. To quote Shakespeare, '*All is fair in love and war*'. However, sometimes it takes a warrior to consummate her love with her beloved. Then, it is not about strategy, but fiery emotion, passion and liberation from all ties that the society holds the mere mortals in.'

Vani broke into an impromptu musical rendition of a poem.

I am burning in fire, like embers in a hearth,
And you play it cool, like flowers in the earth.
I am all passion, emotion, lust and depravity,
While you are reason, rationale, and passivity.

How can you be so naive,
So unknowing of my desires,
And leave me wanting, needing, craving your touch.
I want to run into you, become one with you,
Like a river rushes to a sea, wild and carefree.

I feel the pain of a thousand prickly thorns,
And the softness of a million rose petals.
For your love is like the moon,
Bright sometimes and hid behind clouds,
At others.

If only I knew the secrets of your heart,
And the thoughts that occupied your mind,
I would make you mine, all of you,
And keep you with me, till eternity.

I would build a house in the hills,
And have a secret garden in the backyard,
Where only our love would blossom,
And tenderness would grow in our hearts,
As our eyes melt into each other's
And we look at lands far away.

The dice showed infantile and mature.

Ishika and Ishu

Deeksha went on with description of the infantile.

Prakriti was in seventh heaven.
She had managed to turn the attention
Of Pashupati and Maya's daughters
From their destiny towards love's frivolities.

She now awaited the birth of the first children
Of Pashupati and Jyoti.
She expected Pashupati
To be forever tied in family,
And Jyoti, engaged in raising children.
Knowing what that involved,
She knew that they would soon learn the folly of their egos.

In time, Jyoti gave birth to twins,
A daughter, Ishika,
And a son, Ishu.
Their names were derived from *Ishwar*,
Or God,
For they were truly the images of God.

Ishika had a lovely temperament.
She was kind, docile, gentle, sweet,
Of good nature and humour, and most of all,
A loveable child, who took delight
In life's simple joys.

Ishu was like her in appearance,
Slightly feminine, yet his boyish charms,
Added to his mysterious ways.
One moment, he would be found

Playing in the garden,
An innocent boy chasing butterflies,
While seconds later, you could find him
Singing songs to himself,
Completely oblivious of his surroundings.

From Ishika would descend the first women
On Earth,
While from Ishu, would come the first men.

As Ishika grew up,
She became skilled in the arts, history,
Science, astrology, philosophy,
Music and dance.
She was the apple of the five sisters' eyes
And they never let her
Out of their sight.

Ishu became a man,
Skilled in poetry, literature,
Warfare, drama, agriculture
And the various arts.
He was so handsome,
That the stars themselves
Shone brightly over him
So that the lesser beings could
Get an eyeful of him.

As time passed, the day of
The creation of mankind dawned,
And *Paramatma*, the supreme conscience,
Became the soulmate of both Ishika and Ishu.

From Ishika descended

The first line of women,
While Ishu became the forefather of all men.

The first women looked up to their mother,
And took after her in beauty and knowledge,
Seeking out the best in men, animals, birds, And the flora.

The first men honored their father's will,
And went wherever they were asked to go,
Bringing back bountiful presents for their Women folk,
Their fields and their livestock.

As men and women began
To form marital alliances,
The first children were born.

Divine Lovemaking and Jealousy

Vani chose a poem on maturity.

Madhumati woke up from her sleep,
And in her dreams she had dreamt of Sibu,
She was dancing and singing
And making love to him too,
She could not get much rest, could not keep,

Patience by her side,
For she longed to be,
In this life, Sibu's bride.
When the anguish of separation from him got,

More than she could take,
She took to running towards him,
For her love for him was not fake.
She wanted to feel his body next to her, on a whim,

To caress his hair with her hands,
And to lie with him on the river shore's sands.
She found Sibu practicing at the auditorium,
And ran into his arms in her delirium.

She confessed her love for him,
And he spoke the same,
For he remembered the night of love making,
And the dance they played as a game.

He suggested they practice again,
She could sing and play music,
And he would dance,
In environs, rustic.

Madhumati left and brought,

A plethora of instruments,
The Veena, the sitar, the flute, the shehnai,
The harmonium, the banjo and the drums.

She started playing a beat,
That was, in style, latino.

For she felt like dancing to a mojito,
She brought out her clappers and did a flamenco.

She made a whirl,
And did a twirl,
All hell was let loose,
As she put on her dancing shoes.

After playing the beats,
She took to playing the lead,
And held of Sibu's hands,
To start dancing the salsa,
As well as lead the band.

The salsa as a dance form,
Had yet not found its origin,
But Madhumati found salsa to be norm,
And tango, like the tangerine.

She also invented, in a jiffy, the waltz,
For she had listened to the classical music,
That Sibu had performed in the play,
'The Fakir's Chrysanthemum'.

She took to the dance floor,
And swung Sibu around,
For what seemed like forever,
And arrested his fall from the ground.

In a move which made her look clever,

She took out a clover,
From her wallet,
And ground it with a mallet.

And put the clover,
In Sibu's mouth with her own,
Seeming like a rose in the bower,
While he looked like a loaf of bread out of the oven.

Madhumati told Sibu, 'Let's invent
A lot of dance forms',
And hence she took to dancing
What looked like the Lindy Hop,
The Bacchatta, the Jive and Hip Hop.
She also danced the Mambo,

And made it look like a fish gumbo,
For she was moving like piscine,
In a form that looked pristine.
She then made some movements
Which looked like the Rhumba,

And soon took to dancing the Samba.
Samba gave way to Disco,
For it seemed like fireflies had invaded
The hall, which was lit, as if with moonshine.

With all these dances,
Sibu felt like he was on a roller coaster,
He jumped and waltzed and hip-hopped,
And jived and tangoed.

He would, every now and then,
Clasp Madhumati's thighs,
Or let go of her like a mother hen,
And then suddenly look her deeply in the eyes.

Madhumati suddenly let go,
And started playing the Veena,
She played a devotional Bhakti Geeta,
And they started swaying,

To bhajans of Radha and Krishna,
And to songs of Meera and her love.
At times, Sibu took to flight,
As if he was a sprightly dove.

Sibu had love in his eyes,
And what lay in Madhumati's heart,
Only a poet can surmise.
For her heart beat fast and furious,

And synchronised to the beats of Sibu's feet.
When he let her swing,
His eyes did cheat,
A glance, a look, or a mere motion.

Oh, through dance, there had been a promotion,
Sibu had escalated to the form of Krishna,
And Madhumati to Radha,
For all to witness the Rasleela.

At times, Madhumati played the sarod,
And made her song *sufi* with some notes.
Sibu took to whirling like a dervish,
And acquired the persona of a saint that was churlish.

At times, Madhumati played beats
That sounded Africano,
And mimed the voice of the jungle,
The lion and the monkeys from Dominicano.
And Sibu let himself mingle,

With Madhumati's person,

For her eyes,
Were Sibu's very own prison.
With her eyes,

She danced, a million dances,
That looked like romances,
And the furtive glances that she gave,
Made him look like a knave.

Sibu, at times, looked like,
He would dance to the grave.
Or finish at the end of a pike,
If he could, himself from Madhumati, save,

Some grace, for sometimes,
He looked like a fool,
Who had fallen for her charms,
As if fallen from a stool.

He got some gall,
And gave Madhumati a kiss,
Which caused Madhumati to acquire a shy pall,
And she longed to break from his embrace.

Together they danced again,
And this time he held her close to him,
And let his hands wander,
From the small of her back,

To her bosom, her neck,
And her wide swaying hips.
He gave, at times,
Butterfly kisses with his eyes,

And then, looking at her like a jealous swain,
Who would not refrain,
From taking what he pleased,

He did not heed,

To the fact that amidst the tender kissing,
Madhumati had started crying.
Sibu felt tender, gentle love for her,
And ended the dance at once to let go of her.

Together they sat,
As if they had had a lover's spat.
Sibu's protective arm around Madhumati,
Seemed like flowers and confetti.

All this time,
Kamakshi, Menaka, Ritambhara and Urvashi,
Had been watching from a distance;
The dance, the drama and the romance.

In their hearts,
Jealousy and animosity grew.
Kamakshi, who was a love poet,
Started feeling like a shrew.

Urvashi who was a warrior,
Began to live in fear,
Of losing Sibu's love,

And Ritambhara, who was gentle like a dove,
Started feeling like a preying falcon,
To rid Sibu of what he felt for Madhumati, the emotion.

Menaka lost all notions of magic,
And lay frozen
As if she had experienced something tragic.

All the five sisters,
Now experienced hallucinations.
Was this for real,

Or was the love between Madhumati and Sibu surreal?

They began to think of a plan,
Something that would rid them of this love couple.
In their hearts, Sibu was the man,
Who would feel the heat of trouble.

Discourse on a Child

Vani was so in love by now that she felt like an infant craving the touch of her mother. She cooed, 'Darpan, I am beginning to fall in love with the story, now that we have children. As soon as she said that, she realised the interplay in words and blushed. Quickly correcting herself, she said, "What I meant was, now that Pashupati and Jyoti have Ishika and Ishu, the tale seems to have taken a whole new meaning. Also, the lovemaking between Madhumati and Sibu is just beyond description, don't you think?'

Darpan was lost in the words that Vani had created for him and he responded shyly, 'I do love children myself and I hope Ishika's and Ishu's children, the race of mankind, are as loving as their names. I can't wait to hear what happens to Madhumati's and Sibu's love story. Can you please explain the metaphors of infantile and mature?'.

The change of topic made Vani breathe a sigh of relief and she continued, 'The birth of Ishika and Ishu speaks of the infantile nature in the story of Pashupati and Riu's sisters, as opposed to the beastly and natural traits that it had so far. Meanwhile, Madhumati's and Sibu's love is beginning to acquire a mature hue as they begin to understand more of each other and do not feel awkward in each others' presence. It now seems like they were made for each other from the start.'

Darpan added, 'I agree. Ishika and Ishu, the names themselves sound so childish and innocent. While Madhumati translates to sweet mother, Sibu sounds like sweetoo or sweetie, as if it's the name of her child that she mothers.'

Deeksha affirmed, 'Yes. The story does have a very strong mother child aspect to it. While Pashupati is like an enfant terrible chasing his five mothers around, Madhumati plays the doting mother to Sibu. The birth of Ishika and Ishu and the descent of mankind just adds to the maternal element of the story.'

Darshan confirmed, 'God could not be everywhere, so he created mothers.'

Vani started cooing like an infant seeking a mother's affection.

I love you mommy with all my heart,
But I guess, this you have known from the start.
Did you know that I wrote this poem for you?
I have known you like an angel
Who saves me from monsters hiding in the dark.

Don't leave me out in the crowd, Momma,
For I might never be able to make it back to you.
Am I your naughty child, the one you did not want,
The one you separated from, and did part?

Do you remember the time we made swings in the Spring,
Or the puddles we jumped on, when it had rained all day?
I still feel lost on warm nights, as I toss and turn,
And wish for you to sing and turn my fears away.

Of all the things I hold close to my heart,
It's the thought of having you by my side, I hold on to,
And your smile, your kisses and your embraces too.
They help me face the struggles of my day, and for this,
I want to thank you, Momma, for being the best mother,
There ever was and ever will be.

The roll of dice showed separation and union.

Part 3
The Odyssey

Rohini

Deeksha raved about the pains of separation.

Prakriti meant to upset the family life of Pashupati.
He had acquired the love of the five daughters of Maya.
She started to poison Maya's mind,
By telling her that her daughters never asked
For her permission before starting to live with Pashupati,
And Jyoti even decided to go ahead and have children.
'I think it's high time you punished them
For their waywardness.'

Maya began to see the logic in Prakriti's plea.
She thought of a plan to separate Pashupati from Jyoti
And all her other daughters as well.
She began to increase the power
Of the Rohini Nakshatra.

The Rohini Nakshatra represents agriculture,
Materialistic desires, Kama or love,
And indulgence, as symbolised by the ox.
Rohini is symbolic of Prajapati or Brahma,
The supreme creator.

Rohini is derived from Roh, which means,
To rise or to bring into existence.
Rohini is sometimes shown
As Chandra (the moon) personified.

Rohini is also the wife of Chandra,
Apparently fond of fine dresses,
Decor and cosmetics.

Rohini resembles Saraswati,
As Prajapati Brahma himself chased Saraswati
And the latter took the form of a deer.
Thus, Rohini tends towards sensuality.

As the powers of Rohini increased,
It became the largest shining star in ether,
And its gravitational pull was such,
That its tidal forces began to attract Pashupati.

Soon, he began to lose interest in Jyoti and the sisters,
And decided to depart for Rohini.
He bestrode the glorious star,
And was met by the sage Kama.

Kama then said to him,
'O Pashupati, you have committed a grave mistake.
You have arrived on a Nakshatra without permission,
And now you must perform certain tasks.'

Pashupati feared the worst,
But knowing very well that there was no way out,
Asked Kama about the tasks.

Kama said, 'You must get the color vermillion,
Which comes from the purest saffron,
For that is what Rohini stands for,
And then perform a *yagna*.
As offerings, you must offer
The Kamadhenu.
This is all that is asked of you.

Pashupati set about finding saffron on the star.
As he was passing by a glade,

He chanced upon a saffron plant.
But as soon as he started harvesting,
An army of bees descended on him,
Stinging him with their stingers,
Caused blood to ooze out from his body.
As he writhed in pain,
A voice boomed from the skies,
'Beware Pashupati, you will not get
Even an ounce of this vermillion,
Instead, you will lose all your red blood to this pasture.'
Worrying for his life, he fled the meadow.

After running for a while,
He came upon a clearing in the forest,
Where there lay a cow,
And to his delight, it was the Kamadhenu.

Kamadhenu was tied to a post on the ground.
As he began unhitching the cow from the post,
Kamadhenu spoke, 'Pashupati, why don't you try milking
Me first, as you have to offer my milk in the *yagna*?

Pashupati began milking Kamadhenu.
When he had collected enough,
He decided to stop,
But to his utter dismay,
The milk would not stop flowing.
Soon enough,
The milk started bursting out in a giant stream,
And he found himself drowning in it.

He tried to make his way out of the milk stream,
But Kamadhenu, with a twinkle in her eye,
Started releasing even more milk,

And he was pushed out by the milk stream,
To the far corners of the universe.

Sikkim

Vani celebrated the spirit of union.

Madhumati's talents led to her growing fame,
And Narsimha began hearing stories about her.
He decided that the time had come,
To make Madhumati a diplomat and to send her
To far away places on missions for the Simha empire.

Narsimha called Madhumati one afternoon,
And told her, 'You must leave soon.
For there is much for you to learn,
From other parts of India under the sun.

You must travel to the north,
The center, and the east.
And take commodities from the Simha Kingdom,
To make trade, that has been done seldom.

You will meet ancient masters,
In each of the Kingdoms.
You must take them as your teacher,
And gain knowledge and wisdom.

Madhumati was surprised and taken back,
Because for trading, she had no knack.
But she knew, opportunity only once does knock,
And in future might never come back.

So she started making arrangements,
Travel things and various accoutrements.
She also pleaded with the King,
To let her take along her best friend Nini.

So the plan was made,

And a hundred camels, fifty horses,
Twenty elephants and forty bullock carts,
Were for the trip, readied.

On the camels went,
Items from the granary,
Barley, maize, rice, wheat,
Sugar, salt, spices, cane,
And other items that make a grocery.

On the horses went precious commodities,
Musical instruments, weapons,
Ornaments, gold, copper and bauxite,
And precious stones like ruby and quartzite.

On the bullock cart were piled,
Silks, cottons, wools and garments,
And wood works from the carpenter.
Also on it edible oils and extracts,
As well as fragrances were to be plied.

Madhumati took a map and charted out a route.
First, she would visit the northern state of Sikkim,
From where she was to head towards Bengal in the east,
And finally she would land in Madhya Pradesh
To finish the odyssey.

The journey began and the animals took the lead.
To pass her time, Madhumati carried some rosary beads.
She decided to count the beads one by one,
For the journey seemed like a long tour alone.

She decided to take the route of rivers,
As she could easily follow their meandering ways,
And avoid the offbeat track of the jungle,
Where wild beasts of prey could make her plan bungle.

To get to Sikkim she decided to take the following path,
First she would take the Krishna,
Followed by the Godaveri, and then the Wainganga,
Which would lead to the Son, and then the Ghaghara,

Followed by the Kosi and then finally the Tista,
Leading all the way to Sikkim.
The journey was to take two months,
And she began heading north.

The Krishna provided for some spectacular views,
Mangroves, forests, jungles and the wild,
Bison grazing, herds of elephants, deer in a slew,
She wished she had brought more crew.

The Godaveri, true to her name, proved to be a tumult,
As it contained waterfalls, big ravines and gulch.
The Deccan plateau gave way
To the land of Madhya Pradesh.
At Wainganga, Madhumati crossed
A lot of calanques, stalactites and stalagmites.

The Son is one of India's longest rivers,
Originating from *Amarkantak*,
It carried her onward towards her destination.
Ghaghara is a major tributary of the Ganges,
And it cuts through the Himalayan rock.

Onwards went Madhumati on a treacherous route,
The Ghagahra swayed to and fro,
Like a child on a hammock.
It took a lot for Madhumati
To make it across and through.

The Ghaghara merged into the Kosi, the sorrow of Bihar,
It took just moments for this river
To turn from a nullah to a raging river.

The Kosi gave way to the Tista,
And brought Madhumati to the state of Sikkim, a fiesta.

The region is full of legends of the Limbu and the Lepcha.
One legend says that Rang Pa Lepcha,
Who are from a Mongolian tribe,
Were the indigenous people of Sikkim.

These people are shy and live in green forested valleys.
They consider themselves to have originated
From a sacred stone or bamboos.
Their lifestyle is very amiable with nature's ways,
And they hunt and collect wild fruits and roots.

Some of the Lepcha follow shifting cultivation,
For maize, millets and other grains.
They are mostly led by a tribal leader,
Under whom, the village holds sacred order.

There were other tribes like Dukpas,
Sherpas, Magras and Bhotias.
Marriage alliances between tribes,
Helped in maintaining good relations.

The local priest worked as a medicine man and magician.
According to another legend,
The primitive Kirats moved,
From Nepal to Sikkim, as a population.

Another myth is that God created a couple,
Beneath the slopes of the scared mountain Kanchanjunga,
And that all the Sikkimese people
Have descended from the two.
Mayel Nyang was the land
Of the earliest people, the Lepcha.

Hunting and gathering were their primary professions,

Also, they weaved cloth from fibrous plants
Growing in the forests.
That the history of Sikkim began,
With the king Indrabodhi, has been debated by historians.

It is argued that King Indrabodhi's heirs,
Started migrating towards the east
Under adventurous princes.
The Minyak kingdom was founded
By one of the immigrant princes,
And the ruling house of Sikkim
Emerged from them.

A Prince of the Minyak dynasty,
Went on a pilgrimage westward with his sons.
They passed the Sakya monastery
Which was under construction,
And found the lamas struggling
To erect four pillars in the main chapel.
One of the sons of the princes
Succeeded in setting the pillar in its place.

This tremendous feat gave him the title of Khye Bumsa,
The one possessing the strength of one lakh men.
He was offered the hand of Sakya's
High order priest's daughter,
It was suggested that he settle down there,

And he complied with the offer.
He settled at Phari in the Chumbi valley with his wife,
This place became the centre of government
In the Kingdom of Sikkim.
Time passed and Khye Bumsa faced no problems,
It was suggested, that he sought the blessings
Of the Lepcha King, via the various lamas.

The King Thekong Tek was said

To possess prophetic powers.
When Khye Bumsa visited the King,
The King prophesized that even though he was childless,
He would be the father of three sons,

And that his descendants would one day
Reign supreme over Sikkim.
Time passed and the prophecy came true,
For Khye Bumsa had three sons
Who came to settle down in Gangtok.

Khye Bumsa felt a great obligation
Towards the Lepcha King,
A genuine friendship resulted between the Lepchas
And the newcomers.
Together, Thekong Tek and Khye Bumsa swore
Brotherhood amidst mingling,
And a pact was signed in blood at Khabe Longstock.

The third son of Khye Bumsa, Mipon Rab,
Became the Chieftain,
After his father's death. He had four sons,
To whom we now owe
The origin of the four principal clans.

Mipon Rab was succeeded by the fourth son,
Guru Tashi, who moved his base to Gangtok.
The Lepchas on the other hand,
After the death of Thekong Tek,
Broke into minor clans and looked towards Guru Tashi
For the leadership of their clan.

Sambre, a Lepcha, was appointed as chief adviser,
By Guru Tashi whose rule marked the absorption
Of a foreign ruling house,
Onto native ground and thus paved the way for,
A regular monarchy.

Thus Guru Tashi was crowned the first ruler of Sikkim,
And was followed by Jowo Nagpo,
Jowo Apha and Guru Tenzing.
The next ruler was Phuntsog Namgyal,
Son of Guru Tenzing
Who was born in the 16th century.

It is said that there was an entry
Of three venerable lamas into Sikkim,
From three different directions.
There was a meeting at Yoksam,
And they debated the possibility
Of religion over paganism.

Claims were furthered by two of the lamas,
But the third one, remembered the history and prophecy,
Of Guru Padamsambhava, that a man
From the east,
By the name of Phuntsog, will rule Sikkim.

To look for Phuntsog, messengers were sent out.
He was found near Gangtok and the lamas
Took no time to crown him King.
He was seated on a nearby rock
And water was sprinkled on him,
From a sacred urn.

With such a rich history,
The state of Sikkim beckoned Madhumati,
And she approached the ruler,
The Lhongse Lama and sought his advice,

He told her to enjoy the local cuisine, the festivals,
The trade fairs, fun fairs and the dances.
He urged her to indulge in trading,
And when the time was right,
He would teach her some art of lovemaking.

Madhumati left for Gangtok's town square,
Where there was a festival going on.
It was a street parade,
And there were masked people who looked like animals
Singing a song.

The entire street was full of colors;
Red, green, blue, turquoise,
Azure, cherry, peach and shades of greys.
Suddenly a float arrived full of mountain forms,

The mountains were colored sap green,
To denote the arrival of spring,
And there was a sprinkler mounted on,
Which suddenly started to spray water
On everyone like rain.

Another float followed,
And this one was full of children.
Their faces in the center of flowers, formed a garden,
And a sweet perfume flowed,

From the fruits on trees,
Apricots, cashews, pine nuts,
Almonds, raisins, kiwis and apples.
The whole float looked like the garden
Of Eden on wheels.

The next float had a temple built on top,
With girls dancing the Manipuri around it,
Their faces hid beneath a veil
Making a visual pot-pourri.

The last float had a lot of animals,
Mountain lion, bears, asiatic monkeys,
Macaques, wild dogs and yaks.

The animals were all animated and performed a circus.

The floats passed by,
And after them arrived a band of people,
Carrying drums, flutes, trumpets,
Bugles, castanets and guitars.

The band played a tune
Which sounded like the Bihu,
Which could be likened to the cooing of a Cuckoo.
After the band, came the traders carrying goods,
Which they set up in colorful stalls.

The stalls sold everything
You could imagine being in a household,
Like shawls, candles, bedsheets, gold,
Trinkets, cushions, winterwear, curtains,
Upholstery, bicycles, books, furniture and condiments.

The parade stopped as the stalls were set up,
Madhumati decided to trade her items.
She started bargaining and took to barter;
One sack of wheat for the table,

One sack of sugar for the chair,
Lapiz lazuli for gold,
Guitar for winterwear,
Condiments for shawls,

Silver for wooden artifacts,
Edible oil for condiments,
Sacks of rice for bicycles,
And sacks of maize for books.

She invented a curious system of trade.
She would weigh the item
She wanted to purchase in seconds,

And then she would calculate a unit price.
Later, she would multiply it by the weight
To arrive at the actual price.

Similarly she calculated the prices of items,
That she had and found which ones came close.
When a negotiation was finalised,
She closed the deal and bought the goods.

She ended up with more items,
Than she had picked,
Which caused her to panic.
But soon, she came up with an arrangement that worked.

She decided to offload the goods
That she had purchased,
At the local traders,
Along with some other items to be bartered,
And then carried off with her trade.

Knowing the total load that she could carry,
She did the numbers in her head,
And then tallied and bartered
Accordingly, so that she was left,
With only as much as she could keep.

She ended the trade for the day,
And decided to attend a fun fair,
Where the game of Khopar was being played,
With leather coins or Kaudis.

The game is similar to Monopoly.
The idea was to win as many Kaudis,
Or equivalent things as possible.
One could do that by throwing a dice,
And landing on certain squares and performing trades.
Madhumati started the game by bartering

A sack of maize for 10 Kaudis.
She then threw the dice,
And on it came the number five.
She moved five squares and won a shop.
She acquired the shop,
And waited for her turn again.
The next time the dice rolled to a stop,
She got a seven.

She moved and this time
She acquired a piece of land.
Slowly the game got her busy,
And she got more than one or two winning hands.
She ended the game with a profit of 20 Kaudis.

Satisfied with her trading skills,
She decided to return to the lamas.
She reached the monastery
On top of the Tchango Hill in Sikkim,
Where she was greeted by the Lhongse lama.

He congratulated her on winning
Good trades and the game of Khopar.
He said that they must leave for his private chamber,
Where he would teach her how monastic life,
Can be turned by love making into a beautiful life.

Since Madhumati was a bachelorette,
He decided to tease her by discussing matrimony,
And wondered if she liked to be tested.
He asked her, 'Madhumati, do you know
About the various kinds of marriages?'
Madhumati, being naive, said that she did not know
Much about marriages.

The lama told her, 'Let me then tell you
About marriage of the form Gandharva.

When in privacy, a girl cannot meet her lover,
And a maid should be sent over to the lover,
Who, upon meeting the lover,

Should describe the nobility, high birth,
The education, status, good qualities, skills, talent,
Knowledge of art, music, cuisine,
Human nature and affection,
Present in the girl to her lover
So that he grows in his affection towards her.

Likewise, when the maid meets the girl,
She should describe the handsomeness,
The chivalry, the attitude, and other qualities,
Of the man to the girl.

She should not talk about the girl's other lovers,
Or the impracticality of their parents.
She should then quote from history,
Of women like Shakuntala,
Who, with the relentless pursuit of their chosen lovers,
Were married to them and were happily assimilated
Into the society, without any drama.

She should continue to speak
About the good fortune of the man,
His obedient nature, his chastity and the promise
Of happiness that he holds for a woman.
In other words, she should build such a case for the man,
That if he were to take away forcibly
And unexpectedly, the woman,

It would not be a shameful deed.
When the girl is gained over and all is agreed,
And the woman starts acting like the man's wife,
He should bring fire to the house
Of a Brahmin, without strife.

He should spread Kusha grass upon the ground,
And offer his salutation to fire all around.
He should then proceed to marriage
Within the precepts of religious law,
Upon informing the parents of the fact,
And let the ice thaw.

It is of ancient knowledge
That a marriage solemnly performed,
In the front of fire cannot afterwards be condemned.
After the marriage has been consummated,
The relations of the girl should be informed.

They should be made aware of the fact,
In such a manner that they give their approval;
In other words, by use of tact.
They should be reconciled
By giving appropriate gifts and presents,
And this is the Gandharva marriage process.

If the girl is in doldrums and in doubt,
The man should do the following, as a roundabout.
On a suitable occasion, he should have the girl
Contacted by a female friend,
And then have her unexpectedly
Brought over to the house of his friend.

Fire should then be arranged in the house of a Brahmin,
And the man should proceed as above
And begin the marriage procession.'
Nini broke in and said that she had some confusion.
She said, 'It looks like I will always be the maid
And hence the friend in the procession.'

The lama corrected her and said,
'Well, social status has no say,
A maid can perform the role of the friend,

Or a lady of high birth can play.
Now tell me, do you know about the life
Of a virtuous woman?'
Nini piped in, 'Do you mean a virtuoso,
A genius woman?'

The lama corrected her again, 'No,
I meant one that is free from vice.'
Madhumati said that even though she knew a bit,
If he elaborated, it would be nice.
So the lama began, 'A virtuous woman
Should treat her husband like he is divine.
She should maintain cleanliness,
And arrange flora in various parts of the house.

She should maintain a neat and clean, well-polished floor,
And should surround the house with a garden,
Because it meant so much more.
She should place in the garden, things
Like incense, needed for the daily rituals.
She should be religious
And should pray daily to the various Gods.

Towards the sisters, brothers, cousins,
Uncles, aunts and other relatives,
She should behave in a manner that is suitable and nice.
She should plant vegetables, clumps of fig tree,
Bunches of sugar cane, the mustard plant,
The parsley plant, the mango tree,

The fennel plant, the xantochymus pictorius,
And clusters of various flowers,
Such as the yellow amaranth,
Trapa bispinosa, jasmine,
The jasminum grandiflorum,
The china rose and the wild jasmine,

The tulip, the nadyaworta, the dahlia, the marigold.
These should be planted
With fragrant grass angropogon schaenanthus,
And the fragrant root of the plant andropogon miricatus.
She should also get arbours made
Seated in the middle of the garden,

Also, a tank, a well or a pool should be dug.
The company of beggars should be avoided
And so should the company of thugs.
Unchaste and roguish women, female fortune tellers,
Female Buddhist mendicants and witches,

Should be avoided as well.
She should consider the choices
Of her husband, while taking meals.
She should always be ready to greet him,
When she hears him coming,
Or she should order her female
Maid servant to keep him company.

The female maid servant can wash his feet,
Or the wife can do it herself.
She should always put on her ornaments when she
Is going somewhere with her husband.
She should never give or accept invitations,
Without taking his consent,
On attending marriages, sacrifices and rituals.

She should never engage in games,
Or sports against the will of her husband,
Or sit in the company of her friends,
Or visit Gods in the temples.
She should always take a seat after him.
He should never be woken when he is asleep,
While she should always get up before him.

The kitchen should always be clean,
And in a quiet and secluded place,
So that it cannot easily be accessed by strangers.
In the event that the husband misbehaves,
She should not put blame on him in excess.

She should never curse or abuse him,
Instead, she should use conciliatory words
While she rebukes him.
She should never scold him too much,
And should avoid sulky looks, bad expressions,

Looking at passers-by, speaking aside,
Standing in the doorway,
Remaining in a lonely place for a long time,
And conversing in pleasure groves.
Also she should keep her hair, body and teeth
Very neat, clean and tidy.

The Lama asked, 'Tell me Madhumati
What do you know about examining
The state of a woman's mind'.
Madhumati replied, 'Well, holy lama,
I know a bit, but I like listening to you
So much, that I would rather have you
Carry on teaching me as such.'

'So listen, dear child,
A man should examine the state
Of a woman's mind as follows:
If she listens to him,
But does not let him know of her intentions,
Then he should use a go-between.
If she meets him once,
And comes dressed in much better clothes again,

He should become aware

That she can be pleasured with a much greater force.
However, a woman who lets her man
Talk to her about things,
But does not reveal much for a long time,
About what her heart holds,
It is to be considered a trifle in love.

But since the human mind is fickle,
Such kind of a woman can also be acquired
By keeping a close acquaintance with her.
When a woman starts avoiding a man's affections,
Because of the respect she holds
For him or pride in herself,
She can still be gained over in confidence,
With the help of a very clever go-between.
If a man tries to approach a woman,
And she rebuffs him with harsh words,

She should be abandoned at once.
However if the woman approaches
A man affectionately,
Then the man should try to act
Lovingly and calmly with her.
A woman who sets up a meeting with a man
In lonely places,

And starts touching him with her toes,
But because of the doubt in her mind,
Pretends to be unaware of it,
Such a woman should be conquered
With patience as follows.
If she happens to go to sleep
When he is present, by chance,
Then the man should put his left arm around her,
And see whether she is repulsed by him when she wakes.
In such a way, one can come to know whether
She is desirous of the things being done to her.'

Nini, at this point interrupted and said, 'What if she slaps?'

'Well,' the lama said, 'We do not consider violent
People my child, only loving ones.
To continue, what he is doing with the arm,
The foot can be used for the same.
If the man is successful, he should embrace
Her more closely,
But, if she does not enjoy this and gets up,
Yet behaves the same with him, the next day,

Then the beloved cannot be coerced
Into a relationship by the man.'
Nini interrupted again, 'But lama,
Why are you teaching Madhumati, what you should
Be teaching a man?' To which the lama replied,
'This is good knowledge that can be passed on,

By Madhumati to her lovers
When they intend to read her mind,
And the same principles
Apply to reading a man's mind too.'
This quietened Nini's perturbed head.
The lama continued, 'When an opportunity
Is provided by a woman to a man,
And her love is revealed to him,

He should proceed to establish a union of love with her.
Some of the revealing signs of love are,
She calls out his name
Without being spoken to in the first place,
She reveals herself in secret places,
She speaks to him trembling and with trepidation.
Now Madhumati, I shall ask you, do you know
How to adorn yourself?'
To which she replied, 'I know only a little bit
About getting ready and looking good,

But it would be of great help
If you teach me yourself.'
The lama began again, 'When you fail to get the attention
Of the beloved, as previously related,

He has to follow a different path to attract the partner.
Good qualities, youth, liberality and good looks,
Are the chief and the most natural means
Of making a person agreeable in the eyes of others.
But, if these are not present, a man or a woman
Must resort to artificial means.

An ointment made of tabernamontana
Coronaria arabicus,
Or costus speciosus and flacourtia cataphracta
Can be used,
As an unguent of adornment.
On making a fine powder of the above plants,

Applied to the wick of a lamp,
Lit with the oil of blue vitrol,
Produces a black pigment or lamp black,
Which, when applied to the eyelashes,

Produces a beautiful effect in appearance.
The oil of hogweed, the sanna plant,
The echites putescens, the yellow amaranth,
The leaf of the nymphae, on application,

To the body has the same effect;
A black pigment from the same plant,
Produces a similar effect.
On consuming the blue lotus, the mexna roxburghi,

The powder of nelumbrium sepciosum, ghee and honey,
A man becomes beautiful in the eyes of others.
The things mentioned above,

Together with tabernamontana coronaria
And the xantochymus pictorius,

On being used as an ointment, produces similar results.
The bone of a hyena or a peacock is covered with gold,
And tied on the right hand.
It has the result of making a man
Lovely in the eyes of others.

Similarly, a bead made of the jujube seed,
Or of a conch shell, enchanted by incantations,
Mentioned in the atharva veda,
Or by the incantations of those
Well skilled in the magical sciences,

And tied on the hand,
Produces the same result as described earlier.'
With this the lama told Madhumati
That he had described love enough,
However, he had to give her a gift.

He went inside the temple
And brought out a fish in a fish tank.
He told Madhumati, 'This is *Angel*,
I shall give you an incantation by which you can summon her.
Nini, curious again,
Asked, 'But how will it come? It can't walk.'

The lama calmed her curiosity by saying,
'Don't worry, the fish will appear.
The fish is a creature of love and is magical.
Just chant, *Swim swiftly for the tide is low, Angel,*
And the coast is clear for you to beguile,

The hearts of men, women, princes, kings and paupers,
Bring forth your ornaments, your voice,
Your eyes, like saucers.

Use your discretion in calling upon the help of Angel,
For she can help you in the matters of love
With her powers magical.'

The lama then made a humble request.
'Your arrival has indeed been fortunate.
Our princess Radha has been captured
By the evil wizard Kamsa.

He has cast a spell on her,
Which makes her want him as a lover.
We must rescue our princess Radha,
And for that we need your help.

Will you please go out into the dark forest,
In the foothills of the Kanchenjunga,
Where Kamsa has his castle mid-air,
And rescue Radha from his lair?

The knowledge that I have given you,
Will come of use,
And so shall Angel,
I hope that it all ends well.'

Madhumati thought for a while,
And then looked at Nini,
Who frowned and gave a despairing look.
But soon, they agreed together,
To look for Radha in the dark forest,
And onward to the trail, they took.

Nini was curious and asked Madhumati,
'How in heaven's name do you intend to free Radha?'
To which Madhumati replied,
'I am as clueless as you are.

But I will think of something on the way.'

Meanwhile, the forest started to become dense and stark.
Strange voices and creepy shadows leapt from the dark.
Nini squirmed and hung on
For her dear life, to Madhumati.

Out of nowhere suddenly, an arrow flew
And missed them by inches,
And struck a grazing doe.
The doe breathed its last in moments.

'Hush', Madhumati whispered to Nini,
'Don't make a noise, or move a bit',
As behind a thick tree trunk they hid.
She squinted and leaned her neck forward
And caught a glimpse of satyrs looking for the hit.
The satyrs were mythical creatures,
That were half man and half horse-like in features.

They were armed with bows and arrows,
And were combing the forest,
As if looking for an intruder.
Madhumati whispered to Nini,
'It seems like we are not welcome here'.

A ladybug whizzed past Nini's nose,
Who tried to hold it in,
But gave way and sneezed loudly. The satyrs arose
From their march and fired an arrow in her direction.

Their hideout had been given away,
And now the arrows came like pelting raindrops,
Madhumati was quick on her feet,
And ran towards her cache of weapons.

She grabbed a Bindipala for herself,
And to Nini, she offered the Cakra.
They unleashed the might of the weapons

Onto the onslaught of arrows,
With Madhumati chopping the arrows with her Bindipala,
While Nini sliced them with the Cakra.

The satyrs were now losing out,
As their arrows had come to naught.
They took out their swords,
And charged towards the fighting couple.

Madhumati knew the satyrs' weak spots,
And instead of attacking the swords,
Bent down on her knees,
And used the Bindipala on their legs.

Nini completed what was remaining,
By destroying their swords with the Cakra.
Madhumati felt pity for the satyrs
And did not want to cause them wounds.
So she came up with a plan that would settle the score.

She had brought with her casks of fine wine,
And knowing the satyrs' fondness for wine and song,
Decided to put it to use, in a method fine.
She carried on her person water guns
Much akin to the *nalika*.
She filled the water guns with wine,
And started showering the satyrs in *varsha*(rain).

Nini brought out a guitar,
And started playing tunes folksy and whimsical.
Pretty soon, the whole scene turned comical.
Satyrs lay belly side up, on the ground,
Some started climbing trees,
While others, trying to take to the skies, were found.
Some others started singing songs, dancing,
Skipping, hopping and fooling around.
Madhumati left the clownish troop,

And decided to trudge forward in her quest.
The forest had trees of all kinds,
Oak, rhodenderon, willow,
Cedar, pine and redwood.
Also to be found were flowers, shrubs,
Moss, lichen, wild grass, canopies,
Cacti and an assortment of herbs and spices.
Madhumati collected herbs like rosemary,
Fennel and thyme which she found in the wilderness,
Along with some fragrant spices like
Pepper, cardamom, clove and cinnamon.

Out of the corner of her eye,
Nini saw a lush green meadow,
That beckoned her mysteriously.
She saw a kaleidoscope of butterflies,
Of brilliant hues, viridian, ocher, umber,
Scarlet, magenta and ivory black flitting amidst the flowers.
The flowers were the kind she had never seen before,

They grew in a glorious bunch,
And sprung straight from the ground,
While flowers that shot above from stalks,
Bended in a droopy manner at the end of them.
An alluring perfume that smelled most heavenly,
As if it had been distilled from the Garden of Eden
Wafted from the meadow.

Before Madhumti could stop Nini,
And tell her to consider the dangers lying ahead,
Nini threw caution to the wind,
And ran towards the mysterious magical meadow.

Little did she know that the meadow was an artifice,
A cleverly constructed trap where lay fauns,
Creatures that were half men, half goats.
They were armed with swords,

And went straight for Nini's throat with their cleavers.

She shrieked in horror and collapsed on the ground,
As swords descended on her from all sides.
Luckily, Madhumati was prepared to take them on,
And she changed her weapon to the Mudgara.

She lodged it squarely on Nini's chest,
As she lay on the ground in her vest.
The swords came down on the Mudgara,
And with one swift movement of the weapon
Madhumati threw them all away.

Immediately, she passed the Sira,
Which she had been carrying in her other hand,
To Nini and pulled her towards herself,
By giving her a hand.

Nini wasted no time and swung the Sira at the fauns.
The Sira's curved and sharp edges
Cut deep into their skins,
And they lay slaughtered in a pile.

It was Madhumati's turn now,
And she started targeting the fauns' heads and horns,
With the Mudgara and Nini's prowess,
Together the duo drove the fauns away.

There were no more skirmishes on their way,
And soon they reached the castle gates.
They were attacked, in no time, by exploding fireworks,
That were thrown at them by the castle guards.

Madhumati resorted to the *VarshaBana*,
And doused the blazing fireworks with water.
Before the guards could resort to more drama,
Madhumati sent a note tied to an arrow flying over.

The note revealed their friendly intentions to the guards,
Who opened the gates and let them enter.
Onwards they went and Madhumati sent Nini to Kamsa.
Nini announced herself as a maid and extolled the virtues
Of Madhumati, making her look like a prima donna.

She spoke about her charming nature, camaraderie,
Good fortune, kindness, grace, humour and beauty.
But most of all, she spoke of her odyssey,
And that she was looking for a lover, her sweetie.

Kamsa was delighted and told Nini
'Just like your madam, Madhumati,
I am sending for her, perennial flowers,
That she can adorn herself with.'

Nini bid goodbye to Kamsa
And returned to Madhumati with the flowers.
Madhumati took a look at the flowers
And decided to put them to various uses.

Some of them she crushed and made a perfume.
With others she made a garland, much like beads.
With some others she made a bracelet.
And the rest she used to adorn her feet.

She doused herself liberally with the perfume,
Put the garlands around her neck,
The bracelet around her hand,
And the anklets around her feet.

She decided to pay a visit to Kamsa,
And upon reaching his castle,
Made her intentions clear to the guards.
Kamsa summoned her inside.

Madhumati didn't waste any time,

And immediately began regaling him with a tale.

'The story is about a boy, Abhinaya and a girl, Vismaya.
Abhinaya is a naughty boy, a wizard.
He captures Vismaya and holds her captive.
Soon he tires of her charms
And decides to capture another girl, called Maya.

Maya is a wizard herself.
Seeing the plight of Vismaya,
And the evils of Abhinaya,
She decides to put up a fight.

Abhinaya summons the spirit of Zeus,
And causes thunder and lightening.
Maya summons Aurora,
And makes a magical display of the northern lights.

Abhinaya then summons the Goddess Aphrodite,
And creates Nature's plentitude to overwhelm Maya.
Maya summons Perseus, the God of destruction
To destroy the excesses created by Aphrodite.

Maya then starts playing a game with Abhinaya
She speaks, 'By Ergin, I summon Herodotus',
Abhinaya mimes her and says, 'I summon Herodotus.'

Maya then speaks, 'By Ergin, I summon Achilles',
Abhinaya imitates her again,
And says, 'I summon Achilles.'

Maya then plays a trick on Abhinaya and says,
'By Ergin, I am a frog.'
Abhinaya falls for the trick, and mimes her,
Saying, 'By Ergin, I am a frog.'
Instantly, he is converted into a frog.
Maya then frees Vismaya from her captivity.

Kamsa, upon listening to the story,
Squealed with laughter,
And then asked Madhumati,
'Are you going to play the same game with me?'

Madhumati batted her eyelids at him, as if in love,
And replied, 'I only wish to play love games with you.'
She asked him for a dance,
And began to sing *Raga Milan*,
The raga of togetherness.

Together they danced,
The Ntriya, the Nritta and the Natya.
She pretended to be a lotus,
And like a humming bird, he hovered.
She danced like a peacock,
And like a *bahalia*, or the hunter, he hunted.

She played a weeping willow,
And he danced like the eager woodpecker.
She imitated a truant infant,
And he played the caring father.

Soon, they dance close to each other,
And hold each other in a warm embrace,
Looking deep into each other's eyes,
Wishing they were not on Earth,
But somewhere far away, in the stars.

As things begin to get really hot,
Madhumati, always true to her naughty self,
Decided to retreat from Kamsa's embrace.

She pushed him away,
As if she did not want him to hold sway
Over her heart and her mind.
When he grew impatient and lost his mind,

He began to leave a trail of bites,
All over her body, her hands, her chest,
Her thighs, and her forehead.
Kamsa was then in an ecstasy, he could hardly believe,
That a beauty like Madhumati was in his arms.
And before he could say anything,
She took a betel nut leaf with a sweet meat
And inserted it into his mouth with her tongue.

He felt like he was atop the seventh heaven,
As he tasted her inside his mouth,
Her fragrance and the aroma of her hair,
Emanated from her and surrounded him.

Suddenly, Madhumati broke free from his embrace,
And starts laying Kusha grass on the floor.
Kamsa was perplexed and asked her the reason for it.
To which she replied that she wanted to marry him, right there.

He was ecstatic, and started helping her with the task,
In moments, they had finished laying the Kusha grass.
Madhumati then lit a fire on the Kusha grass,
And asked Kamsa to sit next to it and repeat the hymns.

As Kamsa sat close to the fire, he felt dizzy,
A certain smell from the fire began to invade his nostrils.
In moments, he passed out and was unconscious.
Unknown to him, Madhumati had mixed intoxicants
With the kusha grass; such had been her plan.

Madhumati rushed to Radha's chambers
And along with Nini, they escaped the palace.
Madhumati raised a glass of wine to her lips,
And as she fell to a dreamy stupor,
She composed her first poem for Sibu, and the verse,
Was titled "*The Beat of my Heart*", a poem full of longing.

The beat of my heart,
Betrays my love, my darling,
For it calls your name
And remembers the warmth of your voice.

The beat of my heart
Is like a thousand drums,
Whether you are near or far,
For it celebrates in joy, our union.

The beat of my heart
Is like the falling of the first rain drops,
Pitter-patter on the rooftops,
As they bring our love from the heavens.

The beat of my heart
Is like a songbird,
A thrush, a lark, or perhaps a Mynah,
As it croons in a drowsy love-infused orchestra.

The beat of my heart
Is like shoals of fish,
Angelic creatures of the mighty ocean,
As they glide, glisten and glitter in the warm sunlight.

The beat of my heart
Is like the Cupid's bow,
Taught, tense and gentle; all at the same time,
Catching lovers off-guard in the bowers.

The beat of my heart,
Is like you and I,
As we partake in eternal love,
And seek bliss in togetherness.

Discourse on Love

Vani did not feel very comfortable breaching the subject of love, instead she chose to talk about something else, 'So tell me Darpan, what do you think about Rohini, the fact that the name stands for love and attracts Pashupati? Did you like the history of Sikkim and the rescue of Radha by Madhumati?

Darpan had love in his eyes as he spoke, 'I wish I could travel to the stars myself, but then I am not a God. I also wish I could learn the art of love like Madhumati did so I could rescue the princess and perform a good dead. Can you please explain the metaphors of separation and union?'

Vani averted her gaze from Darpan, feeling that she would simply melt if her eyes met his. She spoke with tenderness, 'Well, Pashupati in Rohini's story is not looking for a union, he is always running away, half committed to his tasks. He is asked to fetch simple things like saffron and a cow, which is a docile animal, yet he fails. He gives up the saffron as he cannot stand being stung by the bees. When it comes to Kamadhenu, she senses his disenchantment and perhaps also his lust and teaches him a lesson by drowning him in an excess of milk. On the other hand, Madhumati applies her lessons perfectly. Not only has she mastered the art of love, she is also in love with Sibu, which makes her feel the pain of Radha and relates to her as a person. Hence, she offers herself as a sacrifice to the evil Kamsa and liberates Radha, which goes to show her as a truly loving person who is ready for union with her lover.'

Darpan guessed, 'So being in union is being in love, while separation is denying love.'

Deeksha answered, 'You are right. Unless you are seeking union with your lover, you cannot be in love. You will be in a state of separation and hence, incomplete and devoid of love.'

Darshan added, 'Shall I say, love makes the whole world go round and round and round ….,' making everyone laugh.

Vani broke into an impromptu lyrical rendition of a love poem which made everyone sigh.

When I fall in love,
The world will sing melodies,
Of a time when,
Lovers met in secret.

In the tavern,
Where poets dream,
And children scream,
And kisses are stolen.

When I fall in love,
I will feel lonely,
Without my love
By my side,

To keep me company,
In the cold nights
And warm days
And in the moonlight.

When I fall in love,
It will be forever,
And I shall feel
Like a flower,

That has sprung in June,
Like a well lit moon,
That takes to the sky,
When the clouds are nigh,

To play hide-and-seek,

Amidst waves and creeks,
Where desperate lovers meet
And their fancies take to dreams.

Krittika

Deeksha summed up the fallouts of arrogance.

Pashupati was lost, hovering in the milky way,
When Prakriti and Maya thrust him
Into the orbit of Krittika.

Krittika nakshatra is the ruling enclosure
Of Agni, the fire God.
Krittika is considered to be the center
Where power is born.
She is the birth star of the Chandra.

Krittika is also the foster mother of Karthik,
Who is an able commander in battle
And is handsome in appearance.

Krittika is also known as the Star of Fire
And is identified as a foster mother, commander, warrior,
A glow of power, lustre, physical and creative force.
She needs outer energy from circumstance
To achieve her true powers.

Krittika destroys dark thoughts, while purifying,
And preparing that which is not yet ripe.
She rules over wars, battles and disputes.

Krittika denotes the capability
To obtain a transformation,
By destroying the impure and the vile from life,
And giving birth to purity, morality and virtues.

Pashupati descended onto Krittika

And upon alighting on the star
Was greeted by the seven sisters,
Maia, Electra, Alcyone, Taygete, Asterope,
Celaeno and Merope.

The sisters took his approach to their home as a threat,
And challenged him to a duel
If he wished to stay there.
Pashupati, cursing his fate, accepted the offer.

The duel was to be a battle of wits,
Courage and sportsmanship.
Maia began first and challenged him to ride a horse,
Bareback while chasing game.
The first to get the game would be the winner.

The chase began and Pashupati
Had hardly managed to secure the reins,
When Maia leapt on her horse in one swift jump,
Held it by its mane,
And chased after the game, a small piglet.

The piglet leapt and bounded about in fear,
As Maia quickly covered the ground to it,
While Pashupati was still struggling
To break into a gallop.
The contest was over in seconds,
As Maia caught the piglet by the scruff of its neck
And headed back to the starting line.

With a sinking heart, Pashupati readied himself
For the next challenge with Electra.
The challenge was to fence with light sabres.
Electra chose her favourite red laser sabre,

While Pashupati chose an infrared one.

Electra brought down her sabre in a flash
On an unprepared Pashupati,
And she missed him by inches.
Pashupati had not even managed to switch
His sabre on, and was caught off guard.

The laser burned through his body,
And he felt a searing pain shoot up his back.
As he began to regain composure,
Electra's sabre striked again,
This time like a rap on his knuckles,
And he felt like a schoolboy
Being punished by his teacher.
He was now injured in his hand and back.
Once again the laser saber flashed over him,
And took a swipe at his scalp,
Removing a thick clump of his hair.
The rest of his head was on fire!

He decided to quit the fight,
And found some water to heal his wounds.
By this time, the sisters had reached a decision.
If he was to lost one more contest,
They would throw him out of Krittika.

The deciding contest began,
And it was the most challenging of the three,
As it was mixed martial arts with Alcyone.
Before he could even greet her,
She took him by his hand and twisted it,
Throwing him back down, hard on the ground.

Pashupati felt emasculated
Surrounded by such powerful women,
And his pride in his powers began to fade away.

Alcyone launched a volley of punches,
First, at his beating heart,
Which almost made him throw his guts out.
The punches felt like a never ending assault,
At his stomach, shoulders, the side of his head,
Thighs and knees.
Whenever he threw in a counter punch,
She blocked it with a shell guard.
Alcyone, with a final blow,
Landed an upper cut,
On Pashupati's chin,
And he fell down like a severed timber log.

Somehow, he managed to get himself up,
Only to find himself at the receiving end
Of Alcyone's kicks,
Straight out of the repertoire
Of a skilled martial artist.

She landed a flying kick on his head and
A front push kick on his chest,
But when she did a Wushu Butterfly kick,
Pashupati staggered and simply collapsed.

The sisters then threw him out of Krittika's orbit
And set him on a voyage
That seemed to lead nowhere.

Bengal

Vani sang paeans of humility.

Bengal stretches from Himalayas in the north,
To the Bay of Bengal in the south,
To the Nagar, the Barakar,
And the lower reaches of Suvarnarekha in the west,
And the Brahmaputra, the Kangsa, the Surma,
And Sajjuk rivers in the east.

The province includes the States of Hill Tuppera,
Cooch Bihar, Sikkim
And the areas under large rivers and estuaries.
A large portion of people
In the western districts are Hindus,
While the majority in the east is of Muslims.

The parts inhabited by people
Speaking Bengali stretches,
Far beyond the political boundaries
Of the province of Bengal,
It extends east into the district of Goalpara,
Sylhet and Cachar,
Which belong to the province of Assam,

To the west into Santal Parganas,
Purnea, Manbhum lands,
Which are included within the boundaries of Bihar.
The northern boundary touched the summits
Of Himalayas at the time of the Gupta Kings.
The province of Bengal has no deserts,
No hills, nor ridges, except on the fringe,

It cannot take pride in the purple waters
Of the Kashmirian lakes,

Or display the marvel of Haramukh,
Cental India's gushing stream,
Which leaps into falls
Between marble rocks near Jabalpur,
Or the backwaters and waterfalls of the Malabar,

That lend their aura to the scene of the western sea board
Of the Southern Presidency.
However, it takes pride in the snow capped peaks
Of Darjeeling,
The vast river-irrigated plain which forms
A delta between the three great river systems,
Broadening into a visual feast of irrigated fertility,

With flats and swamps cut in the south by thousands
Of coves and creeks,
At one time, the royal seat of Kings,
And now, home to the Royal Bengal Tiger,
The Rajah of the Jungles.
The mysterious hand of nature
Has divided the province into four major divisions,

Which roughly corresponds to the major political divisions
That the historical eras have seen.
North of the main tributary of the Ganges,
Now called the Padma,
And west of the Brahmaputra,
Lies the exclusive region which forms
The modern Rajshahi Division,

And parts of Cooch Bihar.
The most immanent part of this area
Is the land of the Pundravardhana.
West of another tributary of the Ganges,
The Bhagirathi, or the Hooghly,
Stretches the mighty Burdwan Division.

Between the Padma, the Bhagirathi
And the lower reaches of the Brahmaputra,
And the estuary of the Meghna,
Is the central region of Bengal containing
The majority of the Presidencys area.
In the east, beyond the Meghana, stretches
The Chittagong division,

Within the folds of which, lie the buried remains
Of the royal seat of Samatata.
The most defining trait of Bengal is its river system.
The two gigantic rivers, the Brahmaputra and the Ganges,
With their numerous tributaries and branches,

Have played a pivotal role in shaping its destiny.
The vast deposits of silt carried down from the uplands,
Have created huge areas of deltaic lowlands,
And the process is still in flow, in full vigour.

Changes in the river course has built
And unbuilt teeming cities,
And flourishing marts, often times
Changing the whole outlook of large areas.
The Ganges enters Bengal at a point
Where the low lying Rajmahal hills,
Almost touch its waters.

The present course of the Ganges,
The curve it makes
Around the spurs and slopes of the Rajmahal hills,
Is very different from how it was
Before the sixteenth century.
In those days is flowed further north and east.

The Ganges shifted towards the south and west
Before reaching its present course,
And it is still possible to trace some of the dry beds

Of its old channels.
Today an enormous volume of the waters of Ganges
Is carried mainly by the Padma,
While the upper part of Bhagirathi has shrunk
To a very narrow and shallow stream.

Historically, the Bhagirathi was
The more important channel of the Ganges,
But, by the beginning of the sixteenth century,
It was replaced by the Padma.
Bhagirathi is venerated in Hindu mythology,
While Padma, despite causing much havoc and terror,
Does not have any mention credited to it in mythology.

There was much difference in race and culture
Among the primitive people of Bengal.
An interesting commentary on the orthodox view of the origin
Of the early people of Bengal,
Is made by the Sunahsepa episode
Of the *Aitareya Brahmana*.
A Brahmana boy was adopted as his son
By the Rishi Visvamitra.

His fifty elder sons disapproved of him
For the act,
And were cursed by the father, as a consequence.
The offended guru prophesized that their offspring
Shall inherit the ends of the earth.
Thus came the Andhras, Sabaras, Pulindas,
Pundras and Mutibas,

Who lived in large numbers
Outside the confines of Aryandom,
And were identified as *dasyus* or outlandish barbarians.
A different account of the origin of the Pundaras,
And other tribes like the Suhmas and the Vangas,

Is found in the first book of the Mahabharata.
A raft drifting along the Ganges and carrying a blind old sage,
Passed through many kingdoms,
Before it was picked up by a king named Bali.
The monarch, who was childless,
Asked for the boon of an offspring.

The sage complied and in due time, the queen
Gave birth to five sons,
Vanga, Kalinga, Anga, Pundra and Suhma.
From their name are derived the names of the five kingdoms.
Which together comprise the modern provinces
Of Bengal and Orissa.

The primitive tribes of Bengal were regarded as *dasyus*,
Or transgressors by the sages.
The Mahabharatha describes the Bengal sea coast
As inhabited by the Mlechchas,
The Bhagavat Purana classes Suhmas as a sinpul (papa)
Tribe along with the Kiratas,

Hunas, Andhras, Pukkasas, Abhiras,
Khasas, Yavanas and Pulindas,
While the Dharmasutra of Bodhyana prescribes,
Expiatory rites after mingling
With the Vangas and the Pundras.
The wild traits of the people of Bengal
Are also documented by the Jainas.

It is stated in the *Acharanga-sutra,*
That Mahavira travelled through the pathless land of Ladhas,
And in Vajjabhumi and Subbhabhumi,
Many natives attacked him,
And dogs leapt at him.
Few people kept the beasts at bay,

While striking the monk, they said,
"Chu chchhu" and made their dogs bite him.
Many others had to eat bad food in Vajjabhumi.
They carried a long pole to ward off the dogs.
The Jaina writer mentions how tough it was to go
About in Western Bengal.

The Bengal kings suffered much
At the hands of the conquerors,
While also utilizing opportunities to wreak
Vengeance over their enemies.
They participated in the battle between
The Pandus and the Kurus,
And appeared in the epic Mahabharata
As allies of Duryodhana of the Kurus.

There is a thrilling account of a lively encounter
Between a scion of the Pandus,
And the mighty ruler of the Vangas.
Some Bengal kings fought on elephants,
While some others rode on ocean-bred steeds.

As the Gupta empire was established,
It brought an end to
The independent existence of the various states
That had flourished,
In Bengal. Excluding Samatata,
The rest of Bengal was acquired,
By the Gupta empire, by the time of Samudragupta.

The ruler of Samatata
Pleased the emperor Saumudragupta,
By payment of all kinds of tributes,
Obeying his commands,
And reaching out to pay court to him.

Samtata then became a child state,

Acknowledging the sovereign rule of the Gupta Emperor,
Although it had full autonomy of its internal affairs.
The exact bounds of Samatata can't be determined,

But it can be said that
It was approximately the size of Eastern Bengal.
Whether Samdugragupta subjugated the whole of Bengal,
Or whether his father's reign had some role to play in it,
It is difficult to say.
An inscription mentions military exploits
Of a king called Chandra,

Who won battles in the Vanga kingdoms,
Against his enemies,
Who fought together. His identity is a matter of debate
Amongst scholars.
He is often identified either as
Chandragupta or Chandragupta II.
In the former case, we must conclude
That Samudragupta's father,
Had already added Vanga to the Gupta empire,

While in the latter case, it is assumed that Vanga had
Shaken off the Gupta empire,
The task of reconquering which, by defeating
A combination of people,
From different states of Bengal had
Been left to the son of Samudragupta.

It is clear that even though Bengal
Was split into a number of independent states,
They got together and offered a solid resistance
Against a foreign invader named Chandra.
It could either be one of the two Gupta emperors
Named Chandragupta,
Or an earlier ruler whose aggressive policy
Helped the Guptas,

By weakening the resources of Bengal
And its power of resistance, through his policies.
The latter argument appears to be more likely
Since it makes more sense
That a portion of Bengal was included
In the original kingdom of the Guptas,
Which gave them a foundation
For further conquests and rallies.

There is sufficient evidence
That Samadudragupta himself,
Led his victorious army into Bengal.
For we find the name of Chandravarman,
Among the kings of Aryavrata,

Who were, according to the Allahabad Prasasti,
Uprooted By Samudragupta.
Chadravarman may be identified as the king,
Mentioned by name in the Susunia inscription,
As the ruler of Pushkarana.
This Pushkarana is further identified
With the village named Pokharna,

25 miles north-east of Susunia on the southern bank
Of the river Damodar.
It has yielded antiquities from way back
Into the Gupta period, perhaps even earlier.
Chandravarman thus, may be regarded
As the king of Radha,
Or the region immediately to its south,
Any by defeating whom, Samudragupta,

Paved the way for the conquest of Bengal.
The copper plates from Damodarpur
Of Buddhagupta indicate that northern Bengal,
Formed an integral part of the great Gupta empire,
All the way to the end of the 5th century.

Another inscription from Damodarpur,
Dated way back to the year 544 A.D.,
Refers to a Suzerian ruler,
Whose name ends in -gupta.

Thus the history of Bengal is rife with Kings,
Tribes, local people and conflict.
In such a region Madhumati
Arrived to carry out her edict,
And she went straight to the Purulia market square.

It was the time of Durga Pooja,
And there were festivities all around.
Devi Durga is a Hindu Goddess,
Who is worshipped as a manifest,

Of the creative feminine forces or Shakti.
She is also believed to be an incarnation,
Of Lord Shiva's wife Parvati in her fiercest form.
She is the mother of the Universe,

Venerated for her grace as well as her horrifying form.
Originally held in spring, or *basanta*,
Durga Pooja is also called the Basanti Pooja.
All around, temples and stages
And *pandals* were decorated,

Processions, revelry, performance arts,
And recitations featured.
Durga Puja stalls showed the goddess Durga,
Along with the deceptive, shape-shifting
Powerful buffalo demon Mahishasura,
Who was defeated in battle by her.

The festival signifies the victory of good over evil,
Besides being a harvest festival
That celebrates the Goddess,

As a matronly power that presides over all life and creation.
The Durga Puja festival arrives
At the same time as *Vijayadashami*.

Nini, who was enjoying the festival, out of curiosity,
Asked Madhumati, 'what is Vijaydashami?'
Madhumati explained that it was a day
Which marked the celebration of the victory of good over evil,
To which Nini remarked that to her, all festivals
Seemed that way.

Soon, Vijayadashami celebrations began all over
The market square.
There was an actor dressed as Lord Rama,
And another dressed as the demon Lord Ravana,
And they soon engaged in a dance of war.

Rama got the better of Ravana,
And shot an arrow to his heart.
After that, effigies of Ravana,
Were burnt all over the town square.

A big effigy of Ravana housed in the ground
Next to the town square.
A missile rocketed its way towards the effigy's center,
Causing a fire to be lit and the effigy
Soon went up in flames,
Followed by the sound
Of exploding crackers.

The main Goddess worshipped
During the festival is Durga,
Although, there are other deities
Such as Lakshmi, Ganesha,
Saraswati and Kartikeya who are worshipped too.
Ganesha and Kartikeya are considered
To be children of Durga.

Lord Shiva is also worshipped during this festival.
Floats passed around town square, carrying all these deities.
The display gave way to prayers at twilight,
And offerings to Saraswati,
The Hindu goddess of music, poetry, knowledge, wisdom, inner knowing and creativity.

She is considered to be another incarnation
Of the same multi-handed goddess Durga.
The eyes of Durga on all the floats
Were painted such that they looked as real as life.
Afterwards, prayers to Ganesha
Were offered in the temples of Durga,
Followed by remembrance
And preparations for other manifestations,

Of the Goddess, like Mai (mother),
Laskhmi (Goddess of wealth),
Kumari (Goddess of fertility), Ajima (the grandmother),
Saptamatrikas (the seven mothers) and Navdurga
(The nine manifestations of Durga).
After that, the Goddess is welcomed,

And festive Durga worships and celebrations,
In elaborately decorated temples and pandals,
Are conducted all over the town.
Shlokas (verse), Mantras (incantations),
Arati (prayer) and offerings are then made.

Durga shlokas praise the Goddess as the manifestation
Of nourishment, memory, power, wealth, emotion,
Forbearance, faith, peace, forgiveness, satisfaction,
Beauty, righteousness and fulfilment.

Madhumati found this the right time to begin trading.
She first traded her musical instruments for candles,

Bags of wheats for idols of the Goddess,
And a bag of sugar for the Goddess's ornaments.

She followed the same system of calculation again.
She calculated the number of items in her inventory,
Leave the excess with the traders at their stalls,
And calculate the cost based on the unit's price.

She traded bags of cotton for bags of perfumed rice,
And she acquired coconuts, Bengal's famed produce.
She acquired edible oils for gunny sacks of barley,
Dried fruits for religious books,

And books for vases made from mud.
She traded her wood works for pitchers,
And acquired glass beads,
And bottles of fine wine for muslin.

She got into playing a game with the locals,
Which involved drinking a local under the table.
She had to drink all the concoctions,
And later recall the names of all those drinks.

She started having one drink after another,
The english rum, french brandy,
Some exotic cocktails,
Toddy from the south,
Hooch and arrack from the east,

And Feni from the west.
Someone had brought gin,
Which even Nini said yes to.
Nini got one too many drinks and puked.
And then said that she needed to rest.

The puking episode paused the game,
Madhumati's opponent had passed out,

It was quite a shame,
But the game was not over yet,
As she had to still recall the names of the drinks.

She did it with ease,
And made her case.
She had won the competition.

She won cases of bottles of wine
From the local traders.
She piled up the cases on to her bullock carts,
And then decided to make her way to the Kings palace,
On reached there, she requested his presence.

The King, Swarbhanu, had heard of Madhumati's arrival,
Her success at trading and at the gambling table.
He welcomed her with open arms,
And invited her to a banquet with his knights.

After the banquet was over,
Swarbhanu called Madhumati over,
And said, 'I will teach you the ways of war,
And then I shall let you have my prized possession
As a gift to take away from here.

Let me tell you first about an army on the march.
An army on the march must pass quickly
Over mountains and valleys,
It should not wander over barren uplands,
Instead, should keep close to water laden grasslands.

An army should camp at high places,
Preferably hillocks or knolls,
Elevated above the surrounding areas.
It should never fight after climbing the mountains.

You should get away as far as possible

From a river after crossing it,
And if the enemy marches into the river, do not meet
It halfway down the stream,
Instead, let it cross half the stream,

And then deliver your attack.
If you are in the state of anxiety,
You should never go close to an enemy,
And meet near a river for an attack.

Always moor your raft higher up the river,
Than your enemy and let it face the sun.
Never move up-stream and confront the enemy
Up the river.
When crossing salt flats,
You should have the singular concern

Of crossing them as fast as possible.
In dry and level country,
One should acquire an easy and accessible position,
With raised ground at the rear and the right.
The four useful subjects of military knowledge
Are mountains,

Rivers, plains, and marshes.
It is common military strategy to prefer high ground
To low lying areas,
And sunny areas to dark ones.
One must always arrange for fresh water and food
For men.

If the army arrives at a bank or a hill,
It must always take the sunny side,
With a slope on the right rear.
If, as a result of heavy rains, a river is in swelling tide,
One must wait until it subsides
And then, there is nothing to fear.

One must leave the following places as soon as possible,
Places with cliffs,
With torrents and deep natural hollows,
Quagmires, crevasses,
Tangled thickets and confined areas.

While it is beneficial to remain away from such places,
It can be advantageous if the enemy is approaching
From such places.
If you camp in a place, where there are ponds,
Surrounded by aquatic grass, shallow basins
Filled with reeds,

Or a thick undergrowth with woods,
They must be routed carefully and searched.
If the enemy is nearby and remains quiet,
He has the natural strength of position on his side.

When he keeps away and tries to instigate a battle,
He is provoking the other side to advance in battle.
If it is easy to find his camp,
Then it is being offered as a bait.
Signs of movement among foliage in the forest,
Shows that the enemy is on the move.

An ambush can be gathered
From the sudden flight of birds.
Another sign of a sudden attack is startled beasts.
An oncoming of chariots can be gathered
From dust rising in columns.
Quiet words and advancing preparations
Are signs that the enemy is about to attack.

A proposal of peace unaccompanied by a sworn covenant
Indicates a plot,

When there is much running about,
And all the ranks of the enemy are being filled,
It means that the critical moment has arrived.

When some of the enemy troops are seen retreating,
While some are seen advancing,
Then it's a lure.
When the soldiers stand against their spears,

They are famished and need water and food.
If the soldiers begin drinking water first when sent,
Then the troops are suffering from thirst.
If there is much commotion in the camp,

The general's authority is weak.
If an army kills its cattle for food,
And feeds its horses with grain,
And when the men do not use camp fires,
With hanging cooking vessels,
It means that they will not return to their tents,
And have resolved to fight till death.'

Nini interrupted, 'But it can also mean,
That they are out of food and will starve soon.'
To which Swarbhanu replied, 'No my dear,
Battle hardened soldiers
Will always find food and shelter,

And are used to eating vermin and snakes to keep alive.'
He told Madhumati, 'Now let me explain the terrain
Which can be like a bee hive.
There are six kinds of terrain that can be distinguished,
Temporizing ground, accessible ground,

Entangling ground, narrow passes,
Precipitous heights and positions
At a great distance.

Accessible ground is that which can be freely
Traversed on both sides.
About this kind, it is advised to carefully
Guard one's line of supplies.

Entangling ground is one which is hard
To reoccupy once abandoned.
If the enemy is not prepared,
You may rally forth and slap defeat.
Temporizing ground is one from which neither side
Will gain by making the first move.
In this case, even if the enemy is offering ground,
It is wise not to make the first move.

If one can occupy first the narrow passes,
Then one must garrison them,
And then wait for the enemy's arrival.
Should the enemy be the first in reaching
And acquiring a pass,
Go after them only if the path has a weak garrison.

For precipitous heights, one must occupy the sunny
And raised spots,
And then wait for the enemy to arrive to you.
There can be insubordination when the common soldiers
Are stronger than the officers.
While the regiment can collapse when the officers
Are strong and the common soldiers weak.

The result is ruin when the higher officers
Are angry and insubordinate,
And when they meet the enemy, they take to battle
With resentment,
On their minds, before the Commander-in-chief
Decides whether it is right to fight.
The result is disorganization when a general
Is weak and without authority,

Or when his orders are not clear and distinct,
And the officers and men end up with no fixed duties.
The result is rout when a general
Underestimates the strength,
Of the enemy and allows a weak army
To fight a stronger one.

Such are the six ways for a sure defeat.
He, who knows these things,
And puts them to use, will never see defeat.
If fighting is sure to lead to victory,
Then the army must battle on,
No matter what the ruler's decision is.

That General is the jewel of the kingdom,
Who goes forward without the promise of fame,
And without worrying about disgrace,
Whose only thought is to do his kingdom service.'

Nini interrupted again, 'But should a General
Not think about reproach from the masses,
When the body bags start arriving in numbers?'
To which Swarbhanu replied, 'A good General,
Will never have to face that day,
As he has taken into account, the collateral.'

Swarbhanu continued, 'Madhumati,
You are very quiet and I am pleased,
You are a good listener and Nini keeps me amused.
Now let me tell you about the Nine situations in war.
There are nine varieties of ground recognized
In the ways of war, that lead to certain situations.

The open ground, the facile ground, the serious ground,
The difficult ground, the contentious ground,
The dispersive ground,
The desperate ground, the hemmed-in ground

And the intersecting highways ground.
The facile ground is had on penetration into
Hostile territory at a small distance.

Dispersive ground is acquired when fighting
In one's own territory.
Contentious ground is that whose possession
Gives no advantage to either side.
Open ground is that on which each side
Has the freedom of movement.
Intersecting highways ground is that which forms
The key to three contiguous states.

Serious ground is had when an army has infiltrated
Into the center of the enemy,
Leaving a number of armed and barracked cities,
To its rear.
Difficult ground consists of rugged steps, mountain forests,
Marshes and country fens, that are hard to traverse.

Hemmed-in ground is that which is approached via
Narrow gorges,
And from which one can only return via tortuous paths.

Desperate ground is that from which one can be saved
By fighting quickly.
The strategy therefore, is to not fight on
Dispersive ground,
Not to halt on facile ground,
And not to attack on contentious ground.
One should try on open ground,
To not block the enemy's way.

One should gather and plunder on the serious ground.
One should resort to stratagem over the hemmed-in ground.
The following principles
Should be observed by an invading force.

You should try to penetrate as deep as possible
Into enemy lines.

One should study carefully,
The health and sobriety of their men.
You should humor them,
Make them feel at home and be a doting mother hen.
In desperate situations,
Soldiers lose all sense of fear,
And stand firmly by their leader.

One should prohibit the taking of oaths,
And do away with superstitious beliefs.
On the day of battle, it is allowed for soldiers to weep.
It is not enough to ride horses and chariots,

Instead, one must learn the proper usage of ground.
A general must ensure secrecy, be upright and just,
And have a calm demeanour
Thus maintaining law and order.
He must be able to charm his officers
And keep them in ignorance.

He should be able to alter his plans and arrangements,
And keep the enemy guessing about his movements.
At the crucial step, a leader of men,
Behaves like a mountaineer,
Climbing up the highest rock,
And kicking away the helping ladder.

He breaks his cooking vessels, burns his boats,
And doesn't allow the enemy to know his plans,
Even by the wildest guess.
You find yourself on critical ground,
When you leave your own land,
And take your army across to the enemy's side.
Serious ground is when you penetrate deeply

Into into the enemy's land.
When you penetrate only a bit, it is facile ground.

The ground is hemmed-in when you have narrow passes
In front, on the rear you have the enemy's strongholds.
It is best to inspire men with a unity of purpose
On dispersive ground.
There should be close interconnection
Between the various army segments on a facile ground.

I would hurry up my rear on contentious ground.
I would keep an eye open for my defences on open ground.
I would integrate my alliances
On the intersecting highways ground.
I would keep pushing forward on difficult ground.

I would drive into my soldiers,
The hopelessness of saving their lives
On desperate ground.
I would confront the soldiers with my acts,
Not with my design, on the ground.
Throw your army in the tumult of war and it will survive,
Plunge it into the fire of battle,
And it will come out safe and revived.'

Swarbhana finished his discourse on war,
And then summoned his horse.
Out came Chetak, the flying horse with wings,
And he told Madhumati,
That now, he belonged to her.

He revealed to her the incantation for Chetak,
'Oh might Chetak, the winged horse, akin,
To a devilish satyr or an angelic fawn,
Come like a mighty steed, a stallion,
And lead us to victory on a chariot.'

Swarbhanu then took Madhumati into his confidence
And told her about the abduction of prince Krishna.
He told them about the evil king Ravana.
Ravana had his eyes on the kingdom of Bengal
And had abducted the crowned prince Krishna
As he wanted the throne for himself to rule.

Swarbhanu pleaded with Madhumati to help him.
Madhumati was stupefied as Bengal was mighty
And powerful, while she was just one single entity.
How could one single person make a difference?

She asked Swarbhanu why had they not managed,
To liberate the crowned prince Krishna by themselves.
Swarbhanu replied that Bengal's mighty prowess,
Had come to naught, as Ravana was evil and wretched.

He had managed to secure various kinds of grounds,
The open ground, the facile ground, the serious ground,
The difficult ground, the contentious ground,
The dispersive ground,
The desperate ground, the hemmed-in ground
And the intersecting highways ground.

He always kept the whereabouts of Krishna a secret,
And when the Bengal army mounted an attack,
He moved Krishna between the grounds.

'Ravana follows perfect strategy,
He does not fight on dispersive ground,
He does not halt on facile ground,
He does not attack on contentious ground.
He does not block the enemy's way
On open ground.
He gathers and plunders on serious ground.
And resorts to stratagem on hemmed-in ground.'

Ravana's army consisted of trained infantry
Possessing extremely good weapons,
Like the *agni bana* and the *varsha bana,*
Trained cavalry, soldiers on elephants,
And cannons ready to launch missiles in seconds.

Moreover, Ravana himself was skilled in Maya,
And could create creatures that were like shadows
Ready to fight long after they were dead.
Some of these creatures were those from the underworld.

Ravana himself had been given a boon by Lord Shiva
That promised him safety from death,
Which made him a formidable opponent.

Madhumati considered all and her heart sank,
Surely trouncing Ravana in battle seemed like a difficult task.
Nini started crying and her tears wouldn't stop.
It took all of Madhumati's efforts
To make her hold back her tears.

Together, they headed towards the delta of the Ganges,
Where the army of Ravana was camped.
A plan had started to form in Madhumati's mind.

She came up with a strategy called the 'deep blue'.
The whole idea was to drown Ravana's army in water.
With the entire army submerged,
Madhumati would benefit from the resulting confusion.

Ravana's perfect stratagem over open ground,
Facile ground, serious ground, difficult ground,
Contentious ground, dispersive ground,
And the other kinds of grounds
Would stop operating
As all kinds of grounds would then be submerged under water.

Madhumati nocked a *varsha bana* on her bow,
Pulled back the bow string and let it loose skyward.
She followed it by a volley of *varsha banas*
And the sky became blue with them.

Soon, a massive downpour fell on Ravana's army.
It rained so hard that the horses in the cavalry
Got washed away and so did the elephants.
All hell broke loose in Ravana's army ranks,
As every foot soldier ran for cover.

Madhumati had scored her first victory,
And she felt a step closer to administering Ravana's defeat.
She summoned angels with her trumpet
And warriors with her bow.

She then ordered the warriors to cut the coconut trees
In the mangroves of the Gangetic deltas,
And to collect the leaves as well.
The warriors started felling the trees with their axes,
And in no time, a large stockpile of trunks
And leaves was amassed.
The trunks were to be used for making hulls,
While the leaves were to be used
For making sails, masts and rudders.

Madhumati then ordered the angels,
To build various kinds of boats,
Amphibious assault ships,
Battlecruisers, destroyers, dreadnoughts,
Schooners, Galleons, Cutters,
Clippers, cogs and caravels.

As the ships formed her naval armada,
Madhumati became its Commander-in-chief,
And Nini, after some argument,
Assumed the position of the second-in-command.

The two girls first took the inventory,
As they began amassing their infantry,
Cavalry, horses, elephants,
Gunpowder, armaments,
Canons and missiles.

After the inventory had been dealt with,
The girls divided the navy
Into the forward regiment,
Which comprised of the infantry and cavalry,
The second regiment,
Which had the cannons and the elephants,
And the supporting regiment,
Which had the missiles.

Madhumati then looked into the crystal ball
And came to know that Krishna
Lay captive in the now submerged difficult ground.
Since Ravana did not have a navy,
He had no way of moving him around.

Madhumati began organizing her navy
Into a *matsya vyuha*,
And started preparing the scene
For a guerrilla attack on Ravana's army.

The strategy was simple,
They were to form small teams of ships,
Like shoals of fish,
And sneak on to the various grounds,
In the late hours of the evening.
They pounced on the enemy,
Dealing with heavy blows from all sides.
Madhumati intended to give Ravana
A dose of his own medicine,
By using his own strategy

On the various kinds of grounds.

As light began to fade and evening fell,
Madhumati's naval armada slipped into darkness,
And began their assault at the same time.

The assault ships rained *cakras*
On the infantry stuck on open ground,
Always keeping their way out open.

Soon all the infantry surrendered, fearing for their lives.

The battlecruisers then began pelting *Agni banas*
On facile ground, while moving at all times.
The battle ended even before it had begun.

The destroyers zeroed in on dispersive ground
With the *satghani*,
Making sure that they did not fight for long,
And left Ravana's cavalry bleeding and screaming.

Whenever Ravana's canons fired in retaliation,
Madhumati's navy changed their formation in the *vyuha*,
Taking the form of a big fish.
This maneuver of the *Mastya Vyuha* confounded Ravana,
As he did not know where to hit Madhumati's navy.

As soon as the canon fire stopped,
The dreadnought broke formation,
And started launching missiles
At serious ground,
While plundering at the same time.
This foray left Ravana's canons in tatters.

The final blow to Ravana's army
Was delivered by the schooners,
As they launched a volley of *varsha banas*,

Drowning the remnants of Ravana's army
On the hemmed-in ground,
While they resorted to the strategy
Of sneaking in on the difficult ground
And liberating Krishna, just in time,
Before the difficult ground
Got completely submerged.

Madhumati consumed some fresh home-brewed liquor
And thinking about Sibu waiting for her,
She penned her second poem,
'Will You be There My Love?'

Will you be there my love?
When this dreamy odyssey ends,
And hold my hand in yours
As we walk down the aisle.

Will you say sweet nothings in my ear?
As you kiss me tenderly,
And take me in your arms,
To end this long period of absence.

Will you sing a love song?
And hush me to sleep with a lullaby,
As you cradle me like a child,
And dance with me,
Till eternity comes to a stand still.

Will you bring me flowers, carnations and posies?
And write love notes to me,
Poems of Herodotus,
Fluttering in sheaves of butter paper.

Will you lead me into the moonlight?
For a fairy tail romance,
And tell me the legend of Endymion,

As you shepherd children through the valley of the Gods.

And most of all, will you marry me, darling?
And make me your blushing beatnik bride,
Leading me to a house in the hills,
Where we make sweet love forever.

Discourse on Pride

Vani carried on her conversation with Darpan, 'Darpan, could you see the fire of Krittika being reflected in the seven sisters and how easily they humbled the mighty Pashupati in a duel? Did you feel proud of Madhumati as she displayed her abilities as a skilled commander-in-chief, while we only knew her as a singing and dancing childish girl?'

Darpan agreed, 'Yes, I absolutely loved the description of the Krittika Nakshatra and the fertile Gangetic plains of Bengal. I am fascinated by the rich history of the province. Its comes as a bit of a suprise, that a warrior like Pashupati is defeated so easily by some girls. Madhumati is getting better and better with time and it seems like she has been really listening to her gurus, including Durvasa. Can you explain to me the metaphors of arrogance and humility?

Vani explained, 'Remember Darpan, that pride is the most common of emotions, and that of false pride is even more common. Pashupati is proud of the fact that he is a warrior and thinks little of the seven sisters. His pride leads to his undoing in battle. Madhumati on the other hand, is humble and approaches battle with a cool head on her shoulders. She assesses each and every scenario and devises strategy based on her learnings thus emerging on top.'

Darpan spoke with vehemence, 'I agree completely. Madhumati deserves everything that comes her way. Pashupati has a lot to learn from her. In fact I am beginning to wonder whether Madhumati was Pashupati in her past life and has learnt from his mistakes.'

Deeksha laughed as she spoke, 'Well, you are free to draw whatever conculsion you wish about her past life. All I can say is that pride leads to demise while humility prevails.'

Darshan added, 'I guess, one must not become extremely humble or extremely vain; a balance is the order of the day.'

Once again Vani began singing a rhyme.

I am such a child without you,
Thinking that I can go on and on.
But, the fact is that I need you by my side,
To keep my head where it belongs.

Or else, I walk with my head in the skies,
And fall hard on my face.
So don't leave me love,
Even if I come off like Narcissus.

And a flower does bloom,
Standing for my pride,
As vanity is my favourite sin,
And you are my bride.

I want to hold your hand,
And hold my head high,
As I learn from you,
How to be humble.

And yet, remain a man
Of this world and others,
As we look out for each other
And brave the storms,
Of a life on Cassiopeia.

Swati

Deeksha described the stupors of the body.

Pashupati was travelling through a sea
Of never ending nothingness,
When Prakriti and Maya
Thrust him again, into the orbit of Swati.

Swati stands for art, freedom and creativity.
Swati means purity,
Like the first drops of rain.

The arena of Swati is owned by Lord Vayu,
And is also influenced by Rahu.
Both leave their impact on Swati,
Imparting to her, traits like
Complete freedom, independence,
Spontaneity and restless behaviour.

Swati was the name of one of the wives,
Of the Sun in Hindu epics,
As well as the sanskrit name of Arcturus.
Because of its brightness,
It is also referred to as the real pearl.

Swati is considered auspicious
When starting an educational venture,
Social activities and events,
Learnings in general,
Financial transactions,
And dealings with the public.

She deals in pursuits that require

A calm and flexible approach,
The important thing being to go with the flow,
In grooming and self adornment,
Actions that require diplomacy,
Buying and selling in general,
And in the pursuit of arts and sciences.

As Pashupati landed on Swati,
He was greeted by the high priestess
Of magic and illusion, Kaya.

She agreed to let him stay on Swati,
Provided that he succeeds in certain tasks.
He was to brave the fierce eternal storm,
That was a constant apocalyptical occurrence on Swati,
And then to cross
The realm of dark spirits,
To reach the grotto of grandeur,
From where he was to fetch her the chalice of magic,
Which would grant her unlimited powers of magic.

Pashupati made a weak approval, almost refusing her.
He started negotiating the difficult terrains of Swati.
He had to make an arduous journey
Through the barren sandy desert,
Followed by climbing over the sheer rock faces,
That hung over deep rifts in the mountains.

He headed towards the valley of Yurba,
Where the fierce eternal storm lay waiting.
As he slowly got closer to the storm,
Little tornadoes began to appear out of nowhere,
Running amok, kicking dust and sand in his eyes.

He could barely see farther than his hands now,
And began to look for water to wash his eyes.
Little did he know that the pool of water
That he was heading towards
Was surrounded by murky quicksand.

As soon as he stepped into the quicksand,
The ground began to give way under his feet.
He felt like it would disappear and dissolve,
Like salt in water,
And he would drown in it.
He kicked his feet and flew his arms to stay afloat,
But the more he fought,
The faster he got sucked into the mushy mess.

He realized that he had to stop fighting,
And hence stood still,
His breathing being the only movement.
The quick sand had now reached upto his neck,
He lay neck deep in the mess.
He was about to make his last prayers,
When a furious wind cleared the sand,
And picking him up in a swift movement,
Threw him flat on his face on the ground.

He did say his prayers,
But instead of being the last ones to God,
They expressed gratitude for having his life spared.

No sooner had he thanked his stars, when a blast of wind
Carried him high up,
Where the air was churning in a vortex,
And began throwing him around
Like a rag doll.

He squinted his eyes to let a little light in,
Fearing that dust would trespass into them.
At the center of the vortex,
Was a blinding light,
And a voice boomed from it,
'Go back, Pashupati, this is the realm of magic
And you will find nothing but pain.'
As the voice finished talking,
A bolt of lightening flashed from the center,
Straight at him and struck him hard.

He found himself on the ground,
His body scalded, bruised and battered.
The vortex had vanished,
And a clear blue sky,
That dazzled with a brilliant display of aurora lights,
Took its place.

The ominous sounds and lights,
Had brought all of Pashupati's childish fears to life,
Yet he trudged on his journey.

Soon he reached the borders of the underworld,
The dark, mystical and haunted abode of dark spirits.
He knew from his studies,
That no one could survive there long enough.
So he set a sand timer,
To help him decide,
When it was appropriate to turn back.

As he went in, shadows started darting all around him.
Eerie voices, interspersed with blood curdling screams,
Shattered the haunting silence of the underworld.

He began to lose his mind.

He started hallucinating,
And saw flesh eating plants,
Creepy, crawling, scavenging insects from hell,
Demons with such horrifying appearances,
And dark bodied spawns of the devil,
That ran helter-skelter,
Mouthing foul abuses,
And singing bawdy songs.

He began to wish that he had never come there,
As the underworld smelled rotten
Like decaying flesh.
He had to brave certain narrow passageways
Where garbage and slime rained
From above,
And made him run for shelter.
It did not help at all
When the places of shelter that looked appealing
Turned at once, torturous and hideous.
They reeked of country liquor,
Of sewage and filth.

He could not bear it any longer,
And started to puke all over,
Copious amounts of vomit,
And bile that came out of his bowels.

The sand timer was running out,
And he decided to run back, out of the depravity
That was the underworld.
Suddenly, however, he felt chained to the ground,
As dark spirits began to hover around him.

They began whispering in his ears,
Such blasphemy, that he felt his mind would explode.
At that moment he remembered,
The magical sound of Aum,
And with his failing energies,
Began uttering Aum,
Aum, Aum, Aum Tatsat.

Suddenly, he found himself free of the dark spirits.
He fell, scampered and ran like a mad man,
Not knowing in which direction he was headed.
In these moments of insanity,
He managed to cross the underworld.

He had, however, run into the grotto of grandeur.
He kept running in the direction of light,
And arrived at a chamber,
Which seemed to be lit in neon, bright.

He entered the chamber,
And at its center,
Was kept the chalice,
A golden cup, studded with precious jewels.
It was so brilliant,
That he could not keep his hands off it,
And he removed it from the center.

Boom! A sound exploded in the grotto,
And the establishment started collapsing in on him.
The pillars, walls, the ground, all started caving in,
While he stood stupefied, frozen still.

When he realized what was happening,

He ran on the double.
Ghouls, spirits and ghosts descended on him,
As they tried to make their way out too,
From the recesses of the grotto,
And Pashupati screamed in horror.

In his delirium, he spotted a small crevice,
From where he could make an escape.
He crouched down on his knees,
And brushing off the evil spirits and ghouls,
Managed somehow to get out in time,
As the grotto came down in a massive explosive collapse.

He was about to explode with joy,
When he remembered that in his hurry to get out,
He had forgotten to take the chalice,
And left it inside.
He let out a cry of anguish,
Feeling that all was lost in that one moment,
And all of his efforts had come to naught.

When he returned to the high Priestess,
She fumed and raged and burst into flames,
And eventually, she kicked him out of Swati.

Little did he know that this was just the beginning
Of his troubles as Prakriti and Maya
Had hatched an even more evil plot.

They had captured Jyoti, Ishika, Ishu,
All of humanity and their children
And had trapped them far away from the planet.

They met Pashupati, Ritu, Pavan, Jal and Dhara

To explain the deal to them.
They would have to brave all the seasons on Earth,
Which included Sheeta (winter),
Basanta (spring), Grishma (summer) and Varsha(rain).
Each season was now to look like a calamity
Because with Jyoti gone,
The balance of fire was missing from the elements.
They would have to work together,
And if they managed to survive the harsh climes,
They would be reunited.
On being asked the reason for doing so,
She replied that she had done such a deed
To teach them the importance of staying together,
And the futility of inflated egos.

Madhya Pradesh

Vani made music on the vagaries of the mind.

The state of Madhya Pradesh, being centrally located,
Is often called the heart of India.
The state has a rich cultural heritage, a large plateau,
Numerous monuments, meandering rivers,
And forests that run for miles.

It also inhabits a curious mix of flora,
And wildlife in Sylvan surroundings.
Historically, it was known as Malwa.
The climate of the region is pleasant
And moderate throughout the year,
Seldom interspersed with extremes of weather.

The primary regions within the area are Malwa,
Nimar, Bundeklhand, Baghelkhand,
Chambal and Mahakaushal.
The chief language spoken here is Hindi,
While in and around the areas of Sironj, Bhopal, Kurwai,
And Burhanpur, Urdu mixed with Hindi is commonly used.
Different dialects are spoken in different regions,

In Malwa, Malwi,
In Baghelkhand, Bagheli,
In Bundelkhand, Bundeli,
And in the tribal areas, Bhili and Gondi.

The main crops cultivated here are soybean, wheat paddy, tuar,
Gram, maize, mustard, jowar and masur.
Major rivers here include Narmada, Chambal,
Sone, Betwa, Tapti,
Banganga, Ken, Pench, Shipra, Tawa and Mahi.

Madhya Pradesh has the largest forested area in the country
And a lot of it is protected.
The province is a part of the peninsular plateau of India,
Lying in the central north.
The boundary of the province can be marked,

In the west by the Aravali,
In the east by the Chhattisgarh plains,
In the north by the Ganga Yamuna plains,
And in south by the Maharashtra plateau
And the valley of the Tapti.

Majority of the province lies on the tableland
Of Central India bounded,
In the west by the Gujarat plains,
In the east by the Chattisgarh regions,
In the north by the Upper Gangetic plains,

And in the south by the Godawari valley.
The state is traversed by the Satpura, Maikal
And Vindhya Hill ranges, running east to west.
The highest point is at Dhupgarh, near Panchmarhi,
Most of the province has an elevation
Of between 305 to 610m above sea level.

In general, the state
Is at an elevated position geographically.
It can be divided into seven regions
Based on its topography.

Covering nearly the entire western section,
Of Madhya Pradesh, is the Malwa plateau.
Formed by the Deccan rock traps, the plateau,
Begins north of the Betwa and Narmada rivers,
And covers in Rajgarh, Mandsaur, Dhar, Guna,
Dewas, Sehore, Ujjain, Raisen, Jhabua,
Shahpur, Sagar and Vidisha.

Its average elevation is 350 to 450 meters,
But attains the height of 800 meters at some peaks.
The main rivers of this region are,
Chambal, Kshipra, Mahi,
Betwa and Parvati.

Covering the northern part of the lower basin,
Of Chambal river, is the Central Indian Plateau.
It is bound in the east by Bundelkhand's gneiss rocks,
And in the south by the Vindhyan rock groups.
Western boundary is formed by the Karuali and Bundi hills.
The region presents a mixture of low land,
And upland topography.

Deep ravines of the Parvati, Kalisingh and Chambal
Rivers mark the area.
This region spreads out in Bhind, Morena, Gwalior,
Shivpuri, Sheopur, Guna and Mandsaur.
The maximum height achieved here is 500 meters.
In the north and the north east,
The plain reach a height of 150 – 300 meters.

Lying to the east of the Central Indian Plateau,
Bounded in the northeast by the Rewa-Panna plateau,
Is the Bundelkhand plateau.
Granite rocks from the Arabian era
Can be found in the area.
The topography is smooth and undulating,
And the plateau is flat with marginal slopes.

A third of the northern plain area is flat all around,
And presents a stark contrast to the Vindhyan table land,
Which rises in three well marked escarpments
Roughly delineated by the rivers Sindh, Dhasan,
Betwa and Ken.

This region in Madhya Pradesh is spread over,

Tikamgharh, Chattarpur,
Datia, Shivpuri and Gwalior.
The height of the region is between 150 to 450 meters.
The highest point touches 1172 meters at Sidhababa peak.

Also known as the Vindhyan plateau,
Is the Rewa and Panna plateau,
Which lies to the northeast of the Bundelkhand plateau.
The maximum height here reaches 750 meters.
The Vindhya state group's Bhander hills
And Kymore ranges have a number of waterfalls,
With heights upto 450 meters.

The area is drained by the rivers - Ken,
Sonar, Berma and Tons.
The covered area has its spread in regions - Panna,
Damoh, Rewa and Satna.

The Narmada-Sone valley is drained by the rivers Narmada
And Sone, extending from the northeast
To the west with an average elevation of 300 meters.
It is bounded by the Kymore,
Vindhyan and Bhander hills
In the north valley,

In the south by Satpura and Maikal hills,
And in the east by the Baghelkhand highlands.
The valley is sharp with trap falls
Within the Narmada river, which do not allow navigation.
The cities included in this area are Mandala, Jabalpur,
Hoshangabad, Barwani, Harda, East Nimar,
Raisen, Dewas, Dhar and West Nimar.
Parts of Shahdol, Rewa, Umaria,
And Sidhr district form a part of the Sone valley too.

To the south of the Narmada Valley is the Satpura,
And Maikal region.

It has an average elevation of 300 meters.
The peak of Dhupgarh is the highest point in the state.
The Satpura slope is gentle in the north,
And sharp in the south.
The area includes Betul, Chhindwara,
Seoni, Balaghat, Khargone, Mandla and Khandwa.

The Eastern plateau is spread over the eastern
Parts of Madhya Pradesh,
Which is called the Baghelkhand Plateau,
In the Sidhi region.
In this region, the elevation ranges from 400 – 1000 meters.

Madhya Pradesh has three major seasons,
Summer, Monsoon and Winter.
During summer, the temperature
Ranges above 29.4 degree Celsius.

Generally, the eastern parts of Madhya Pradesh,
Are hotter than the western parts.
Regions like Datia, Morena, Gwalior
Record temperatures of over 42 degree Celsius
In the month of May.

The humidity is relatively low
And the region experiences frequent dust storms.
The south-west Monsoon breaks out in mid-June,
And the entire state receives a major share of its rainfall
Between June and September.

The south and south-east regions tend to experience
A higher rainfall, whereas,
The parts in the north west, receive less of it.
Sidhi, Balaghat, Mandla, Jabalpur and other eastern parts
Receive more than 150 centimeters of rainfall,
While the region of western Madhya Pradesh receives
Less than 80 centimeters.

The winter season stars from the month of November.
In the northern parts, the temperature remains low,
As compared to the southern parts.
The daily maximum temperature in most of the
Northern parts in the month of January
Is limited between 15 and 18 degree celcius.
Generally, the climate is dry.

Tribal people form a large demography in Madhya Pradesh.
They are called by different names,
Such as the indigenous, aboriginal, native,
Tribal and primitive.

The major tribes are the Gonds, the Bhils,
The Santals, the Minas and the Oraons.
The have their own language systems,
And live in different regions of the forest.

Tribals are the autochthonous people of the land,
And are considered to be the foremost settlers
Of the Indian Peninsula.
They are called *Adivasis*, which means the first settlers.

Before the caste system came into place,
People were divided into different tribes.
Each tribe was a homogenous,
And self-contained unit functioning without
Any hierarchical discrimination.

Gradually, the chief started assuming military and political powers
And was recognized as the ruler.
These led to the emergence of monarchies and republics.
Tribes began to be associated with large kingdoms.

Each tribe had its own system of administration.

Amongst the tribes, all authority is decentralized.
The Maniki and Munda systems
Are examples of tribal institutions.

Tribes in India belong to three major stocks,
Mediterranean, Mongoloids and the Negritos.
The Negritos are believed to be the
Earliest inhabitants of the Indian Peninsula.
The Mongoloid race is represented by
Tribal people in the sub-Himalayan region.
The Mediterranean tribal population forms a majority
In the country and are known as Dravidians.

With the advent of the Aryans,
A long struggle started off between the Aryans
And the Dravidians, then referred to as Dasyus.
The conquered Dravidian were reduced to a servile status,
And were regarded as Sudras.

A section of the Dravidians who escaped defeat,
And did not surrender to the Aryans,
Still maintained independent existence in hills and forests.
They are believed to be the forerunners
Of the various tribes in India

As Madhumati came to this region of plateaus and tribes,
She witnessed the *Brahmaur yatra*.
The yatra (pilgrimage) is a fair-cum-festival journey
Celebrated by the Brahmaur.

On the day following *Janamashtmi*, the fair
Commences and is celebrated for six days.
It is dedicated to Ganesh, Lakshna,
Narsingh ji, Keling, Harihar (Shiva) and Sheetla.

An assembly of people gathers in the Chaurasi area,
In their most attractive and gay dresses.

The high priest of Brahmaur heads
The procession and is dressed in the Gaddi dress,
With a silken *pagri* and a golden *kantha*
Round his neck, along with golden earrings.

Musicians play various musical instruments
At the beginning of the fair.
The musical instruments include
Narsinga, shehnai, dhol, nagara and karnar.

The high priest leads the people,
And performs *puja* at all the temples
In the Chaurasi area and then
Goes around the temple three times (in parikrama).
The evenings are reserved for folk songs and dances.
People make offerings to the temple
And receive *purshad* of *halwa* and *luchis,*
Which they carry to their homes.

Madhumati found this a good time to begin her trading.
She bartered *dhols* for *nagaras*,
Beens for *shehnais*,
Sitars for ektaras,
And flutes for bugles.

She started trading artefacts,
And exchanged statues of folk people,
For those of local gods and goddesses.
And traded woodwork for pottery.

She bought glasswork in exchange of ceramics,
And at one point, Nini convinced her
To trade a pair of oxen for horses,
But she wizened up and thought otherwise.

After one week of the *Brahmaur yatra*,
Came the very important *Mani Mahesh* Fair.

Mani Mahesh is a sacred pilgrimage place for the Gaddis,
As it is believed to be Lord Shiva's residence.

Snow covers the peak at all times,
And it is believed that no one has been able
To scale the summit.
Before beginning the *yatra*,
The *chelas* of Keling and Mani Mahesh
Are consulted to check if the *yatra*
Will be successful.

After getting permission from the *chelas*,
The pilgrims start the *yatra*.
Every pilgrim is required to take a dip
In the *Brahmi Nullah* and offer dhoop,
And a goat is pledged as *manauti*.

Pilgrims must finish the yatra in two stages.
They must first be present at the lake
On the morning of Radha *asthmi*
Which falls fifteen days after Krishna's *Janam ashtmi*.

It is believed that this day is very sacred
For taking a bath in the Mani Mahesh lake.
Pilgrims take a dip in the *Gauri Kund*
Before starting for the final dip in Mani Mahesh lake.

The yatra is begun barefooted.
This shows that the pilgrimage is very sacred.
Songs are song by the pilgrims
In praise of Lord Shiva, during the *yatra*.

Male goats are sacrificed on the way
And their meat is cooked and eaten nearly raw,
Since it is difficult to cook meat
At such high altitudes.

Dhoop is offered by all the pilgrims,
And all together
They pray to catch a glimpse
Of Kailash's magnificent sight.

Madhumati found an opportunity again
And traded sacks of wheat for a goat.
She also traded incense for *dhoop*,
Various ornaments for bangles
And silk garments for decorations.

Nini got curious and asked her,
'What will we do with the goat?'
And Madhumati replied to her,
'We will make cheese by milking the goat.'

There were more festivals and fairs
But Madhumati had grown tired of them,
And felt like meeting the tribal chief
Who, it turned out, was a shaman.

He introduced himself as Anirban,
And said that he was the local shaman.
He had heard of Madhumati participating
Actively in the fairs and trading, he said.

He told her that he would teach her magic,
And began with the method of invoking spirits.
He brought up ancient manuscripts
That were relative to the fact of spiritual intercourse.

He spoke, 'For invoking of the spirits,
One must prepare for high and mysterious
Ceremonies, by living in a manner
Secluded from the rest of the world.

One should be disposed towards religion.

For three days, one must live
Without sensual gratification,
And burn temple incense and candles that are waxen.
One must choose a place that is solitary and secluded,
Where no business is carried on,
Where there is no entrance for unhallowed eyes.

For this purpose, unused buildings,
Free from wandering people,
Or lonely caves in the midst of forests,
Or rocks by the sea shore,
Or ruins of ancient structures,
Where nocturnal birds have taken tenancy,
Or any place, the general appearance of which
Indicates desolation and darkness,
Is ideal for invoking spirits.

After choosing a place, secure and free from interruption,
The Theurgist or the Invocator must choose
A proper day and hour for invocation,
According to the order, nature and office of the spirit.

He must remember that the good are raised
During the increase of the moon,
And he must raise the dead and the bad,
During the decrease of the moon.

He should have with him earthly seals,
The spiritual seals,
Sacred pentacle or lamen,
The Magic Sword, vestment,
And other instruments for performing his rituals.

After having decided the day and the hour,
The Theurgist must get the Temple incense himself.
And consecrate or exorcise the place
By burning for a week the Temple incense, each evening.

After this, he must draw his circle, nine feet in diameter.
Inside the outer circle, should be placed,
Two concentric circles
On a piece of Virgin parchment.
Four inch squares must be inscribed then,
And the four quarters of the world,
Marked within by an accurate compass.

In the middle, to ensure divine protection,
One must describe the names of God,
Jehovah, Adonai,
Tetragrammaton and Sadai
In appropriate inscriptions,
Taking care that the circles
Are formed correctly,
And jointed duly,
Fortified with sacred crosses,
Within and Without;
The coal or the chalk first properly consecrated.

Wax must be used as the source of light,
And each waxen candle set in a brass candlestick,
Enclosed in a magic pentacle.
The sword must be made of pure steel,
Forged specially for the occasion,
And none of the instruments used
Must ever be devoted to any other purpose.

All things begin ready, one must, along
With his associates, enter the circle
In the proper planetary hour,
On entering, one must consecrate with the sword
And close the circle in an appropriate manner.

After this, one can proceed as one considers fit,
To constrain, adjure or force the spirits

To make an appearance.
In doing this, one must be firm, confident,
Undaunted, not despairing or impatient,
But determined to bring his purpose and will
To the desired effect.'

Anirban finished directing and said,
'Now Madhumati, I will teach you the spirit
To invisible appearance.'
Nini questioned like a foolhardy student,
'Is there a spirit that can grant everything I want?'
Anirban laughed and said,
'If you are good, perhaps it will be revealed.'

He began chanting the incantation,
'I conjure thee Egin, Rex Borealis,
And also charge thee,
That thou shalt make your presence felt before me,
And before this circle,
By the sufferance of the Almighty,
And by virtue of sentences,
And his passions,
Which here shall be rehearsed,
To bind and constrain thee.
I conjure thee, Egin, by the Father, the Son,
And the Holy Spirit,
And by the earth, the sea, the air, and heavens,
And by all that is contained therein,
That thou come again,
And make your presence felt to me and my friends,
Not fearful and terrible,
But in a mild and peaceable form,
Without envy or hurt against any of us.

I conjure thee, Egin,
By all the holy words,
That God spake in creating the world,

And by all invisible and visible creatures,
And by the virtues of heaven
And by the four elements,
And by all the holy words that God spake to Moses,
And to all the other prophets,
And by the incarnation, passion, death and resurrection,
Of the mild and ineffable saviour of all mankind.

I conjure thee, Egin,
By the general resurrection,
And by the horrible day of judgement,
I conjure thee Egin,
By the appearance of the Holy Spirit,
I conjure thee also,
By virtue of all the spirits of the just,
And by the most holy apostles,
Evangelists, patriarchs
And by the holy saints.

I conjure thee, Egin,
By the power, grace and mercy
Of God;
I conjure thee, thou spirit Egin,
Under the pain of condemnation,
And thy horrible doom at
The great day of the judgement;
I conjure thee Egin
By all the high names of God
I conjure thee, Egin,
By the great curse of God;
I conjure thee by the high power,
And strength of our lord Jesus Christ,
The Son of God,
In all his heavenly glory;
And I conjure thee in the entirety of these,
To appear before me in an instant
Like a child of merely three years,

And without envy, hurt or fear,
Thou fulfil my request.'

Having said the incantation, Anirban continued,
'And now I shall teach you how to raise the soul of the dead.'
He started chanting an incantation again,
'By the virtue of holy resurrection,
And the torments of the damned,
I conjure and exorcise thee, spirit of the deceased,
Whose body is put here,
To answer my life's demands,
Being respectful unto these sacred
And mystical ceremonies,
On the pain of everlasting distress and torment.'

Then he began chanting,
'Berald, Beroald, Blbin gal gabor aguba,
Arise, arise,
I charge and command thee.'

Nini began shivering with a fright,
And complained, gathering all her might.
'Oh, all this is too scary,
Can't we talk of something beautiful like the stars?'

To which, Anirban replied,
'Good idea, let me now tell you,
The science of Astrology.'

'Canst thou the sky's benevolence restrain,
And make the Pleiades to shine in vain,
Or when Orion twinkles from his sphere,
Thaw the cold season and unbind the year?
Bid Mazzaroth his destined station know,
And teach the bright Arcturus to glow?

The highest level of the celestial science,

Astrology may be defined as the art
Of knowing before hand and predicting
Future events by the motions, positions,
And influences of the heavenly bodies,
And other heavenly phenomena derived
From experimental and rational observations,
Made by the wisest philosophers,
Of all ages and in most of the civilized world.

Poets and philosopher have been
Among its firmest votaries.
Chaucer, the father of English Poetry writes,
For in the stars clearer than in the grass,
Is written God wot, whoso, could it read,
The dethe, but that men's witts ben so dull
In stars many a winter before
Was writt the dethe of Hector, Achilles,
Of Pompey, Julius, or they were bore;
The strife of Thebis; and of Hercules,
Of Samson, Turnus and of Socrates,
The dethe, but that men's witts ben so dull
That no wight can well rede it at the full.

There are principles on which astrology is founded.
I'll find it hard to believe that the principal architect,
Decked the heavenly arches with all these fires,
Only for show; with these glittering shields,
To amaze poor shepherds watching in the fields.
I'll not believe that the least flower which pranks,
And the least stone that in her warming lap
Our mother Earth doth covetously wrap,
Possesses not some peculiar virtue of its own,
And that the stars in heaven have none.'

With this, Anirban brought the discussion on magic to an end,
And spoke about his prized possessions,
That he wished to hand over to Madhumati. He beckoned

Kaalia the snake and *Robyn* the bird,

He spoke to Madhumati,
'I am handing over to you,
The magical serpent Kaalia,
And the illusionist bird Robyn.
To summon them here are the incantations.

Starting with Kaalia,
Hiss, slither and wind yourself Kaalia,
Come to me from the dungeons underground.
You are magical, whimsical, a creature of Maya.
Tell me the secrets of magic and reveal the ace of spades.

And now for Robyn,
Fly to me, like a rush of wind, O Robyn,
You are a deceiver, a creature of illusion.
Build me castles, fairy tales and lands of promise.
And come to me in one of your many disguises.'

Madhumati thanked Anirban, while Nini,
Sheepishly asked a question again,
'Can we summon both of them together?'
And Anirban laughed saying, 'You never fail to amuse me
But there is no such incantation,

To summon the two together,
You must chant the incantation for one,
And then for the other.'

Anirban, then asked Madhumati
To lend him a ear.
He described his woes.
The *Mata Rani* (Queen Mother) Yashoda
Of the province had been captured
By the great Tantrika, Asura.

Asura, a demon and a Tantrika,
Was well versed in the art of Tantra,
That ancient science of secret rituals,
That summoned dark spirits and powers.

He also held sway over the underworld,
And had a large army of demons.
He had taken Yashoda *mata*,
To that weird world, called Dystopia.

Dystopia was a land,
Where effect preceded cause,
Where darkness prevailed over light,
Where the bad ruled over good,
Where evil spirits created havoc,
Where demons trounced angels,
Where Asura revelled in hedonism,
As clouds of death and destruction
Rained putrid, prurient phlegm
And bile that made a sensitive soul
Nauseous and hateful towards the surroundings.

In order to reach Dystopia
Madhumati had to climb to the summit
Of all the plateaus of Madhya Pradesh.
Anirban told her the hymns,
That she would have to elicit
At the top of each summit,
To complete the magical spell,
That would then take her to Dystopia.

She started with the foothills of the Malwa Plateau,
She swam the Betwa river with ease,
And reached the Narmada river's banks.
The Narmada river was raging with fury.
She had to negotiate with the Naramada at its banks.

Then, she began climbing the walls of the Raisen ravines.
Wherever she found a foothold, she latched on to it.
At times, holding her weight only by her fingernails.
Finally, she managed to scale the Malwa plateau.
Once on top, she screamed the following hymn,
At the top of her lungs,

'By Ergin, And by the Lord of the underworld,
Grant me passage to Dystopia,
Grant me passage and grant me rights,
To the secret recesses of the underworld.'

Her ascent of the other plateaus,
The Central Indian Plateau,
The Bundelkhand Plateua,
The Vindhyan Plateau,
The Baghelkhand highlands,
The Satpura and Maikal region,
And Eastern Plateau,
Can be described as treacherous,

As she had to scale sheer cliffs,
Negotiate rivers full of dangerous beasts like crocodiles,
Wade through dangerous swamps,
Evade capture by indigenous cannibal tribes,
Avoid poisonous snakes, reptiles,
Mountain cats, wild dogs, bears,
Nettles, wasps, hornets, wild bees,
And the occasional swarm of army ants.

The forests of the region were full of dangers
That lurked in hidden recesses,
Like quick sand, moats full of filth,
Swamps full of flesh eating piranhas,
Pools carrying box jellyfish,
Desert like terrain with rattle snakes,
Vipers and mambas.

At times, she ate fruits,
That seemed luscious and sweet,
But turned out to be poisonous
And she had to use all her knowledge
Acquired from her guru Drona to administer
An antidote in time and save herself.

But somehow, she managed
To scale all the plateaus,
And arrived at the gates
Of Dystopia, safe and sound.

Anirban had told her about Dystopia,
Being guarded
By seven demons
Who were like the seven deadly sins;
Ahankara (pride), Lobha (greed),
Vasana (lust), Irshya (envy),
Kopa (wrath), Lolupta (gluttony)
And Alasya (sloth).

These seven demons
Were the servants of Asura.
If one were to defeat the seven,
One could put causality in the right order,
Convert Dystopia to Utopia,
And end the evil rule of Asura.

Madhumati had contrived a strategy.
It involved acting like a child,
And invoking some spirits
That could counter the very nature
Of these demons.
And then playing games with the demons.
She reached the house of Ahankara,
And took the form of a little girl.

She invoked the spirit of Namratha (politeness),
By chanting, 'By Ergin,
I invoke the blessed child of Shanti(peace),
Namratha, to bless me with her presence.'
She spoke to Ahankara,
'Let's play the game of Patience.'

Seeing the little girl,
He laughed at her,
And agreed to play the game.

The game of patience
As outlined by Madhumati, the little girl,
Involved picking matching pairs of cards.
The one who picked the maximum pairs, won.

The game began, and true to his nature,
Ahamkara started cheating.
Madhumati and Namratha,
Politely ignored the fact that he was cheating
And continue to play the game
As if nothing had happened.

In due course of time, Namratha started to pay off,
While Ahamkara's cheating amounted to nothing,
Madhumati won the game.

Ahankara was stupefied,
And fell at Madhumati's feet.
He felt belittled and defeated.
He vowed to correct his nature.

Madhumati left for Lobha's quarters.
She now invoked the spirit of Tripthi(satisfaction),
By chanting, 'By Ergin,
I summon, the daughter of Satiation,
Tripti, and ask for her blessings.'

Together, they asked Lobha,
To join them in the game of Nim.

Lobha laughed at their childishness,
But succumbing to his greed,
Agreed to give them a chance.

The objective of Nim,
Was to remove either one or two stones,
From a pile,
And the last player remaining,
With no stones to remove,
Would be declared the loser.

The game began,
And true to his nature,
Lobha started removing as many stones as possible.
Madhumati and Tripthi were on fire,
Understanding the game's stratagem
Only picking as many stones as necessary.
Soon, Lobha emerged as the loser.

He realized that the girls
Had made a fool out of him,
Knowing very well, his nature.
He promised to change his ways.

Madhumati proceeded to the lavish lodgings of Vasana,
And found him lounging with a bevy of ladies.
She summoned the spirit of Saralta (simplicity)
By chanting, 'By Ergin, I summon
The daughter of Prakriti,
To guide me in victory over Vasana.'

Along with Saralta, she invited Vasana
For a dwanda (a duel).

Vasana, in his stupor of power,
Laughed a throaty laugh,
And derided the ladies,
Mocking them for their stupid decision
Of challenging him to a duel.
He agreed nonetheless, and the duel began.

Vasana was drunk and could barely walk two steps,
When Saralta grabbed his arms,
And lifting him over her shoulders,
Brought him crashing down on the ground.

As soon as his shoulders touched the ground,
The duel was over, it only took an instant.
Vasana was now rising out of his inebriated state
And realized the folly of his ways.
He promised to give up his promiscuous days.

Madhumati then headed towards Irshya's house.
She found Irshya lost in thought,
Planning something against her enemies.
Madhumati summoned the spirit
Of ShubhKamna(Good Wishes),
By chanting the hymn,
'I summon ShubhKamna, the daughter of Kamna(Wishing),
And wish that she alight on Dystopia.'

Madhumati and ShubhKamna together,
Invited Irshya to the simple game of Hopscotch.
Irshya, laughed at their foolishness,
As they were only children,
And she was an adult.
Clearly, they were no competition,
But she wanted to see them defeated,
And readily agreed, taking the first turn.

The game began, proceeded and ended,

As Irshya had expected,
She won with ease.
All this time,
She felt like Madhumati and Shubhkamana
Were throwing the game away.
She was surprised,
When ShubhKamana came to her,
And said 'Congratulations, Didi(Sister).'
It was then that it dawned on her,
The little child only wanted good things for her,
While she was being selfish and cruel.
At that moment she changed,
And promised them
That she would reform herself.

Madhumati played similar games
With Kopa, Lolupta
And Alasya.

With Kopa, she summoned Shanti(Peace)
And played the game of Prema(Love).
With Lolupta, she summoned Upawasa(fasting)
And played the hunger games,
And with Alasya, she summoned Karma (Work),
And played the game of Bhaagya (Destiny).

One by one, all the demons,
Succumbed to her childish charms,
And as the last demon fell,
Causality was made right,
And Dystopia became Utopia.

Asura'a throne started shaking
And he began quivering with fright.
He fled from Utopia,
Fearing for his life,
From the angels,

Who had now taken over,
And Madhumati freed Yashoda Mata.

Madhumati emptied a decanter
And poured wine into an empty goblet.
As she drank the last dregs of the rose wine,
She penned her third poem to Sibu,
'I Miss You'

I miss you like the rivers miss the rain,
Like the devils miss a refrain,
And like fateful events set in a chain
Which bind lovers to each other again and again.

I miss you like the clouds miss the sun,
When its dark and gloomy, because hun,
I have become one with you in body and mind,
In soul and in the very essence of my being.

I miss you like the flowers miss a bee,
When spring arrives and nature looks on with glee,
At blossoms in the bower and fruits give power,
Of flesh, fragrance and nourishment to children.

I miss you like the sea misses the shore,
As wave after wave of joy crashes at my door,
To bring news of you, a brave knight in shining armour,
Who will rescue me in my darkest hour.

I miss you my love, like a lover misses soulful eyes,
As they cast a spell on the onlooker
And hold him besotted.
For they have been moist
With the pain of solitude,
And twinkle with stars,
As they accepted love's gratitude.

I miss you my love, as if I am a child,
Who is running towards an angel from heaven,
Brought down to the land to bring yuletide,
Pomp, show and glamour,
And most of all, the love in my life.

Discourse on the Mind

Vani eyes were fixed on Darpan's face as she spoke, 'Darpan, did you like travelling to the dark underworld of Swati? I was scared out of my wits, to be honest. What did you make of the hilly terrain of Madhya Pradesh; its tribals, the colorful festivals and the spiritual world?'

Darpan was lost in thoughts, while Vani's question caused a break in the chain of his thoughts. He woke up with a start and spoke, 'The underworld gives me the creeps. As a child, I used to think there were monsters underneath my bed and I always slept between Dad and Mumma, holding onto her tightly, lest the monsters should decide to pounce on me in the dark. I find Madhya Pradesh enchanting, to say the least, if not fascinating, as it sounds saturated with legends. I wish I could travel with Madhumati to the province when she sought to inculcate correct behaviours in the demons and fix Dystopia. Can you please explain the metaphors of the body and the mind?'

Vani spoke and her voice was full of wisdom, distilled over the ages, 'Pashupati lets the underworld get the better of him because he lets the spirits take over his body. He does not use his mind, the most powerful of his possessions, his sparkling intellect. Madhumati is wise beyond her years and transforms herself into a child, making the demons overconfident of themselves. At the same time, she does not get intimidated by them, as she is not listening to her bodily instincts. Instead, she lets her mind take over the interactions and summons the appropriate spirits, recalling her learnings and then with the help of those spirits, emerges as the victor, the superior mind.'

Darpan surmised, 'So we must always exercise our minds, not the powers of our body.'

Deekha cautioned, 'It's always mind over matter. One must use the body to do the physically demanding, strenuous tasks, but in situations that demand mental rigour, the mind must be called into action.'

Darpan summarized, 'It takes love over gold and mind over matter, to do what you must.'

Vani started singing a lyric.

I was walking alone,
Lost in the thought of you,
When I came upon a child,
And held his hand.

I asked his name,
And he said,
'What's in a name, Ma'am?
Am I not someone you know now?'

Now I know him like I know you,
For we spoke of names,
Games, loves and rhymes,
And sang till the moon came out.

He then looked at me,
And told me, 'I am your soul,
And your mind, and your heart,
And your lover, and your child.'

Tears rolled down my eyes,
I took his head in my lap,
Kissed him gently,
Lulled him to sleep,
And as the stars came out
He faded away in my arms.

Part 4
Battle for Togetherness

Sheeta

Deeksha described the bleakness of sorrow

Pashuapti, Ritu, Pavan, Jal and Dhara
Found themselves on a cold and bleak terrain.
The planet had become dark and desolate,
The trees shrunk to hardened stumps,

Water streams had become frozen,
It snowed so much,
That animals succumbed to frostbite
And birds fell like flies from the air.

Cold and dry winds blew in from the north,
Carrying with them, hail and snow,
Piling up mountains of frost
On the Earth, making it ice laden.

Life had come to a standstill,
All of humanity and children had disappeared,
And the lands looked haunted,
As if they were home to dark spirits.

Pashupati and the girls were in a limbo,
Not able to decide what to do.
Without Jyoti, there was no source of warmth,
And with the cold biting at them,
They were not able to think clearly.

Suddenly, Ritu came up with a plan.
She decided on a game of love.
If Pashupati could make love to Ritu,
To begin with, and then with each of the sisters

The heat generated could dispel the cold.

Pashupati did not need any instructions on the matter.
He pulled Ritu towards himself,
And started teasing, tickling and toying with her.
He removed the pin that held her hair in a bun,
And her hair loosened down in a streaming cascade.

He began caressing her silken hair,
Taking time to knead her temples with his thumbs,
At the same time, stroking her neck gently.
Their foreplay caused heat to build up in ether,
And it seemed for a while that their plan would work.

But, unknown to Pashupati and Ritu,
Something was happening to Pavan, Jal and Dhara,
The heat caused Pavan to blow hot,
Jal to release steam,
And Dhara to break into hot geysers.
It seemed like they were envious of the love
Between Pashupati and Ritu.

Suddenly, Pashupati pulled Ritu by her hair,
And gave her a passionate, imploring kiss,
That made her lose her senses,
And she almost lost her balance,
Falling to the ground.

As a result, the seasons became troubled even further,
And the heat began to rise.
Wind now became hot and cold,
Leading to the formation of fog.
Water started flowing faster as it was now hot,
Colliding with icebergs and breaking them into icicles.

The Earth exploded in various places,
As the heat trapped inside burst forth.
But the steam soon condensed in the cold
To form droplets of rain which provided more water
For snow, icicles and icebergs to take form.
The end result of all this was even more cold.

Pashupati and Ritu saw all that happened,
And broke free from their kiss.
They were surprised to see Prakriti and Maya,
Who had come to announce,
That Pashupati and Ritu, along with her sisters
Had failed at their first task.
Now, they had to prepare for the next,
Which was to control nature's abundance
Arriving in the form of Basanta.

The Chandras

Vani celebrated the colors of happiness.

Madhumati came back from her odyssey,
And she had only one thing on her mind.
She could not stop thinking about Sibu lovingly,
The thought of him had her in a bind.

As soon as she entered Simhagadh,
She rushed to Sibu's quarters.
But he was not to be found,
And hence, she ran towards the auditorium.

Not being able to find Sibu anywhere,
She began to despair.
Could anything have happened to him somewhere,
While she was away, Oh! how much for him she cared.

She went back to her house,
And found her four sisters laughing and chatting.
Unable to contain her curiosity,
She asked them the reason for their laughter.

To which Urvashi replied,
'Now that Sibu has been dispatched,
I am sure you have another task at hand.'
Madhumati was aghast and suddenly collapsed.

When she came to her senses,
Kamakshi explained everything to her.
While she was away,
The four sisters got busy.
They put Sibu in a hex,
From which he was to be freed,

And Madhumati was to be his liberator,
Since he was so in love with her,
And she with him.
When asked why, they said they had done it on a whim.
Madhumati put two and two together,
And understood that the sisters could not bear,
Their love for each other.
She asked them, 'Tell me about the hex.'
To which the sisters replied,
'Oh! for you, it will be a simple quest.

You must journey to the four kingdoms,
Of the Meenas, the Ashwas,
The Suryas and the Chandras.
And finish some tasks laid out by us.

You shall meet one of us at each of the kingdoms.
Now hurry up and rush towards the Chandras.
To make it easy for you,
We offer our gifts from our gurus to you.

You may have Kamakshi's book of potions,
Urvashi's bow and arrows,
Menaka's wand and Ritambhara's crystal ball.'
With these words, the sisters left her and she looked pale.
However, she gathered herself immediately,
And decided to leave for Chandra's country.

She arrived at the Chandra capital, ChandraKumari,
Where she was met by Kamakshi,
Who explained to her the first part of the hex.

She said, 'You begin at the temple of ChandraKumbha,
Where you are to enter the first chamber,
It's the temple's guest chamber,
And once you solve the dilemma in there,
You will be led to other chambers,

Where more puzzles await you.'

Madhumati asked, 'What kind of puzzles are these?'
To which, Kamakshi replied, 'It's just quarrels of lovers.
At each chamber you will meet a couple,
At a different stage of their love affair.
You must help them in the best way possible,
Taking into account what they need most at that time.
Before entering each chamber, you shall meet me,
And I will explain to you the task ahead.
For instance, in the first chamber,
You shall meet Romeo and Juliet, the fabled lovers.

Let me tell you about the lovers now,
They are from Italy and their families are sworn enemies.
The two families, Montagues and Capulets
Are from the city of Verona.
They are enemies, masters and servants alike.
The men who work for Montagues and Capulets,
Often get into street fights with swords and knifes.

Prince Escalus rules over Verona.
He asks the families to stop fighting,
Or face a punishment not to their liking.
Romeo is the only child of the Montagues,
A young teenage boy.

Juliet is the only daughter of the Capulets,
A fourteen year old svelte girl.
Since Juliet does not go anywhere,
Without her nursemaid taking care,
She does not know Romeo.

There is a masked ball at Juliet's parents' friends'.
Romeo attends the ball with his friends.
He meets Juliet and they fall in love.
To avoid trouble, they do not talk about their love.

Now when you meet Romeo and Juliet,
You must help them out.'
Saying this, Kamakshi retreated and faded out,
While Madhumati headed towards the ChandraKumbha.

She entered the guest chamber,
And found a sad, morose and desolate Romeo.
He said to her, 'My life has no meaning here,
I have been trying to meet my Juliet,
But her parents have confined her to their house.'

Madhumati thought for a while,
And then brought forth her crystal ball.
She gazed into it and said, 'O Crystal ball,
Show me other lovers who feel Romeo's pain.'

The Crystal ball displayed various other lovers,
Across many eras, who were separated from their beloveds.
Madhumati paused the ball's vision,
To take a look at a particular couple in union.

A girl confined to the balcony,
And a boy serenading her underneath.
This gave Madhumati the idea for victory,
And she told Romeo to come with her.
They went to Juliet's house together.

Madhumati waved her wand and asked for a guitar.
Poof! Appeared a brilliant classical guitar.
With the body of cherry wood,
And sound, most amazing,
She began with the first strum,
A song for lovers, she did sing.

'Juliet, my love, come out to the stars,
For they are near, not far,

Just like the stars in my eyes,
When I look at you with love's surprise.'

Suddenly the light switched on in Juliet's room.
Romeo got excited and started jumping around,
As if, flying on a witch's broom.
He snatched the guitar from Madhumati's hand,
And began to play a sweet serenade.

'Juliet, Julia, Julie! How many names shall I give to thee,
You are all that is meant for me.
I shall never be away from you,
And I shall give my heart too,
For you are the light of my life,
The apple of my eye,
And the morning sun doth shine,
Because it knows you are mine.'

Suddenly, Juliet appeared on her balcony,
And Romeo nearly fainted.
Soon however, he became aware of his victory,
In getting Juliet tainted,
With his love song and pleadings.

He sang again, 'Drop me a line my love,
So I can climb and meet thee,
For tonight is the night of the moon,
And of love's sweet glory.

Juliet dropped him a rope,
And Romeo climbed and hung on to it.
Soon they were together on the balcony,
And gave a flying kiss to Madhumati.

Her task completed, Kamakshi appeared.
'Well done,' she said.
'But now get ready for the second chamber,

Where you shall meet Majnu, the lover,
And Layla, who's tender.

Layla and Qays fell in love with each other,
When they were quite young,
But when they grew older,
Layla's father became against Layla and Qays
To be in each other's company.

Qays' obsession with Layla,
Led to their community give him,
The epithet of Majnu, as one was given to
Ibn-al-Maluwwa of the 'Amir tribe.

Qays started composing lyrical poems for Layla,
His efforts led to the locals calling him
Majnu or the madman.
He asked for Layla's hand in marriage,
But Layla's father refused saying,
'It'll be considered wrong to have one's daughter
Marry someone mentally challenged, like you.

Soon, Layla was married off to a nobleman,
Who was a merchant, loaded with riches.
He belonged to the Thaqif tribe in Taif.
His name was Ward Althaqafi,
And Ward means rose in Arabic.

Upon hearing of Layla's marriage,
Majnu left the tribal camp,
And began wandering the desert.
Now you must go and meet him and see what you can do.'

Madhumati entered the second chamber,
And found Majnu in a distraught state.
He was being chased by a crowd that thundered,
Beat him and scolded him; they were so full of hate.

'Pelt him, pelt him with stones, that's his punishment,'
They chanted, 'He is evil, Majnu is evil.'
Madhumati realized that she must save him from the pelting,
And from the punishment ordained by these evil people.

She immediately charted out a plan for rescue.
She chanted the incantation for Chetak,
And the flying horse appeared in time due.
She mounted the horse and held him by the reins.

Instantly, the horse started galloping,
She raced towards Majnu, who was now floundering,
And pleaded with him to get on top,
Together they galloped away and did not stop.

Soon after, the horse spread its wings,
And started to soar through the clouds.
Majnu was delighted, he had escaped by a thin margin.
He was now free to go wherever he chose.
He begged Madhumati to take him to Layla's house.
They flew across the village and reached her house in no time,
Only to find it surrounded by guards
Appointed by her rich husband.

Madhumati invoked with an incantation,
Kaalia the serpent, who appeared in a jiffy.
She tied a note around its neck,
And told him to get to Layla in a hurry.

Kaalia slithered past the guards,
And found Layla's chambers.
In the meantime, Madhumati gazed
Into the crystal ball's visions.
And she became aware
That the guards would find out about Layla's escape,
She summoned Robyn,

And told him to be ready.

Kaalia delivered the note to Layla and upon reading it,
She came to know that Majnu was waiting.
Kaalia changed his form to a female friend,
And together, they walked out of the house like fiends.

They gave the guards a slip, but not for long,
For they heard Majnu singing one of his songs.
They rushed to grab hold of Layla and Majnu,
By now Robyn had created a fog and it grew.
Madhumati, Laila and Majnu, with Kaalia and Robyn,
All mounted the horse and flew away.

The task being complete, Kamakshi came again,
'Excellent Madhumati,' she said, 'You've done it again.
We have a final task and for this stage,
I'll see if you have come of age.

You must have heard of Mahiwaal and Sohni,
But if you haven't, then Madumati,
Sohni and Mahival's love caused quite a commotion,
Within the Kumhar community because the notion,
That a daughter of this community,
Must marry a person who is an outsider.
So a marriage was arranged by her parents immediately,
And Sohni was send to the house of an elder.

Mahiwal renounced the world,
And began living as a hermit.
Eventually, he moved to a small hut,
Across the river Chenab from Sohni's homely world.

In the middle of the night,
With everyone fast asleep,
The lovers would meet.
Sohni made a vow that she promised to keep.

Mahiwal would wait by the river everyday,
And she swam across the river,
With the help of a baked earthen pot,
Baked, so that it would stay afloat.

In the next chamber you will find them,
Go help them if you can, with your stratagem.'
Madhumati entered the next chamber,
And took out the crystal ball given to her.

She gazed into it and saw Sohni's sister-in-law,
Replacing Sohni's pitcher with a half baked one,
And after the evil woman had a private guffaw.
Madhumati became aware of the wicked plan, however.

She immediately materialized Robyn,
And told him to go to Mahiwal at dawn,
And tell him to wait a little longer than usual,
For the night would be long.

She told Sohni about the half baked pitcher,
And indeed Sohni found it out.
Madhumati then used her bow to create warriors,
And asked them to chop wood with their axes.
She summoned the angels with her trumpet,
And asked them to be the wood carriers.

Together with Chetak,
The angels carried the wood to the riverside.
They lay it down there and started building a raft.
In no time it was made.

Madhumati now asked Robyn to fly across the river,
And inform Mahiwal of Sohni's raft.
He waited on the shore to receive his beloved,
And soon Sohni was united with Mahiwal.

On completing the task, Kamakshi arrived again.
'You have passed the test, Madhumati,' she said.
'Now you must head towards the Kingdom of the Ashwas,
Where Urvashi awaits you and so do their warriors.'

Discourse on Joy

Vani's eyes were tired with sleep, but she carried on the conversation with Darpan, 'Darpan, have you ever liked snow and extreme cold? Could you see the contrast between the cold weather and the heart warming tales of the lovers Romeo and Juliet, Layla and Majnu and Sohni and Mahiwal?'

Darpan gushed, 'I love it, the winters I mean. It's my favourite season. I love making a snowmen and putting carrot noses on them. I also love making snowballs and pelting my dad and mumma with them. I am fascinated by love stories too, always wishing that the lovers be united at the end in some sort of an epic climax that makes a supernova look weak in comparison. Can you please elaborate on the metaphors of sorrow and happiness?'

Vani lovingly nudged thoughts and words in his direction, stirring his childish mind to enlightenment, 'Sheeta stands for extreme cold, a dark place that we all run away from, a metaphor for sorrow, exemplified by the story of Pashupati who is not able to stir up enough love with Ritu. While Chandra, the moon, is also a cold place, yet it has some semblance of joy as it brings us tidal waves and a pleasant coolness instead of bitter cold. Madhumati is able to unite the lovers by bringing in their life music, science and art.'

Darpan exhaled and felt better, 'I can see why Madhumati excels at tasks as she is sweetness exemplified, while Pashupati stands for the exact opposite, a beast amongst men. So it makes sense that one brings happiness, while the other bears sorrow.'

Deeksha added, 'Sorrow and happiness go hand in hand. One must experience the bitterness of sorrow to understand truly the sweetness of happiness.'

Darshan spoke poetically, 'In my opinion Keats summed it up well in a line, 'A thing of beauty is joy forever.''

Vani started singing and dancing again.

Don't leave me child,
For you are the apple of my eye,
The joy of my life,
The cherry on top.

If you go away,
It will be cold all day,
And snow shall fall
Over the hearth where embers once burned.

One look from your eyes,
Is all I seek all day.
One touch from your hand,
And my body burns like the sun's rays.

Since you've been gone,
My days are empty and sad,
And my eyes are dreary and wet,
'Cause without you, nothing looks well.

The day you'll be back,
The garden shall sing,
The flowers will play,
The sunlight will dance,
And the stream of joy
Will flow on and on.

Basanta

Deeksha described the harshness in ruthlessness

Pashuapti, Ritu, Pavan, Jal and Dhara
Found themselves looking at a hedonistic Nature.
Everywhere they looked, there was excess.

Flowers were popping out of the ground
Like tadpoles teeming in puddles.
Trees began taking over as forests,
Not a patch of land was left untouched.

Lakes began to overflow with water,
Fish began to pullulate,
Swarms and shoals began to swim
All over the overflowing oceans and seas.

The atmosphere expanded beyond the horizon,
Birds began mating whenever they got a chance,
New species of birds were sighted too,
Along with grasshoppers, nymphs and crickets.

The whole environment buzzed with the sound
Of whistling parrots, cooing cuckoos,
Chirping crickets, screeching bats,
Howling dogs, meowing cats,
Roaring lions, neighing horses,
Trumpeting elephants, mooing cows,
Bleating sheep, cackling crows,
Barking deer, hooting owls,
And roosting birds.

Pashupati, the King of Beasts himself, was flummoxed.

He had no idea how to control these wild beasts.
Even if he could calm them down somehow,
He wondered how he could ever control the elements.

Out of ideas, he turned towards the sisters.
The sisters, in their desperation, came up with a plan.
They started squeezing all the resources.

Pavan began sucking air out of the atmosphere.
Jal started extricating water from the land.
And Dhara started to make the earth itself recede.

Pashupati considered the plan an excellent idea.
Little did he know that the plan would soon backfire.

As Pavan began to remove air,
Birds began to drop down and die,
Trees began to droop and fall,
And animals began to choke and breathe their last.

The removal of water by Jal had similar consequences.
Trees stopped sprouting fresh leaves,
Birds' songs turned to noise,
And animals started running for their lives.

The final straw on the camel's back
Was recession of the land itself,
As entire trees became fodder for the planet's belly,
Animals began to sink down marshes and swamps,
And the last remains of life dwindled.

Once again, Prakriti and Maya appeared,
And declared that Pashupati, Ritu and her sisters
Had failed at the task of controlling Basanta.

They still had a chance,
As their next task was to rein in Grishma.

The Ashwas

Vani basked in the happiness of forgiving.

Madhumati reached the Kingdom of the Ashwas,
And was greeted there by Urvashi,
Who jumped straight to explaining the tasks to her.
She said, 'In the palace auditorium,
You will meet Singh's general and get an ultimatum.

You must thwart the invading forces of Aryan.
The battle of Samarkand has been lost by him
And he has turned his attention to India,
Since reaching the banks of Chenab.
He wants to expand his empire into Punjab.

The northern parts are under the rule of Bir Singh.
But the empire is falling apart,
And has had many defectors revealed.
Aryan was invited by Sher Singh and Vikram Singh.
He sent an ambassador to Bir Singh too,
Claiming himself the heir to the throne of India

The ambassador was held at Lahore and released later.
Aryan began for Lahore and Punjab,
But discovered Sher Singh's dismissal
By the armies sent by Bir Singh.
On Aryan's arrival at Lahore,
The Singh army marched to Dibalpur
And placed Maan Singh as the governor.

Maan Singh was deposed and he left for Kabul.
Troops were supplied to Maan Singh by Aryan,
And these troops joined Sher Singh,
As they laid siege to Bir Singh at Delhi.
He defeated them and drove away Maan Singh's army.

Aryan understood that Singh
Would not let him have Punjab.

Now Madhumati, you are supposed to join the battle.'

Madhumati turned to her crystal ball again.
She analyzed the size of Aryan's army,
And took over the command of Bir Singh's forces.
She secured the right flank against the city of Ranikhet.

She took the help of her angels by sounding the trumpet,
And dug trenches, covering them with tree branches,
To secure the left flank.
Further, she invoked with her bow, the warriors,
And tied together hundreds of carts with ropes.
Between carts, she placed the woodwork for men on horses.
She surveyed the trenches with Chetak, the horse.

When Aryan's army arrived,
They were trapped and found the approach,
Too narrow to get through and attack.
Madhumati quickly took advantage of the field,
And surrounded them.

A lot of Aryan's forces were rendered useless,
And fled to the neighbouring forests.
Madhumati had also used her wand to summon cannons
And muskets.

Made to face cannon fire and musket fire,
The troops of Aryan were in circumstances dire.
The cannons were extraordinary,
The could be fired without any fear of getting hit,
As they were shielded by the carts
Held in place by ropes.

After the cannon fire and musket fire,

Madhumati let loose a line of archers.
A volley of arrows descended onto the Aryans,
And they ran helter-skelter.

Later, to trounce the Aryans completely,
Madhumati ordered a cavalry charge.
With armed bayonets the cavalry charged
At full steam to bring the battle to a victory.

This task being accomplished, Urvashi appeared.
'Bravo Madhumati, you have done well,' she said.
'Now get ready for your second task.
This is a battle at Chaurashi,
On the banks of the Bhagirathi River,
North of Calcutta and south of Murshidabad.

The armies are those of Bengal's Chandragupta
And the invading forces of Mongolia, of Ogdai Khan.
The Mongol has formed a pact with the deposed chief
Of Chandragupta, BirPaani along with others,
Forming a formidable force to combat Chandragupta.

Chandragupta's army has 40,000 soldiers,
50 cannons, and 20 war elephants.
This battle is gauged to be substantially relevant
In the control of the Indian subcontinent.

Ogdai Khan had first landed with his armada off the coast
Of Madras and the weak garrison there had surrendered.
The Nawab of Carnatic tried to retake the Madras coast,
But despite superiority in numbers, he was easily crushed.

Later, Ogdai Khan laid siege to Pondicherry,
And attacked and seized Arcot, Carnatic's capital.
The Raja Sahib of the Marathas sent reinforcements
To battle against Ogdai Khan, but his armoured elephants,
Caused a stampeed when faced with Ogdai's musketry.

With successes at Conjeevaram, Trichinopoly and Arcot,
Ogdai Khan secured the Carnatic.
Further, a large force under Ogdai Khan
Sacked the town of Hooghly,
North of Calcutta.

On learning of this attack,
Chandragupta garrisoned his forces
And reached Calcutta.
He was clearly outnumbered.

Your task is now to help thwart Ogdai Khan.'
Madhumati, having understood the task,
Entered the chamber and immediately took
The forces of Chandragupta under her command.

She chose the tactic of guerrilla warfare,
As it suited an outnumbered army.
Besides Chandragupta's army,
She summoned her own warriors, using the bow.

She divided them into *agrasena,*
Visheshsena, nipunasena,
Bheetsena, and *vanasena.*
For each sena she made factions,
Called the guna or multiples,
Each guna, or multiples of warriors,
Functioned and attacked as a unit.

They took their orders
From their unit's leader.
They used the tactic of surprise attacks.
The vanasena used jungle warfare,
The agrasena used frontal warfare,
The nipunasena used skilled warfare,
While the bheetsena and the Visheshsena

Used martial warfare.

Together, these forces started attacking
Ogdai Khan's troops in tandem.
Madhumati supervised the overall formation herself,
While riding the horse Chetak, at random.

Soon, all hell broke loose,
As Ogdai Khan's troops started
Suffering massive casualties,
And their morale took a beating for good.

The tactic of guerrilla warfare had paid off,
As Ogdai Khan's troops did not know,
Where the attack would come from,
And where they could be let off.

The battle was over soon,
And Chandragupta emerged victorious.
Madhumati had done it again,
And Urvashi appeared looking frazzled.

She said, 'Good job, Madhumati,
But don't rest on your laurels,
For again you have to pick your shovels,
And start digging war trenches,
Because the next battle is the battle of ChandraTati.

One army is that of Rana Kanwar,
Whose main commanders are Man Singh,
Krishndas Purohit and Surjit Singh.
His army also includes Afghans led by Pasha Khan,
And Bhil tribals led by Nakul Gond.
He is also accompanied by Vikram of Marwar.

The Rana's army has 10,000 soldiers,

Of which 5000 are horse-borne,
3000 are part of the infantry,
1000 are on top of elephants,
And another 1000 are spearmen.

Besides this, there are the Bhil tribesmen,
500 in number, led by Nakul Gond along with Afghans.
The Army formation is thus,
Harawal (front portion) led by Man Singh,
Chandrawal(back portion) led by Surjit Singh
And south (right) adjacent led by Pasha Khan.

Rana himself is at the center of things
Along with his minister, Veer Bahadur Singh.
The surrounding mountains hide the infantry of the Bhils.

The other force is that of the invading Moghul Taimur,
He has deputed his General Shakur,
To lead a large army against Rana.
Rana has advanced with an army
Nearly half in size as that of Taimur,
And has reached Chandratati.

Anticipating the attack of the Moghul,
Rana sacked the entire region upto Chittor,
To prevent the Moghul
Army's access to food and shelter.

Your job Madhumati, is to thwart the invading forces.'
Madhumati takes control of Rana's armies.
Since she is outnumbered by a large margin,
She makes an engimatic *vyuha*.
It is the *chakravyuha*
With all the commanders at the center,
And soldiers are laid out in the form of a *chakra*,
That is, in the shape of a spiral.

With their spears drawn,
And standing shoulder to shoulder,
They made for quite a sight from dusk to dawn,
And looked as if they were made of rocks and boulders.

She placed the cavalry and the elephants at the periphery,
And then let Taimur's forces attack.
For she knew she could have a sure victory,
If her soldiers kept to their barracks.

The battle began and Madhumati sent out the Bhils,
And the Afghans
Out to initiate the battle,
And to bait Taimur's forces
Into her maze, like herded cattle.

They fell for the trap,
And chased the Bhils and Afghans,
Straight into the *chakravyuha*,
Where they were met with the cavalry, the spearmen,
And the elephants too.

The first onslaught on Taimur's forces
Was that of the spearmen.
They brought down his horses,
With their spears drawn.

The next wave of assault,
Was the cavalry,
Which led a victory
Charge over Taimur's infantry.

This was followed by a complete rout,
By elephants that were stout.
Within moments, Taimur's armies were shot.
The task being completed, Urvashi came out.

She exclaimed, 'Stupendous, Madhumati! Well done again.
You have bettered yourself time and again.
Now is the time for your last exercise at this stage.
It is the battle between Paxter and Horus.

It is the Battle of Corinthus,
Fought at the banks of the river Corinthus,
Which is close to the north west border of India.
Paxter's army has decided to cross
The monsoon swollen Corinthus,
Despite it being under the surveillance of Horus.

The location of the battle, according to a Buddhist source,
Is where an ancient road,
Crosses the Corinthus river's banks,
And is perhaps the modern city of Fuschia.

After defeating the Arachnid Empire's forces
Under the great Theseus,
Paxter began a new campaign to extend his empire
Towards India.

Possessing a large army, an estimated,
50,000 infantry, 6000 cavalry,
He crossed the river to fight and conquer.
However, Paxter was outnumbered 3:1 or 4:1.

Paxter's column entered via the Shuber Pass,
But a smaller force went through the northern route,
Taking the fortress of Minkonos enroute,
A place of mythological significance to the Greeks.

Paxter has to subdue Horus in order to march east.
It would endanger further exploit,
If he were to leave such a strong opponent at his flanks.
Horus has to defend his kingdom
And pick the right spot to halt Paxter's advance.

Paxter crossed the Corinthus river,
And Horus lay waiting across the river.
Paxter set camp in the town of Palem,
On the right banks of the river.
Horus drew up on the southern bank of the Corinthus river,
To thwart any crossing troops.

The Corinthus was swift and deep enough,
That any opposition to a crossing would
Have spelled disaster for an attacking force.
Paxter knew that a straight approach had little chance,
Of victory and tried to look for alternative fords.

He moved his cavalry up and down the river
Bank each night,
While Horus shadowed him like a fox.

The most historical event in the battle
Was Paxter's crossing of the Corinthus.
The devious preparations for it
Were managed with the help of numerous feints,
And other sorts of deceptions.
Horus was kept continuously on the move,
Until he called it a bluff and relaxed.

His portion of the army was led upstream
By Paxter and then he traversed in secrecy
Using skin floats filled with hay,
And smaller vessels cut in half.

Crotus, Paxter's general, engaged in frequent feints,
Regarding crossing the river.
Paxter soon landed on an island,
And then crossed to the other side.

News of Paxter's crossing reached Horus,

And he readied his forces
To meet Paxter in battle.
It's now your task Madhumati, to defend against Paxter.'

Madhumati gazed into her crystal ball again,
And took command of Horus's troops.
She deployed her forces
And commenced with the attack.

Horus's forces were poised with cavalry at both flanks,
Their center consisting of infantry,
With war elephants,
Rising above them in equal intervals.

Paxter's infantry was outnumbered 1:5.
And the heavy armour-piercing bows
Of Horus were proving their strength.
Paxter's army, located across from Horus's
Army, crossed the river to meet the elephants.
Madhumati herded the elephants
And their large number
Prevented a frontal attack.

Madhumati, destroying Paxter's right flank,
Circled around to Paxter's left flank
And began a massive attack against him from there.
She correctly guessed Paxter's maneuvres
Of moving the cavalry from the right to the left flank.

She used a trap for this cavalry movement,
By building a gulch from which, the archers
Could target the massive movement
Of cavalry riders.

As soon as the cavalry began moving,
The archers let go of their arrows.
Soon, the cavalry was finished,

And Paxter was in a bind.

Whatever was left of his army,
Madhumati finished off with her elephants.
She led a rout on the infantry,
Leading a battle charge with a victory cry.

The final task being over,
Urvash arrived again,
And congratulated Madhumati, albeit with a sigh.
She said, Now you must head over to the Suryas,
And then to the Meenas,
Where you will meet Ritambhara and Menaka,
To perform the final tasks
Before you and Sibu can unite.

Discourse on Kindness

Vani's eyes gazed on at the distant horizon as she spoke, 'Darpan, did you like the blazing, blooming burst of Basanta, bringing with it the fragrance and colors of its blossoms. Did you relish the battles that Madhumati fought?'

Darpan blurted out, 'I must admit, the child in me, in its depravity, enjoyed the excesses of Basanta, half wishing that it would take over the entire planet. I am beginning to wonder whether Pashupati is Madhumati's child, the erring infant who is not wise at all and is prone to fits. Pashupati's behaviour is based on a kind of an animal instinct, indicating that he has a reactive mind prone to risky behaviour which leads to poor results. Madhumati, his mother, is always cool and considers every scenario before she arrives at a decision, thus achieving success. Can you please explain the metaphors of ruthlessness and forgiveness?'

Vani explained, 'Ritu and Pashupati together as a team, are animalistic, moved only by their instincts and hence ruthless. When Basanta manifests this ruthlessness in her external behaviour, they are not able to come to terms with it. What Basanta needs, is someone to soothe her. Instead, they deprive her of essential elements, leading to further chaos. The Ashwa or the horse, is the King of animals who stands for forgiveness, a virtue displayed best by Madhumati. She takes to battle, but only to thwart the attacking forces, never to inflict harm on anyone. She is always a gracious victor, letting the defeated armies retreat in peace, thereby forgiving them.'

Darpan questioned, 'So, is it better to forgive and forget, than to punish and regret?'

Deeksha replied, 'Yes. Kindness is the best policy, especially in the face of hate and ruthlessness.'

Darshan summarized, 'The pen is mightier than the sword.'

Vani remembered something that she had penned and started singing.

Kindness in your eyes,
Is not a surprise,
As I have known you,
Since I was a child,

When you took me in your arms,
Told me sweet stories,
Held me tight,
And made my fears go away,

And what have I known,
Other than your beaming smile,
Shining down on me like the sun.
I never felt about anyone,
Like I feel about you,

Tender, sweet, soft, delicate, cool,
Mumma, you are the one,
I thought about all day,
At school, at play and at work.

If I could ask God,
For one thing,
I would ask for you,
And only the thought of you.

Grishma

Deeksha described the fire of destruction.

Pashuapti, Ritu, Pavan, Jal and Dhara
Found themselves looking at nature on fire.
Everywhere, heat was taking its toll

The the land sprouted hot geysers,
And steam whistled out from the cracks.
Hot magma started flowing from open crevices.

As the terrain became warmer, trees began to die.
All plant life started to wilt,
And the roots of trees were made bare and exposed.

Air began to heat up and vortices began to form.
Dust storms, sand storms and cyclones started brewing.
It became difficult for life forms to be without shelter.

As air became hot, flowers began to droop,
Birds fell from the sky,
Bees and the insect kingdom suffered much harm.

Water started to boil and currents began to form,
Fish began to come to the surface and die.
And all kinds of aqueous plants withered to bits.

Most of all, ether itself began to heat up,
And the entropy, enthalpy, inertia and gravity,
Started to get affected.
Stellar systems seemed like they would fall apart
As pressure began to build up in the stars.

The sisters thought it would be easier this time,
As Jyoti, the very source of fire was missing,
So they came up with a plan.

Their plan was to make Pashupati
Work with each of the sisters in a separate team.
With Pavan and Dhara he would drive winds.
With Jal and Dhara he would bring water.
And with Ritu he would calm nature's fury.

Pashupati started with Pavan,
And together they materialzed fast winds,
Which began to absorb heat
And currents started to form in the atmosphere.

Pashupati then worked with Jal,
And together they made ebbs and tides of water.
The waves that formed, soaked the excess heat,
And a stream of water began to flow to the oceans.

Pashupati then teamed up with Ritu
And together they danced the cool waltz,
Channelizing the heat in all directions,
Making it flow from their arms and feet
Towards the stars, into the outer atmosphere.

For a while, they thought their plan had worked.
To their dismay however,
Everything they had done had a flip side.

The wind current formed a permanent storm
That started feeding on itself,
And increased the heat flow even further.

The stream of water,
Started channelizing the heat out
Of the hot geysers, from the Earth's core.

And the heat flow from Ritu's dance to the stars
Was reflected right back,
As the stars intensified their glow.

Prakriti and Maya appeared,
And declared that they had failed in this task as well.
Their last task and perhaps the sole saving grace,
Was to hold together the season of rains.

The Suryas

Vani delved in things cool.

Madhumati reached the Kingdom of the Suryas
And upon reaching, found Menaka waiting there for her.
She was standing on delicate wisps of cotton candy clouds,
That seemed to disappear with misty sprays of water.

She descended from the clouds and started talking,
'O Madhumati, you have your task cut out.
This stage is full of magic and may leave you wanting.
You shall begin at the great colosseum,
Where you'll meet your first challenge,
Of which, I shall explain only a bit,
As it is in the form of a chimera,
An aggressive beast, half lion-half goat.'

With that she left Madhumati,
Who then proceeded to the colosseum.
She entered the building and found herself facing
The beast, its paws spread out, breathing fire
From its nostrils and spewing foul invectives
From its mouth.

Not having any clue as to what to do,
Madhumati turned towards the crystal ball.
However, the crystal ball did not turn
Out to be of much help either,
For it just showed an image of the Chimera.

Madhumati picked up her magic wand
And summoned a magic sword.
She took a giant leap with the sword in hand,
And cut the head of the chimera in half.

The chimera lay chopped,
Head somewhere,
Body elsewhere.
Madhumati thought she had vanquished the beast.
But to her surprise,
The head and the body suddenly came together.
Thus began a new day of fighting, a new sunrise.

Madhumati summoned a fireball with her wand,
And burned the chimera to dust with it.
She thought, this time she had the beast for good.
But, like a phoenix rising from its ashes,
The chimera came to life again and stood tall.

Madhumati was now in a fix,
And summoned tremendous wind with her wand,
Trying to blast the chimera to the skies upward,
And then brought it down to the ground.
The chimera was crushed, fractured and destroyed.
But this time, Madhumati was skeptical of its demise.
And she was right, because from the splintered bones,
The chimera reassembled
And became its ferocious self again.

Madhumati realized that the Chimera was truly diabolical
And could not be destroyed with methods simple.
She came up with an idea, to make it fight itself.
She swerved the magic wand and created a clone of itself.
Out came a chimera, equally ferocious looking and inimical.

The opponent chimeras began fighting each other,
And what a sight it made.
It was fit for a camera,
A shot, panorama,
As if a martial arts gymkhana,
Fists flying, tails cracking,
Jaws biting and finally,

The chimera was demolished.

The task being finished,
Menaka appeared again,
And said,
'Well done,
But now, you must handle the angry birds,
So please proceed,
To the next chamber.'
Madhumati entered the next chamber,
And found herself facing Red,
Bomb, Terrence and Chuck.

Red has just come out of anger management,
Because of his resentment with the green pigs,
Especially their captain Leonard.
The pigs were from an island,
And had introduced the birds,
To new technologies,
Such as helium balloons and slingshots.

The pigs were holed-up in city walls,
And the birds wreaked havoc all over the place,
By throwing themselves with slingshots
At everyone who came, especially the pigs.
They caused a lot of damage with their bombs.

Madhumati's task was to rein-in the birds.
She talked to Kaalia,
Who suggested a plan that involved,
Capturing the birds in nets.

Thus, together they lay bread crumbs on the ground,
And spread a net on top of them.
When the birds would come to eat,
They'd get stuck in the net on the ground,
Forfeiting their flight forever.

The plan was all set,
The birds arrived and got stuck as planned.
But they were very clever,
And decide to take off with the net.
They manage to fly a small distance,
But then, got tired and stayed put.

Suddenly Red had an idea.
He decided to put Chuck and Bomb to use.
He asked Chuck to light Bomb up,
Who proceeded to light Bomb's fuse.
Bomb exploded and the net got blown away.
The birds escaped and Madhumati's plan was foiled.

Madhumati now looked into the crystal ball,
And it showed a bird singing in a cage.
She immediately thought of trapping the birds in cages.
With a wave of her want she produced gold cages,
Each with a clever trap inside to hold the bird in place.

Time came and the birds, upon finding the cage,
Were attracted by the food tantalisingly kept inside.
Bomb rushed into the cage and got trapped first.
Red became furious and assembled a team.
Together they catapulted themselves
Against the cage holding Bomb.
As they crashed against the cage,
The metal gave way and Bomb was freed.

Madhumati began to lose heart,
And started to wonder,
As to why the crystal ball showed,
Her the bird in the cage and the music.
She began whistling to herself,
And suddenly noticed a change in demeanour
Of the angry birds.

Suddenly it all came to her,
The birds were affected by music,
It had a calming effect on them.

She now had a new plan.
She waved the wand,
And materialized a huge cage,
Big enough to house all the birds,
And inside she placed a gramophone.
She then started playing a whistling melody
On it.

Soon the birds began flocking to the cage,
And as soon as all of them were inside,
Madhumati locked the door of the cage,
With all the birds becalmed and secure inside.

The task being complete,
Menaka arrived and gave kudos to Mahumati.
She also told her to leave for the Meenas,
Where the last set of tasks
Would be explained to her by Ritambhara.

Discourse on Cool

Vani felt a cool breeze hit her face and a chill ran up her spine. Instinctively she turned towards Darpan, hoping that he would hold her, as she whispered in a soft voice, ' Do you like the summers Darpan, the heat beating down from the sun, causing the animals and plants to yearn for shelter in cool winds and the occasional showers? Can you see how the magical kingdom of the Suryas, the sun metaphor that stands for heat, is paired opposite Grishma. Did you enjoy Madhumati's encounters with the magical creatures?'

Darpan's eyes shone like a child as he spoke, 'I don't like the summers. I can't bear the heat, it gives me heat strokes. If my mother had not smothered me with her mango *pannas* and lemonade, I would not have survived those unbearable summers. I feel that Pashupati, Ritu and the sisters are somehow jinxed. With Jyoti, the very source of heat in the seasons, gone, they should have been able to brave the summers, but they failed miserably. Madhumati has become magical, from the romantic warrior we knew. I guess, she understands the concept of duality better than we do. She materialized a dual of the chimera which is exactly what was needed. Please explain the metaphors of destruction and cool to me.'

Vani spoke in a sing song voice, 'Grishma stands for fire, the season of destruction, when life itself is destroyed so that it can be renewed and start afresh. The Surya empire stands for the sun, which is hot and yet cool at the same time, for it stands for something magical, heat, life giving rays that do not rain fire. Instead, they bring joy and happiness and carry away sorrow and depression. Madhumati has now become the epitome of cool, as she wields the wand and the sword with equal finesse. She is full of magic and love and is able to handle fearsome creatures, such as the chimera, as well as the naughty and tiresome angry birds, thanks to her cool demeanour.'

Vani began hearing voices in her head, and gave those words her voice.

C.O.O.L,
Baby you look so swell.
Hold me close, I like your smell.
Make me dance, the quick step.

I need you, you know it well.
If I were you, I could tell,
That I was falling apart
At the mention of me.

And yet, there was a certain
Coolness to me.
Bring me flowers.
Bring me wine.

Baby, you look so fine.
I want you to be only mine.
Till the very end of time,
As we dance, sing every rhyme.

How did you become so hip?
Master, sailor, captain of the ship.
Turn it around, starboard,
Flag on the mast,
We are star bound.

Varsha

Deeksha described the beauty of simplicity.

Pashuapti, Ritu, Pavan, Jal and Dhara
Now faced a downpour
Like nothing they had ever seen in their entire lives.

It seemed like the clouds would themselves fall,
Along with the stars and the heavens,
On top of them in the massive torrential rain.

It had started with clouds beginning to gather,
Dark ominous symbols of nature's power.
And then, it started to pour from all corners.

When it poured, little streams began to form,
Toads began to croak, crickets began to screech,
And birds changed their song to the *Raga Malhar*.

Narrow *nullahs* turned into surging rivers,
Ponds transformed into massive lakes,
And lakes seemed to extend to the seas.

The oceans began to swell,
Waves crashed on the shore,
Reaching a height of hundreds of feet.

Pathways on the terrain got slushy and muddy,
Roots of trees and plants began to rot,
And standing crops were decimated.

Fruits fermented, flowers floundered,
Birds took to shelter,

Animals slipped and suffered injury,
While some lost their lives in floods.

Pashupati was on the verge of tears,
Watching the demise of his livestock.
He had to think of something and think fast.

He recalled the story of Lord Krishna
Who, in similar circumstances,
Bore the weight of the mountain Govardhana
On his pinkie,
And saved his village Gokul from nature's fury.

Inspired by the story,
He asked Ritu and the sisters,
To start building a dam,
One that would stretch across the land
And hold all the water together.
The dam was to be so massive,
It would tie together all the mountain ranges,
Run through their valleys,
And form a wall between their folds.
The catchment area of the dam
Would then be the mountainous regions,
And it would hold back water,
Until they came up with another plan.

Dhara began piling up earth,
Pavan started blowing wind to spread the matter,
And Jal took to binding it.
Ritu was the craftsman who put it all together
In a final moment of artistry,
And the dam was ready.

They rejoiced in their victory,
As the dam seemed to hold its ground.
But their happiness was short lived,
As water from the bowels of the earth
Started to ram against the wall of the dam.

They had not taken into account
The belly or the underground,
Of the terra firma,
Where the geysers had started to spew
Water and steam.
As the pressure from the underground water
Started to build at the walls,
The dam started showing cracks
And finally, it gave way.
The situation became worse than ever,
As all of land was now submerged in water.

Prakriti and Maya arrived and had a hearty laugh.

The Meenas

Vani began to describe the virtues of delusion.

Madhumati reached the Kingdom of the Meenas
And upon reaching, found Menaka waiting there.
She stood on a carousel with a sphinx on top,
And the whole apparatus was lit up in flames.

Menaka alighted from the carousel,
Like an angel moving from a shroud.
She came to stand next to Madhumati,
And spoke, 'Your next task is to tame the Griffin.

The beast is one with the tail,
Body and hind legs of a lion.
It's got the wings and head of an eagle,
And the fore feet are but an eagle's talons.'

She continued, 'The griffin is believed,
To be the king of all creatures.
They are associated with gold,
And are said to lay eggs in burrows on the ground,
With gold nuggets in their nests.
Griffins are guardians of the divine,
And a symbol of power that is divine.

The Griffin is supposed to protect
From witchcraft, evil and secret slander.
Not only do Griffins mate for life,
But if either of their partners die,
The other one continues,
The rest of their life alone.
Thus the Griffin became a symbol,
For churches in opposition of remarriage.

A Griffin's claw is said to have medicinal properties
And can bring eyesight to the blind.
The curious mix of a lion and an eagle in their self,
Draws on boldness and courage
And makes it akin to the fiercest monsters.
You, my dear Madhumati, are supposed to tame
One such Griffin which has become a monster.
Enter the next chamber and meet your game.'

Madhumati entered the chamber with much trepidation,
And there it was, a massive hulk of a monster,
Breathing fire. A heaving sight, ready to tear
Her limbs apart, or so it seemed, in his animation.

Madhumati was quick on her feet and invoked Kaalia.
She sent the serpent to fight the megalomaniac
That was the Griffin.
The serpent spread its hood and hissed,
Biting the monster and emptying its venom inside.
But Madhumati was dismayed,
As the beast displayed
No signs of the venom's effect on the outside.

Madhumati then conjured a cage with her wand,
But the demon used fire on the cage,
And it burned down as if it was wood.
Madhumati had now truly come of age.

She realized that the demon was not easy to beat.
She began to think of a plan that was neat.
She peered at the Crystal ball
And gazed into the depths of the Niagara Falls.
She thought about building such a ravine
And if she could get it done fast, she would do fine.

She summoned up warriors with her bow,
And angels with her trumpet low.

She asked the angels to dig a ravine deep,
And to build it like a crevasse
From where no one could crawl or creep.

She ordered the warriors to engage the beast,
Who then began to take the heat.
Meanwhile, the angels got the ravine ready,
And Madhumati only had to get the beast feel needy.

She felt that the monster would love to eat some meat,
So she arranged in the ravine some raw goat meat.
The monster smelled food and fell for the plot,
He fell in the ravine and tried to come out.

But alas! he was trapped,
And Madhumati had triumphed once again.
The job being done,
Ritambhara appeared yet again.

She said, 'You are very close to Sibu,
You now have only one final task in front of you.
But it is the hardest,
You will meet the opponent who is the toughest.
It's a trinity of dragons; white, red and black.

The white dragon is peaceful and likes to help.
It represents understanding and purity.
Red dragons are symbols of the terrible storms
Caused by fighting with one another at night.
While the Black dragons are the most evil.
They use destructive powers to meet their evil ends.

Dragons are mythical creatures,
Generally fire-spewing and with reptilian traits,
That feature in the myths of various cultures.
Most of them are depicted with six limbs;
Four legs and a pair of wings.

In folklore, dragons are said to guard gold.
They have also been recorded to get introduced
In village granaries, to deter mice and rats.
Some dragons are supposed to be poisonous,
Or breath fire from their throats,
As in the old English epic Beowulf.

They are sometimes portrayed as hoarding treasure.
Some myths feature them with a row of dorsal spine.
Dragons are supposed to be a significant part of cultures
And religions around the world.

They are said to be wiser than humans,
And are believed to possess some sort of magic
Or supernatural powers.
They are often associated with rain, wells and rivers,
While in some myths, they are said
To be the reason behind human speech.

Narratives about dragons,
Often involve them being slain by a hero.
The blood of a slain dragon
Is said to be both good and poisonous
In medieval legends and literary fiction.

Go on Madhumati, rescue Sibu with your last act.
In the next chamber await the trinity of dragons.
Remember that we have a pact,
If you finish this task, Sibu will have his liberation.'

Madhumati stepped into the chamber,
Her heart beating fast,
And the sight inside left her aghast.
For the dragons were like thunder,
Three of them, like the three heads of a monster.

With the help of Angel,
She quickly materialized a She Dragon,
That the three could fall in love with, in communion.
The She Dragon was a delight to look at,
It had lovely hair and eyes like that of a cat.
It swayed mysteriously
And drove the Black and the Red Dragon
Mad with desire instantaneously.

The White Dragon seemed
To be at peace with himself and walked
Close to the She Dragon to sit beside
Her and nudged her playfully with his tail.

Pretty soon, a fight broke out between
The Black Dragon and the Red Dragon.
All this commotion
Gave Madhumati ample time to think of a solution.

She came up with one in the nick of time.
As the dragons were now leaving the fights,
She came up with the idea of a singularity.
Not a naked one however, a covered singularity.

She conceived one with the help of her wand.
The idea was to make one which could
Pull the dragons into another universe,
If only she could draw them close.

She then remembered that dragons like music,
And asked Robyn to fetch her a lyre,
And the angels, to form a choir.
Together they started making divine music
Close to the covered singularity.

The dragons, on listening to the music,
Lost all sense of time and started making merry.

They started rushing towards the singularity in a hurry.
No sooner had they reached the point of music,

They hit the spot of the singularity
And started dissolving into the vortex.
Their flesh started peeling off slowly
And they seemed to disappear, as if in a solvent.

Soon, they had all gone down the vortex.
This task settled, Madhumati had finally solved the hex.
All the four sisters now appeared.
Their faces looked flushed and smeared
With sadness because now they feared
That they would have to reveal where Sibu lay hidden.

They all spoke together,
'Madhumati, you have proved us wrong, my dear.
Now you must not fear,
Go ahead and be united with Sibu for all years.'

Discourse on Self

Vani was in a philosophical mood as she spoke, 'Did you like the rains, Darpan? I always feel down and depressed for some reason, when it rains. Oh damn the rains, pun intended. Don't you think that Madhumati's final nemesis, the Griffin and the Dragons are symbolic of perhaps, her deepest darkest fears?'

Darpan voice made a soft droning in the silence, 'I enjoy the rainy season a lot. I like the pitter patter of raindrops and I love getting drenched when it pours. My mother scolds me a lot, as I tend to get sick later. It's a pity that despite Pashupati's finest attempt at the task, the dam fell apart. It's really amazing to be alongside Madhumati, and watch her surmount all her obstacles. The Griffin and the Dragons were especially difficult but again, kudos to Madhumati for thinking wisely and not applying brute strength when faced with such beasts. Can you please explain the metaphors of simplicity and delusions?'

Vani carried on the conversation, 'Simplicity and delusion are like the two sides of the self. The self can either be simple or we can delude ourselves into imagining it as something grand or grotesque. Pashupati's task looks daunting at first, but if you look closely, it's a simple one, to control the ebb and flow of a deluge of water. The problem is that the approach he takes is also a simple one. He decides to hold all the water in a reservoir, not thinking of the consequences if the reservoir were to fall apart. Madhumati's task is full of grandeur and delusions, with a Griffin and dragons which do not seem real at all, and the approach she takes is also a bit surreal, involving a chasm and a singularity.'

Darpan spoke with a childish curiosity, 'So, what you are telling me is the concept of duality in self, that of simplicity and delusions?'.

Deeksha answered, 'Yes, you understood it correctly. But you must also understand that the self, or the *atma*, is one conscience and is simple. Once you get rid of your delusions, you realize that it is one with the *brahman*, or the universal conscience.'

Darshan summed it up, '*Aum* is the sound, and the soul or the self, answers as one'.

Vani spoke parts of an epic poem.

My love, you are me.
And I am you.
You are my child,
And I am the mother.

I am the cradle,
I am the wind,
I am the fodder,
I am the mind.

You are the cattle,
You are the child,
You are the rattle,
You play all the time.

As we wake up,
Every day,
Just you and me,
I look into your eyes,
And see me.

Prithvi Lok (Planet Earth)

Deeksha described the beauty of wilderness.

Prakriti and Maya beckoned Pashupti,
Ritu and her sisters,
And told them that they had failed
At all of their tasks.

Since Maya was mother to Ritu
And her sisters,
And Prakriti was godmother
To Pashupati,
They arrived on a mutual decision.

They would liberate Jyoti, Ishika and Ishu,
Along with all of humanity and their children.
Although, together with Pashupati,
Ritu and her sisters,
They would be asked to leave the heavens
And descend to *Prithvi Lok.*

There, they would have to begin life anew.
Ironically, they would first have to learn,
How to make fire,
Which would be akin to their first task,
That of liberating Jyoti.

After liberating fire,
They would have to seek shelter.
And then learn how to hunt and gather.
From there, they would learn,
How to build the first tools,
From wood and stone.

Later, they would learn the art of forging metals,

And build weapons for hunting.
With an excess of meat,
They would take to sheltered houses,
And soon learn the first form of farming,
While also keeping cattle for dairy and work.

They would invent the first form of language
And symbols to communicate with each other.
They would form the first notions of family,
And learn how to build societies.

From societies would sprout the first villages,
Where they'd soon learn governance,
And invent seals, paper and some sort of military.

Some amongst them would take to building cities,
And invent books to read,
In which they would document knowledge,
And build schools for higher learning.
They would learn from the mistakes
Of their past lives.

Soon enough, they would have built,
An entire human civilization.

As Maya and Prakriti left them,
Pashupati and the others descended to Prithvi Lok.

Pashupati held Jyoti's hand.
He felt the warmth of her hand
Course through his veins,
And in the other hand, he held two stones.
He struck them together,
And sparks flew, hitting some dry grass,
And everyone screamed,
FIRE!

The Look of Love

Vani sang about togetherness.

The sisters led Madhumati to the next room,
And explained to her with a mischievous look,
'We have created a pagan paradise for the two of you,
Look Madhumati, it's heaven and Sibu waits for you.'

Madhumati could not believe her eyes,
For wherever she looked, there was bright light.
That filled the surroundings as it glittered,
And the air was so clear, it felt like it was filtered.

A stream of water flowed and it made lovely music,
Madhumati was thirsty from all her work and took a sip.
It was the sweetest water she had tasted in a while,
Hungrily, she lapped it up and then did smile.

For her eyes fell on an orchard,
That was laden with fruits.
Each one full of color and nectar and smelled sweet,
And had a beautiful taste to boot.

She took a bite and drowned in its sweetness.
It was lusty and full fleshed,
And smelled of roses, peaches and apples.
She then heard a sound coming from a shed.

She ran towards it and found a sled,
On which some pixies were drinking mead,
Who then took to flying and singing,
Oh! what joy to Madhumati, this place was bringing.

In a distance, she saw children playing some games.
They had precious stones in their hands;

Emeralds, rubies, topaz,
Quartzite, sapphire, corals,
Every which one, that you could name.

They were playing hopscotch,
And looked merry as can be.
Suddenly they called out. 'Sibu uncle,
Come out! Look, it's Madhumati!'

Madhumati almost fainted with delight,
For it was Sibu who came out, to stand in her sight.
When she came to her senses,
She rushed into Sibu's arms,

And cried, 'O Sibu darling,
Now we are together,
What was I becoming,
Apart from you, it seemed like forever.
I have written a poem for you,
Let me read it out.
Its called 'The Look of Love'.

The look of love,
When I am by your side.

I see the light of the moon
In your eyes
The look of love,
It could be what I see
When I see what I adore

And what I have felt I need more
Because it's you my amore
I can wrap my arms around you
Hold you close and feel you

How long I've been without you

And now that we're together
You're all I can think of
You're all I need

Don't ever let go
I love you so
Finishing the poem, she looked deep into his eyes,
And they kissed.
She closed her eyes,
And felt like she was in heaven.

When she opened her eyes,
She heard the chirping of birds,
And they held their hands together,
And looked at the distant, far away lands.

Discourse on Art

Vani's hands gestured like an artist holding a brush as she spoke, 'Do you like waking up to the reality of life beginning afresh on Earth with only fire to start with, Darpan? Can you imagine Madhumati and Sibu, playing with children holding precious stones in paradise?'

Darpan woke up from his dream and blurted, 'I believe in Pashupati, Ritu, Pavan, Jal, Dhara and Jyoti. I love Ishika and Ishu. I believe they can take humanity forward and make paradise on earth. Isn't that the whole idea? The story leaves Pashupati to create the paradise that Madhumati and Sibu are now dwelling in? Please explain the metaphors of wilderness and togetherness.'

Vani felt relieved explaining the last parts of the story to Darpan, 'Pashupati is wild and so is Ritu and the sisters. They have been like children, messing up the tasks assigned to them. They have been playful and naughty, not responsible and mature. Hence, they have inherited the wilderness of planet earth, so that they can treat it as their playground; a vastness they can forge any way they want to make it suit themselves. Madhumati has, time and again, proved herself to be an epitome of humility, courage, compassion, perseverance, knowledge and leadership. She deserves the pagan paradise and togetherness with Sibu.'

Darpan spoke with happiness in his eyes, 'I feel happy for both of them. I guess, Pashupati will find his happiness in the wilderness of Earth with his five lovers, while Madhumati and Sibu will find bliss in their pagan paradise'.

Deeksha added, 'Perhaps the two stories will merge together in the distant future when earth itself becomes a pagan paradise.'

Darpan summarized, 'True paradise lies in the heart of lovers and attaining that is an art.'

Vani began sining her last poem,

I am your story,
I am your song,
I am your picture,

Its been so long
Since you painted me
And made me art.

Your brushes came down
With the flourish of Caravaggio
And I was your Venus de Milo.

You took your time,
And I gave you my heart.
You breathed life into me,

And I stood tall.
You gave me language,
And taught me music.

You wrote poems,
And I was poesy.
You drank from my lips,

And the heavens became artsy.
You taught me philosophy,
And I became wise.

You made love to me,
And I drowned in your sweetness.
And now, my love,
I am all you've got,
I am your true art.
Just listen to your beating heart.
You've known that from the start.

The Beginning

Epilogue

Everyone looked at one another, as if they had been drugged by opium. The story Vani had begun to tell them had ended and it had taken their breath away.

Darpan broke the silence with his childish words, 'I get it, let me summarize the discourse. Isn't that what the story is all about, the philosophical musings? It has the following discourses: materialism, realism, limbs, sensory organs, feeding organs, *mukha*, motion, feelings and metaphysics in the first part of the story, where the discussion is on Madhumati and her sisters. Then the discourse is on human nature, seasons, music, affinity, desire, attraction, Eros and child in the second part, which focuses on Love. The third part of the story which is about the odyssey has discourses on love, pride and the mind. The fourth and final part of the story, which tells us about the battle for togetherness, the discourses are on joy, kindness, cool, self and art. So I guess, this is a philosophical tale about a girl who is looking for love, and discovers philosophy in the process.'

Vani looked at Darpan as if admonishing a child, 'You have hardly understood the story. When you and Darshan were struggling with the concept of the dual, I came up with the simplest of duals, the mother and the child. Then I made a mother like character and gave her a name, one which sounded like sweet mother, or Madhumati, and gave her a lover on which she could shower her affections, perhaps in a child-like manner, Sibu. Feel free to draw parallels between Madhumati and Sibu, and Pashupati and Ritu, for Pashupati is wild and infantile; perhaps it is fitting that he gets the love of five women, thus destroying the dual and demonstrating the fact that in life, dual may not be the only existing scenario.'

Vani continued, 'I gave Madhumati all the qualities that I could think of in a lover. She had wisdom, beauty, education, kindness, patience, a strong will, knowledge of the arts of love, magic, illusions and song and dance. But if you look carefully at the discourses, they describe the development of a child along with the love shared between the child and the mother.'

Vani carried on, 'The material world paves the ground for the child to be born and realism must exist for his birth as well. Perhaps, first the seed and the egg are materialized in the womb and then the limbs begin to take shape, followed by the sensory organs, the feeding organs and the mouth. When the child is born, he takes to motion; the infant crawls on all fours and rushes towards his mother, carried forth by pure instinct. He starts developing feelings for her in his soul and thus the first chapter ends with the genesis of the child. The second chapter describes the love between the child and the mother, for it is defined by human nature, affected by the seasons and emotions guided by listening to the music of his heart. This leads to various kinds of attractions and perhaps even lends a slight erotic flavour to love as he grows up under the loving eyes of his mother. The third chapter in the child's life is when he learns to love someone other than his mother, while also learning about the second most important emotion in life, taking pride in his accomplishments. Along with these emotions, he begins to develop a mind of his own. In the final chapter, the child is now a mature adult and has learnt to feel joyful, be kind towards others, be cool in times of trouble, understand himself and perhaps to look at everything as if it is born out of art.'

Darpan, Darshan and Deeksha were all amazed at Vani's narration of the hidden meaning in the story.

Darpan, who simply could not be put down, spoke again, 'Can you tell us the story again, Vani?'

Vani's eyes twinkled as she gently held Darpan's gaze. 'Perhaps, I will tell you another one soon.'

She held hands with Darpan and they walked away.

Darshan looked at Deeksha with a shy smile and Deeksha winked at him.

Glossary

A

Aakrosh : Angst
Aalingam : Entwining of the lover's limbs
Abhaya : Fearless
Abhinya : The art of expression in Indian aesthetics.
Achilles : Greek Hero of the Trojan war
Aditya : King of Surya dynasty
Aghasura : Demon from mythology
Agneya Astra : Fire arm
Agni bana : Chief fire weapon
Agnicurna : Gunpowder
Agni dharana : One of the recipes of the Agni Bana
Agrasena : Standing army
Airawat : Lord Indra's mythical elephant
Amrita : Divine potion granting immortality
Amukhta : Weapons that were not thrown
Angasudda: Perfection of limbs and movements
Angula : A measure equal to one's finger's breadth
Ashwas : Of the horse (equine) dynasty
Astra : Missile
Atma : Soul

B

Bakasura : Demon from mythology
Basanta : Spring
BharatNatyam : A form of classical dance which originated in Tamil Nadu
Bhangi : Gait or posture
Bhava : Facial expression
Bheetsena : Troops of allies and friend
Bhumispara : A gesture symbolising victory over Mara
Bindipala : A heavy club with a broad and bent tail end

Bol : Indian Rhythmic mnemonic
Brahmins : Highest class in hinduism, specialising as priests

C

Cakra : A circular disc with a small opening in the middle
Calique : A double edged ritual knife used to cut energies
Chaitya hall : Prayer hall.
Chakram : Teacher of Menaka
Challava : Deception
Chandrapani : King of Chandra dynasty
Chandras : Of the Moon (Lunar) dynasty
Charawahas : Cattle lifting marauders
Chor Police : A game of thieves and police.
Colline : Sickle used to cut herbs used in spells and hexes

D

DantaKantha : Weapon of war in the shape of a tooth
Daanava : Demon
Deepika : Princess of Surya dynasty
Deep Mala : Warrior's arrangement in which they are armed with Agneya Astra:
Deva : Deity
Devadasis : Dancing girls dedicated to gods,
Dharma : Religion
Dhyana : Profound meditation
Diorama : The book of illusions used to keep a journal of spells
Drona : Guru of Madhumati
Durvasa : Guru of Urvashi
Dwanda : Duel between opponent warriors
DwarPalak : GateKeeper
DwarRakshak : GateKeeper

E

Ergin : A sharp instrument like a cleaver for inscribing various other tools of magic.

F

Fakir : A Muslim or Hindu religious ascetic who loves solely on alms.
Float-pots : Consecrated cauldrons for mixing lotions and potions

G

Gada : A heavy rod of iron with one hundred spikes on top
Garbhagraha : Sanctum of a temple typically housing a diety
Garuda : A giant divine eagle
Gilli Danda : A game much like cricket played with a bail called *gilli* ,and a bat called *danda.*
Goliath : Bible character described as a giant Philistine warrior.
Gopuram : Lofty gates of a temple
GrihasthaSamhita : Verses related to household functions
Grishma : Summer
Gurukul : Residential school.

H

Hasti Vyuha : Warriors are arranged in the shape of a group of elephants
Hercules : Roman adaptation of the divine Greek hero Heracles who was the son of Zeus.

K

Kaarkhana : Mill, factory
Kamadhenu : Divine bovine goddess
Kalapam : A poem written in one metre

Kalpavriksha : Wish fulfilling divine tree in Hindu mythology
Katlasa : Pitcher
KalaMandapa : Courtyard in a temple for cultural activities
KalyanMandapa : Corridor in a temple for marriage ceremonies
Kamakshi : Madhumati's sister blessed in the art of love
Kansa : Krishna's Uncle and a Demon King
Kathakali : A form of classical dance with origins in Kerala
KhelSamhita : Verses related to Play and Games
Kho Kho: A game where one team sits/kneels in the middle of the court, in a row, with adjacent members facing opposite directions. The runners play in the field, 3 at a time and the team that takes the shortest time to tag/tap all the opponents in the field, wins.
Ksepyo Agni Yoga : One of the recipes for Agni Bana

L

Laya : Rhythm
Luna : Moon Goddess

M

MaitriSamhita : Verses related to friendship
Mandapa : A hall with carved pillars
Mandir : Temple
Mantra : Incantation
MantraMukhta : Weapons that were discharged by a mantra
Masundi : Cudgel
MatsyaKreeda : Wrestling fish out of the waters
Matsya Vyuha : An arrangement of warriors in the shape of reefs of an ocean
Maya : Illusion
MayaJaal : Intricate web of illusion and deception
Mayavi : Teacher of Ritambhara
Meena : Of the fish (Piscine) dynasty
Menaka : Madhumati's sister, blessed in magic.
Milan : Union
Mohiniattam: A form of classical dance that originated in Kerala

Mrigya : Chase
Mudgara : A staff in the shape of the hammer
Mudra : A symbolic or ritual gesture in Hinduism and Buddhism
Mukhta : Weapons that were thrown
Muni : Sage

N

Nadi Pahad : A game of land and rivers, where one must stay on land and avoid the rivers.
Nalika : A hand gun or a musket rightly piercing the mark
Narsimha : King of Simha dynasty
Natya : Dance Drama
Nayanmars : Group of 63 saint poets
Nipunsena : Bands of soldiers from guilds and mercenaries
Nritta : A pure dance where the spotlight is on tala or time measures
Nritya : In this dance, there is a fusion of Nritta or pure dance and facial expressions
Nrityangana : Dancer
NrityaSamhita : Verses related to dance

P

Pachisa : A game in which notes of denomination 25, 50, 75, 100 have to be exchanged to make up 100.
Paramatma : Supreme soul
Paramhans : King of Meena dynasty
Parasu : Battle axe
Pasa : Noose
Pinjara : Cage
Poornima : Full moon night
Putana : Demoness from mythology

R

Raga : A musical note
Raga Viraha : The music of separation

Rati: Hindu goddess of love and desire
Ravi: Sun god in hinduism
Ritambhara : Madhumati's sisters, a master of Maya or illusion

S

Saarthi : King of Ashwa dynasty
Samantas : Feudatories, or big landlords
Samhita : A methodically, rule based combination of text or verses
SangeetaSamhita : Verses related to music
Sataghni : A weapon which had the power of killing a hundred at a time
Shankh Vyuha : Warriors arranged in the shape of a conch shell
Shastra : Scriptures
Shatrusena : Enemy troops
Sheeta : Winter
Shehnai : An Indian musical instrument similar to the oboe which has a double reed.
Shikhara : Lofty tower or Spire
Shiksha : Education
ShukKashi: A wild boar chase
Simhas : Of the Lion Dynasty
Singham : Prince of Simha Dynasty
Sibu : Madhumati's love interest, a dancer
Sira : A bucket like instrument curved on both sides, with an opening made of iron
Suryas : Of the Sun Dynasty

T

Tala : Rhythm
Theurgists : People who practice a system of beneficent magic followed by Egyptian Platonists
Tomara : A javelin, or an iron club.
Toranas : Gateway to stupas.
Tona : Witchcraft
Tupak : Small gun

U

UmaSamhita : Verses related to Uma
Urvashi : Madhumati's sister – a warrior

V

Vadya Mandapa : Corridor in a temple for musical performances
Vanasena : Forest tribes and warriors
Vanawasis : Foresters and tribesmen
Vatsyayana : Teacher of Kamakshi
Varsha : Rains
Vihara : Monastery
Vimana : Stories atop the sanctum of a temple, also a sanctuary
Visheshsena : Troops recruited for special occasions
Vismaya : Amazing
Visvasghati : One of the recipes for Agni Bana with powder of zinc, khumbi, lead, with turpentine, oil wax and charcoal
Vyuha : Arrangement of warriors in a pattern
VyuhaBheda : Deciphering the arrangement of warriors

Y

Yantram : Engines of War
YudhSamhita : Verses related to warcraft

About the Author

Anshuman Rai teaches computer science and dabbles in software consultancy, where he puts to use a decade of experience acquired writing software for various firms in India, America and Europe. He holds a Bachelor of Technology in computer science and engineering from IIT Kanpur and a Master of Engineering in computer technology and application from C.S.V.T.U. He is also pursuing his Ph.D. in digital image processing from C.S.V.T.U.

In his spare time, he likes to make some noise with his guitar and a harmonica. Writing is a hobby and an acquired talent, developed in the spare time he gets away from his laptop.